FABULOUS HOLLYWOOD BABYLON

In 1920, Hollywood was Majestic, the studio with all the stars. Majestic picked them off the lot, frosted them in fantasy, sold them to America's devouring love.

They were the most beautiful girls in the world, boy-next-door heartthrobs, silent clowns, child stars eager to sleep their way up. Lost in the glittering frenzy, seduced by adoration. With money they couldn't throw away fast enough.

It was Ben Sommers' job to cover up the scandal, the wild sex parties, the liquor, the cocaine. To play up the stars, their Hispano-Suiza automobiles, their fairytale palaces and all the crazy marvels of their make-believe world.

MAJESTIC

Ray Hubbard

MAJESTIC

A Bantam Book / January 1981

ISBN 0–553–13218–0

Published simultaneously in the United States and Canada

Bantam Books are published by Bantam Books, Inc. Its trademark, consisting of the words "Bantam Books" and the portrayal of a bantam, is Registered in U.S. Patent and Trademark Office and in other countries. Marca Registrada. Bantam Books, Inc., 666 Fifth Avenue, New York, New York 10103.

PRINTED IN THE UNITED STATES OF AMERICA

0 9 8 7 6 5 4 3 2 1

A Note to the Reader

Most of the characters in *Majestic* really lived and made moving pictures. Many of the events actually happened or could have happened. I have taken a few liberties with chronology and some literary license with real events and characters for dramatic purposes. I have tried to make the language and the style of the fictional events as true to the period as possible. If there are any factual errors, they are entirely mine.

Each chapter starts with a clipping from a newspaper or magazine or trade journal. They are created entirely by me, although the ideas for some of them came from real news items. In many instances I have used the actual name of a newspaper or magazine for documentary effect.

I would like to express my deepest gratitude to those who helped me in the research and the writing of *Majestic*. Special thanks are due to Mark Olshaker who gave me the original encouragement to write; to Jay Acton for his faith and good advice; to my editor, Ursula Brennan, for her unflagging patience, understanding, and skill; to Ted Solotaroff for his sensitive final editing.

At the Library of Congress, Division of Motion Pictures, I am indebted to Barbara Humprys, David Parker, Patrick Sheehan, and Paul Spehr. They not only pointed me toward original sources and made valuable suggestions but made it possible for me to view the films in the collection of the American Film Institute.

Mary Corliss, of the Museum of Modern Art Film Library, gave me invaluable help by searching out stills from vanished films and found wonderful photographs of Hollywood motion picture studios of the 1920's. Tony Slide, of the Academy of Motion Picture Arts and Sciences, was very helpful in tracking down dates.

The librarians who administer the microfilm newspaper collections at the Los Angeles Public Library and the San Francisco Public Library were generous with their time, stretching library rules so that I could take as much advantage of the collections as possible on short trips to the West

Coast. They cheerfully made hundreds of photostats of materials I could not read on the spot because of time limitations.

Librarians at the Beverly Hills Public Library allowed me to search through their uncatalogued photo collections, and librarians at the Montgomery County Library in Rockville, Maryland, kindly ordered special microfilms.

I would like to thank W. Landon Banfield, Larry Klein, and Ben Wolf for specialized assistance.

Above all, my wife, Marion, deserves my gratitude for putting up with my lifelong infatuation with the silent film. *Majestic* is dedicated to her for other reasons as well. She knows what they are.

Potomac, Maryland 1979

1

January 1919, Hollywood

The Los Angeles Examiner*

BREAD LINE OF DESPAIR

HOLLYWOOD. The postwar depression has forced many vets into bread lines. But in this city the human wreckage of "movie madness" is seen everywhere. The tragedy is intensified by the bright sunlight and the banks of flowers that bloom riotously around each cottage. Despite national pleas to stay home, they still come to Hollywood to realize their dreams.

The long white Hispano-Suiza 16-cylinder two-seater sped around the corner from Hollywood Boulevard onto Majestic Way. The strange canoe-shaped tail flashed in the early morning sunshine and the wicked looking chain drive slackened momentarily as the driver shifted gears, then tightened, and the rear wheels bit into the gravel. Perched on the left front fender was a large silver Chinese dragon holding a trombone bell in its jaws. The loud Klaxon that sounded from it was capable of freezing a pedestrian's blood at twenty feet.

The driver, dressed in white, sported an English cap with goggles pulled down against the dust. Despite them he was instantly recognizable as Wallace Reid, the most popular romantic lead in motion pictures. The motor car did not slow

---

*Each chapter starts with a clipping from a newspaper, magazine or trade journal. They were created entirely by the author, although the ideas for some came from real news items. In many instances I have used the actual name of a newspaper or magazine for documentary effect.

down as it took the curve at high speed yet Reid grasped the steering wheel lightly, almost carelessly with one hand, the other draped casually over the back of the passenger seat. This was the hand he waved cheerily at fans when they shouted, "Hi-ya, Wallie!"

Reid loved automobiles. He loved to look at them, drive them, simply lean against a fender and talk about them. He owned six motor cars—massive, expensive, powerful. No one else was allowed to drive them. "Like some horses and women," he was quoted in *Photoplay* magazine, "they are too much animal for most men to control." And skill, as well as nerve was needed to master the elaborate patterns that shifted the gears; then too, only a delicate touch could make the precise adjustments of the fuel mixture levers on the steering wheel and the dashboard.

The white speedster swept down the graveled road shadowed on either side by fragrant eucalyptus trees planted two decades earlier by the rancher who sold his bean field to Saul Rubin for a moving picture studio. Beyond the border of tall trees lay endless fields and citrus groves. In the clear early morning light glimpses of other studios flickered between the blurred tree trunks—to the south was Paramount, and to the west Metro flourished among the orchards and spreading knots of bungalows and houses. Out of vision over the hills to the north lay Universal. Scattered between were a dozen smaller clusters of studio buildings jumbled with business districts springing up along the tracks of the Pacific Electric Railway. Here and there abandoned outdoor sets from the past spectacles made impressive ruins against the sky.

The studio gates were spanned by an arch pierced by cutout letters spelling the word **MAJESTIC.** On either side were identical stucco buildings with Spanish tile roofs. Behind lay the rest of the studio buildings, cheap frame structures painted a faded yellow ochre, the same yellow used on Southern Pacific depots the length of California because it had the virtue of not showing dirt. Over it all was the endless, incredible blue of the Hollywood sky, more brilliant than any paint.

A small crowd had gathered before the gates, as they did at every studio in town, a hundred or so men and women hoping for a day's work as extras. Dressed in their own finery to earn an additional dollar, they shivered in the chilly California dawn. They wore beaded and embroidered evening gowns, polo whites, satin lapeled dinner suits, crepe de chine afternoon frocks; clothing as necessary to their survival as food.

2

Reid accelerated and the gateman swung the gates wide and stood back. The extras surged forward, eager to be seen by the star. Reid scorched through the gate, sixteen cylinders pounding, waving and smiling. The gates slammed shut.

The Majestic Studio lot was a maze of blacktop streets closed in by shabby buildings that crowded on each other. Reid came to a stop as two workmen carried a large gilded chair across the street. Concealing his impatience Wallie waved back as they shouted good morning to him. He was very popular with the crews, drinking beer with them, joking and playing ball between takes, lending money, advising on love affairs, being godfather to their children.

Oscar, Willie's dresser and valet, looked out to see the white racer stop in front of the dressing room bungalow. Standing up on the seat Wallie jumped gracefully over the side of the car door, as if performing on camera. Oscar came out onto the porch.

Wallie stopped and looked at his valet warily. "Don't yell at me, Highpockets, my head is splitting." He jogged up to the porch. The dressing room bungalow, built especially for Reid, was Hollywood's interpretation of a Cotswold cottage, complete with a simulated thatched roof. He ran through the parlor and into the dressing room. While Oscar waited with a large turkish towel, he hurriedly showered in the glass stall, pounded by streams of cold water from eight nozzles. His powerful torso gleaming wet, he emerged and toweled himself vigorously while the valet poured black coffee in the kitchen.

Eating breakfast in his private dining room in the Executive Bungalow, Saul Rubin removed his gold pocket watch and snapped the cover open.

Rubin was torn between acting like a father to his awkward stars and being the firm and purposeful leader whose job was to turn out a hundred pictures a year. As president of Majestic Studios and, next to Abe Weiss, the biggest shareholder, he ruled the lots in much the same imperious way that Weiss ran the financial headquarters in New York. After all, the studios had been his own property until his merger with Weiss. He still felt the pride of creating them out of the dusty bean fields nearly a decade ago.

He pushed the plate back, eggs half finished. He loved having breakfast in this room, looking out over his back lot, and usually lingered there planning the day. But everything this morning would be rushed. First, he would make a ceremonial visit to Stage Three where Reid's new picture, *The Roaring Road,* was starting production. If there was time he'd watch a few scenes. James Cruze, the director, was on his first big picture and a little attention from the boss himself wouldn't hurt.

Then he would be driven to the station to take the Overland Express to New York. At this point Rubin's spirits dropped. All he seemed to do these days was ricochet back and forth between Hollywood and New York. After four long nights in a Pullman compartment, fighting for sleep, he would have to take on Abe Weiss. Weiss didn't travel. He stayed comfortably in New York. Then when there was trouble he would make his presence felt by a string of nagging telegrams.

Lunch on Friday. That was something to worry about. Lunch with Weiss was difficult at best—the man specialized in turning problems into tests of his will. Now, with the Douglas Fairbanks–Mary Pickford mess still unresolved, their meeting would be pure hell. The old man must know that the queen of Hollywood and her famous stud would do what she damn well pleased. Besides, Pickford had never been his star. She'd belonged to Weiss right from the start.

Rubin stood on the verandah for a moment looking out into the sunlight. He tried to cheer himself up by remembering the old days in the East, trying to make films under the drab skies of Queens. This was more like it. Sunshine every day. He walked briskly across the lawn toward Stage Three. Watching a picture in production was one of his main pleasures in life. All that equipment, artifice, people being pulled into order. He felt a special affinity for the actors and the crews. People. That was his particular skill. Working with them, encouraging them, creating a climate of friendly concern so that they felt at home and did their best work.

Also fitting the picture to the star, that was another skill he took pride in. Look what he'd accomplished with Gloria Swanson. And Wallie. He'd been right on the automobile thing. Put Reid behind the wheel of a racing car and the picture would pack every theater. There was something about the sight of Wallie's profile, the set of his jaw as he hurtled into danger, pulling off breathtaking stunts with all that trick driving. It drove audiences wild. The man was a gold mine. The grosses were wonderful.

Reid lay back in the barber chair and closed his eyes, as Herbie spread the spill cloth over his costume.

"Lie back, dear boy," he said. He looked at Reid's face and frowned. "Honestly, what did you do last night? Never went to bed, I'll bet." He spread lather over Reid's face as he scolded, then shaved him with a straight razor. "I'll have to speak to Dottie. Roscoe Arbuckle can get away with that sort of thing—partying all night and then coming to work. It's all that fat." The lather was wiped off with witch hazel. "But, Wallie, you're different. Every little line shows up on a muscular face right away." He spread thin layers of grease paint. "It's all I can do to cover 'em up these days."

He worked with tints from many jars and tubes. "Don't expect me to resurrect all that sagging tissue," he sniffed. "I do makeup, not work miracles." He darkened the famous eyebrows. "You're no kid, Wallie. You're pushing thirty. It's about time you started conserving. I can't do it all."

Wallie merely smiled at the nagging. Herbie would work a miracle with his creams and paints and fix him up like new. In the old days only light makeup could be used so that facial expressions would register on the slow film. Eyes had to be outlined so the whites could be distinguished in the pale faces. Herbie had changed all that with subtly colored grease paints; now each actor had his own tint, and the rows of jars were labeled with star's names.

"Do your stuff, Herbie," Reid muttered softly. "If you don't, I'll have to get to bed regular like some hick." He tried to keep from laughing so as not to move his face.

"That's exactly what I'm talking about!" said Herbie. "Lie still." He stepped back. "There," he said, "It's absolutely the best I can do under very unfavorable circumstances."

Reid opened his eyes as the chair swung up into sitting position and he looked across at the mirrors. Herbie had done exactly what he said he couldn't do—a resurrection.

Every morning, Wallie thought, I walk in here and leave as if the previous twenty-four hours hadn't happened. Other men have to watch themselves grow old. It's there every morning when they shave. He smiled at his reflection in the mirrors. Herbie sees to it that I always look twenty-four, not a day older. Not only do I stay young forever, but every time the script changes, there's a new Wallie Reid. If I get tired of this month's Wallie, there'll be a new one for the next picture.

He stood admiring his reflection, then sucked in his gut and turned sideways. "Great!" he said softly. "Great." He appraised the beautiful image in the mirror. "What a lucky son of a bitch I am," he whispered.

5

"Send a wire to the Coast," Abe Weiss said to his secretary. "I want it should arrive there this morning." He leaned back in the swivel chair, a movement that lifted his tiny legs off the floor.

TO THE ROARING ROAD COMPANY MAJESTIC STUDIOS HOLLYWOOD CONGRATULATIONS AND BEST WISHES ON THE BEGINNING OF A GREAT AND IMPORTANT PICTURE IN MAJESTIC HISTORY STOP I KNOW AND SHARE YOUR EXCITEMENT AS YOU START OFF ON THIS ADVENTURE STOP BEAT METRO AND FOX TO THE FINISH LINE STOP MAY YOUR SPIRIT NEVER FALTER WALLIE STOP LOOK LOVELY WANDA STOP BE BOLD IN YOUR DIRECTION JIMMIE STOP REGARDS ABE WEISS

He nodded curtly at the secretary who picked up his pad and left the office. Looking down at his buffed fingernails, Weiss could see a blurred reflection of his own face. That was how he liked things. Neat and precise.

Then his face darkened. That idiot, Rubin, would be getting on the train just about now. Probably pick up some dumb twat in the lounge car and *yentz* all the way to New York. What a mess Rubin had made. Dumb *schmuck!* What could he be thinking of, a studio head yet, to let the greatest star in pictures slip through his fingers. It took a real idiot to lose a Mary Pickford. Well, soon he would pay. Even as he scowled, Weiss savored the thought.

On Stage Three six movies were being shot simultaneously and the noise was deafening. The cameras were already cranking on all but *The Roaring Road*. Down the line of sets directors were shouting instructions to actors and cameramen. A piano and violin duo belted out Shubert to help Winifred Westover cry in her big scene. Shots rang out and doors slammed. Screams and sobs echoed from the glass ceiling. "No, no no!" someone yelled. "Hit him harder!"

James Cruze shouted across the chaotic stage. "Who's Elsie Wright? Anybody named Wright around here? Goddamn it!"

A pretty dark-haired girl ran to his side and stood attentively.

"I'm right here, Mr. Cruze. I'm sorry, but I was asking the cameraman what kind of notes he wanted. I've never worked with him before, either." Heads together, they spoke loudly above the din.

"You ever done script before with anybody?"

"Oh yes, sir. A lot. I just never worked with the two of you before." She looked at him directly. "I know exactly what to do, unless of course, you want something very unusual." She smiled sweetly.

The director returned the smile. "Good. When they said I'd be getting a new script girl, I thought they meant inexperienced." They both laughed. He lowered his voice. "This is a big picture. What's your name? Elsie?" She nodded. "I can't afford any slipups." He looked at her meaningfully.

"I'll help all I can, Mr. Cruze." Out of the corner of her eye she saw Rubin watching them. She tugged at Cruze's sleeve and her eyes directed his attention to the tall figure standing by the edge of the set. Cruze hurried over and they shook hands.

"Any advice for a new director on his first picture?" he asked.

Rubin put his arm around Cruze's shoulder.

"My best advice to a new director on the first day is to fire somebody off the set—an assistant of some sort, nobody important. In front of everybody." He smiled. "Puts the crew on notice that you mean business. You'll be surprised at the effect it'll have."

"Thanks for the advice. Sounds good. I'll do it first thing after lunch."

Wallace Reid hurried up to them and put his hand on Cruze's arm.

"Honest to Christ, Jimmie, I'm truly sorry. Hell of a way to start out." He flashed the famous Reid smile. "I promise to be better." He turned to Rubin and punched him playfully on the upper arm.

Rubin didn't smile back and moved away slightly. Wallie hit too hard. He nodded at Cruze. "Let me make my little speech and get out of the way."

Reid eyed Rubin's back speculatively for a moment, then made a mournful face at Cruze over Rubin's shoulder, playing to the crew. Cruze pretended not to notice. Wallie followed them across the studio floor to the center of the set, shadow boxing in the air, thumbing his nose as he punched. The crew watched laughing. Rubin stopped and turned to see why everyone was so tickled. Wallie froze, an angelic look on his face.

Everyone gathered around Rubin to hear his speech over the noise from the adjoining sets. From somewhere off in the huge studio a chant began. "One, Two, Three. Squirt!"

7

Rubin looked toward the yells of laughter that followed. "Roscoe Arbuckle must be using seltzer bottles this morning instead of cream pies." Everyone smiled. Rubin cleared his throat and raised his voice.

"I'll only take a minute. I want everybody to get to work or this picture'll fall behind schedule on its first day.

"I just want to extend my congratulations and best wishes to all of you on the start of this picture. If it is as successful as Wallie's previous racing pictures, exhibitors will be dancing in the streets." Reid executed a fast fox-trot. Rubin tried to ignore him. "I have such high hopes for these pictures that we have—and you are the first to hear it—purchased the rights to all of the Dusty Rhodes racing stories from *The Saturday Evening Post*." There was a little stir of approval and a few handclaps. "So I have only one more thing to say." He paused for what he hoped was a moment of drama. "Get in there, drive like hell, and come out winners!" He smiled nervously, stepping back to indicate that he had finished. Everyone applauded politely.

Cruze held up his hand. "All right, you heard the boss," he called out resolutely. "Let's get going." His decisive tone let the crew know that although the president of the studio was standing by, this was his set and he was in charge.

"Wallie. Wanda. I want to rehearse this scene for a minute before we shoot it." Two men snapped white chalk lines on the floor as guides. The actors checked their positions so they wouldn't step over the chalk lines and out of camera range. Then they took positions for the establishing master shot.

Rubin loved seeing Reid work. He was so smooth and professional for all of his horseplay. Rubin had watched Reid's popularity grow slowly but steadily since his first role, that of the Indian in Vitagraph's *The Deerslayer*. Chosen for the part because he had the physique of a natural athlete, Wallie was willing to appear on camera wearing only a skimpy breechclout, displaying his trim rump to advantage. Women had been delighted by the young savage. Exhibitors hurried to notify the head of the Vitagraph Company, who quickly featured Reid in a series of adventure films in which his shirt somehow was always ripped off.

Audiences had grown tired of the sturdy, rough, honest farmers and toilers of humble but decent origins that filled the photoplays of the early years. Now they wanted the new breed of smiling, trim, muscular young men with quick wits and charming ways with the girls. Impressed after seeing him as the blacksmith in *The Birth of a Nation,* his partner Abe Weiss had signed Reid to a long term contract at Majestic.

Soon Reid came to typify the new leading man. Always playing a devil-may-care college man of rich parents, Wallie smiled, wisecracked, and flattered his way into a million hearts. Men watched him to learn how to be confident and sophisticated with women. Girls watched him to flesh out their fantasies.

"Motion picture stars are wishes come true in the flesh," Saul Rubin was fond of saying. He found stories for Wallie Reid that combined the best of Teddy Roosevelt's strenuous life and the new worship of elegant clothes, manners, and the motor car. The Majestic publicity department coined a word to describe him—"Pep." And he was peppy. Unfazed by defeat, heedless of obstacles, he charmed his way through six or eight pictures a year.

The best part, Rubin thought, was that he was not a *schmuck* like most actors. He was cooperative, the highest compliment Rubin ever paid an actor. Just make sure the girls saw the bulge of his *gid* once in every picture, and they'd double last year's grosses for sure.

"Camera! Action! Now, Wallie!" Cruze crouched in the canvas chair waving his arm at Reid. "Walk to the desk. That's right. There she is sitting behind the desk. Step back. You didn't expect to see her there. Fine. Faster. Good reaction. She looks like a hot number to you. Smile. Think. Very casual and self assured. That's right. Now perch on the corner of her desk.

"Wanda, sweetie, look up and recognize him. The fast-driving devil who nearly knocked you down. He's good looking, but you don't want him to know you think so. Not too much. Cut!" Cruze ran over to Wanda and, crouching beside her, took one of her hands. "Underplay, honey," he said gently. "Wallie turn ever so slightly so we can really see you giving her the eye." He jumped up. "Roll cameras!" he shouted as he ran toward his chair. They repeated the scene and went on to the next.

"Come on, Wallie! Those eyebrows are famous. Use 'em, for God's sake!"

"Too bad you're the boss's daughter," Wallie said archly.

"I'll thank you to park your carcass off my desk," Wanda sparred.

"Wallie, mock alarm. Pretend you're a little afraid of her. Kid her." Cruze was yelling through a cardboard megaphone.

9

Wallie, smiling, jumped up then leaned across the desk, charming, debonair.

"How'd you like to go for a little spin?"

"Elsie, mark that for a close-up and a two shot later," Cruze muttered.

Wanda's eyes grew large as she smiled up at Reid. "That line might work with some cookies, big boy, but my father owns this auto agency, and *fast* doesn't only mean cars around here. When Daddy says he wants *fast* workers, he doesn't mean that kind!"

Laughing, Cruze shouted, "Cut!" At the desk he said, "Very cute, kids. Lots of spunk, Wanda. Keep it going and we'll be back on schedule by lunch." He backed away saying, "Now let's set up for close-ups and reverses, so stay put. Cameras," he called out, beckoning. "Elsie, check positions."

Saul Rubin watched for another minute, then got into the waiting limousine. Wallie and Wanda were very attractive together, a nice spark in their banter. He settled down for the drive to Pasadena, feeling satisfied. Weiss needed him to turn out class product like that. That's what he did. Turned it out with more pizzazz than anyone else in Hollywood. Let the old man grouse about Mary Pickford if he wanted to. The pictures were what counted. He looked at the brilliant gardens on the outskirts of Pasadena. That was another thing. It would be cold and grey in New York.

Cruze worked rapidly but systematically. After each scene was filmed in a master shot, the detail shots were made—close-ups, reactions of one actor to another. Each shot was described by Elsie in her notebooks, so the film cutters had an outline to follow. She also put down other details—which hand was on the telephone, hats on, hats off—so incongruities would not appear in the various shots that would be spliced together into the final scene.

By noon, six complicated interior scenes had been completed. The production schedule called for all of the studio interiors to be finished during the next four weeks, then the entire company would go on location for the racing shots. When they stopped for lunch, Reid and Cruze were joined by Marion Fairfax, the writer of the scenario.

"I love the way you and Wanda are hitting it off, Wallie," Marion said as they walked to the bungalow. "The scenes just crackle with energy."

Lunch from the commissary was delivered to Wallie's

bungalow by a waiter on a bicycle. As they ate Marion jotted down some new dialogue for that afternoon's scenes.

"I didn't see Rubin leave, did you, Wallie?" Cruze asked.

"God, no. I was trying not to look at him. He always makes me nervous, anyway. He tries too hard and it just doesn't work."

"Oh, Wallie!" Marion swatted at him with a celery stalk. "Don't be unfair. He only wanted to give us his best wishes. He was smiling, after all."

Reid laughed. "That's when you have to be on guard. You have to understand one thing. If this picture finishes early enough, he'll try to rush me into another one." He blew out his breath. "Yesterday was my only day off after *Alias Mike Moran*. I'm pooped." Then he held his arms out, stretching like a warm cat, flexing his muscles. "But Christ almighty, I love being a star."

2

The New York World, Jan. 12, 1919

HOLLYWOOD NOTES AND NEWS EVENTS
CONSTANCE TALMADGE'S LAUNDRY PROBLEMS!

Beautiful motion picture star Constance Talmadge has solved a worrisome laundry problem in a unique way. Dirty diamonds were the big problem that faced the petite younger sister of star Norma Talmadge in one of her new romantic comedies, *The Veiled Adventure,* now being filmed. In the photoplay Constance plays a young woman who teaches her fiancé a lesson by involving him in a theft and a big black lie. The family jewels play an important part.

Miss Talmadge decided to use her own precious stones for the picture, but they were too dirty from constant use to properly reflect the light. She solved the problem neatly by washing them in imported champagne!

As the train gathered speed Polly turned hoping to catch one last glimpse of her mother and father waving good-bye. But they were lost in the midday gloom of the valley and all she saw was a burst of orange flames as it belched from the mouth of a furnace lighting up the grey sky. She cried quietly for a few miles.

If only. That's all she could think about. If only Pa hadn't gotten burned so bad. Then she wouldn't have to go stay with an aunt she'd never even met. It wasn't fair. Why her? She'd been a good girl.

The dark landscape rushed past the windows, strange and

even scary. The train had already taken her farther from home than she'd ever been. She sat, hardly moving. An occasional tear ran down her cheek.

A man sat down beside her. He smelled good. Like spice.

"Why don't you blow your nose and wipe your eyes?" He held out a clean white handkerchief.

She looked up at him. He was bald and a fringe of red hair ran around his head just above his ears giving him a cheerful look as he smiled down at her. She took the handkerchief and used it. He wore a dark speckled suit, little flecks of color in it, she noticed, like a bird's egg. She looked away and handed the handkerchief back to him. "I'll be all right."

"No, you keep it, honey."

"Thank you."

"I got little girls of my own. Just your age. You traveling alone?"

She nodded.

"Everything'll be all right. You'll see." He smiled at her again. "Is the conductor looking out for you?"

She nodded again and hugged her shawl closer. "I guess so."

"My name is Hopkins. I'll be in a car up ahead if you need anything. Compartment 2B." He smiled at her over his shoulder as he left the car.

Toward the middle of the afternoon Mr. Hopkins returned and asked if she would enjoy sitting with him in his compartment for a little while. Polly nodded and followed him through the cars to the Pullman. After exploring the compartment, which enchanted her, she sat by the window and looked out, hands folded politely in her lap.

"What's your name?"

"Polly Walenska."

He sat opposite and told her about his three daughters, only one of whom was really her age. After a while he casually put his foot on the seat next to her. She moved closer to the window, feeling strange, as if he had imprisoned her somehow with his shoe. Now quiet, Mr. Hopkins stared at her.

"And how old are you, dear?" he whispered.

"Thirteen . . . and a little."

"You're very pretty, Polly. Very."

Polly was thrilled by Mr. Hopkins' invitation to have dinner with him in the dining car. She had never been offered a choice of food before and didn't know what to order. They

13

didn't have stew, the only thing she knew she would enjoy, so Mr. Hopkins ordered for her, and the food looked so elegant she was almost afraid to eat it. He tried to make pleasant conversation at dinner to put her at ease. After dinner, he took her hand and led her back to his compartment, like a kindly uncle.

The porter had made up the lower berth. Mr. Hopkins closed the door to the bedroom and then locked it. He took off his coat and vest and hung them up, while Polly stood uncertainly by the window. Mr. Hopkins lowered the shade with both hands, his face level with hers, looking directly into her eyes. Again she felt imprisoned, only this time by his forearms, bristling with red hair.

"Polly," he whispered, "you know what I'm going to do. You can make it a very wonderful experience for both of us, or it can be miserable for you. I would like it to be nice for you, your very first time." There was a pause. "It is your first time isn't it?" He lifted her chin so she had to look at him. "Little sweetheart? Yes," he smiled, "I can see that it is. Good."

Polly could hardly speak, her stomach churned and she felt sick with fear—it was not knowing what would happen next. She hoped it wouldn't hurt.

Mr. Hopkins spoke so softly, he might have been talking to a kitten. "I'll show you everything you have to know. You'll like it, you'll see." He ran his tongue over his lips and began to unbutton her blouse, very slowly, as if afraid to startle her. He then unbuttoned her skirt and let it fall to the floor. He took off her blouse and she stood there in her camisole and stockings. Two more buttons and the camisole fell open and he began to fondle her breasts.

"There's my good girl." Hopkins stepped back and undressed. Polly looked at the floor, afraid to look at him. She sat on the edge of the berth, eyes closed, and waited. He was so gentle that Polly was unprepared for the stabbing pain. Mr. Hopkins was unprepared for so much blood. He finished quickly, then washed himself at the small fold-down basin while Polly watched horrified.

The porter knocked at seven-thirty announcing that Chicago was next.

"Who is Emily?" Polly asked as she buttoned her skirt.

Mr. Hopkins took his gold watch from the shelf and put it in his vest pocket carefully adjusting the chain across his stomach.

"My little girl—why?"

14

"That's what you kept calling me," she said evenly. "While you were sleeping you grabbed me and called me Emily."

Hopkins' arm shot out and he slapped her across the face.

"Don't say that." He spat the words out. "Don't tell me that. What a terrible thing to say to a man!" But as a red welt spread across her cheek, he was sorry he hit her, then worried. He wet a towel which he made her hold on the bruise. As they got up to dress Mr. Hopkins turned his back to her.

From the center of the Grand Concourse Mr. Hopkins pointed toward the Ladies Waiting Room. He held out his hand to her, again the kind smile. "Good-bye, Polly."

Polly faced him and ignored the hand. "What about my money?" She stood still, feet planted squarely, her anger growing with each word. "You owe me money. Girls get paid for letting men do what you did to me." She paused, unused to the fury inside her. "Want me to yell?"

Hopkins looked as if he had been struck. The girl hadn't said ten sentences to him. Now this. He quickly reached for his billfold and took out ten dollars. This wasn't turning out at all as he had planned it.

"More, or I'll yell. You did it to me more than once," she snapped, looking him in the eye.

He took out more bills. "Here's fifteen more, you little slut." He shoved the bills into Polly's hand. "Take it. That's it." She took the bills and still raging, he grasped her arm and roughly pushed her away. She was off balance, tripped and fell.

When she got to her feet, Hopkins was hurrying away. She felt something running down her leg. Looking down she could see a line of blood beginning to spread out on her stocking. She looked around and saw a desk with a little sign that said TRAVELER'S AID.

"Please, ma'am, I'm hurt."

3

January 1919, New Orleans

The doors of the Loyola Avenue trolley car opened, and Ben stepped down in front of the Southern Pacific railroad depot. Once inside, it took a minute for his eyes to adjust to the cool darkness. There it was, listed on the departure schedule: THE SUNSET LIMITED, DESTINATION: LOS ANGELES. He hesitated for a few minutes to see how other passengers handled the tickets, not wanting to seem like a rube.

Most of the men and women boarding looked very swell. He pulled down his jacket. At least it was new and his tie was real silk. He glanced at his shoes, decided they looked scruffy, and rubbed them against the back of his trouser leg.

The conductor at the gate glanced at the ticket and told the porter in which car to put Ben's suitcase. He smiled pleasantly.

"Welcome aboard, sir. Would you like to go to the smoker

or to the observation car for the departure? If you haven't had breakfast, the diner is serving. Take your pleasure."

Ben thought of the immense breakfast his mother had insisted on serving him. "Thanks." For an instant he weighed the smoker against the observation car. The brochure included with the tickets had described the observation car, listing among its features the library, lamp shades hand-painted with scenes of California, and the telephone. He especially wanted to see a telephone on a railway train. His mother didn't have one and neither did anyone else he knew, so there was no one for him to call. There wasn't even anyone he knew left at the city room of the New Orleans *Times-Picayune*. His friends had all enlisted when he did. No telling when they'd get home or even if some of them ever would come back from France.

Ben drew a deep breath, stepped up onto the observation platform, and glanced inside. It looked as though a party was going on.

All the passengers seemed rich, the men in white flannel trousers or business suits, the women wearing jewelry, although it was still morning. Two women were even smoking, and everyone seemed to be holding a cocktail. Sunday morning, too. That would come to an end if prohibition was ratified. He settled down into the chair, happily enjoying the atmosphere of the car; the perfume of the women, cigars, whiskey, the low, polite sound of their conversation. Although everyone was talking, it was not noisy, and there was a special—he thought genteel—quality to the sound.

A very pretty girl was already using the telephone.

"But you said the offer was for three pictures at the new rate. What kind of friend are you? You got four for Bunny." There was a pause, then the girl bumped her hips. "Don't I do that for you, too?" Another girl, evidently a friend, stood listening and stifled a giggle behind her hand. "Here's Bunny." She handed the phone to her companion.

Ben heard the word "fuck" twice. He stared at Bunny, since he'd never heard a woman use that word before who wasn't a whore. She was certainly prettier than any whore he'd ever had. Seeing an empty chair he moved closer. As the conversation developed, he realized they were both picture actresses of some sort talking to someone in Hollywood.

A soft voice came from behind him.

"They're being pigs about the telephone, aren't they?"

Beside him sat a girl, smiling. He smiled back, almost catching his breath. She was wonderful, black hair tied up behind her head, huge violet eyes that looked deep into his, as

17

if searching out some secret. No girl had ever looked at him that way before. She was so beautiful he was unable to answer. What could he possibly say to such a lovely creature? He gulped and stared, frantically trying to think of a reply to her perfectly simple remark when a man about his own age reached out his hand to her.

"Stuart is about to leave, Olive, dear. We should see him off the train."

"All right, Sam," she answered. Turning to Ben, she smiled again and said, "Excuse me." She said it as if they were friends. He watched her retreating figure, feeling a rush of regret.

The porter struck a small gong announcing their departure, and the conductor stood patiently waiting for the two girls to finish with the telephone. One of them was smoking a cigarette, holding it high in the air, elbow crooked in a theatrical manner. Against the light, Ben could see the silhouette of her thighs through her sheer dress. Lordy!

He heard someone exhale loudly beside him. "God Almighty!" said the conductor. "Look at that. I bet that's a fancy snatch," he whispered to Ben. "Well, I got to break it up," he sighed. "Excuse me ladies. It's time to say good-bye. I've got to unplug the phone."

The blonde blew smoke into his face and said, "Go peel your banana!"

The conductor reddened and his mouth opened slightly as if to answer her, then he thought better of it. Face set, he pulled the plug and dropped the connecting wire out the window.

"You dumb son of a bitch!" She walked toward the conductor. Ben felt sure she would slap him. He evidently did, too, for he backed away.

"I ought to kick you right in the balls! Come on, Bunny. Let's get the hell out of here."

The conductor picked up the telephone and wound the wire into a neat coil. "Dirty mouths. Tough as nails. Put your pecker in that and she'd grind it off. Stay away from that kind."

Ben grinned. "I'd take my chances. God damn! Beautiful girls, tough or not."

4

January 1919,
Luncheon at Delmonico's, New York

The doorman at Delmonico's nodded deferentially to Abe Weiss and an attendant from the cloakroom took his hat and stick, then pulled his gloves, finger by finger, from his extended hands. Another attendant helped slip off the fur-lined coat and carefully blotted the drops of slush from its shoulders before hanging it up. A young woman stepped forward and tucked a red carnation into his buttonhole. In turn he tucked a bill into her shirtwaist. She smiled and curtsied but Weiss's remote expression did not change. Inwardly he was still boiling with rage.

Delmonico's lobby glowed with a pale rose light reflected on brocade walls from flickering gas globes held aloft at the foot of each staircase by a life-sized bronze amazon. Gas illumination was more flattering to beautiful women than glaring electric lights.

Weiss ignored the bowing maitre d'hotel as he made his

way across the dining room. He could not, however, ignore his competitors. Walking from table to table Weiss seemed full of good spirits, jovial, making quips about business, exchanging stories. Delmonico's was the principal meeting place for the titans of the New York film industry, and as many deals had been made across the linen damask as on the fabled million dollar rug in the lobby of the Alexandria Hotel in Los Angeles.

Today Adolph Zukor introduced him to Enrico Caruso, with whom he was lunching. Weiss asked after Marcus Loew's wife at one table, and at another assured Lewis Selznick that he wasn't really trying to steal his star, Olive Thomas, away from him. Actually the deal was almost set, but why ruin Mr. Selznick's lunch? Finally he congratulated William Fox on the great success of Tom Mix's new picture, a high-class western at the Strand. It was a small industry and each one knew what the other was up to. Weiss finally sat down at his table overlooking a grey Fifth Avenue.

Saul Rubin lounged in the backseat of his limousine, using the short ride from the Astor Hotel to Delmonico's to prepare himself to face an Abe Weiss who, by now, would know that Mary Pickford, Douglas Fairbanks, and D.W. Griffith were leaving Majestic. They were joining Charlie Chaplin to form their own company, United Artists Corporation.

Losing Mary Pickford would be a major blow to any studio. An entire industry stood on her tiny shoulders. Movie audiences went to see stars, certain stars, no matter what the picture was about. And Majestic had the stars. Weiss had been correct, there was no antitrust law against cornering all the stars. For six years Abe Weiss had been able to force exhibitors to take a year's run of Majestic pictures by promising that six to eight of them would star Mary Pickford.

To keep Mary happy Weiss was paying her ten thousand dollars a week, with a fifty-thousand-dollar advance on thirty percent of each picture's profits. He had set up a separate company to handle her pictures and paid her mother, Charlotte, fifty thousand dollars a year to advise. Even Mary's brother, Jack, and her sister, Lotte, had been given their own picture contracts with Majestic. But none of it had turned out to be enough.

The chauffeur opened the passenger door. With a deep breath, Rubin stepped out into the slush. He looked up to the second-floor windows of the dining room. Abe Weiss would already be up there, watching him and waiting.

Rubin crossed the dining room, stopping at many of the same tables as Weiss had. Weiss remained seated as his partner from California arrived at the table and slid into his chair.

"Sorry I'm late, Mr. Weiss. Slept badly on the train, as usual, and I dozed off at the hotel. How have you been?"

Weiss glared at him. "As well as could be expected."

Rubin became more uneasy. "You sound piqued," he said lightly. "How is Mrs. Weiss? And the girls?"

"Mrs. Weiss is always fine, and the girls spend money. You think I'm in business to make pictures? I'm in business to make money so they can spend it."

Weiss looked as elegant as ever. He was a thin, tiny man in his early forties. But his body was trimly muscled, and the delicate arrangement of his face seemed to be held together by the tautness of his skin. As he held up the menu, his perfectly manicured fingernails gleamed and the jade ring glowed as if illuminated from within.

"Lake Erie whitefish and a boiled potato," Weiss said to the waiter.

Rubin ordered lavishly from the house specialties.

Weiss looked at him accusingly. "While you were enjoying the train ride, Mary announced that she was leaving Majestic. You must have had some inkling, Mr. Rubin, and you didn't send a telegram, even?"

"I got the wire in Omaha. Yes, I suspected. There were rumors all over the lot before I left, but when I asked her, she only smiled and shook her pretty curls at me."

Weiss leaned forward, almost spitting every word. "The worst is yet. Mary is going to First National for six pictures while whatever United Artists is gets itself organized. Six hundred thousand dollars a year, fifty percent of the gross. The girl I brought to Hollywood goes over to my worst enemy. Tom Talley. *Gevalt!*" He lowered his voice and growled, "And you, Mr. Rubin, you let it happen."

Rubin felt a chill. "Mr. Weiss, that is not true. No one could have stopped her. The two of you go back years. If you couldn't keep her out of friendship, loyalty, and mutual respect, not to mention ten thousand a week and a cut of the gross, how could I?" Rubin leaned forward. "I did everything I could. I found great stories for her. Assigned her favorite directors. I stopped Mickey Neilan from acting because she liked his directing. I took William Desmond Taylor off another picture in the middle to put him with her." His voice had risen and he stopped to control it. "The truth is nothing

21

would do. Mary wants everything her own way. No controls, no supervision, and all of the profits."

"What about Fairbanks?" Weiss asked.

"Where Mary goes, Doug goes. Their affair is very hotsy-totsy now. If both of them could ever get divorced, they would probably marry. In the meantime, they manage. No one is supposed to know, of course." He held up his middle finger. "Doug sold more than bonds on that tour." He winked.

Weiss shook his head. "Divorce is out of the question. They'd be denounced from every pulpit in the country. Their careers would go down the gutter. No nice lady will go to a picture starring a divorced woman, and that's that! She'll see if she tries it."

"Mr. Weiss," Rubin began, trying not to sound anxious. "I never thought it would really happen. The stories I heard, everybody heard. During the negotiations Fairbanks wired the chairs so everyone would get shocks. Griffith called him a buffoon, sulked out there on the lawn, refused to come in and talk again." Rubin snickered. "Then Fairbanks crawled around under the table grabbing the ladies by their ankles. Cute? Chaplin wouldn't trust anyone; even when his lawyers said it was OK to sign, he wouldn't." He leaned back in his chair. "You see why I thought they would never pull it off. McAdoo must have made them see sense."

"When the rumors first started," Weiss said reflectively, "I invited Mary and her mother out to the country house at Sands Point. I *mutched* her around the rose garden and tried to talk to her like a father. I even offered her five thousand a week to retire for five years. Better off the screen than working for somebody else." Weiss looked past Rubin as if into the distance. "The answer was 'no.' She had a God-given duty to make pictures. God would strike her down if she retired, even at such a salary. She hoped the pictures would be for Majestic. But no, she had to go to First National! *A bone in my throat!*

"Well, Mr. Rubin, what do you plan to do? I have contracts with exhibitors and Mary starts her last picture for us next week. Doug has six months to go on his contract, then he is gone, too. With both Reid and Fairbanks working, we could count on a light adventure every four weeks. Now what?"

Rubin watched him absently pushing the food from one side of his plate to the other.

"I plan to speed up production on the Reid pictures,"

22

Rubin announced. "We'll give him more money instead of time off. How have your conversations with Maxwell's mother gone? Mary May Maxwell could be the new Mary Pickford, if we groom her right and give her the right directors."

"Maybe it will all fall through," Rubin said. "Maybe Mary will hate having her own company and come back."

"Don't kid yourself." Weiss fixed him with a glance. "Mary will make it work. She is smart enough to make up for all of Doug's stupidity and Chaplin's suspiciousness. She thinks like a man, and she'll pull them all together, and they'll make it work despite themselves. I taught her." He smiled ruefully. "To keep her happy, I taught her."

He poked grimly at the table cloth with his butter knife. "Well, now they got it all. All those exhibitors who complained that I paid her too much, the fancy productions to keep her happy. Now they'll see what it's like. Now *they'll* be paying little Mary's bills. All those First National exhibitors will be sorry they ever hired themselves a star and got into picture making. I found it all out ten years ago. What a surprise they'll get!" He almost sounded happy. "Then they'll wish they'd stuck to the theater side of the picture business and left the making to us."

Rubin finished eating in silence, glancing at Weiss from time to time. It hadn't been as bad as he'd expected. As he finished, Weiss took his napkin out of his collar and pushed his chair back, preparing to leave. He turned back to Rubin.

"Nine tomorrow morning. Be in my office. Don't be late *yentzing* around. 'Dozed off!' What do you think I am? A child? By the way, I want you to fire Mandel. I don't like the tone of his wires to the office. When I buy a property that I think will make a fine picture, I don't want him refusing to give me a scenario."

It was as if someone had spilled cold water on Rubin. Mandel was his brother-in-law and the studio supervisor. "You can't be serious, Mr. Weiss."

Weiss stood up.

"Sit down, please. You can't say something like that and then walk off, just like that."

"I paid $6,500 for *Old Wives for New* and asked when he would have a scenario ready for me to look at." Rubin could see Weiss's teeth as he spat out each word. "I only wanted him to get commercial to the extent that he is able to see the value in a modern story. He only wants to do period crap. He sent me this." He threw a rumpled telegram onto the table.

OLD WIVES FOR NEW WASTE OF TIME STOP WHILE THERE IS NO QUESTION IN ANYONE'S MIND THAT NEW YORK OFFICE IS SEAT OF GOVERNMENT STOP THERE IS CONSIDERABLE DOUBT IN OUR MINDS THAT IT IS THE SEAT OF GREAT LITERARY AND DRAMATIC DISCERNMENT STOP REGARDS MANDEL

Weiss snorted. "I am the chairman and the biggest stockholder. Many of the company's properties are under contract to me personally. I was making and selling pictures successfully when Mandel was still selling off a pushcart. What gives him the idea that he knows so much? I said what I got to say. Fire him. I hear things aren't too good between him and your sister, anyway. Maybe it won't make that much difference to her. Get him off the lot by the end of the day. You hired him. You fire him. Tomorrow morning in my office. At nine."

Rubin nodded.

Weiss walked across the dining room touching shoulders and beaming.

5

January 1919, Somewhere in Arizona

The stationmaster at Cochise looked directly into the rising sun. Down the straight tracks that led into the sunrise, he could see a point of white light and a finger of smoke. Right on time. All those swells, sound asleep, most likely. In a moment the smudge would engulf half the town in a cloud of black smoke. The train would not slow down until it reached the rail yard in Tucson.

The train sped toward him and the agent stepped back into the doorway of the freight office as the dark cloud hit the platform. Through the mixture of coal smoke and steam the cars were a blur as they roared past. Some details stood out clearly, some were lost in a sense of dark speed. A cook in a white hat stood at a half-opened door. Then a private car passed, and standing directly in front of its windows was a naked man. He stood there, his arms grasping the window casing, as though to steady himself. Then the image was gone, erased by smoke.

Another momentary vision appeared suddenly through the dark cloud. It was a face—the stark white face of a beautiful woman looking out of the window of a compartment. She stared straight ahead, certainly not comprehending the town of Cochise or the details of the Southern Pacific depot there. It was only a glimpse, a fragment, but the image was very powerful. A pale oval, two dark shadows of eyes, the merest suggestion of rose-colored lips. Vanished. The agent experienced an overwhelming sense of sadness from that moment of vision. Months later he would recognize the face looking out at him from the Phoenix newspaper.

The waiter had already taken Ben's breakfast order when the door at the end of the empty dining car opened. A large man entered and paused, deciding where to sit. After Ben nodded an almost imperceptible good morning, he came over to the table and held out his hand.

"Thomas Bascomb. Mind if I join you? If you'd rather be by yourself and read the paper, sing out." He stood waiting.

Ben jumped to his feet with a grin. "Not at all, not at all. Name's Sommers. Ben Sommers." He waved his hand at the chair opposite. "Please sit down."

Bascomb sat down and smiled back at his breakfast companion. Young kid, he thought, not more than twenty-four at most. Husky. Probably fresh out of the army going home.

"What part of the South you from, Mr. Sommers?"

Ben could feel his ears start to get hot. "I guess you can tell from my accent. I been tryin' to lose it. I'm from New Orleans."

"Thought so. I noticed you here on Sunday night looking at that great cookie with the dark hair, the movie queen."

"Movie queen? That girl?" His mouth fell open as he stared at Bascomb. "The one sittin' back there in the corner?" He grinned. "I couldn't keep my mind on eating dinner, for lookin' at her."

Bascomb laughed. "You weren't the only one staring. Every man in the car practically had it out in his hand." His voice became confidential and he leaned forward. "That's

26

Olive Thomas." He sat back smiling as if he'd just played his best card.

Ben was stunned. "Olive Thomas?" The Ziegfeld girl, the movie star. "Jesus H. Christ!" He whistled softly. "I talked to her," he said, brightening. "In the observation car on Sunday morning. She talked to me. As if I was anybody."

Bascomb flagged a passing waiter and ordered a bourbon and water.

"They all look different off screen, I'm told," he said. "I think it's the makeup."

Ben rested his elbows on the table. "Who was the gent with her? Anybody?"

"I dunno. Not her husband. Think they're separated. Husband's Jack Pickford. Little Mary's baby brother." He winked at Ben. "Jack's kind of a notorious stud around Hollywood." He tasted his drink. "You heading for L.A.?"

Ben nodded. "Lookin' for work. I used to be a reporter for the *Times-Picayune* before I enlisted. Got out just before Christmas. Thought I'd try California, have me an adventure." He wiped up egg yolk with some toast.

Bascomb ordered a steak, then sipped the bourbon. "You see any action?"

"None at all. I barely got to France before it was all over. Didn't see a thing." He laughed self-consciously. "Mostly saw New Jersey and it wasn't much. Just a bunch of farms."

Bascomb watched the scenery glide past and Ben finished his breakfast. The waiter put a huge steak in front of Bascomb. "What made you decide on L.A.?" He cut into the steak and decided it was done properly.

"Couple of buddies in camp came from there. Honest, to hear them carryin' on, it's God's country. If it's only half that good . . ."

"How you gonna keep 'em down on the farm . . . ?" Bascomb sang in a flat voice.

Ben settled back and watched Bascomb eat. He was interested in this man. He'd taken this expensive train to California, an all-Pullman train he couldn't really afford, hoping to meet important people who might give him contacts for getting a job in Los Angeles. The Sunset Limited was like a little private club, and he had talked to a lot of successful men in the past two days, accepted their cigars, drunk their brandy. Every time he met one of them he wrote the name down in a little notebook. Bent over in his upper berth each night he jotted down affiliations and addresses. He had been given a lot of free business advice in the smoking lounge or in the observation car. Mostly, "Buy land, watch out for water rights."

"You live in California, Mr. Bascomb?"

Bascomb shook his head. "No, Washington, D.C." He swallowed the piece of steak he'd been chewing. "I'm heading for California on business. I'm in the public relations racket. Traveling with my boss." He jerked his head toward the front of the train. "He's up ahead in the private varnish."

"Varnish?"

"Yeh. Private car. That's railroad lingo for private car. Varnished wood. Get it?" Ben nodded. "My boss is William Gibbs McAdoo. President Wilson's commissioner of railroads." Ben looked impressed. Bascomb was airy. "Travels like this all the time." He chuckled. "At government expense." He chewed thoughtfully. "Always order a steak on a train that goes through Texas. The railroads compete with each other to see who serves the biggest one." He ate very rapidly. "What kind of job are you looking for? You're a pretty good-looking lad, but you hardly seem like the matinee idol type. Know anybody at any of the studios?"

Ben was puzzled. "Actually, I thought I'd try a newspaper in Los Angeles. That's what I'm good at." He looked Bascomb squarely in the eye, encouraged that this successful man seemed interested in him.

"Jesus, not work in the movies?" Bascomb stopped, fork halfway to his mouth. "You must be the only kid in the States that doesn't want to work in the movies."

"Hell, I'm a newspaperman, not an actor," Ben said. "I got a letter from my old city editor at the *T-P*. He didn't want me to leave."

Bascomb resumed eating. "You're lucky. But that letter might not be much help." He smiled slyly. "I'm not sure if anyone at any of the L.A. papers can read." He guffawed at his own joke.

Ben smiled weakly. "What do you do when you do public relations?" Ben asked, to change the subject.

"Darned if I know," Bascomb replied. "It's a pretty new field. I just make sure nothing terrible gets in the papers about my boss and the good things he wants to read about get put right up there on page one." He grinned. "And I try to influence reporters like yourself to say nice things." He winked. "It's going to be grand having a friend on an L.A. paper."

28

Ben wished the man would be serious for a minute. The coffee was all gone and in a few minutes there would be no casual way to continue this conversation.

"What do you and the commissioner expect to be doing in Los Angeles?"

Bascomb glanced up at him, speculating for an instant. "Well, it's kinda secret for the moment," he answered offhandedly.

"Have you lived in Washington a long time, Mr. Bascomb?"

"Yep. A few years now. I went with Wilson when he got himself elected president. I was a front door in his campaign. You know, hired halls, got bands for torchlight parades." He took a toothpick out of his mouth, held it up and examined the point, then selected another. "Got involved with Creel and the war films. Handled some of his Liberty Bond rallies." He looked out of the window as if remembering. "That's where I first saw young Pickford. He was with his sister and Doug Fairbanks on a bond tour." He thought for a minute, then said, "I kept my hand in. First thing, I knew, William G. says to me, 'I got a little job on the coast. Come on along.'" He smiled. "The weather in Washington is lousy this time of year, the women are easy in Hollywood. So here I am.

"Kid, this is the only way to travel. None of that upper and lower berth nonsense." He brought the chair forward, looked around and lowered his voice. "I got my own bathroom." He made it sound like a genuine achievement. "'Want to take a crap?" He pushed his plate away.

"Not right now," Ben said. "But I've never been in a private car," he added.

Bascomb nodded. "Most people haven't. Come on and look." He signaled the waiter and stood up. "Let the commissioner buy your breakfast. I'll put it on the tab for the car." He signed the check.

"Gee, thanks a lot, Mr. Bascomb. I've got to be careful how much I spend. I may not be able to land a job right away." He hoped he wasn't being too obvious, but maybe Bascomb did know somebody on a newspaper in Los Angeles.

Near the front end of the train a velvet rope hung across the passage between the cars. From it hung a sign with gold letters, PRIVATE. Bascomb unhooked the rope and they stepped through.

"That little red rope marks the difference between the classes," he said. "Those who can and those who can't. Those who do and those who don't. The haves and the have-nots. May not look like much, but when you cross that line, the sky's the limit. Anything you see can be yours."

Opening the door beyond, Ben could see what Bascomb was talking about. It was a private world. Thick carpets muffled the sound of the wheels. Windows frosted with elaborate designs allowed him to see out, but no one could see in. Bascomb pointed to the other end of the corridor.

"That's his nibs's room up there. Got a bathtub, a double bed, fireplace, parlor, the works." He opened the door to Bedroom C. "Here's my place. The sofa makes up into a bed. Comfortable. Sure you don't want to use the crapper?"

"No thanks," said Ben, a little embarrassed.

"Excuse me, then. The only orderly thing about me is my digestion." He tossed a newspaper to Ben, opened a small door and closed it behind him. Ben sat on the sofa and watched the desert roll past.

Bascomb came out and washed his hands at the small sink. "We must be getting into Tucson." He bent slightly and looked out of the window. "Ben, why don't you just sit there and enjoy the comforts? I got to go up and see McAdoo. He'll be up by now and there are always telegrams to be sent whenever the train stops. If there's anything you want, just push that button and order from the waiter. We got our own kitchen and it won't cost you a dime."

Ben sat down to read the paper and enjoy himself. This was a lot more than he'd bargained for when he'd bought his ticket. He didn't know much about public relations, but he intended to parlay this meeting into something good. Next time he traveled across the country, he wanted to go first-class.

6

January 1919, The Streets of New York

The Hollywood Reporter

CHAPLIN IN NEW ROLE

Charlie, who was visited on the set of *Easy Street*
by dancer Nijinsky, has completed filming a ballet
dream sequence for his latest First National release,
Sunnyside. Knocked unconscious by a cow, Charlie
dreams that he is the god Pan. He dances with a
bevy of lovelies in classic Greek costumes. Playing
on a flowered pipe, Charlie-Pan dances with the
nymphs until he backs into a cactus, waking him up
from his dream. Leave it to Chaplin to try new
ideas and make them into socko popular entertainment.

Bessie Weiss lay in bed listening. Abe was standing by the
window looking out into East Thirty-first Street.

"What's wrong, Abe?"

"Why are you awake, Bessie?"

"You should ask, why? Who could sleep with your fussing
around? Come back to bed, Abe."

"I'm going out to walk for a while. The storm's finished
and it's clearing. Looks cold, but nice."

Bessie sighed and closed her eyes. "Bundle up, for God's
sake. Wear your overshoes. Try to be back by six and I'll
have a little something fixed warm for you." While he dressed
she wondered what was bothering him now.

"Abe, don't slam the doors. You'll wake up Hannah and
she threatens to quit every time you wake her up."

Park Avenue was never quite deserted, but at three A.M.

31

there was less movement than usual. The sleet had started to freeze dangerously, Weiss thought, horses will fall.

Abe Weiss had been walking the streets of New York at night since he arrived in the States in the winter of '93. The tenement flat was so crowded and his bed in the windowless room so uncomfortable, he spent many of his nights walking and thinking. Restless, ambitious, dreaming always of some way to get ahead, Abe had followed his nighttime thoughts in leasing an empty store for a nickelodeon in 1903. At first open only at night, it used chairs rented from a neighboring undertaker for a penny each. At the end of three months he owned his own chairs.

He liked to think that he solved all his problems with the same reasoning. He examined each problem as if it were unrelated to him, held it up at arms' length so that he could view it from all sides as the Talmud did. His greatest decisions had come from these marathon sessions in the cold or hot nights, for he walked in all seasons. Now, he shivered slightly, wishing for a little summer warmth on this freezing January night. Somewhere in the back of his brain an idea was beginning to form. As yet he was unable to articulate it and question its merits, but it continued to tease him. After thirty blocks he realized what it was. After fifty blocks he was busily questioning it. On the way back to the house he was beginning to feel pleased with himself.

"Send a telegram to Moses Klein in Washington," Weiss said into the speaker box on his desk, "and tell him to take the Congressional up this afternoon. Then get Greenglass into my office." He looked out of the window for a moment.

A moment later Nathan Greenglass was standing before the desk.

"Good morning, Mr. Greenglass. Sit down. I've been thinking. What do you know about Charles Grossman over at Vitagraph?"

"He has the reputation of a very smart lawyer."

"What else?"

"He knows theaters like he knows his hands. He's also done a good job of building up the Vitagraph percentages by various deals he makes because he knows more about the local theaters than the exchange who books them knows." There was a slight pause. "I think some of the deals he makes are questionable. But then they have worked for Vitagraph."

"They must have somebody good over there to do as well as they do with that trash they turn out. They don't deserve the grosses they get." He sat and looked at the top of the desk, then spoke slowly, "I got an idea and I need a man who really knows theaters and houses all over the country. Would he leave Vitagraph?"

Greenglass shrugged. "Any man will leave anywhere for the right money and the right job. I only hear good about him."

"Get him over here tomorrow morning at nine. Rubin, Klein, you and Goldman along with Grossman."

Saul Rubin stood in the doorway. Weiss beckoned him into the office. "You wired Mandel?"

"No, Mr. Weiss. I felt more discussions were in order. He is central to so many projects, I doubt I can keep production going without him."

Weiss lifted his hand. "How much do you want to continue as president of Majestic Studios?" In an otherwise motionless face Weiss raised both eyebrows and looked at Rubin blandly.

"But I'm a partner! I own half!"

Weiss shook his head slowly. "I would take the name Majestic and my various properties and leave; you could have what was left," he said quietly. "You would find, Mr. Rubin, that much of what is listed as an asset of Majestic is really held in my name, or owned by one of my companies. Stars are under personal contract to me, not you or Majestic. Directors, the same. I've even bought story properties. All of them, they only work *at* Majestic. They work *for* me."

Rubin closed his eyes. I can't afford a showdown with him, he thought. Everybody loses against him. Everybody.

"Can it wait until I return to the Coast? I hate to do it in a wire."

"Mr. Rubin, it's because of a wire the bastard sent me that this is happening. If he's not sensitive about telegrams, why should you be?" His voice hardened. "I wanted him off the lot yesterday. If you can't manage that and want to wait five days, you can. But I want him out. After yesterday, you're paying his salary personally."

Rubin looked at him, started to speak, then closed his mouth, breathed deeply and said, "I'll send a telegram."

Weiss nodded. "When you've done that, we can start the nine o'clock meeting."

Nathan Greenglass stood in the doorway. "Mr. Grossman just arrived, Mr. Weiss. Everyone is here now. Shall we come in?"

Weiss stood up smiling, his arms out in a gesture of

welcome. "By all means, by all means. Sit down, everyone," he said, indicating the circle of chairs drawn up around his desk. He beamed as he shook Grossman's hand. "Thank you for coming. Thank you."

Charles Grossman sat down directly opposite Abe Weiss, his mouth clamped firmly on an unlighted cigar. He felt in danger. Everyone knew how slippery Abe Weiss could be, and he was determined to be on guard.

For the first few minutes Weiss exchanged idle studio gossip. He told a story about how Sam Goldwyn never carried any money so the lines of his trousers wouldn't be disfigured by the bulge of things in his pockets. They all laughed.

Moses Klein said, "There's only one bulge he wants the girls to look at." More laughter.

Abe Weiss nodded at Grossman. "Do you know everyone, Mr. Grossman?"

"I haven't had the pleasure of Mr. Klein, here."

Weiss smiled reflectively.

"Mr. Klein and I go back a ways together. I found out that despite the fact that Majestic gave substantial sums to certain congressmen to help defeat legislation aimed at interstate taxes on prints of moving pictures, no one knew who Majestic was. We know each other from the days when I was in Washington making pictures during the war. In the Creel office."

Klein nodded at Grossman. "After Mary Pickford sold a million dollars in Liberty Bonds, and it was discovered that more people knew her name than the President's, they found out who Majestic was pretty quick."

"Mr. Klein reminds official Washington who we are in various ways." There was a moment of silence. Then Weiss said, "Well, Mr. Grossman, do I have horns?"

"I didn't expect horns at all. Claws, maybe."

Weiss held up his hands and laughed. "Sometimes I wish they were." He lowered his voice and looked at Grossman directly, his tone confidential. "Stop worrying. I want to hire you, if you are as good as I hear. I am not a bad man to work for. I want to make Majestic the biggest and best moving picture production and distribution company in the world." He shrugged. "Such a little ambition. I will be very generous if I succeed."

Grossman nodded and chewed on his cigar.

"What I am going to tell you, Mr. Grossman, you probably know already, our business being what it is." Weiss laughed.

"We spend twenty percent of our effort on making pictures, then with the other eighty we make gossip. It's a small business. Everyone knows what's going on with everyone else."

Everyone laughed dutifully except Grossman. "Majestic is losing two of its biggest stars. One of them, Mary Pickford, is the biggest in the business. It is a terrible loss. So I ask the question, how do we stay on top? Naturally . . . don't misunderstand . . . we still have big, big stars. More than anyone else. Cecil DeMille says he can make great pictures without stars, that one great picture will create its own stars. Right, Mr. Rubin?" Rubin nodded.

"What element of success are we missing? What does our competition have that we don't have? Fox, Metro, Paramount, Triangle, and all the rest, especially the big new threat, First National, what do they have?" He tapped at his forehead with one finger.

"How did I get into this business, I ask you? By owning a theater, like everybody else. I bought a nickelodeon and I couldn't get a steady supply of pictures. Sixteen years ago, I went looking for pictures, better than the crap that I was buying for lack of anything at all. I squeezed and pressured, demanding two new pictures a week. Sometimes I got them, sometimes not. So, I started to produce. First, I bought what I could from any source, then filled in. But even I could produce better crap than was being turned out by those *schmucks.*"

Klein broke in. "Mr. Weiss is too modest. What he won't tell you is that he studied the problem of what made a good picture. He stood at the rear of his theaters for hours analyzing what made an audience laugh and cry. He left nothing to chance."

Weiss continued. "It was a business, a problem to solve. After I bought the second house, I used the profits to make a few pictures. First thing you know, I was in the picture business as well as the theater business, and soon I was selling pictures to other theater owners."

Greenglass said softly, "And here we are one hundred million dollars later."

"Give or take." Weiss beamed and looked at his fingernails. "The next thing I was in the distribution business as well and needed a lot of good pictures. That's where Mr. Rubin and I joined our companies. He had the best studio on the Coast and I had the biggest distribution setup. So there we were—manufacturing and distribution.

35

"Last night it came to me. What we are missing. Theaters! Outlets of our own. We only own a few theaters. Everybody shows one of my pictures and makes a profit on it that I don't get." He leaned across the desk and his voice became intense. "What would happen if I start buying a theater in every city and town in the country? Where I can't buy, build new ones. Where owners won't sell, squeeze them a little. Get more rentals, play two theaters against each other, force them into exclusive contracts. Make them sell, in the end."

"It's wonderful," Klein said. "Just like Rockefeller and Standard Oil or Havemeyer and sugar. A little illegal, not too much. But maybe, by being smart, we can get around that."

Weiss bore in on Grossman, who had shown signs of relaxing a bit. "Now you see why I need a smart man like you, Mr. Grossman."

Weiss became expansive, charming again. He leaned across the desk, joking. He sat back in his chair painting dreams of success and wealth; visions—animated, effusive, intimate.

Klein, watching him sell, thought to himself, this is how he wins a star. This is how he got Roscoe Arbuckle away from Lewis Selznick, charmed Charlotte Pickford into signing Mary again, pulled the rug out from under Sennett and Triangle and took Gloria Swanson. When the man wants to be charming, Klein thought, no one is safe.

By noon, Charles Grossman had decided to become a vice-president of Majestic in charge of a new theater division. At twelve-thirty, Weiss stood up.

"Time for lunch, gentlemen. I will take us all to Delmonico's. We can continue talking there. You be thinking while we walk up the avenue, Mr. Grossman?"

"About what, Mr. Weiss?"

"About First National and their theaters. I want to kill them off."

7

January 1919, At the Arcade Station— Los Angeles

Ben stayed in Bedroom C most of the morning, embarrassed to be there by himself, afraid someone might come in and ask him what he was doing there. At last Bascomb returned, looking concerned.

"I just knew it wouldn't keep," he said furiously.

"Something wrong, Mr. Bascomb? I was beginning to worry a little."

Bascomb slammed the door. He stood looking out of the window for a minute. "I'm in a spot. It's the big picture deal. Word's out somehow and McAdoo's furious. He's still a cabinet member, after all." He perched on the windowsill. "But I'm afraid it's gone beyond that point. Damn!" He sank into the armchair and grasped the arms.

"What deal?"

Bascomb looked at him as if trying to make up his mind whether to speak out or not. He took a deep breath. "McAdoo was asked to be the attorney and front for one of the biggest deals in movie history." He quickly sketched in the Pickford, Fairbanks, Chaplin, Griffith alliance.

"Well, who talked? They're the ones to blame, not you."

"Fairbanks and Chaplin blabbed to the skies." He sounded disgusted. "Movie people don't know how to keep their mouths shut, for God's sake!" He sighed deeply and, in resignation, sat down again. "I guess I can't blame them. They live for gossip and to see their names in print. Studios spend fortunes making sure everybody's name hits the papers and magazines once a day. And I'm getting paid to keep it quiet." He laughed.

But Ben could see the worry and distress in his eyes. What had seemed to be just a story was evidently a serious matter.

When the waiter arrived Tom said, "Charlie, why don't you just bring some ice and a bottle. Save your steps in the long run." He looked at Ben. "Want a beer? Sandwich?"

"No thanks, I'm full." He reconsidered. "On second thought, maybe a beer'd hit the spot."

Tom watched the waiter retreat, then hit the arm of the chair a powerful blow with his fist. "Oh, hell!" There was resignation in his tone, "I'll fix it when we get to L.A. A few denials in the right places, pay off a few columnists. I can fix everything."

He put his feet up on the side chair and looked over at Ben.

"Now, how about you? You gonna be a cub all your life?"

Ben felt slightly miffed. "Hey, I'm no cub. I was a full fledged reporter on the *T-P* for four years before I enlisted. I was only a cub for a few months after high school."

Tom looked at Ben as if he had underestimated him. "You're lucky. Not too many guys make it through high school."

"I was the only kid I knew who was still going to school after he was fourteen." He sounded slightly smug. "The guys I went to grade school with were all out working and spending all their money on girls and such." He poured himself a glass of beer. "I didn't have a real girl until I moved away from home and went to work and made a little money. I guess that's what money is really for, girls." He looked up and caught Bascomb's understanding grin.

"There's one thing certain, Ben, if a girl goes with you and you got no money, it's love for certain." Tom went on. "You liked being a reporter? You must have—you're still at it."

Ben's eyes gleamed. "Hell, yes. Rough and tumble. First few times I saw real excitement, I got so het up I couldn't sleep for hours." Smiling, he said, "Kinda grown up and dirty, if you know what I mean." He leaned forward, confidential. "I'm kinda like two people. I learned to try and think things out. My pa was a very deliberate man. I've tried to be." He grinned. "I don't do as well, but I try." A rough section of track made the crystals in the chandelier tinkle, and he looked up.

"Reporters are a funny lot," Bascomb said as if remembering a specific person. "You a good one?"

Ben cocked his head and thought a minute. "Yeh. I am. I always got a lot of ideas. Things jus' come to me. Angles, you might say." He was laughing as he spoke, remembering. "Every time I'd hear a rumor or a piece of gossip, Lordy, I'd translate it into a bunch of stories, quick as a wink. Couldn't sleep sometimes, thinkin' up ways to handle stories. Used to drive my editor crazy."

"Sounds like you was a one-man newspaper."

"I guess I thought I was. What I really was," he lowered his voice, "was a pain in the ass. Speakin' plainly."

The train chugged slowly into the Arcade Station in Los Angeles, amid noise and confusion, bells, the hiss of steam. And in the distance, a brass band playing. Ben looked out the corridor window.

He gasped. "Look!" he yelled. "Oh, my God, Tom, they know everything."

Across the front of the train shed hung a brilliantly colored banner, on which was spelled out in huge letters, CONGRATULATIONS TO UNITED ARTISTS. Beneath it stood the band, resplendent in bright blue uniforms, playing "Columbia, the Gem of the Ocean." And standing on the platform, baton in hand, and having the time of his life, was Douglas Fairbanks.

"Oh, Christ," Tom said softly. "Christ! Now he'll never believe me."

Ben froze, Bascomb's fingers digging into his shoulder, as a roar of fury erupted behind them. McAdoo stood halfway down the corridor shaking with rage.

"Bascomb! Is this your doing? Smacks of you, the carny feeling to it. Flashy. Tasteless. The improper gesture at a perfectly inappropriate time." He fished in his pocket for a dime and threw it on the floor where it rolled under a radiator grille. "That's all your work is worth!"

Bascomb stepped forward. "Mr. McAdoo, I assure you this is none of my doing! I'm as shocked as . . ."

"Get the hell out of my way!"

At that moment, Fairbanks, jumping up and down on the

platform, spotted McAdoo through the window. As his head popped up into view he rapped for attention on the glass. McAdoo stopped in confusion. Fairbanks' face continued to bob up and down.

Bascomb grabbed Ben's arm. "Let's get the hell out of here." As they reached the top of the steps in the vestibule, Fairbanks appeared at the bottom, surrounded by a growing crowd. Suddenly, as Ben shrank back against the wall, he gave an astonishing leap and landed lightly on the top step in front of them.

"My name is Doug Fairbanks. I'm pleased to meetcha." It was as if he didn't have one of the most famous faces in the world. He bubbled with enthusiasm and shook hands. McAdoo pulled him into the car and slammed the door. Tom and Ben stood for a moment on the platform with the porter and their suitcases. McAdoo opened the door and thrust his face toward them.

"You're fired, you son of a bitch! Fired! Pick up your check at my office tomorrow. You Judas!"

Fairbanks, all smiles, pushed his way past. "Can your man get me a glass of orange juice? I'm a little dry. We do a nifty Sousa's 'Liberty Bell March.' Wanna hear it?"

McAdoo sputtered and tried to push Fairbanks back into the car. "Douglas, please! I'm trying to be discreet about my arrival here. I didn't think it wise to let the news out just yet. No one is supposed to know; after all, I'm still in the President's cabinet!"

Fairbanks looked puzzled. "Discreet? Bill, this is very discreet, only a few cowboys and the stagecoach, a few girls, the band. Gee, Bill, if I'd wanted to draw attention to your arrival I'd have put a press agent on the job and done it up right. This is plenty quiet for Hollywood." He leaped off the steps and ran toward the band, jumping over luggage and trunks in his path.

Bascomb turned to McAdoo. "It's your zoo now," he grinned. "You be the keeper. I'm getting out of here. Come on." He pulled at Ben's arm. As they reached the bottom of the steps the porter pointed to a distant arch. They headed toward it as the band started up "The Liberty Bell March" and the cowboys lifted McAdoo to their shoulders, shooting into the air. He wore a stricken look.

As they walked through the station toward the taxi stand, Bascomb was shaken with fits of laughter every few steps. He gave the porter five dollars and they were on their way.

"The Alexandria Hotel, driver." Bascomb slumped down in

his seat and little gasps of laughter continued to bubble up out of him.

"I give them a couple of months at best. That's like oil and water. Even with Oscar Price as president and with Abrahams and Schulberg running it, McAdoo can't last. He has no sense of humor. Wait till Doug wires up his chair." He started to laugh all over again.

Ben looked out the window, surprised by Los Angeles. It didn't look like a town in a western movie at all. It looked like a city.

The Alexandria Hotel was at Fifth and Spring, a block long and very elegant. The doorman took their bags and ushered them inside. Here it was ten at night in January, and the doors were standing wide open. There were hanging baskets of fern and flowers everywhere. The lobby was filled with people, many in evening clothes, conversations and laughter coming from all sides. It was an impressive sight, massive marble columns, sweeping curved stairways, balustraded balconies, glittering crystal chandeliers.

"Gosh, it might be any big city. New York, even," Ben said.

Tom looked around. "Yeh. People always think they're coming to a hick town. There's lots of money in L.A. Land speculation, water, oil right within the city limits. Then there's the movies. Millions to be made there. They may not be considered cultured, but they're plenty rich." He spoke to the desk clerk. "You have a reservation for Bascomb?"

The clerk looked up. "Yes, sir," he said, checking. "A single."

"Well, make that a double. My assistant is staying with me." He turned to Ben. "What's your name, kid?"

The clerk raised one eyebrow. "We don't encourage that sort of thing, sir." He glanced at Ben, then down at the register.

Bascomb leaned toward him. "As soon as we're registered," he muttered, "send up a couple of girls."

The clerk flushed. "The bell captain will help you, sir." He turned to Ben and asked politely, "Your name please?"

"Sommers. Benjamin Sommers." Embarrassed, he turned to Bascomb. "Listen, if this is going to be inconvenient, I can find me a boarding house."

"Skip it, kid. You're staying with me."

He tipped the bellboy another dollar. As soon as the door to the room closed Ben took Bascomb's arm. "Tom, it's none of my business, but you're out of a job now. This room costs

41

ten dollars a night and I've only got about twenty dollars left. Please stop throwin' your money around."

"Thanks, kid, for worrying about me. But I got an idea that will pull us out of the soup. I know who will pay for all this."

"Who?"

"Abe Weiss, the chairman of Majestic. Meanwhile, let's hit the hay. We gotta be up at six. I want to call New York by nine their time. It may take a few days to make arrangements."

"What will Weiss and Majestic pay you for?"

"Information, my friend." Bascomb gave him a long look. "You want to work in the movies? . . ."

"Tom, I'm not used to jumpin' like you. I have to think things out."

Tom propped himself up on his elbow. "Listen kid, remember what you told me about meeting Olive Thomas in the observation car? How you only got so many opportunities in life and you'd just let one pass? Well, this is an opportunity. You better not let it pass." He lay back on the pillows and closed his eyes. In a few minutes he was asleep and snoring.

Ben lay awake in the darkness. He'd only met this man today and already he was sharing a room, maybe getting a job.

The smooth sheets felt good on his skin. He ran his hand across them. Not too bad. In two months he'd jumped from a rough army blanket on a steel cot, between two doughboys who didn't smell too good, to a berth on a fancy Pullman car with a manservant who ran his shaving water for him, then to smooth sheets in the fanciest hotel in southern California. Tomorrow, maybe the movies.

8

January 1919, Chicago

ELECTRIC THEATER
LAST TWO DAYS! LAST TWO DAYS!

ABE WEISS PRESENTS
A MAJESTIC PICTURE

THE WOMAN GOD FORGOT

Geraldine Farrar
Wallace Reid

Directed by Cecil B. DeMille

THRILLS, LAUGHTER, TEARS,
SPECTACLE, ROMANCE, HISTORICAL!

The lady from the Traveler's Aid Society summoned a nurse and the two sat Polly down and questioned her. Their mutual opinion, when Polly told her story, was that Mr. Hopkins should be arrested if not castrated. The nurse decided that Polly should go to the Florence Crittenden Home for examination in the event some damage had been done.

"Don't you worry one bit, dear. That's what Traveler's Aid is here for. You just go along." She hesitated. "God bless you, dear. You'll need His help, I'm afraid."

Polly couldn't imagine what she was talking about. The worst part was over and Mr. Hopkins was gone.

After a phone call, a woman from the home arrived to escort Polly in a taxicab.

A doctor examined her and cleaned her up, recommending a thorough hot bath. He said he hoped Polly would not get pregnant and she gasped. In all of the past twenty-four hours that had never occurred to her. She imagined a baby, bald like Mr. Hopkins, a thatch of wiry red hair on its tiny chest.

She had never seen a bathtub before, only the galvanized tub on the kitchen floor close to the stove. This tub looked just like the one in her hygiene book, with its little animal feet and had faucets with hot and cold water in them.

"Get in there and scrub yourself well, young lady. Get as much of that man out of your crotch as you can." The nurse turned off the water and left. Polly slipped out of the robe and sank into the hot water, luxuriating in the warmth. First the water turned pink from blood, then as she began to wash, grey from grime. She had never been so clean.

"Well, you look cleaner." The nurse motioned to a girl with heavy eyebrows that met over her nose. "This is Mavis, Polly. Mavis is going to let you share her room for the few days you will be here, until we can be sure you have no infection." She turned to Mavis. "Help Polly get some supper, then she probably should try and get some sleep. I don't think she slept much last night." The nurse gave Polly a meaningful look. "There's a nightgown for you on the stool."

"Who fucked ya?" Mavis asked. "Ya get knocked up, that why you're here?"

"Oh, a man on the train. I don't really want to talk about it."

Mavis led the way to the kitchen where the cook fixed sandwiches for Polly. There were mountains of food everywhere in the huge room. She had never seen so many things that looked good to eat.

She slept the rest of the day and through the night. Awakened by Mavis the following morning, she was given new underpants and stockings. After a huge breakfast of eggs and sausage and milk, she went to see Mrs. Waterson.

"Polly, dear, I don't think you ought to tell your folks any more than you wish to. I'll enclose a little note with more of an explanation." She thought for a minute, then added, "I think it best just to say that you were molested. If you want to, sometime, you can tell your mother you were raped. But I think you should think about that. We've had a lot of bad experiences with mothers and fathers."

Polly sat at the little desk in the front parlor and wrote her letter. It was hard to concentrate because of the traffic on the street outside, but she wrote as neat a letter as she could, forming each word carefully. Mrs. Waterson approved and added her note, sealed and stamped the envelope.

"I can't say they'll be relieved when they hear what's happened, but at least they'll know you are safe and well cared for. Now run along and find something to do." Mrs. Waterson smiled at her.

Polly sat on her bed and looked at a pile of magazines recommended by Mavis. "This here's my favorite. *Photoplay.*"

Slowly turning the pages Polly saw incredibly beautiful women and handsome men smiling at her, dressed in expensive clothes, standing in gardens, by automobiles, in wonderful rooms. Polly didn't know who they were but they were glorious.

Mavis sat beside her clucking her tongue in approval as she turned the glossy pages. "I just love going to the pictures, don't you?"

Polly looked up. "What're they?"

"You mean you never seen a movin' picture? Where you been? Where'd you live? Pictures are absolutely everywhere. Everywhere!"

"Not in Iron Valley they ain't. That's where I been."

Mavis sat down shaking her head. "Hey, if you want, we could go and see one. They let us go twice a week if two or more go together." She stopped suddenly. "You got forty cents? I'm busted."

"I got two dollars sewn in my jacket. We could use that."

"Jeez. We could both go. We could go to the Electric. It's only two blocks away. They change pictures there three times a week. Wanna ask tonight?" She was trying to appear nonchalant.

Mavis found Mrs. Waterson.

"Polly's never been to a movin' picture show. Be good for her to get out." Mavis grew confidential. "You know. All she's been through. Give her something to take her mind off it."

Mrs. Waterson nodded. "Yes, she mustn't dwell on her situation."

Polly spent the rest of the day poring through Mavis's movie magazines. She cut the dollar bills out of her jacket and took them to Mrs. Waterson.

"Could you keep one of these for me in case I need it? I'll use part of the other one to take Mavis and me to the picture."

"That's very generous of you, Polly. I'll put the dollar with the rest of your money in the cashbox. When you get ready to leave you can take it all with you."

45

After supper four girls started out for the Electric Theater. As they turned the corner Polly stopped, staring at the blaze of light bulbs that outlined the theater. She had never seen anything so thrilling. Mavis assured her that the outside was nothing compared to the inside. Inside it was like a palace.

"Just to walk into the lobby is a real treat," Mavis said, "but with a picture, too, it's the grandest place you can go. A good picture show makes life worth living."

The outside of the theater was entirely covered with posters. "Who are they? What's happening?"

"They're the stars. Don't you know anything? In the fur dress, there, that's Geraldine Farrar, the opera star. The guy in the armor is Wallace Reid. God, isn't he wonderful! Hey, you can read, can't you?"

"Sure, why?"

"I hate reading the titles out loud to some dummy who can't read."

Because Polly seemed to be in a daze, Mavis snatched the money out of her hand, bought the tickets, and gave them to the doorman. In the lobby Polly stopped again, stunned by its magnificence. Tapestries and gleaming oil paintings covered the walls. Electric candelabra stood on marble plinths, throwing soft lights over the painted figures of nymphs and satyrs that chased each other across the ceiling.

Mavis tugged at Polly's arm. "Come on, we'll miss the overture."

Polly longed to look at the details, the great crystal chandeliers, the gilded furniture, the pots of palm trees, the soft lighted nooks where comfortable settees nestled. But Mavis rushed her into the archway. On either side of the blue velvet curtain was a dimly lighted archway holding shining clusters of golden tubes.

"Those are the organ pipes. Wait till you see it come up out of the floor." She wiggled with delight. "Isn't this just the cat's pajamas?"

The lights began to dim and the organ console rose out of the orchestra pit into a pink spotlight. The light picked out the silhouette of a man seated at a mass of keys and buttons that curved out to either side of him as far as he could reach. There was a magnificent roar of sound that shook the auditorium.

Mavis nudged Polly. "See? What'd I say?"

After they applauded the overture the curtain came to life, drawing up in little gathers, bathed with a flickering white light. Out of the darkness of the sky, stars twinkled and

46

formed themselves into a constellation, the Big Dipper. The words A MAJESTIC PICTURE appeared shimmering among the stars. That's why Mavis wondered if she could read. Polly grabbed Mavis's arm.

"It says, 'a Majestic picture.'"

"Don't read out loud. It's annoying as hell." Mavis jabbed at her and concentrated on the screen which had come to life.

THE WOMAN GOD FORGOT
Directed by Cecil B. DeMille
Starring Geraldine Farrar
and
Wallace Reid

No experience in her life had prepared Polly for what happened to her in the next hour. She had seen a Bessemer converter tapped and watched the glowing river of molten steel pour out while sparks flew in every direction. She had clutched at her father's hand as great sheets of red hot steel sped past between rollers with a roar that made it impossible to speak. But these spectacles were nothing compared to the sweep and grandeur of the incandescent images that moved before her eyes. She gripped the arms of her seat as Farrar, playing an Aztec princess, swept down a ceremonial staircase dressed in floating gauze edged with ropes of glittering jewels. Preceded by hundreds of beautiful girls spreading her path with flower petals the princess moved through great halls where the walls and pillars were covered with thousands of grinning skulls.

Polly was stunned. Spectacle after spectacle flashed before her startled eyes. As the sun rose upon the day of battle, the army was called by a huge bronze gong struck by a naked slave. Fantastic temples and pyramids were silhouetted against the sky. The princess fell in love with a dashing Spanish soldier, Cortez. They kissed on a bed of jaguar skins in a shadowed room lit by great urns of glowing coals. Muscular slaves pulled on silken ropes and a soft curtain floated down around them so that human eyes might not see their lovemaking.

The titles compared Reid to a tiger—but he was like a god. When he prepared to do battle with Montezuma, Reid held his sword handle up to make a cross, and a sudden shaft of sunlight illuminated his beautiful face in such a way that Polly felt faint.

47

Montezuma, on the other hand, was a frail old man. As he painfully struggled up the endless steps to the top of the pyramid to be tortured, Polly wept at his decision to die for his people. When the princess offered herself to Cortez if he would spare Montezuma, Polly found herself wishing that she could die for all of them. She cried out at the scenes of torture, Montezuma's feet pressed against red hot irons. At his death Polly was sobbing aloud.

"Jeez, it's only a movie," Mavis whispered. The tears on Polly's cheeks reflected the flickering light from the screen. "Don't worry, honey. It's not real."

As the words THE END appeared on the screen, Polly sank back in her seat exhausted and transformed. There was so much more to life than she had ever imagined. Whatever Wallace Reid had done to the princess behind the curtain must be totally different from what Mr. Hopkins had done to her. Life in Iron Valley was so ugly and dull, while in this foreign land it was so grand and exciting.

Mavis, amused by Polly's powerful reaction to the film, told her how movies were made while they walked back to the home. Dismayed that all she had seen was artificial, created for an hour's entertainment, Polly was silent and embarrassed. But when she closed her eyes she could see the beautiful princess drive the sacred knife into her breast. It must be real, she thought, it had to be real.

9

January 1919, A Private Room at Delmonico's

The private rooms in the towers of Delmonico's were not intended for business meetings. But Abe Weiss thought the main dining room would be too full of competitors, so they found themselves lunching in an ornate parlor.

"Well, Mr. Grossman, you've had two blocks of a nice walk and a few minutes while we ordered, plenty of time to think." There was a sly note in Weiss's voice. "What do you suggest we do about First National?"

Grossman, eyes bright with excitement, said, "I didn't need any walk, Mr. Weiss. I know how to bring your competitors to their knees. No one else can do it, except maybe Paramount. No one else is big enough. But with your rate of production, your stars, your organization, the exchanges, the booking offices, the theaters you already own, you can get a monopoly of theaters and you can knock out First National at the same time."

Grossman spoke softly, his mind racing. Quiet, respectable, bald, nearsighted, happily married, and the father of three lovely children, Grossman had the instincts of a killer. In Abe Weiss he saw the opportunity to wreak the havoc he had dreamed of in his years of working for organizations tottering on the brink of failure. He had always lost out to distributors or studios that were not more shrewd or more clever or even more crooked; they were just bigger and more powerful. Now was his chance to get back at them all with the power of the biggest of them all. Majestic. He stopped eating and described his plan.

"Fear. That's your tool. You don't really have to be a monopoly. Just act like one. Start buying up theaters. Do it in a splashy, dramatic way. Also be mysterious about it—rumors will leak out. Buy a few really big ones in strategic locations, the Rivoli, say, and the Rialto, you sew up Broadway. Freeze everybody else out of the showcase of the world. Buy up as many theaters as you can afford, then threaten to buy up all of the rest. Force them to sign exclusive contracts. Name your own price on rentals. The little exhibitors will figure that if they're a Majestic house you'll leave them be. As soon as First National starts losing a few houses out of their contract list to Majestic, they will be so afraid they will fall apart."

Grossman paused to gulp some wine.

"Theater owners are a bunch of clods, and especially the theater owners that make up First National. They run million-dollar houses as if they were corner candy stores. Not knowing business methods, they are afraid of lawyers and contracts. Many of them are self-made men who distrust everyone else in the business. They cheat on rentals, even on their own pictures, for God's sake, trying to gyp their own bookers and exchangers. First National is ripe to be taken."

Weiss was delighted. Grossman's ideas dovetailed perfectly with his theater acquisition plan. Two birds with one stone.

"Just think of the trouble Williams and Talley had putting First National together," Grossman continued. "Imagine getting twelve owners of theater chains together in one hotel room. I'm told the Astor had to redecorate the suite. It was worse than the Battle of the Marne!" He laughed at his own joke. "It may still fly apart after two years. Think of such a business; a dozen ill-paired bedmates, not suited to get along, facing staggering commitments. A million here to Chaplin, a million there to Mary Pickford. And they both leave in a few months for United Artists. Who do they have then? When the First National theaters closed during the flu epidemic, Talley had to borrow. They have no reserves, and they're using a river of money to keep those new studios going. Buy up theaters and threaten their shaky structure, and you'll see."

Weiss's eyes gleamed. This was the kind of talk he liked to hear. Disaster to his worst enemy. They'd be sorry for enticing Mary away from him. Pay, that's what they'd do. He gave orders.

"I want a list of cities and towns. In each city, the names of the three biggest theaters. In smaller towns, the name of the key theater. Owners, mortgages, loans—facts, facts, facts. A list of exchanges and booking offices and who they service. Who services each theater on the list? Our own people will know much of this, but it's never been put together before. Take chains. If we buy a chain of theaters, what does that give us in population, in potential audiences? Who will sell his theater to Majestic? Who will have to be encouraged to sell? Maybe a man dies and leaves his theater to his widow, does she only need a little encouragement to sell or a lot? If Havemeyer could burn up cane fields and Rockefeller oil depots, we could be able, somehow, to convince a few widows to sell, no?"

Klein, alarmed, said, "Be careful of violence. Since those days there are new laws. If you get caught now, you don't only go to prison for arson but for violation of the Sherman and Clayton Antitrust Acts as well. Watch your step, Mr. Weiss."

Weiss stared at him steadily. "I certainly won't condone violence, Mr. Klein. If, by chance any happens, I won't be the one who does it." He turned toward Grossman. "Figure out the details."

Klein, almost inaudible, said, "It will cost millions. Where will the money come from?"

"We only need to buy certain theaters," Grossman said, "the others will fall into line. What do you earn from a theater?"

Nathan Greenglass answered. The financing of theaters was his subject, his only subject. "If you stick to certain guidelines in paying for the house, for example, ground rent no more than thirty dollars a year per seat, a theater seating three thousand will return at least twenty-five percent on its investment each year." He grinned. "Pretty good?"

Weiss cut into his potato. "Cheap bastards. They complain whenever we increase the rentals on the pictures."

Greenglass continued. "Twenty-five is actually very conservative. It's a figure below which Majestic will not operate a theater. Sid Grauman, in Los Angeles, will earn profits of

51

nearly ninety percent this year on his Million Dollar Theatre. The Rialto, here on Broadway, will earn eighty."

"Now, where will the money come from?" Weiss looked around the table. "I can't swing that much cash. But I can borrow."

Klein said, "Kuhn, Loeb is getting ready to lend Sam Goldwyn some money. He needs it to expand."

Weiss nodded. "Poor Sam. He lost out on all that Du Pont money when Zukor kicked him out of Paramount. Du Pont decided not to try and fight Morgan over control of Kodak and film." He shrugged. "Besides, I wouldn't go there anyway. They know too many people in the picture business. Word gets out. You go in and ask for a loan and meet a competitor in the revolving door. He puts two and two."

"Have you thought about selling shares to the public?" asked Grossman.

"Not unless I have to. If I own it all, I don't have to answer any questions. It's bad enough to borrow. A bank will demand a man on the board as it is."

"Most bankers are frightened of our business, anyway," Klein said. "We're too undisciplined for them." His face brightened. "Hey, you know what? Here we are, America's fifth biggest industry in terms of dollar gross, and we're self-financed. This hasn't happened in a hundred years in this country. Not since the days of Astor and Vanderbilt. Think of that, Mr. Weiss, you own it all."

"Not quite all," Weiss grunted. "But I intend to." He got up and walked over to one of the narrow windows overlooking Madison Avenue, pulling the heavy draperies aside. "No one would have us. That's the only reason we got it all. I'm worth twenty million and I can't get inside a single club in New York. Mrs. Weiss does not shop in certain stores where she doesn't feel welcome. There's a reason we own it all." He underlined each word. "No one else wanted this business. When you been a secondhand clothes dealer, you know dirt and are not afraid of dirty people, people who don't want to be dirty but can't afford to pay for a bath. I lived there. I knew the people. I knew what they liked."

He let the drapery fall, face intense with emotion. "You know what they liked? They liked pictures. I decided that if there were twenty million poor and dirty people with a nickel to see a picture show each, that's a million dollars. And so I took it and gave them the world in return. I gave them decent entertainment that nobody else gave them. You know what they did before pictures? Got drunk and hit their wives." He laughed. "That's entertainment? I lifted them out of their miserable steaming and freezing holes for one hour a week and made them kings and queens. And the nickels poured in. The rich bankers never even knew what was happening. It wasn't until a couple of years back when J. P. Morgan got interested enough to try and control Kodak and the manufacturing of film that the banks even knew we were using fifty million dollars' worth of film a year! Nobody saw the potential, nobody but us."

Grossman said quietly, "You mean you, don't you, Mr. Weiss?"

Weiss smiled gently and sat down. "Thank you. No. That's not true. I wish I could say I had that kind of vision alone by myself. There were many of us, Jesse, Sam and Adolph, Willie, Uncle Carl, Marcus. Mostly friends, even relatives. We're still friends, some of us. It got too big too fast for there to be only one or two. Nothing like it in history. It was an explosion of money.

"Gentlemen," he said, standing up, "we got work to do. Mr. Grossman, welcome. *Mazel tov.* Draw up your plans and I will put them into action. Come on. Let's buy picture houses."

10

January 1919, New York and Hollywood

"Mr. Weiss, there is a man on the telephone calling from Los Angeles. He says to tell you he knows all about United Artists. Name is Thomas Bascomb."

"Send Greenglass in and shut the door."

After a moment Nate Greenglass opened the door quietly, and as Weiss picked up the receiver, Greenglass picked up an earpiece that hung on the side of the telephone and began to listen.

"Hello? Mr. Bascomb? This is Abraham Weiss. What is it you want to tell me?" After almost ten minutes Weiss interrupted. "Just a moment, Mr. Bascomb. I wish to discuss this with an associate. What is your number there? I will call you back in one-half hour. Please remember how difficult it is to arrange a long distance call. It may take me longer, but please wait. I will get through this morning." He hung up.

Leaning back in his chair he half closed his eyes and said, "So now we know. Have Mr. Grossman check on this Bascomb. He sounds genuine, but you never know. Make sure. Call Moses Klein in Washington. Bascomb said I should remember him from the Creel office in Washington during the war. See if he was actually there. The name is familiar." He sat thinking for a moment then said softly, "That dumb *schmuck*, Rubin. All this happening under his nose. Maybe we'll give Mr. Bascomb a chance to show what he can do."

Bascomb replaced the receiver with a yell. Standing up, he extended his hand. "Weiss believed me. We both got jobs. Congrats, kid. Two hundred a week for you, OK?" He snapped his fingers.

"OK! Thanks. Thanks a lot," Ben said slowly. "I'm not sure I can be worth that much." He shook his head and smiled. "Hollywood salaries are certainly crazy."

"It's a bullshit business in a bullshit town. And I'll work your ass off. Publicizing movies isn't just wild stunts, it's hard work. Let's grab some chow. Weiss ordered the studio to send over a car for us."

The Indian Grill Room of the Alexandria Hotel was a dramatic adventure designed by a scenic artist from the Fox Studios.

"Jesus Christ, we'll be lucky to make it through breakfast without getting an arrow through the heart," Bascomb said, trying to settle into a chair held together with rawhide lacings. Ben pushed a particularly dangerous looking potted cactus further away with his shoe.

The studio driver sought them out and stood respectfully by while Tom finished his coffee. A mob of men milled about in the lobby as he stopped at the cigar stand and bought a copy of each Los Angeles newspaper.

Settled into the backseat of a dark blue Pierce-Arrow limousine, they headed out into the traffic. The driver looked at them in the rearview mirror.

"Notice all them gents in the lobby? That's called the 'million-dollar rug.' Those are all independent film producers and distributors; most of them don't have offices. They work out of the lobby and their hatbands. Sometimes a million dollars' worth of business is done on that rug in a single week."

Tom looked at Ben and grinned. "Crazy bus'ness, crazy town." He jabbed a finger at the pile of newspapers in Ben's lap. "That's your new morning and evening assignment. We have to know every word that's printed about Majestic. We'll hire clipping services in other cities to cut out articles and mail them in. But here in home territory, it'll be your job.

You'll get so you can spot the name in fine print at fifty paces." He picked up *The Los Angeles Examiner*. "Pay special attention to this one." He opened the second section. "As long as you don't let the journalism get to you. Willie Hearst loves the movies. His girl friend, Marion Davies, is a star in his picture company, Cosmopolitan, and he spends millions producing extravagant turkeys for her, then millions more publicizing them. He pays real attention to the industry, though, and he was the first publisher to assign reviewers to pictures and run screen gossip columns. More than you can say about the papers of note in Washington, New York, and Chicago." Laughing, he continued. "You got to be careful, though, a big movie story can knock an international crisis right off the front page in a Hearst paper."

On the entertainment page Ben found a long story about McAdoo's arrival at the Arcade Station the previous evening, with all the details of Doug Fairbanks's welcome. He read it aloud to Tom, mocking the style in which it was written.

"Hold on there one minute, kid. That paper is going to be your bread and butter and some jam, too. You can't ask them to print the stories you plant and then make fun of them."

Ben flushed. "I didn't mean . . ."

"You did too. Listen, kid. Those cow-town reporters are going to be your best friends. Don't try to upstage them with your fancy eastern dude ways. Any success you have is going to depend on those people and you better find out who they are and why they are valuable to you—even if they write with cactus spines. If that's what sells pictures, just make sure they spell the name right. You can't have any kind of honest relationship if you have contempt for them."

"OK," said Ben after a moment's reflection. "I get the point."

Something had been bothering him since the telephone calls to New York. "Tom, how did you know that the Majestic publicity man was quitting and going over to United Artists?"

Tom cranked up the glass partition so the driver couldn't hear. "I didn't. I lied to Weiss. When I said his man Bamberg was going to U.A. it was a wild guess. Pickford and Fairbanks are going to need someone, and they both know Bamberg from years of working with him at Majestic. No matter how much he protests to Weiss now, after my call no one will believe him. Probably out looking for a job right now."

"Kinda hard on Bamberg."

"Oh, don't worry about him. He'll get hired fast. To have worked at Majestic is a good recommendation, and if Weiss fires you that's a good reason for somebody else to hire you. It's that kind of business. Besides, you have to think differently now. It's us first, everybody else second."

Saul Rubin, an intense man with great dark circles under shifting black eyes, looked coldly at his two new employees.

"I understand your deal and I have been told your salaries by New York. I have officially fired Bamberg. He won't be back. I don't mind saying, I certainly dislike the way you went over my head to Mr. Weiss. I wouldn't have hired you, you're not nearly as experienced as Bamberg was, but let's get something straight. I run the studio and you're in Hollywood, not New York. You don't work for Abe Weiss, you work for me, and I call the shots out here. Mr. Weiss is three thousand miles away. So, we'll try to get along anyway. You do your jobs and there won't be any trouble."

Bascomb relaxed back into the comfortable chair.

Ben glanced around the gothic library at the fireplace and the leaded glass windows. "Like it?" Rubin suddenly said. "I had it copied from one I saw in a Metro picture with Connie Talmadge. The boys did a nice job."

Tom cleared his throat and Rubin looked toward him expectantly.

"As long as we're getting things off our chests and clearing the air, so as to speak, Mr. Rubin—can I call you Saul? Please call me Tom. I am here because Mr. Weiss put me here. You take that up with him, if you want to. I assume you didn't want to, because you accepted us and the deal he made with me. We are replacing a man who was working for you under false colors and divided loyalties, helping denude this great studio of three of its grandest talents and box office draws. Mr. Weiss was outraged to learn all of that from me, an outsider, not from you, the studio supervisor and president. I intend to publicize and promote Majestic from coast to coast and I can't do it only from an office in Hollywood. I expect to be in New York from time to time and I'm told Mr. Weiss gets out here once a month. I'll appreciate any help you will give me, but if you choose not to, it won't make a hell of a lot of difference. Harder, yes. Impossible, no. Any questions, Saul?"

Rubin looked at him intently. "I like a man who knows

exactly where he stands and what he is doing. Someone will take you to your offices and give you a tour so you don't get lost. Good morning, gentlemen."

In the messy loft that was their new home, a dozen girls and men seemed to be talking on their telephones at the same time. Bascomb sat on the edge of a desk and rapped for attention. Quickly, everyone hung up and sat waiting.

"I assume you were calling all of your friends at other studios to find out what happened to Bamberg and who the new man is. I'm the new man. My name is Thomas Bascomb. This here's my assistant, Ben Sommers. Ben and I go back a long ways together." Ben shot a sideways glance at Tom who nodded at him and winked.

"Today is my first day. I must have your complete cooperation and help. If you feel, for any reason, that your loyalties cannot be switched from Mr. Bamberg to me, please resign at once. It will save on bloodshed in the long run.

"I have a lot of ideas about how I want to run this department. But I can't have all of the ideas. I'll welcome any you have and will give you credit if they're used. I'll get credit anyway if the department works well and we do a good job. So I can afford to be generous with credits. If we fail, I'll get all the blame. I don't intend to make a long speech, but let me ramble on for a minute, then we can all get to work." Bascomb looked around. Sure now that he had their attention, he intensified his pitch.

"Back when today's big motion picture executives had the same status as sideshow operators, we were like barkers with checked suits and diamond horseshoe stick pins. We can look back fifteen years now and laugh at those days as being prehistoric. Actually, we two were made for each other. The barker was the right man in the right place at the right time. He had a knowledge of human psychology, both as regards editors of papers—he was trying to get them to run his stuff as now—and the general public to whom he was trying to sell the product. He did stunts. So will we. I hope the zest and drive that the sideshow men had to such a vital degree has not gone out of this crowd. We're going to have fun and make a big noise. I may not still wear a checkered suit, but I'm still full of beans. I hope you're with me." There was scattered applause.

Bascomb was shown his office, sat down and put his feet up on the desk. He motioned Ben into a chair. "Ask one of the girls to find a bottle of bourbon. We got plans to make."

11

February 1919, Wall Street, New York

What could they be thinking of, having a meeting with this kike? Cyrus Cotton sat behind his desk and stared at the notice. He couldn't understand why the firm would meet with a Jew to begin with—and a Jew in the movie business at that. Maybe a Rothschild or a Loeb, even a Meyer, somebody responsible, solid. But in the movie business? He took out his pocket watch. Nearly three now, better not be late. Some of the senior partners were coming to the meeting. A junior partner of Falcon, Wilde, Renfrew and Tanner, Investment Bankers, Cyrus Cotton rarely saw any of the senior partners.

He walked upstairs through dim corridors, where the only color came from oriental runners on the floors. Just as Cyrus sat down in the conference room, Walter Falcon and his secretary entered. Cotton was surprised, the Jew must be important to get Falcon into a meeting. The secretary bustled forward and pulled out the center chair. Cyrus noticed that there was only one chair on the opposite side of the table. For the Jew, he guessed. Falcon lit a cigar.

"Good afternoon, Mr. Falcon. Cold day, isn't it?"

"What do you expect in the dead of winter?" Falcon did not smile.

"See what's keeping them. A client is waiting, and his time is as valuable as mine." When Falcon closed his mouth it became an almost invisible line across his face. The secretary hurried out.

Within a short time four men entered, the three other senior partners, and another junior partner, Fred Walsh. Samuel Wilde, a tall beefy man with a red face and a wide expanse of vest decorated with a gold chain from which trophies dangled, sat down next to Cyrus and nodded.

"Afternoon, Cyrus. Is Weiss outside?"

"I believe he must be the small man I saw waiting as I came upstairs."

Alvin Renfrew and William Tanner nodded curtly at Cotton and sat down further along the table. He was not quite sure they knew who he was. Walsh smiled at Cyrus. The secretary hovered. Renfrew exhaled loudly in an impatient sound.

"Well, we may as well hear what he has to say. I hope we can understand him, hear he has a terrible accent." He inclined his head briefly at the secretary who pressed an invisible button under the edge of the table.

Carrying a leather envelope, Weiss opened the center door and looked in. There they all sat in a row waiting for him. Weiss looked from face to face. *Goyim.* Not a Jew in the place. Good. Just as he'd suspected. He would get by, he thought, as he stepped to the front of the table and waited. No one stood to welcome him.

Walter Falcon indicated the chair. "Good afternoon, Mr. Weiss. Please sit down."

Weiss placed the leather envelope on the table so they would see how expensive it was.

They sat watching him, sizing him up, studying his face. Weiss felt like an animal in a zoo, a freak, someone in a sideshow. There was no sound in the room. Weiss suspected they didn't see too many Jews. He slid forward so his feet would touch the floor. He always felt more secure if his feet

60

were on the floor, even just toes touching. He crossed his hands and waited. He'd be damned if he would speak first.

"What can we do for you?" Tanner asked.

"I want to borrow thirty million dollars." That would make them sit up and pay attention. Not everybody started out like that, he bet.

Wilde blew out his breath as if he had been holding it a long time and blustered, "That is quite a lot of money!"

Weiss looked at him as if he was a bright child making a sudden discovery and smiled patiently.

"I'm aware of how much money it is. If it wasn't, would I come to a bank?" Weiss paused, then added lightly, "A few millions I could handle myself. But for a big amount I come to you."

Falcon, with a genial condescension in his voice, asked, "Why do you need the money, Mr. Weiss?"

"I want to build a theater chain from coast to coast, the greatest collection of theaters ever assembled. There's a lot going on in the picture business now. Lots of changes, new companies starting up, new competition. You got to keep one step ahead, stay in front. Two years ago it was all different. I was the first one who combined production with distribution and everything was going smoothly. The biggest in the business. Now it's all up in the air. You know how we are set up?"

"Why don't you tell us, just to make sure?" There was a note of patience in Falcon's voice that Weiss disliked. He looked at him sharply.

A goy bliept a goy, thought Weiss. What could he expect? He would have to be precise, explain carefully. They obviously didn't know his business, so he would tell them, from his point of view, the best point of view.

"It might take some time, you got the time?"

Falcon nodded. Then the others did.

"Up until 1913, all moving picture production was under the control of a patents trust. The men who owned the patents would only rent the equipment. You couldn't buy it. They told you what to make, how long, who could sell pictures, who could show them. Like a vise, they were. William Fox broke the trust in 1913." Weiss laughed. "The last public-spirited thing he ever did. Anyway, things began to settle down. Some men owned theaters. Some men took the pictures that the producing companies made and sold them to the theater owners. They were the distributors— we call them exchanges. Then, to get more and better pictures, some theater owners decided to make pictures themselves. Kept the product coming regular."

Weiss looked at their faces. Here were top bankers, rich men who lent money to other rich men, they knew all about American business. Yet, he thought, I'm telling them for the first time about a business that grosses eight hundred million dollars a year.

Falcon asked, "Wasn't there any regular production schedule, as there is in a plant or factory?"

Weiss smiled at him. Falcon had spotted the golden opportunity, as he had spotted it himself in 1913.

"No. Pictures just got made. Some companies, like Biograph, had a sort of schedule, but it could fall apart easily and the quality was uneven. Some companies turned out two pictures a week, some three, some only one when they could. It didn't make sense. By that time I owned a number of theaters and couldn't get a good picture regular. Besides, the producers only wanted to make two-reelers. You know, short films. I knew the audience was ready for longer pictures, maybe even five reels, six. I imported Duse, the Italian actress, in *Mary, Queen of Scots*, six reels. An immediate hit. I made a lot of money. First picture to play in a legitimate house."

Renfrew, excited, said, "I know. My wife and I saw it. A work of art."

Now you know who I am, Weiss thought, the real innovator, the pioneer, the man who gave the business class.

"I still couldn't get producers to make long pictures so I made them myself. Started in a warehouse in Queens. Hired actors. Then I put together groups of theaters in various cities and towns and supplied them on a regular basis. Occasionally I would buy another theater myself, if it was a good buy, but mostly they were chains owned by men I knew. Faced with the same problem of demand and lack of product."

Walter Falcon looked at the small, dapper figure balanced on the edge of the chair before him. Interesting. Weiss was completely in control. Falcon had never seen anyone ask for so much money with so little show of nerves.

"If I did one thing, I made it a business. I regulated production. I turned out two—not one or three—two pictures, either five or six reels long, each and every week. Dependable. Like a railroad. You could set your watch by my production schedule. Exchanges liked it. They knew where their next dollar was coming from. From Abe Weiss. Then I started buying exchanges.

"Gentlemen, the idea is simplicity itself. I make a picture and rent it to my own exchange for a profit. I distribute that same picture through my exchange and make another profit. I exhibit that picture in my theater and make a third profit. I rent that picture to an independent theater owner and make a fourth profit. Then come overseas sales. England! France! It's endless. Then came the problem."

Tanner interrupted with laughter. "A quadruple profit on each product. Jesus God! A vertical industry, just like oil and steel. Very shrewd, Mr. Weiss. What in heaven's name could your problem be?"

Weiss drew his shoulders together in an offhand way. "Everybody has started doing the very same thing. Now a group of theater owners, who have their own exchanges, First National, is finishing a big studio in Hollywood. Now they're hiring stars. Now they are buying more theaters. I must have more theaters of my own to compete."

"But, Mr. Weiss," Tanner asked, "how many theaters do you need?"

"All of them." Weiss smiled at him.

Tanner laid his cigar on the lip of the ash receiver. "Be reasonable. Surely you're joking? No one wants competition, ever. But no one can own everything, no matter how desirable it might seem from a business point of view."

Weiss looked at him. "About First National, I never joke. Look at it my way. If there is only one theater in a small town and tonight it is playing a Paramount or a Metro picture, my Majestic picture is sitting on a shelf in some exchange somewhere getting dusty. I plan to own a theater in every town, in every village, on the main street of every city in this whole country. If First National owns the only theater downtown, I have to play second-run houses. I will go broke."

Falcon held up his hand. "You mean you must have first runs? Does a picture have to run in a first-run house downtown to make a profit?"

"Now you said it. I got to have a first run. No one will go to a picture in a neighborhood house if it hasn't played downtown first. It's human nature. People like to go downtown to a movie palace. Gives a picture class. Then they talk to the neighbors. The neighbors go to the local house, they have to see it, too. People are funny. They go to see the stars.

I got great stars. I got good pictures. I don't have enough of the theaters."

"Who are your stars?" Tanner asked.

"The greatest. Wallie Reid, Tommy Meighan, Gloria Swanson, Roscoe Arbuckle. Olive Thomas just signed up. They are the stars people will pay to see. I used to have Mary Pickford and Doug Fairbanks, but they left to form a new company." Quickly Weiss outlined the formation of United Artists to them. Two of the bankers glanced at each other in dismay.

"But I have an idea. United Artists is starting to make pictures. Do they own theaters? No. Who will own the theaters? We will. If we own key theaters in key cities we will control the product. Let Doug and Mary risk the financing. Let them take the losses when there's a failure. But they will have to show their pictures in our houses. And Majestic's fee is forty percent off the top. I will also rerelease Mary's greatest successes. Doug's, too."

"Why will it take thirty million?"

"Because First National and Paramount are spending twenty. William Fox will spend ten. Everywhere First National is building or buying a theater; Fox is right across the street. Zukor is like a madman buying theaters." He paused, looked at them, then continued slowly.

"The day will come when every major picture company will have to have its own first-run house in every big city in the country. Those companies that also own houses in smaller cities will make more money. If I can buy, I will buy. If I must build, I will build. I will do anything to get my hands on theaters in certain cities. I already have a loose arrangement with some chains around the country. I can depend on them to take my product first and squeeze out the others. But friendships don't last long in this business. Too much money involved."

Tanner looked at his cigar. "What kind of control are you willing to give us?"

Weiss looked at him steadily. "No control. You don't know the business. We'd be broke inside a week. You get one man on my board of directors. I don't give up any control. When may I have a decision?"

"Well, Mr. Weiss, we must first discuss it. We have to look at your assets, your balance sheets, your statements. Did you bring your financial reports with you?"

Weiss patted the envelope. "Right here." He took out a volume that looked like an expensive book bound in blue vellum. Stamped in gold on the cover was the Majestic trademark, the constellation of the Big Dipper against a starry sky. Weiss placed the book on the table. It was a nice piece of showmanship.

"I will wait for your decision at my office. You can reach me there."

Tanner and Falcon stood up and held out their hands across the table. Weiss looked surprised, but reached back and shook hands with both of them.

"Thank you for your time, gentlemen," he said, picking up the envelope and turning toward the door. Tanner was genuinely surprised by how short he was.

"One more question, Mr. Weiss, if you don't mind? Why didn't you go to a bank run by some of your own people? Loeb, Kuhn, or someone like that?"

Weiss turned and smiled. "That is what my competitors are doing. A Jew always turns first to another Jew." He seemed apologetic. "Centuries of mistreatment have made us a little uneasy. We go where we think we will be understood, if not always treated as well as might be. I am a businessman. You are businessmen. If a deal looks good to you, you will not turn down a profit because I'm a Jew. I don't want my competitors to know what I'm doing. If I went to their bankers, they might get an inkling. I'm sure none of the principals would talk. They are men of integrity. But things get out, someone sees you walking in the front door and draws a conclusion. My competitors draw enough conclusions as it is." He smiled. "My request is safe with you until I want to let it out. Any other questions . . . ? Thank you again." The door closed behind him.

12

February 1919, Chicago and New York

Variety, February 22, 1919

MAJESTIC ON BUYING SPREE
FROHMAN ESTATE FINALLY SETTLED BY
WEISS BUY

NEW YORK. The late Charles Frohman's estate has finally been settled by being purchased in its entirety by Abe Weiss to be added to his properties in Majestic.

Included are literally hundreds of stage hits, many boffo Broadway biggies that have had picture studios licking their lips since the picture went down in the tragic sinking of the Lusitania in May, 1915. Loss of ship helped propel U.S. into a warlike spirit.

"Well, what do you think?" Tanner asked.

"I'm amazed," Falcon said after a moment of thought.

Wilde leaned forward in his seat and looked from side to side. "Ignore the short stature, cut through the vaudeville accent, the awful grammar, the man is a brilliant businessman who knows his onions."

"Oh, come off it, Sam," Falcon snorted. "The Jews who've made it in the picture business really have it made. They're not in the street, not traded in any way, they're not public so there's no checking up on them." He grasped the book Abe Weiss had left. "If this is a true statement and not bullshit, this will be our first look at what their business is really like. And let's not be condescending, for God's sake. They could buy and sell some of us personally. You should see the place some fellow, Loew I think, has built out at Glen Cove. We see it right across Hempstead Bay. It looks like it was designed by Henry the Eighth."

"They are smart," said Wilde, thumbing through the financial statement.

"Very smart," Falcon added. "I hate to admit it, but they saw it coming. Somehow they knew the movies were a gold mine and we didn't. We knew all about railroads and oil and mining. How did we miss out?"

"We weren't behind a pushcart on the Lower East Side. We didn't have our finger on the pulse of that crowd. Like the poem says—they may have been hungry and tired and poor, but they always seemed to have a nickel for a peep show and a nickel for a beer," Tanner said.

Renfrew sighed. "Who could have known?"

Tanner almost seemed to be talking to himself. "Well, we missed out in the beginning, but no more. Weiss has a billion-dollar tiger by the tail and can't let go, can't climb on board." An idea was forming in his mind. "Look at the bottom line, Samuel. How much is he worth?"

Wilde examined the report for a minute. "About twenty-five million. Give or take a few hundred thousand. It's a goddamned license to print money!"

Tanner exhaled a dense cloud of cigar smoke. "If he thinks he can double his assets in exchange for just a man on the board, he has another guess coming. But this has to be done carefully. We want to bait the hook, then not let him slip off. Let's organize this. We have to know everything about his business as soon as possible. Who really runs the company? Is it Weiss or someone else? Who is this Rubin?"

Tanner chewed his cigar thoughtfully. "We ought to have a look at that studio. Does it exist? What kind of asset is it?" He turned to Cotton and laid his cigar down on the table.

"Cyrus, get on a train and take a look. We want to know just exactly what is out there and what it's worth, besides the stars, of course. Listen around town. See if you can gather some sense of how Majestic is thought of in the industry, if you can call it that."

Smiling broadly, he picked up his cigar and walked to the door. He turned slowly. "I think that if we can gain control of Majestic by lending them a few million, we should. All of you agree?"

They nodded in agreement.

Renfrew turned to Cyrus. "Who knows, Cotton? You

might even get a lay." They all laughed again. Someone slapped him on the back, which was the biggest surprise of all.

"Mr. Weiss? Mr. Tanner calling. I'll put him on."

"Hello? Mr. Weiss?"

"Yes, I'm here."

"Mr. Weiss, we would like to send our man Cotton out to California to assess your plant there."

"Studio. It's a studio, not a plant. He will see the difference when he gets there. We don't make steam engines. We create an artistic product."

"All right—studio. I'm asking your help in introducing him to your management personnel out there so he doesn't have any trouble."

"Trouble? He would never have trouble. We are very gracious to visitors. Friends who visit us on the Coast have the time of their lives."

Tanner coughed. "Well, we don't expect him to be entertained. He will, of course, have all his expenses paid by the firm. He is there on business."

"What is his name?"

"Cyrus Cotton. He sat in the end chair. To your left at the table. Light colored hair. Plain looking. Thin. He is one of our junior partners and very knowledgeable."

"Have no fear, Mr. Tanner. I assume that if Mr. Cotton's report is favorable, you might agree to further discussions about increasing the amount of the loan?"

"We are always eager to talk to one of our good customers, Mr. Weiss. The partners are impressed with your progress in acquiring theaters. You seem to be buying the right houses, at least according to industry reports." He laughed. "We have started reading the trade press, and I must say it's more colorful than the banking papers. Full of delicious gossip. I've become quite in demand at dinner parties now that I can drop some naughty tidbits at table."

"I'm glad, Mr. Tanner. I'll save up some particularly juicy bits and give them to you at our next meeting. Things you won't find in the trade press."

"Wonderful. Mrs. Tanner will be thrilled." He cleared his throat to indicate that personal matters were over and business was commencing again. "Mr. Cotton will be on the New York Central tonight for Chicago. Be in California on Friday."

"Please have your secretary wire the exact timetable and

we will meet him in Pasadena with a car and make sure he reaches his hotel without incident."

Tanner had a sudden wild vision at the word incident—a western street with shooting, Cotton crouched behind a watering trough ducking bullets. "That's very kind of you." Tanner, despite himself, sounded uncertain.

"Get me Rubin on the Coast," Weiss snapped.

He and Rubin proceeded to plan Cyrus Cotton's tour of the studio, then he added, "Only the prettiest girls. If there is one appearing in a current release, let him screen the picture first at the lot. Then fix him up with her. He'll enjoy it more if he thinks he's got a little star. I want his *schmuck* busy twenty-four hours a day from the time he steps off that train. Like that senator. I want to build a very friendly relationship.

13

March 1919, Riverside, California

Daily News

MAJESTIC BUYS B'WAY THEATERS
RIVOLI AND RIALTO ADDED TO
GROWING THEATER EMPIRE

SPECIAL TO THE NEWS. Moving picture news was
made today by the purchase of two of Broadway's
biggest theaters, the Rivoli at 49th Street, and the
Rialto at 42nd Street. The purchase was made by
Abe Weiss representing Majestic Film Company.
The purchase gives Majestic two first-run houses on
Broadway in the heart of the prime motion picture
district.

The climax of *The Roaring Road* was to be a dramatic race
between a speeding railway train and a fast racing car driven
by Wallace Reid. The sequence was to be filmed at Riverside,
a small town on the banks of the dry Santa Ana River, where
a Santa Fe freight spur could be freed from rail service for
several hours at a time. A locomotive and several cars were
rented for three days and everyone trooped out to watch the
excitement.

"Sure. Go on. You ought to see how it's done," Bascomb
told Ben. "It's only for three days, anyway. Write material for
the press book. You know the sort of thing. 'Thrills, excitement, narrow squeaks, the heat, dust, the hard work and
danger, the dedication of actors and crews who risk their
lives so an audience sitting in a dark theater in Kansas City
can have a few minutes of pleasure.' "

Ben sighed. "Maybe I can figure some new angles. Give it a

lift. I'll ride out with Frank Urson, the second unit director, and see what I can pick up from him. See you Friday."

The logistics of setting up a movie location were like the army going on bivouac. Small sleeping tents for the camera and production crews were scattered across a field. Mess tents stood next to army cook stoves, and local cooks had been hired. Meals were served on rough board tables set up under the shade of large live oaks. Army blankets for bedrolls had been issued to the crews and the men were showing the girls how to make theirs up army style. There was a festive air—it was like a big summer camp for adults.

"This is Ben Sommers, Wallie. He's new with press and publicity and this is his first time out on location."

Wallace Reid held out his hand and flashed the famous smile.

"Don't let anybody invite you for a snipe hunt." He guffawed. "But being on location beats turning up at the studio day after day."

"It looks very exciting, Mr. Reid. . . ."

"Please call me Wallie. Nobody calls me mister except my wife when she gets mad at me."

"Wallie, if there's a chance, I'd like to talk to you about the picture. Maybe at lunch, if you're not too tired. I'm supposed to do a release about the thrills of shooting the racing sequence, and I'd like to get your angle on it."

"Be glad to. When we break for chow, look me up and we can eat together. Be glad to. Anything I can do to help."

Ben liked him immediately. It seemed silly to take to someone who was a stranger on the basis of two or three sentences, but it was more than just an expression and a handshake. Reid exuded an immediate warmth that assured Ben he was really glad to meet him. He suddenly understood the man's popularity.

The only shade was under a big red beach umbrella over a pretty girl making notes as fast as she could write.

"Can I stand here?" Ben asked.

"Surely, as long as you don't talk and distract me," she replied without looking up.

The train steamed down the track toward them as Wallie drove a Stutz along the road parallel to the train, racing it to the crossing ahead. The scene was being photographed from the back of a truck that drove in front of his car. The girl stopped writing.

"What are those big white things?" Ben asked her.

71

"Reflectors. Wallie's face is in shadow. They reflect sun-light on him so the camera can see his reactions."

The train backed up the length of the course so the scene could be shot again, this time with the camera truck following the racer and shooting the scene from behind. Ben wondered what was happening when the train backed up for the third time.

He watched the girl furiously make notes on each shot. While the red umbrella was being planted in a new position Ben asked her what was happening.

"Mr. Cruze and Mr. Urson have worked it all out. To get real thrills and excitement into the race Wallie's auto will cross over in front of the train three times, as the road changes from side to side. Of course, the auto will just barely make it across in front of the locomotive each time." She looked up at him with a dazzling smile.

"But why shoot it over so many times?"

"They're photographing the race from several different points of view. First we'll see the train as Wallie sees it from his car. That view will be intercut with shots of us looking at Wallie from the front, then we can look over his shoulder at the road ahead, then we'll watch him driving as if we were passengers on the train. Get it?" Her voice had a patient edge to it.

"Yeh. Pretty clever. I just thought they'd run along and take one shot of the whole thing."

She shot him a glance from under a raised eyebrow. "It's even more complicated than that. Want to hear?" The um-brella had been set up again and she sat down in her canvas chair. Ben looked at the name painted on the canvas. Elsie Wright. "Sure do, Miss Wright."

"Tomorrow we'll put the cameras and actors on the train and then we'll see them from inside watching the automobile race the train. When each crossover occurs we'll see them run from one side of the passenger car to the other to see if he makes it."

"Why do that?" Ben was paying less attention to what she was saying than to how charmingly serious she was about explaining it to him.

"If you saw him get across the tracks safely from outside there wouldn't be any suspense. Now, the way it's being done, we'll watch him emerge from in front of the locomotive at the same time the girl who loves him sees that he is safe. Seeing it from her point of view helps the audience feel with her, if you know what I mean."

72

"I didn't, but I do now."

She looked up at him. "You're from the South, aren't you?"

"Accent gives me away every time, Ma'am."

She laughed. "It certainly does."

"Do you mind my askin' what you write down in your note book?"

" 'Course not. You don't know very much about making pictures, do you?"

"Does it show that much?"

Elsie put her hand on his arm. "That was mean of me. I'm sorry. We all have to start out somewhere." She smiled. "I've been here almost two years and I keep forgetting I was green myself."

"Ma'am, if you smile at me like that every time you embarrass me, you can do it all the time."

"Now it's my turn to be embarrassed. Most of the regulars have forgotten how to say nice things like that, Mr.—I don't know your name."

"Sommers. I'm Ben Sommers. Publicity. This is the first time I've been on location. It's just great."

"Yes. Everybody loves it. Like a family picnic."

Ben crouched down in the dry grass. "Look here, I have to eat lunch with Wallie Reid to do a story. But has anybody asked you to take supper with them?"

"No one, yet." She had absolutely breathtaking green eyes.

"I'd count it as an honor if you'd let me accompany you."

Elsie looked at him with a mixture of surprise and pleasure.

"Of course. I'd love to."

Ben backed off, reluctant to leave, but knowing that he would be late if he didn't go. Elsie watched him, waved, then bent over her note book as the director began shouting instructions to the camera truck.

Riverside is hot and dry. It sits against the hills to the east of Los Angeles and the ocean breeze that cools the city rarely reaches back to the hills.

By noon of the first day Ben wished he had brought cooler clothes. Everyone but the actors was in shirt-sleeves. He was grateful to eat in the shade. He and Reid sat at a table set slightly apart so they could talk. They had served themselves from the huge crocks of potato and macaroni salad, platters of cold cuts, piles of freshly baked bread. Tubs of lemonade with floating blocks of ice were set off to one side.

Reid proved to be as friendly and easy to talk to as before, but after a half-hour or so his face was beginning to look like a badly painted sunset. "The heat is ruining my makeup, Ben. I've got to get it fixed. Why don't we continue this at dinner? My wife, Dorothy, is driving out with the kids to spend the night. Want to eat with us? We can tie on a steak at the Inn."

Ben hesitated. "Well, I kind of made a date to eat supper with the script girl, Elsie."

Wallie laughed and winked. "Go right ahead. That comes first. One pretty girl in the hand is worth two matinee idols any day."

"Gee, Wallie, I don't want . . ."

"Ben, don't be deferential. I don't like it. If you're going to do publicity for me, take me at my word. We can talk tomorow at lunch or between takes, if necessary. Look . . . why don't you tag along while I go over to makeup?"

Most of the company were taking naps in the shade before shooting began for the afternoon. Lydia, Herbie's assistant, had set up her makeup chair behind a muslin screen, and Wallie sat back in it as she worked on his face.

"Why do you suppose your racing pictures have been so popular?"

Wallie opened his eyes for an instant. "Well, they combine two basic traits in the American public. We love anything mechanical, things that tick. And we love freedom. Autos combine those in the best possible way. I love automobiles. I like their looks, their sound, the way I can move out and feel a sense of release. Free. I feel free. There's no better way to say it."

Ben had never owned an automobile, but he understood. Independence. That would make a swell lead.

A voice called, "Ready for you, Mr. Reid."

Wallie jumped up, handed the bib of striped ticking to Lydia, and loped off toward his racing car. He called over his shoulder, "See you later, Ben. We'll keep this going."

The afternoon shooting was very slow. After each take, the train had to be backed up to retake the shot or get set for the next one. There was no way to turn the locomotive around, so everyone sat in the broiling sun and waited for it. Ben rode on the engine while it was backing up just to try to get the feel of what it was like to be involved in the action. Working on a movie wasn't always the fun he'd thought it would be.

At six-thirty the light began to fade to the point where film could no longer be shot, and the crews broke for supper. Afterward, some went into Riverside looking for girls and excitement; the rest sat around a big fire and talked. Ben and Elsie strolled off together.

"Let's walk up onto that rise and look around." She was wearing a man's white shirt, twill trousers, and puttees like a cavalry officer's. They climbed up a wash to some rocks and sat in the cool evening light.

"Where did you live before you came here?"

Elsie laughed. "I was born here. In Redondo Beach. My folks came here back in '91 when the railroads were selling passage for a dollar to get people to move out to California and buy real estate. Crazy, isn't it? Now, if we could only slow down the deluge."

"Life is sure funny. Never thought in a million years *I'd* be out here working in pictures. Nothing ever happens like you plan it."

Elsie frowned at him. "It does, too. You just can't go around willy-nilly. There are consequences. You have to have plans, some organization, direction."

"I don't agree, Elsie. Before, I always prided myself on looking before I leaped. Now look at me. I didn't plan any of this. And here I am."

"But you can't just float in and out on the tide, letting life carry you back and forth. You've got to take some control."

Ben smiled at her. "Why should a little thing like you have to worry her pretty head over taking control? Some lucky man is going to take all those worries away one of these days."

Elsie sniffed and stared. "I can take care of myself nicely, thank you. My father thinks life is a series of crises. Something happens that changes everything for you. It's how you meet those crises that determines your life. That's your control over fate. You either meet the crisis or it defeats you." She looked at him sternly. "You can bet your boots I plan to meet my crises head-on."

Ben looked at her warily. "I guess you will."

She got up and climbed further into the rocks and tossed a pebble down onto Ben. "King of the mountain," she shouted down at him, laughing.

They scrambled down the wash to where they could see the campfire burning. Someone was singing "Redwing." Elsie held Ben's hand as they walked toward the fire.

In the cloudless sky there had been no real sunset, but in the distant west it turned a turquoise blue-green, and then suddenly it was dark. The air grew colder as the sun went down, and even those sitting around the fire began to feel chilled. Elsie sat very close to Ben and he kept hold of her hand.

14

March 1919, New York and Hollywood

Daily News

MAJESTIC OWNS B'WAY
LOCK, STOCK AND BARREL

SPECIAL TO THE NEWS. Recently Majestic bought two of the four first-run houses on Broadway. The two remaining houses, the Strand and the Criterion, are First National and Metro showcases. This leaves Goldwyn, Selznick, Mutual, and Ince without any chance to play first runs.

Old timers look for new theater construction since present situation restricts profits necessary to recoup costs on each photoplay.

"Where do you think Amos Lynch is now, Mr. Grossman?"

"Think? I know where he is—in northern Georgia, working his way south to Atlanta. He wires in every few days, when he can. Has a gang of twelve men, and they are driving the back roads in three touring cars, following the plan."

"Are you sure his operations couldn't be traced to me or to Majestic in any way?" Weiss seemed fidgety.

"Absolutely. The theater owners think they are selling out to Lynch's company. Then things quiet down, and we buy the theater from Lynch. No direct trace. The money he uses to purchase theaters goes through a dummy company set up in Maryland by Mr. Klein. From there to another company set up in Virginia. You can get away with anything in those southern states, nobody cares. Klein handles it all as film rentals and we actually ship pictures to hide the movement of the money. I think it's foolproof."

Weiss looked at Grossman doubtfully. "I'd like to avoid any more bad accidents. Minor ones can't be helped, probably. Some owners take more convincing than others. I don't want to risk any news of this operation getting back to Walter Falcon at the bank."

Grossman shrugged. "Hell, bankers have accidents, too. They just do it more slowly. Foreclosing on widows and orphans is just as deadly as Lynch's dynamite."

Nathan Greenglass interrupted. "Mr. Weiss, that was a real accident. The rest have been mostly a few bloody noses and some black eyes. That stupid Buford man wouldn't leave his theater. Lynch said he was forced to make that house an example for the rest of the theater owners in the area. So every once in a while he's been blowing up a theater or burning one down—just as a warning. In Suwannee the men couldn't make the owner get out and the fuse burned too short to run back in and snuff out. In the explosion a beam fell on him, and that was that."

"It really upset Lynch and his men," Grossman added. "They were very upset."

"Understandable," said Weiss. "It upset me too. I don't want any more fatalities. Now he has his example and word will travel, believe me. I want that all he should do from now on is to make threats. It's like a director making a western. Show one killing or even just a tableau, you know—a dead woman, her long hair blowing in the wind, a crying baby clutched to her dead breast. That's all you need. Then just show an Indian, his hatchet over a cringing woman, and the audience's imagination will do the rest. Worse, actually, than anything you could show.

"Theater owners are like that audience. Word spreads. Just threaten a little. I want, when Lynch rides into town in those big black touring sedans and puts up at the local hotel, that the theater owners will line up to sell their houses to him voluntarily." He was happy with the scene he painted.

"That's a nice theory, Mr. Weiss," Greenglass said. "But they're not caving in. These are family ownerships. Husbands and wives. They've built a little theater into a nice business over the years, and it's worth fighting for as far as they are concerned."

Weiss sighed. "All right, so some stronger methods may be necessary. But only once in a while. Tell Lynch that. Who's working New England? They won't tolerate rough stuff up there the way they do in the South."

"Black is in western Massachusetts now."

Weiss looked concerned.

"Oh, I know. He's being careful. Has a list of houses owned by Democratic machine members and won't touch anyone on it."

"OK, but tell Lynch to keep moving. I want Georgia sewn up by the end of the month, then he can move into Alabama. I'm thinking of sending him straight across the South and into Texas."

The new blonde secretary dropped a pile of newspaper clippings on the desk. "That's all from last week, Mr. Sommers."

"Thanks, Myrna." He watched her buttocks moving under the light crepe dress and winked at Bascomb. "You sure know how to pick 'em, Tom." He studied the pile of clippings. "Weiss certainly is making a lot of news. Look. Two more theaters, big ones. First the Rivoli and the Rialto on Broadway, now the Million Dollar and the Los Angeles Rialto here in town. That means we've sewn up the prime showcases for both cities. Goddamn! What a move."

"Yeh," Bascomb agreed. "He's empire building. An exhibition empire. Look, when Sid Grauman owned the Million Dollar, he picked the best pictures from each studio and really showcased them. Could have been a Majestic picture, but just as easily one from Goldwyn or Paramount or Metro. Now all those houses will play only Majestic pictures on an exclusive basis. A lot of good pictures just aren't going to get shown in a first-run house now."

Ben reached for a folder of clippings. "Sometimes we buy a theater every few days, sometimes even one a day. You go to staff meetings—what's going on?"

Bascomb shook his head. "I'm not sure. The old man is putting it together very carefully. Nobody says a word at meetings. I don't think even Rubin knows himself. Squeezing the competition out, I guess, and he wants to do it on the sly."

"But he's buying little houses too." He held up a clipping. "Have you noticed that we pick up a few here and a few there in little towns all over?" Ben closed the folder. "Something big's going on. Wanna bet?"

"Mr. Weiss has been anxious to meet you firsthand," Saul Rubin said, smiling at Tom Bascomb. Rubin stood behind his desk in the gothic bay window, silhouetted against the draperies, the shafts of light cutting across his face as if directed from unseen spotlights. He looked especially thin and tall, the black triangles of his peaked hairline looking pasted against the pale skin, dark grey circles masking his eyes. Off to one side, almost hidden in a huge wing chair, sat Abe Weiss, looking steadily at Saul Rubin.

Bascomb walked forward, hand extended, almost bowing, trying to make himself smaller.

"I'm very glad to finally shake your hand, Mr. Weiss. Telegrams are so impersonal, despite the 'regards' at the end." He turned to Rubin. "Is it true that we are to drop 'regards' as an economy move?" Without waiting for an answer he turned back to Weiss. "The long-distance telephone is not the same as a face-to-face meeting, either. I had hoped to get to New York before this to discuss plans and policies with you, but reorganization has been time consuming."

Bascomb then gestured toward Ben, who was standing behind him. "I'd like you to meet my assistant, Ben Sommers, the brightest young man on the lot."

Ben, who had been stunned by Bascomb's forwardness, smiled eagerly and shook hands with Weiss. "I think the theater campaign is brilliant, Mr. Weiss."

"I'm glad you think so, young man. What do you do in the department?"

"I plan and write the press campaigns and prepare the materials sent out to the exhibitors, such as press books and lobby materials, photos, that sort of thing."

Bascomb beamed at Ben. "I've left Ben completely on his own, and the recent campaigns have been his entirely. He did the whole show on *Alias Mike Moran* with Wallace Reid."

Weiss smiled, saying, "Was it your idea for the photos of the bathing girls at the army base?"

"Yes, sir." Ben tried to look modest. "Small-town editors eat them up."

"Everybody seems to. Traveling around the country, I've seen them up on the walls of nearly every exchange and theater manager's office I visited. Not really risqué, just right."

"Mr. Bascomb is very careful about editing what I turn in."

"Yes, I suppose that a young man is more likely to be enthusiastic about girls than an older one. Right, Mr. Bascomb?"

"I'm not that old, Mr. Weiss, not yet at any rate," Bascomb laughed.

Weiss pointed to a nearby chair. "Sit down. What is your name again?" he asked Ben.

"Sommers, sir. Ben Sommers."

"So it's your idea to use bathing girls?"

"Yes, sir. When I was in the army I saw thousands of girlie pictures up on the walls over bunks and inside foot lockers. They were all Mack Sennett girls. I thought to myself, why not Majestic girls? When I was a reporter at the *T-P* before coming west, my old editor was always on the lookout for pictures of pretty girls to spice up the news sections. So I put the two together. Girls and newspapers. It worked."

Weiss turned to Rubin. "Nice. I like that."

Rubin said, "Excuse me, Mr. Weiss, lunch will be ready in a few minutes." He stood up. "Thank you gentlemen for stopping by." He looked at the door and Tom, reading the signal, stood up. Weiss waved him back into the chair.

"Have your waiter set two extra places, Mr. Rubin. I'd like to have Mr. Bascomb and Ben here join us. I want to discuss the new theaters with them and how to handle the publicity."

Rubin attempted a smile, which only made his lean face look more morose. "The roast may be sliced a bit thin, but if you don't mind . . ."

Weiss turned to Ben and asked, "So you like the new theaters, do you?"

Ben nodded vigorously. "They're going to belt First National in the chops."

Weiss roared with laughter. "My thinking exactly."

Ben turned to Bascomb. "Shall I tell Mr. Weiss about my idea for Majestic Week?"

Tom beamed like a proud father, "Go ahead. It's your idea."

Weiss settled back to listen.

"My idea, Mr. Weiss, is to have one week every year in which every theater in the United States plays only Majestic pictures. We can't do it now—not enough houses, yet." He smiled as charmingly as he could. "But I'm counting on you to remedy that." Weiss laughed appreciatively. "But we can start on a small scale in a few of the bigger cities like New York and here in Los Angeles, where we've tied up the major houses. Parades, stars, girls, and new first-run pictures in as many theaters as possible. Eventually all of them." He stopped himself before he got too carried away.

Weiss got up, then turned to Rubin who was standing near the door, waiting to take them to the dining room. "Now, you see, Mr. Rubin, if you had hurried them off, that fine idea might have been lost." He motioned to Ben to walk beside him. "Tell me more, young man. How would you organize it?"

15

March 1919, Hollywood

Polly stood with her back straight. She was wearing a new uniform which fit as well as could be expected. It wasn't actually new, but it was new to her and she considered that the same thing. She had to be careful where she stood. As an usherette on the fifth balcony at the Million Dollar Theater, she was supposed to stand at her station and not move. The steps in the fifth balcony were terribly steep and for the first few days she was afraid to get too close to the railing at the bottom of her aisle. Her eyes soon got used to the dark and after she had seen the feature presentation a few times she found it easier to guide the patrons up and down the steps using her small flashlight.

Polly had been ushering at the Million Dollar Theatre for more than three weeks but the wonders of the theater still enchanted her. A great hall of columns ran the entire length of the building. Grand flights of steps curved in the most unlikely ways. Many of the corridors and pillared balconies ended in a flight of steps that took the stroller back to the starting point. The idea was not to go somewhere—after all, the patrons were in a theater waiting to see a movie—but to have a marvelous adventure.

The day's routine was a stern and rigorous one. The Million Dollar Theatre was meant to be high-class, hence the drill-like precision of the ushers and usherettes. Polly was on the day shift and reported for work at ten each morning. First she changed into her uniform, then combed her hair and made sure her hands and face were clean. Then all the usherettes reported to the mezzanine balcony for inspection.

The captain of the ushers was an elderly ex-marine who had been hired to put some snap and discipline into the staff. Twenty young men and eighteen girls lined up in a long single row and stood at attention, hands by their sides. As Lt. Crowther walked slowly along the line, they held out their hands for fingernail inspection. That their hands would be covered with white gloves made no difference to Crowther. Polly had never paid much attention to her nails, but she did now. Dirty nails were cause for dismissal.

After inspection, they marched in formation to the main lobby, where Orders of the Day were read. These consisted of little slogans to improve morale, suggestions made by patrons about service and politeness, and pointers about procedure.

"Never point to or snap your fingers at a Patron to get his attention.

"Immediately report a Patron who is coughing or sneezing without using a handkerchief. Although the Spanish influenza threat seems to have passed, we cannot be too careful with our Patrons' health.

"Always hold your flashlight down or at a slight angle so it will not shine into the eyes of anyone already seated.

"Flashlight batteries will be tested each morning at inspection."

After the inspection, the ushers and usherettes marched in groups to their stations. Three girls worked the fifth balcony with Polly. The four marched in formation up the Grand Staircase, through the Long Gallery, and across the Esplanade on the third level, where, out of sight of supervision, they broke ranks and straggled up two more flights to the top level. There, a wonderful arched window overlooked the landing of the Grand Staircase three floors below. It was at the cornice level and from it you could not only look down to the carpeted stairs, but also out at the painted cherubs cuddling on piles of roses around the edge of the domed ceiling. The space was filled with a lovely pink light from

84

dozens of clustered, shaded lamps fastened to the pillars at every floor. The light reflected softly from the gold-leafed walls and the French brocade draperies that hung in great folds from the ceiling to the floor far below. Polly loved to stand here and look out. It was like fairyland.

Not many people came up to the top balcony, and those who did usually came up only in the evening to pet. By standing at the door to her station Polly could watch the movie and still appear to be at attention if anyone came up the stairs.

At six o'clock, in a ceremony called The Grand Parade, the evening ushers took over supervision of the house from the day squad. Crowds stood around the balconies to watch. The Million Dollar was the theater to which the residents of Los Angeles brought visiting relatives to see not only a photoplay but the beautiful architecture and works of art, and the superbly trained ushers. Publicity blurbs likened it to the changing of the guard at Buckingham Palace.

The evening squad of attendants, after their inspection, lined up opposite the day squad who, in a flashing nickel-plated flourish, handed over their flashlights while the spectators applauded. Then the day ushers turned and marched smartly in formation down the Grand Staircase and through the door into the locker rooms.

Once through the door the girls burst into yelps and laughed at each other's wisecracks and gossip. Polly found herself listening to a voice that floated down to her from over the top of the row of lockers. It was Velma, the pretty blonde, speaking. Polly listened, one hand smoothing the wrinkles from her uniform. She really loved her uniform. It was splendid looking with its brass buttons and the way the jacket nipped in at her waist.

"My friend Anita, you know, finally got herself a part in a picture," Velma's voice confided in an excited whisper.

"Yeh? No kiddin'." It was Agnes speaking. "Where at?"

"Over to Fox. And it's more than just an extra. She's got lines to speak and two long scenes. She's right up by the camera. She'll get seen."

Polly moved around to the end of the row of lockers and leaned casually against them while trying to tie the bow at the neck of her blouse. Agnes and Velma were just finishing dressing. Velma was rolling the tops of her stockings even with the hem of her skirt so a little bare skin would show each time she took a step, and all the men would turn and look at her.

"Wha'd she have to do?" Agnes noticed Polly and winked at her. "I mean besides the regular." She winked again.

Velma looked up from her stocking rolling and lowered her voice. She seemed to be including Polly in her confidence, so Polly sat down on the bench next to the two girls.

"It's this assistant director she met. He said he couldn't do anything for her if all she did was just plain . . . fucking." Velma looked around to see who was listening.

Agnes's eyes grew wide and she grinned. "Boy, I know what's coming," she laughed. "I hope she had a strong stomach." She nudged Polly with her elbow.

"You guessed it," Velma continued. "She sucked him off."

"I hope he was good-lookin'." Agnes said, snapping her gum.

Polly wasn't quite sure what they were talking about.

"Well," Agnes whispered, "it takes all kinds." Then she drew her mouth down at the corners as if to say ugh and asked, "Did he make her swallow it?" She shivered and giggled.

"You just bet he did. Said it didn't count unless she did."

Polly asked, "Swallow what?"

Agnes looked over at Velma, opened her eyes wide and grimaced in Polly's direction. "This from the kid who talks about being a star all the time. 'Swallow what?' " she mimicked, almost doubled over with laughter.

Velma, her voice patient, answered, "His come, dodo. Wha'ja think?"

"I didn't know." Polly shrugged but she felt a little dumb.

Velma sat down beside Polly and spoke softly. "Look, sugar, it's no secret there's ten thousand of us trying to get into pictures every day. If you want to get a part, not just be a walk-on extra, you got to find some palooka who's got a little pull. Then you do anything he tells you. Especially if you're willing to do something a lotta girls don't like to. It's the only way, kiddo."

Agnes nodded in agreement. "Some girls get in because they know somebody. If you're a politician's daughter, somebody's sister or friend, then you click, you're in and you don't have to go to bed with anybody. But you and me, sister, we got to go all the way, and I do mean all. Otherwise you might as well go back to working in the Woolworth on Main Street. There's too much competition."

"Look at all the girls in the pictures here every week," Velma said. "Lots of them make one picture and you never see them again. They went down on some guy, he paid off with a part, but they didn't click so they're out. No matter what you do to get in, Polly, you got to have something else. Anita told me that."

"So it does mean something if you're talented and pretty and really want to be a star," Polly said.

"Yeh, that all helps. But only after you're in. It's the getting in that'll kill you. Anything's fair game. Some of those guys have real funny ideas, and you got to go along with them or go stand at the gate." She shrugged and made a wry face.

Velma nodded and reached into her locker for her coat. "Lots of girls would rather stand." She paused, thinking. "I don't really know what I'd do." Laughing, she added, "No guy ever asked me to do anything 'specially interesting' yet. I'll let you know, though."

Agnes roughed up her bobbed hair in front of the mirror and drew in a deep breath. "I know what I'd do. If the guy had the right pull and he wasn't too repulsive," she paused and looked at both of them, "he could put it anywhere he wanted." She gathered up her uniform and flung it into her locker. "Ready?" she asked Velma.

"Hey." Velma closed her locker, turned, and waved at Polly. "Don't take any wooden nickels."

Polly could hear them laughing through the closed door as they went down the corridor toward the lobby. She wished she had a friend to talk to, as Agnes and Velma had each other. She wondered about Mavis, where she was, if the baby had come, what it had turned out to be?

Could it be only a month since Mavis had persuaded her to use the money she had gotten from Mr. Hopkins to take the train to California? So much had happened. Her running away from the Florence Crittenden Home in Chicago, the train trip out here, the Traveler's Aid people sending her to another Crittenden Home, then the lucky break of getting the job at the theater. The manager, Mr. Lester, put his hands all over her as he personally fitted her out with a uniform, but it was worth it. Now she was making twelve dollars a week and living in a nice rooming house, Mrs. Bates's, on Olive Street at the top of Bunker Hill. Nearby were even some of the huge old mansions that used to be owned by Los Angeles millionaires.

Now she was waiting for the little cog railway called Angel's Flight that ran up to the top of the hill. On the way she would watch the lights of the city fall away into the darkness as the car clicked its way up the rocky bluff. Everything was new, everything was exciting.

The sun had just set and the sky was turning that peculiar blue green it becomes in California just before dark. She would really have to start going to the casting offices. Her next day off she would see what they were like. Then she could decide what to do next. She wondered how she could meet someone with pull, whatever that was.

16

March 1919, Rome, Georgia

The huge man put a penny in the scale and stepped onto the little platform. The needle on the big dial spun around quickly, shivered, and stopped.

"Aw, shee-it. I'm way down. Roger, you keep me running my legs off instead of riding in that auto and look! I'm down to 281. Gawd amighty."

Roger winked and showed his teeth. "It's all that nookie. Too much exercise, Amos. Gotta cut down to once a day like a white man. You just going too strong there. Entirely too strong." He clucked his tongue. "Just gotta cut down."

They both laughed. "Cut down? Cut *down?* If I'd do that, it would dry up and get all withered up and fall off. Got to keep it lubricated. Only one way to do that."

They both laughed loudly. Amos slapped the smaller man on his back. They wandered down the street until they came to the theater.

Roger spoke. "This the one?" His voice lowered. He looked up at the facade of the building. "Oh, lookie." His face broke into a wide grin. "Jumpin' Jesus. Look at those titties. Must be the biggest in all Georgia."

David Silverman, in a burst of showmanship and imagination rare for the city of Rome, Georgia, had named his motion picture theater The Peacherino. He claimed, when the town fathers were outraged by the sculptured facade, that the theater was named after the Georgia peach, raised on surrounding farms. But everyone knew that the name referred to the two gigantic and lovely ladies that supported the cornice on their heads. Thin drapery fell away from their plaster breasts, each exposing one nipple.

Next door to the theater was the penny arcade where the first moving picture in Rome had been shown. Amos Lynch and Roger Adams stood on the sidewalk.

"Ol' man Silverman keeps it nice," Amos said. "No whores, no loiterers; it's clean, jest right for family trade. Weiss'll like this."

"What if Silverman won't sell? What if he says no? What then?"

"Same as usual. Gotta be a little careful. Make it look good. He'll sign. Do they ever refuse?"

"Yeh, there was that guy in Macon. The one we set fire to. He didn't sign and the theater burned up."

"Weiss doesn't know. Weiss doesn't care. Majestic will build a new theater there. Nice big picture palace. Not some two-holer like that one."

"Do you play Majestic pictures here, kid?" Lynch asked through the hole in the glass.

"Yes, sir. Sometimes. The Mary Pickfords always. But we're the only theater in town so we have to play pictures from everybody."

"Just where is Mr. Silverman?"

"If he isn't in the back of the auditorium, he'll be in his office. It's the door behind the red drape next to the men's toilet."

"Thanks, kid. We'll just go in and see him. We got a picture he may be interested in."

Lynch pulled the drapery aside and opened the door. The room was lit by one bulb hanging from a cord in the center of the ceiling. The walls were lined with cans of film and tin shipping cases. Silverman sat behind a small desk on the far side of the room. He looked up at them and said sharply, "Put that cigar out, you fool. The nitrate film is explosive. Do you want to get us all killed?"

Lynch looked down at his cigar, then dropped it on the rug and ground it out with his shoe. Silverman leaped up.

"What are you doing?" he shouted. "What did you just do to my carpet? I paid good money for that. Cash. I don't do no credit. And now you burn a hole into it. What are you? Some kind of bum? Get out of here!"

Lynch walked over to the desk and put his hands on Silverman's shoulders and pushed him down in the chair.

"Shut up. We're here to buy your theater, Mr. Silverman. It's not friendly to start out our talks with such an insult. Tomorrow it won't be your carpet anymore and you won't care."

"I'm not selling. Good night, gentlemen."

"You didn't listen to me. My name is Amos Lynch. Ever hear of me? You read *Harrison's Reports*? You see the *Exhibitor*? You must know that I'm buying up theaters."

Adams spoke up for the first time. "He *won't* take no for an answer."

Silverman looked at him sharply. "Who asked you? How did you get in this conversation? I won't sell. This theater's my livelihood. If I sell, I got no way to make a living. The answer is no. Good night."

"We'd like you to change your mind. Without making any trouble, that is. We hate to make trouble."

Mr. Silverman's forehead began to shine slightly.

Lynch looked at him. "Roger, Mr. Silverman looks chilled. Why don'tcha shut the window. Then go stand by the door so we aren't interrupted. Now, let's consider the offer."

David Silverman, looking slightly panicky, stood up for a second, then sat down again. "Look here. You can't force me to sell. I told you already I don't want to sell."

Lynch took the only other chair in the room and put it in front of the desk and sat down on it. "I'm very patient, Mr. Silverman. But my patience only lasts so long. Please sign. This here's a deed all made up by our best and smartest lawyer. He's Jewish, too, I think. That ought to make you feel better."

"No, it does not." Silverman looked at him contemptuously.

"Is the price unfair? I thought it was very fair." Lynch looked hurt.

Silverman hesitated. He didn't want to give any advantage. "Yes. The price is fair. It's just that I don't want to sell. I spent my whole . . ."

Adams walked over to the window, glanced out, and then pulled the dark green shade down. Silverman looked over his shoulder at him with fear in his eyes.

"Look. No rough stuff. I'll report you to the police. I'm a prominent citizen here. The chief knows me. He'll find you out."

"Mr. Silverman. What we are going to do to you, you won't want to tell anyone about. Because you won't want your best friend to know." Lynch's voice was quiet and soothing.

Adams stood behind the chair and suddenly lifted Silverman out of it. He locked his arms around the man's shoulders and put both hands across his mouth. Silverman's terrified eyes looked at Lynch over the back of Adams's hands. Adam's thumbs pressed into Silverman's head on each side, just in front of the ears. Silverman's glasses fell off and bounced on the carpet.

Lynch spoke sharply. "Don't break his glasses. He'll need to see to sign the contract. Now, Mr. Silverman. I'm going to unbutton your fly and go inside your underpants. I'm going to take this sharp knife and cut out one of your nuts. Just one. If you still don't sign, I'll go after the other one. You can still fuck with one. It's not such a big loss. But without two, you got trouble." Lynch smiled sympathetically.

David Silverman thought that he was going to faint. How had he gotten himself into this situation? What could he do now? Nothing. Sign. He felt cold all over. Perspiration dripped off his nose and ran down his face. He tried to speak. The hands gripped his mouth tighter. Oh, dear God. He thought. Oh, dear God, help me. . . .

"Take your hands down, Roger. I think Mr. Silverman wants to say something."

"I can't sign. The house is in my wife's name. She has got to sign."

"That's too bad, Mr. Silverman. I'm sure she will want you with both of them rather than none. But she will have to settle for one. Then maybe you will call her on the telephone, and she will come over here and sign. The kid in the box office can witness."

Lynch swept the papers off the desk with one arm. An

inkwell fell to the floor and spilled, the blue ink spreading out on the carpet. Roger wrestled Silverman to the desk and bent him over it backward. He knelt on Silverman's throat with one knee and pressed just hard enough so that there would be no screaming. Silverman gagged. Lynch, at the front of the desk, stood on each of Silverman's feet, spreading his legs apart. He began to unbutton the fly.

"You won't gain anything by not cooperating, Mr. Silverman. We don't lower the price, or anything like that. I'm being very careful of your suit. I don't want you to look funny going out. We don't want you to be embarrassed by doing business with us."

He unbuckled Silverman's belt and spread the pants open. "Still wearing your winter B.V.D.s? Well, it never hurts to be a little careful." Lynch unbuttoned each button of the union suit. He paused and smiled.

"Why, Mr. Silverman, you dye your hair. You got grey hair down here. Well, it's not such a crime to try to look a little younger."

Silverman was crying. Big tears were filling his panic stricken eyes and running down his cheeks. He was desperately trying to speak but Adams's knee made his speech a rasping gargle. Although he couldn't see what was happening, he finally closed his eyes.

With a quick movement Lynch grasped the scrotum in his left hand and slit it open. With the tip of the knife he exposed the testicle. He pulled it free of the sac and cut the tubes. There was surprisingly little blood. Silverman moaned.

"Now." Lynch stepped off of Silverman's feet. "I'll give you a minute to recover and then you can telephone Mrs. Silverman and get her down here." Adams quickly took his knee away. Silverman gasped and his chest heaved and shook with huge sobs.

"I would have signed. I would have signed. Why did you have to hurt me? Oh, my God. Oh, my God." In a sudden frenzy Silverman struggled up and tried to hit at Lynch. The big man simply pushed him back down onto the desk.

"That's not smart. You're not really hurt, Mr. Silverman. Think of all the thousands of farm animals that are gelded every year. They're just fine in a few hours without benefit of a drink of whiskey or anything like that to kill the pain. They're up and around and running off into the fields, don't even know what happened to them, most likely."

"You bastards. You dirty bastards." Silverman sobbed.

"Mr. Silverman, calling names will not help you get your nut back. Now, call your wife." Lynch's voice had a menacing edge to it.

"I don't have to. The theater is in my name. I was just saying that. I'll sign your goddamned contract. God damn! God damn! Let me up!"

"Pick up his glasses, Roger. Let the man up. Give him a little help. Here's the contract. It's very fair. We don't like to take advantage. You'll want to button yourself up before I call in that kid to witness your signature."

Silverman fumbled with the buttons. He was afraid to look down at himself. Lynch sat down on the chair in front of him and helped him button the union suit and then the trousers. Silverman was like a small child who could not yet dress himself. Lynch buckled the belt and straightened Silverman's tie.

"Roger, help the man to sit down in his chair. I don't want him to fall down just yet. Let's get this over, Mr. Silverman. Then you can go home and your wife will fix you a little something to make you feel better. Sit down!"

Dazed, Silverman looked around for his chair. Roger Adams gestured to it and held out the pair of glasses. Silverman was afraid to walk. He didn't know how it would feel, or even if he could. He took a step and fell toward the desk. Lynch stood up quickly but was not in time to catch him. Silverman hit the corner of the desk and rolled to the floor. A hot streak of pain shot through his groin. He moaned. Lynch bent over him and picked him up and carried him to his chair.

"You're making a lot out of such a little thing, Mr. Silverman. Are you ready to sign?" Silverman nodded. "Roger, call in that kid."

The young man stood in the doorway and looked at the wrecked office.

Lynch stepped forward. "Mr. Silverman is selling The Peacherino. We argued a little about price, but we now have a nice agreement and we want you to witness the signature on the contract of the sale. OK?"

"Are you all right, Mr. Silverman? You look terrible."

Silverman closed his eyes. A tear ran down his cheek and hung for a second on the edge of his chin before it dropped off. "I'm fine, Bobby." He took the orange fountain pen that Lynch offered to him and signed two copies of the contract. Then Lynch signed on the opposite side of the page.

Lynch took the pen and pushed the papers toward the boy.

"Sign 'em right there on the line under Mr. Silverman's signature. Thanks, kid. There's a couple of sawbucks for your trouble." Bobby hesitated for a minute, then took the bills that Lynch held out. Uncertainly, he backed out of the room and closed the door.

"Now it's your turn, Mr. Silverman. Ten thousand dollars in cash." He took a huge pile of bills out of his inside coat pocket. "Roger, while I'm counting, clean out the desk drawer. Mr. Silverman won't want to be coming back tomorrow. You can find something to put it in. A film can will do. That big one there."

Adams picked up the can. It had the Majestic trademark printed on the label in full color, a star-filled sky with the Big Dipper picked out in brighter stars.

Adams began to clean out the desk drawer, leaning over Silverman's shoulder to get to it. Silverman was slumped in the chair.

"Four hundred, five hundred, six hundred, seven hundred, eight hundred, nine . . ."

A sad thin wail came from Silverman's open mouth. His eyes were closed, his legs drawn tightly together. His hands were clenched in his lap. A bloody spot appeared on his trousers. The little cry drifted away and his head lolled to one side.

Lynch continued counting. "Nine hundred, one thousand, one thousand one hundred . . ."

17

April 1919, The Casting Office

The South Bend Daily News

WALLACE REID'S THRILLS ARE REAL!

RIVERSIDE, CALIFORNIA. In the blazing sun of this city inland from Hollywood, thrills were filmed every day that will have you hanging on to the edge of your seats when Majestic's new Wallace Reid photoplay opens at the Bijou Theatre on Wednesday. *The Roaring Road* is the exciting title of the sensational torrent of daredevil auto racing that is unleashed when driver Dusty Rhodes goes after the girl he loves.

The only problem is that she is speeding away on a railway train and he must catch the train in his special Stutz! You can hardly imagine what Wallie has up his sleeve for you!

Ben had last minute instructions from Saul Rubin to greet Cyrus Cotton and make sure he got to his hotel. Getting into the limousine on the Majestic lot, he was surprised to find two girls dressed in evening gowns waiting for him. They even knew his name.

"I'm June, Mr. Sommers. This is Edwina. Mr. Rubin thought we would dress up the occasion." She leaned over and kissed him full on the mouth. Ben sat back between the two girls, smiling. This was his fourth month at Majestic and he ought to know better than to be surprised by anything in Hollywood. Rubin certainly thought of everything.

Cyrus Cotton got off the Overland Express at Pasadena and stood looking confused while the chauffeur carried his suitcases to the motorcar. He and Ben exchanged hellos and he asked polite questions about the studio.

For the long drive into Los Angeles, Edwina chose the jump seat opposite Cotton. After a few minutes he felt the pointed toe of her shoe trace a delicate pattern on the back of his thigh, just behind the knee. He smiled at her, politely. She smiled back, winked, wet her lips with her tongue, lit a cigarette.

The hotel desk clerk explained that Mr. Cotton had been moved to the special Majestic suite and his bags would be carried up and unpacked. Dinner was being served in the main dining room. A reservation was being held in Mr. Sommers' name, and they could go in at any time.

From the table in the center of the dining room, Ben pointed out famous tycoons and movie stars to Cotton. He was dazzled.

"Why a suite, I wonder?" he asked. "I'm here to work, not loll around in a hotel room. I expect to be out at the studio every single day." There was determination in his voice.

"All work and no play?" June said, smiling at him. Cotton flushed and paid close attention to his food. He had never eaten a stuffed artichoke before.

Edwina leaned over toward Cyrus and murmured. "I love asparagus. It's so sensual." She began to gently nibble the tip of a stalk.

"Mr. Rubin said you will probably want to sleep in tomorrow to get over the trip," Ben told him. "A car will come for you Thursday morning. I'm afraid we start very early, seven-thirty." He laughed. "The actors are there even earlier, at six for makeup."

"Absolutely kills any hope of parties during the week," Edwina said crossly. "This is a dead town Monday through Thursday."

Cotton gathered courage. "What do you girls do?" He smiled.

June folded her hands primly and looked up at him from under her long beaded eyelashes. "Anything you want us to, sugar."

Cotton's bright smile faded.

"Maybe I ought to send the car on Friday instead," said Ben, grinning at the girls.

At the elevator, Cyrus tried to say good night to all of them.

"We're just going to run upstairs with Cy for a minute to

97

make sure his pajamas are hung properly and his socks all put away," June said, running one finger around Cotton's ear.

"Nothing like a woman's touch to make a hotel room a home," Edwina added. She leaned closer and kissed Ben. "Nighty night, Ben, dear. Sure you don't want to make it a foursome?"

Cotton, eyes wide, grabbed Ben's arm. "Don't leave me alone, for God's sake!"

Ben patted his arm. "You'll have a nice time," he said.

As the elevator doors closed Cyrus sighed, "They warned me to watch out for Indians and Pancho Villa."

The following Tuesday, her day off, Polly got onto the first Pacific Electric car and whizzed out Santa Monica Boulevard toward Hollywood. It was a few minutes before six in the morning, but the car was filled with passengers dressed in fancy clothing. Polly felt shabby. After a few blocks she turned to the middle-aged woman sitting next to her.

"Where do I get off to go to a movie studio?"

"Which one, honey?"

"I don't know. Is there more than one?"

The woman stared at her in disbelief. "Jeeze, there's a dozen or more if you count Poverty Row. But they don't let visitors in, you know." Almost as an afterthought, she asked, "Why do you want to see one?"

"I came to get a job in the movies." Polly smiled at the woman proudly.

The woman burst out laughing. "So did I. So did they." She waved her arm about her head grandly indicating everyone in the car. "So have a million others. Gosh, honey, you got a fat chance. What are you dressed for?"

Polly looked down at her wash dress.

"Looking for work, I guess," she said softly.

The woman let out a hoot. "God help us!" By this time passengers nearby were listening and smiling with superiority. The woman continued, "You got to have a costume. A formal, an afternoon tea gown. A little girl getup. Something. But not your regular everyday clothes." She leaned closer to Polly. "You get two dollars a day extra if you got your own costume. Dress suits get five extra for the men. I'm answering a call at Famous Players-Lasky. They're doing a picture set in prewar Vienna. That's period costuming, see? You can't be expected to supply those. So they do. That's why I'm not dressed special."

"How do you find out? I mean, who tells you what to wear and when?"

"It's posted by the gate at the studio. You go on the day they say and stand there in the crowd and the casting director comes out and picks the best faces." She studied Polly critically. "You got a good face, honey. Pretty." Out of the side of her mouth she added, "But watch those casting guys. They like little girls." She patted Polly's knee.

Polly nodded. "Thanks. Where do you think I should go?"

The woman thought for a minute. "I'd try the big ones first. Little studios on Poverty Row are good, though, because no one wants to work in their pictures. No future. Better stay clear of Universal unless you look Mexican or got Western duds." She settled back comfortably. "Famous, where I'm going, is really Paramount. It and Majestic are far and away the biggest." There was a smug tone to her voice. "Fox and Metro are both pretty good. Only problem with Majestic is that it's a hell of a walk down that road. Then if there's no work you got to walk back."

"What do I do at the gate?"

"Look for the casting window. There'll be a sign and a long line of extras. If there's nothing go over to the casting office and get your name on a call sheet. They'll call you if they need your type."

"What's a type?"

"You know. A vamp, a flapper, snotty kid, tango lizard."

"What type am I?"

The woman looked at her in surprise. "If you don't know, how should I? You better figure that out." She got up. "This is my stop. Why don't you go on to Majestic? It's only three more stops. I know there's nothing here today." She put her hand on Polly's arm and squeezed it. "Good luck, honey."

"You registered?" The man behind the Majestic window didn't look up at her.

"No, I'm not."

"Nothing today. Next."

The man behind her elbowed her out of the way and pushed past her to the window. There was a part for him and he was given a gate pass and went in through the wooden gate off to one side.

She quickly stepped in front of the next person and stood in front of the window again.

"Please, sir. How do I register? I didn't know I had to."

The man looked up, irritated. "Go over to Casting. They'll look you over and give you a form. You can hang around and hope there'll be a general call. But I doubt it today. Next!" he shouted over her head.

"Please, where is Casting?"

"Next! Look, girlie, get the hell out of the way. How can I cast a picture with you taking up room?"

The woman standing behind Polly angrily pushed her to one side.

"Honest to God, some people. Hello, Harry. I got a call for the DeMille. Whatcha got?"

Polly felt like crying. But there was now a line of people that stretched part way down Majestic Way, and she was afraid some of them might beat her to Casting, wherever it was. Rubbing her arm where the woman had grabbed her, she walked up the line and asked an old man wearing jodhpurs where Casting was. He told her politely, and Polly walked past the front gate with its businesslike looking guard in a uniform and found the door in the little building on the other side.

Just inside the room was a waist-high counter. Several men and women were working at desks beyond. No one looked up. Polly stood patiently. After a long while one of the men whose back was turned to her looked at the wall to his right.

"Want something?"

"Yes. I'd like to register. Is this where I do it?"

"Yep. Doris, give her a form."

One of the women got up and without a word gave Polly a yellow paper. She returned to her desk. On an empty desk a telephone rang. No one made any effort to answer it. Besides the telephone and the clatter of two typewriters there was no other sound in the room. No one spoke.

"I don't have a pencil."

"Aw, Jesus Christ! What did they teach you kids in school? Don'cha know how to apply for a job? Don'cha know nothing?"

Polly, although nervous and intimidated, was beginning to be annoyed by the way people were treating her.

"I know enough to fill out a form if I have a pencil. And I'd have brought a pencil if I'd known I'd need one. Please give me one."

100

Doris looked up from her desk, got up and walked to the counter.

"What kind of experience have you had?"

"None. But I learn fast. My teacher in school said I learn fast."

Someone laughed.

"Here's a pencil." Doris looked at her as if memorizing her face, then returned to her desk. She looked back at Polly. "Leave the paper on the counter when you're finished. If you got a photo put it with the form."

"I don't have a photo but I can have one made. I'll bring it next week." She sat down on the bench and filled out the form. She put the form on the counter and opened the door. "Thank you. Please call if there are any parts for me," she called out, as cheerily as she could, and shut the door behind her. Outside, she leaned against the wall and burst into tears of frustration. Then she blew her nose, wiped her face, and walked down to Santa Monica Boulevard to wait for the Pacific Electric car.

Inside the casting office Doris turned and said, "She had beautiful eyes. You should have looked at her. Beautiful eyes, beautiful girl, Paul. Your type." She laughed.

Paul grunted. "They're all my type." His voice rasped and he chewed on his cigar. "I could tell by her voice that she was just another stray alley cat come into the land of milk and honey to make her fortune. They're all alike. Why the hell don't they go back home? Why do they come here?"

"So you can *shtup* 'em," someone cracked.

"Elsie? This is Ben. Can you meet me out by the front gate? I want to show you something."

A few minutes later Elsie came around the corner of the Office Bungalow and saw Ben standing by the side of a bright blue automobile. He waved excitedly.

"I wanted you to see it. It's mine," Ben said, beaming.

"Oh, Ben, it's beautiful. What is it?"

"A Franklin Six. Wallie Reid helped me pick it out. It's got all kinds of extras. Goes seventy-five miles an hour. Get in. We'll go for a spin and a hamburger. Can you take the time?"

"Sure." She walked around the front of the car and stopped. "It's got a kind of a funny front," she laughed.

"I know," said Ben, who was standing by the open door waiting to help her in. "It looks like somebody punched it in

101

the nose. That's called French styling," he added proudly. He closed her door, then walked around to the driver's side and climbed over the door without opening it. "It cost two thousand dollars." There was pride in his voice.

"My gosh! Don't you feel rich?"

"I sure do." The blue Franklin had cost as much as his pa had ever cleared in a year.

"Now watch this." He stepped on the electric starter button and the engine turned over, shuddered, then purred. He held up his hands. "Look, no crank. It starts itself. That was Wallie's idea. It's brand new, costs extra." As if to reassure her he said, "Oh, it's got a crank, in case I ever need one." He laughed with glee as they started forward. "Isn't this the cat's pajamas?"

The gateman saluted them as they drove past, and Ben nodded imperiously. The extras reluctantly opened a path as the machine moved through slowly.

"Oh, look," she said, pointing as he turned into Prospect Street. "It's really falling down now. Kind of sad, like the end of an era."

They were passing the ruins of the vast Belshazzar's Palace setting left standing from the Babylonian sequence of Griffith's *Intolerance,* two blocks long and several stories tall. Huge rotting plaster elephants still sat above the columns, trunks curled toward the noonday sky.

"It must have really been something to see, with clouds of incense and hundreds of extras. Hell, it's still something to see. Somebody told me there's a movement afoot to try and save it, make it into a Hollywood monument of some sort. You know, charge admission. They'd better hurry."

Elsie sighed. "I remember when it was built. Everyone thought Griffith was crazy. But then I never liked the picture."

"Nobody liked it. Everyone expected another *Birth of a Nation.*"

"They'll never save it. Not in this town. Nobody ever saves anything; they only live for this minute. Years from now nobody will even know there was a Hollywood." Her voice was bitter. "It's the same with people. Here today, gone tomorrow. They're not human beings, they're just commodities, like so much canvas or plaster. Use them up, throw them away. The movies should be fun—living and working in a world of make-believe. But it isn't. It's fierce and sad."

Ben looked at her, puzzled. "I sure don't feel fierce and sad! I'm going great guns."

102

Elsie stared at him. "So far you've been lucky."

Just past the Van Kamp bakery on Wilshire, Ben drove into a parking lot. "They serve hamburgers in your car here. I've been dying to try it, but I haven't had a machine to eat in. So I thought we'd inaugurate Magnolia with a cashewburger."

"Alfred or Throckmorton, please. Not Magnolia." She frowned. "What's a cashewburger?"

"The very latest thing. You'll love 'em."

When their trays came, Elsie took a tentative bite. "This sounds awful, looks a mess, but it tastes delicious. I never would have ordered one if you hadn't insisted," she said, poking a stray shred of lettuce back into the roll.

"See, you should always try new things. That's what's so good about California. You can do any crazy thing you want to do, try any new thrill." As if to demonstrate, he held up his cashewburger and took a big bite out of it. "Nobody cares about anything. There's nobody to say anything. It's wonderful. You don't realize it, Elsie, you were born here. But it's so constricting back in the South. So la-di-dah, surrounded by relatives and neighbors who think you have to act just so."

"I guess that's what happens to people who come out here," she said thoughtfully. "They go wild." Elsie grabbed his arm. "Oh, gosh. There's that awful pest, Cyrus Cotton."

Ben said, "Speaking of going wild, he's got Edwina with him."

"Who's Edwina?"

Ben stopped short. "Just a girl. You wouldn't know her."

Elsie stared. "All that beaded fringe looks out of place in the daytime."

"That's Edwina," Ben said as he started the motor. "Let's get out of here before they see us."

Once back on Sunset Boulevard Ben said, "Come to the opening of *The Roaring Road* with me next week. It's a sneak preview at the Alhambra in Riverside. I'll pick you up."

On the Tuesday after her first trip to Majestic, Polly walked into a grubby photographic studio on Hill Street. In a few minutes, the young man in charge asked Polly to call him Lou. He called her Polly. A little while later, Lou remarked that most shots were a dime a dozen, and what she really needed were some special pictures that the casting directors would remember. Polly obligingly stripped to the waist and Lou draped her budding breasts with silk and chiffon. By three o'clock Polly was posing nude for pictures that would end up in Lou's private collection, as well as a few that would be naughty but suitable for the studio files. Lou thought he was working fast, but Polly was working faster.

An hour later Polly negotiated for free extra prints as she lay in Lou's embrace atop a dusty brown velour drapery hastily spread on the floor. Lou was a pleasant surprise. For one thing, it didn't hurt so much and for another, Lou was young, gentle, and kind of cute. It made a difference. This was going to be easier than she'd figured. One of Mavis's remarks came back to her as Lou maneuvered within her. It only takes a minute, you can't wear it out, and men love to fuck little girls.

The following Tuesday the front door was locked again, the "Will Return" card was turned face out toward the street, and this time Polly was prepared with her new device from the Sanger clinic. Lou went to town. He smelled of chemicals, but Polly didn't mind. First he showed her the photographs and she was enchanted by them. Lou made her promise that she wouldn't patronize any other studio but his and was anxious to take more "free" shots. Polly was equally anxious to get her pictures off in the afternoon mail. Another half hour with Lou provided her with mailing envelopes and stamps. She felt she should strike while the iron was hot, so to speak.

18

June 1919, The Screening Room

Every Tuesday Polly got up at five in the morning and rode
the electric cars to visit one of the studios. She signed in at all
the casting offices and stood with the crowds of extras.
Gradually she learned the ropes and grew tough enough to
function in this bitter every-man-for-himself jungle. Grown
men and women clawed, bit, and scratched each other to get
through the half-open gate on a general call. The first twenty-
five through got a day's work. The others went away to try
again tomorrow.

The men who operated the gates or stood behind the
windows calling out names were emotionless, almost inhu-
man. They didn't even blink as men wept and women fainted.
One morning Polly saw extras step over the unconscious body
of a woman who had collapsed in front of the window after
being told the promised role had been given to someone else.
No one made a move to help her to her feet or even pull her
out of the way. She finally crawled into the shade where she
sat, covered with dirt, weeping bitterly.

After a few weeks of appearing at the studios regularly,

Polly began to be recognized. But there was never a part for her. Coming only once a week she couldn't compete with the regular extras. The girls at the theater continued to advise her to find someone to go to bed with. The trouble was she didn't know anyone. It wasn't that she wouldn't, she remarked one lunch hour, with a sigh. No one had ever asked. One of the ushers immediately grabbed her and kissed her.

"I've got an uncle ...," he started. Everyone hooted with laughter.

Polly wiped her mouth on her hand and stared at him unsmiling.

"If you really did, I'd let you do it."

He took another bite of his peanut butter sandwich. "With your looks, sugar, if I believed that, I'd go out and find an uncle."

Polly, still not smiling, said, "You turn up with the uncle, kiddo, and you know where to find me." She turned her back and finished her lunch. The usher pushed his nose up with an index finger and minced off. More laughter.

That afternoon, as she stood at the top of the balcony watching Clara Kimball Young fight off the advances of a Latin villain, she suddenly recalled the chance remark of the woman on the electric car that first morning. What type was she? She truly didn't know. But since she was a nobody, she could create a somebody out of the bits and pieces that she could pick up from the screen.

For weeks she watched and absorbed the gestures and mannerisms of the more polished and talented actresses. She became a catalogue of walks, stances, poses, turns, hip movements, smiles, frowns and tears of a hundred women.

"The screening room is right here, Mr. Cotton. We won't be disturbed. Please make yourself comfortable."

Cyrus sat down in one of the armchairs as Saul Rubin twisted a knob. The lights dimmed and flickering started on the small screen surrounded by red velvet curtains.

"This room for your private screenings, Mr. Rubin?"

"Yes." Rubin smiled gently. "Especially for certain pictures that I want to see alone or with just an intimate friend or two. You'll see."

Images began to appear on the screen and Rubin settled back in his chair as he heard Cotton gasp.

Cyrus Cotton started to slide slowly down into his chair, not quite shrinking, but growing smaller.

"Look as long as you wish, Mr. Cotton. Most men wonder

what they look like while they're doing it. Most never know. That Edwina is certainly some woman, isn't she? She actually performs for the camera. Look at that! Smiled and winked." Rubin reached over and gave Cotton's shoulder an enthusiastic pat. "I must take my hat off to you. You're very good. In another reel you really get her going. That takes a lot of doing with a professional lady. Ordinarily they don't feel a thing. And your powers of recuperation are astonishing. To look at you in your conservative banker's suit, those rimless glasses, one would never suspect you could manage so many times with so little rest." There was only silence from Cyrus Cotton who was absorbed with the film. "Still waters run deep, as they say," Rubin added.

At last Cotton turned and said, "All right, that's enough. You can stop it."

Rubin pushed a button, the screen went dark, the lights came up.

Cotton stood facing Rubin, arms crossed, furious. "What do you want?" he demanded.

"Whatever made you ask that? I thought you'd enjoy a very imaginative memento of two very exciting days."

"Look, Rubin, I'm no fool. You didn't take those pictures because you wanted to please me. I repeat, what do you want?"

"It is very important to Majestic that you send favorable reports to your superiors." The bantering humor was gone now, and Rubin's voice was all business. "We wish to increase the loan by many millions and continue to borrow from time to time. You are the key, as we understand it."

"And if I don't?"

"Mr. Weiss will arrange a screening in New York."

"OK." Cotton took a deep breath. "I just wanted to find out my options. I'll let you see the reports before I send them. I'll have to throw in a few unfavorable comments, of course, so they don't look phony."

Rubin shrugged. "Little things, I suppose. We'll send them out, if you don't mind. As a convenience, of course."

Cotton nodded his head toward the screen. "What happens to the film?"

"Goes into a special vault. We have a superb collection. You must know that you're not the first. I'm sorry that my strong ethics prevent me from showing some of them to you. You'd be astonished as to who does what." He smiled blandly. "Prominent men seem to have no shame."

"I'd like a copy of mine sometime."

Rubin laughed and slapped his knee. "You're the first to ask. I'll order it tomorrow. You can save it for your grandchildren."

Doris in Casting looked up from her desk. "Anyone remember the name of that little girl who sassed Paul?" she asked. "She had gorgeous eyes and a funny name."

Paul Droste looked up. "Wall something. Walla, maybe. Christ, that was weeks ago. Why?"

"William Desmond Taylor is looking for a waif with expressive eyes. She must be here in the files somewhere." Doris stood looking at a wall of filing cabinets, drawers bulging with applications. She sighed, "I remember asking her to send in a photo. Wonder if she ever did."

"Who knows? We get hundreds every month."

Doris looked through the W drawers, maybe she would recognize the girl's picture.

She let out a little yelp of triumph. "Here she is! She did send in pictures." She drew in a shocked breath. "Oh, my God! Paul, do you remember me saying she was just your type? You should have looked under the top photo." She held out the pictures. "Look at what some cheap photographer got her to do. Well, it takes all kinds." She shrugged. "I'll give her a call and we'll see."

Droste's pupils dilated at the nude photos Polly had enclosed with the more conventional portraits. "Well, well, well," he cackled. "You're right. Very pretty." He thumbed through the little stack of pictures. "Her hair needs attention." He looked up and licked his lips. "Guess he wasn't interested in that. But she's young and has nice tits already. He knows what he's doing, and maybe so does she." He smiled at Doris. "Ask her to stop by here first. I'll take a look. Maybe she needs special coaching."

19

June 1919, Majestic Studios

Variety, June 10, 1919

FIRST NATIONAL STEPS OUT IN STYLE

HOLLYWOOD. Abe Weiss may regret the day he gave the final shove to Tom Talley. It was Weiss's abuse of the Majestic preference system that convinced the exhibitor to band together with other discontents and form a production studio of their own.

This week First National added new stars to its galaxy. Lovely Anita Stewart ran out on Louis B. Mayer's new studio and was inked by Talley in a swift move. Topper was the signing of the knockout Talmadge sisters, Norma and Constance, to a three picture deal. Majestic may think it has all the stars in the dipper, but Talley is right out there with his skimmer.

Polly sat on a little bench in the sun and looked around— she was inside the gates at last! Her interview with the casting director, Mr. Droste, had gone well; he'd seemed unusually interested.

Now, a gentlemanly-looking middle-aged man with sandy hair stood in front of her studying her intently.

"Are you the girl Doris said she found for me?" He talked funny but she could tell it was high-toned.

"I was told to wait here for Mr. Taylor, the director."

"Then you must be Polly. You're very pretty. Can you act?"

Her eyes lit up. "You bet I can. I can act like Marguerite Clark, Mary Pickford, Agnes Ayres, Mary May Maxwell." She smiled confidently. "I've been working at the Million Dollar Theatre for months. I've seen 'em all."

Taylor's smile faded. Not another one. Still, there was a glimmer of something interesting there. Maybe he ought to test her anyway.

Polly watched the expression change on his face and added hurriedly, "I'll do *anything* to be in the movies."

Taylor sat down beside her. "Little Miss, I'll give you some fatherly advice. I don't know what you had to do to get this far, but I can imagine. You aren't the first. But don't offer yourself on a silver platter to just anyone who walks past. Everyone will help himself and go on by. If you're determined to sleep your way to stardom—and I don't say that it doesn't work, for sometimes it does—at least only go to bed with those who can help you get there. The rest are a waste of your time and beauty." He smiled sadly. "So don't waste your time with me. If you're any good, you'll get that part. If you're not, nothing you do in bed will get it for you."

Polly looked at the ground for a moment while she decided what to say next. Then she smiled up at him brightly. "I'm still learning. I can't get it all right the first time around. So far only one thing has worked." She studied his face to see if she was getting through. "What works with you?" There was a knowing twinkle in her eye that was irresistible.

"Well," he raised one eyebrow, "I've got a few peculiarities, but sex with children isn't one of them." Watching her closely, Taylor was intrigued by what he saw happen in her eyes. "Hard work before the cameras is what works for me. Are you game?"

"I sure am. Shake?" She held out her hand, overcome with relief, aware of how closely she came to blowing her chance.

"Shake. Get yourself over to Grace in Wardrobe. Then to Makeup. Herbie will know what to do. He'll send you to Stage Four. I want you there in a half hour. Now get going." He pointed toward the steps on a distant building. "Wardrobe is up there." As she hurried off he called after her, "Don't get lost." But he was sure she wouldn't. She wasn't the kind who got lost.

CONFIDENTIAL MEMO

To: Walter Falcon
From: C. Cotton

Date: April 18, 1919
Re: Majestic Studio Operations

I am dictating this to a stenographer at a private bonded service. I wish to be sure that no one at Majestic knows my opinions of that operation.

I must say I am impressed. At first glance the studio seemed to be a madhouse. But after a few days of the sometimes bizarre procedures of a motion picture studio, a pattern of organization begins to come clear.

Majestic turns out one hundred and two pictures a year—five to seven reels each—year in, year out. Considering the high emotional quotient of creative people, it is run quite well. I found some areas where expenses could be trimmed by buying vast quantities of studio supplies wholesale instead of retail.

For every actor before the camera, there are thirteen employees behind it. At first I considered that excessive, but subsequent investigation has revealed that Majestic has the lowest ratio of any major studio.

There is some conspicuous waste in the area of lavish scenery and costumes. One director in particular, Cecil DeMille, spends money as if it was going out of style. But Rubin says extravagance is what audiences want from DeMille. I mean to speak to him directly and try to convince him to be slightly more conservative. I may have some influence.

All is going well out here. I am at the studio every day, making my presence felt.

"Boy, I think that final race with the train is really the cat's meow," Ben said as he drove Elsie home from the preview.

"The audience really loved it. Looks like it ought to be a great success. Especially if they follow your publicity scheme." She laughed. "I couldn't get over how enthusiastic they were when they recognized some local landmark in Riverside."

"I never thought I'd see a grade crossing get a big hand," Ben said, giving her a squeeze.

He slowed down to take a sharp curve. "That conference in

the lobby after the theater emptied out was very interesting. I'm still new enough so that I'm not sure when something has to be cut or added." They drove on in easy silence through almost deserted streets.

"Elsie, what's say we park out on the Coast Highway and look at the surf?"

"Not tonight, Ben dear. Not on our first real date. I just don't feel like getting pawed."

Ben shook his head in exasperation. "Elsie. One minute you act like a really hot tomato, the next minute you're a cold fish." He sighed. "I just can't figure you out." He felt her stiffen and move away slightly. He tried to pull her back but she resisted.

"Is that how you picture me, a hot tomato?" Her voice was cool and she crossed her legs.

"Well, you know what I mean. . . ."

"I don't have the faintest idea what you mean." She took his arm from around her shoulder and, moving away, put it down on the seat between them.

"I wish I knew what you wanted."

"That's easy. I don't want to go three rounds with you on the backseat. But I don't want to be put on a pedestal either. I just want to be treated like a woman and a friend. It's easy."

"I guess so. If you say so. It'll take getting used to, is all."

"Don't be silly. And stop feeling sorry for yourself. Ben, sometimes I do want you to kiss me. But not just automatically, just because we're out together. That's no reason."

He laughed. "That's what I mean. That used to be a pretty good reason."

"Well, it isn't anymore. I'm trying to be a different kind of person." Her voice took on a firm ring. "I am a different kind of person. I have my own rules."

"This is crazy. Here we are on our first real date and I feel like I just went through the wringer. I never talked to a girl like this before."

"That's the trouble. You're not used to talking to girls at all." She sniffed contemptuously. "You just want to keep one around to look pretty under your damned magnolia tree or lay her down to do you know what." There was a long silence.

"You can kiss me now, if you still want to." Her voice was

112

smooth as silk and very inviting. Ben took his foot off the accelerator and looked at her in surprise.

"Is it all right to say that I sure want to?"

"Certainly," she murmured.

The doorbell rang. Ben looked up from the notes he was making at his desk. Eleven-thirty. Must be a drunk.

"Just a minute," he called out and put on his robe. He opened the door and looked out at a girl who stood on the porch. She looked familiar, somehow.

"Hello, sweetie. You Ben Sommers? I'm Bunny Roberts. Can I come in?"

"Sure. I'm forgetting my manners." He looked at her closely. "Don't I know you from somewhere?"

"That's why I came over. So you'd be sure and remember me." She took off her wrap, threw it on a chair and sat down.

He suddenly recognized her. "Bunny! Were you on the Sunset Limited coming out of New Orleans?"

"Yeh, a friend and I took it last winter. You on it, too?"

"You bet. Coming here. Well, it's a small world." She was just as pretty as he remembered. "Can I fix you a drink?"

"Yeh. That's a good way to start."

He went to the kitchen and chipped ice off the block. "Well, what brings you by, Bunny?" he asked carefully from the kitchen door.

"Come on, Big Boy. You're no kid. You hand out a lot of photo assignments that pay pretty well and get a girl's face and figure splashed around plenty. You haven't called me, so I came over to make sure you'd remember my name."

"Gee, I didn't know your name. But I've thought a lot about you since I first saw you in the observation car."

"After tonight, sweetie, I don't expect you'll forget."

"Gee, Bunny, you don't have to. I mean, I'd have called you if I'd only known who you were."

She smiled as she sipped her drink. "That's what the girls say about you. You're a nice guy—don't go forcing yourself on a person. There's a lot of girls who will show you their appreciation if only you nod once in a while. That the bedroom?" She started for the door, but as she passed Ben she stood on tiptoe and kissed him. "You're a big good-lookin' guy. I bet you got a swell one." She had one arm

113

around his neck and slipped her other hand down inside his pajama pants. "I'll bet you're more fun than some of those cold biscuits that slobber over us. Mmmmm." She kissed him again.

"I guess I'm just a bit surprised," Ben admitted as a slow smile crossed his face.

"You mean I'm the first one?"

He reddened. "I'm no virgin," he protested.

"Silly," she laughed. "I mean the first girl to pay her respects."

"I knew there was a lot of this stuff going on, but it never occurred to me that I was important enough to get any."

"Sugar, you control a lot of assignments. I'll spread the word. The girls have been neglecting you."

Later, as Bunny lay smoking a cigarette, Ben watched her hold it up in the air as she had on the train. "You want to know what the conductor said about you when you were standing by the telephone in the observation car?" he asked. "We could see through your dress against the light."

"Nothing flattering, I'll bet."

"Yes, it was. He said he bet you had a fancy snatch."

Bunny lifted herself up on her elbow and let out a howl of laughter. "That old bugger!" She waited for him to continue, then asked, "Well, is it?"

"You're damn tootin'."

Every few nights after that, the door bell would ring and Ben would have a guest. Sometimes it was one of the girls he hired regularly, sometimes one he had never seen before but who came recommended by a friend.

Bascomb laughed when he told him. "If you don't, somebody else will. It may as well be you. They won't expect any more calls than is normal, so don't think it makes you especially obligated. The girls all know it's part of their dues, like staying thin and having decent clothes. Just don't keel over from exhaustion. I'll expect to see your smiling face here every day despite the side benefits."

Most of the girls left a calling card with a picture and telephone number on it, and Ben began calling some of the more interesting ones to escort to the screenings and parties. No one ever went to a party alone. A man who couldn't get a date or didn't want one was suspected of being lacy.

There were occasional embarrassing conflicts, like two girls arriving on the same evening. Ben was willing, but the girls—in competition for his attentions—were not. He solved

114

the problem by letting everyone know that when his porch light was burning, he was alone and eager for company. If it was not lighted, he was either tired or occupied. The system worked fine. And one of the girls suggested that he install a red light in the fixture.

20

July 1919, Sunset Boulevard

Ben had seen the studio gate close behind him in the rearview mirror and had turned toward his parking space in front of the press loft when he noticed what seemed to be a fight off to his right. He pulled up in front of the executive bungalow and trotted toward the small crowd that was gathered around the big publicity billboard. Several planks had already been torn from it and lay scattered on the lawn. Tom Bascomb was standing in front of it, arms flung wide, defiance on his face, looking for all the world like a suffragist protestor.

Bascomb spotted him making his way through the onlookers and yelled at the top of his lungs.

"Ben! Ben, thank God you've come. That prick, Rubin, has the goddamn nerve to order my billboard torn down without so much as a by-your-leave from me. It's *my* goddamned board, not his." The prospect of Rubin and Bascomb slugging it out in the road by the main gate of the studio lot was very appealing.

Bascomb shouted to the head carpenter, who had built the board for him and now was tearing it down. "I know you boys are only following Rubin's orders. But take it easy for a few minutes and let me go over and have it out with the dumb bastard. Ben, hold them off while I run over to the bungalow." He pushed his way through the crowd and ran toward the big square bungalow with its wide verandah and awning-shadowed windows.

The towering board was painted black. Across the top, lettered in gold paint, was the new legend, WRITE NEW MAJESTIC HISTORY HERE. Every two weeks it was repainted with a list of pictures down the left side, arranged in the descending order of their earnings. Stars and other credits were listed to the right of each title and occasionally one of Tom's comments. Ben stepped back and looked up. Sure enough, there was one this week.

POPULARITY OF STAR OVERCAME WEAK STORY

That must have made everyone in the scenario department wince.

Occasionally a director or a writer, distressed by a particularly stinging comment, had stormed in to see Rubin and complain. Nothing like that this week, however. This must be Rubin's own idea.

Abe Weiss had thought the board was just dandy when he saw it less than two weeks ago. Of course Rubin and Bascomb had never hit it off from that first day, and occasionally Rubin did something absolutely unnecessary and spiteful just to remind Bascomb that he was still in charge. This was probably the latest move in a war of nerves. Bascomb had always shrugged off these gestures, laughed them away as if slapping at gnats. Ben looked over toward the bungalow just as Bascomb came out onto the porch. He'd lost the battle with Rubin.

Beckoning to Harry, the head carpenter, Ben said, "I guess

it can come down. But do me a favor, get it down and carted away as soon as you can. I'm sure Tom doesn't want to look at the wreckage." He patted Harry on the back and walked away.

"Sure thing. Tell Mr. Bascomb what I said," he called to Ben. "No hard feelings."

Ben looked up at Tom standing on the porch. Without a word Tom turned, walked back the length of the porch, and disappeared around the corner of the building. A few minutes later he roared past in his racy Lagonda.

At noon Ben's telephone rang. It was Tom, calling from a popular little roadhouse out at the beach in Santa Monica.

"Hey, kid, get away. Come on out here and breathe some clean air for a change. Sky's blue, water's sparkling, wonderful day. Have some lunch with me. OK?"

"Sure, Tom. You sound great. I knew you'd snap back. I'll be there in about forty minutes."

Ben drove out Sunset Boulevard wondering how Tom was really reacting to his defeat. He had never known him to be blue or moody for long. If one idea was turned down, he snapped back quickly with another.

"Gosh, Tom, I'm sorry. Really sorry," Ben said as he sat down at the table.

"Want a drink?"

"I don't think so, don't especially feel like one."

"I sure do." Tom raised a shot glass and looked through it squinting one eye. "Here's to the publicity billboard. Rest in peace."

"Tom, don't be blue because the dumb bastard got in one against you. You're still a number one guy with Mr. Weiss. That's what really counts."

Bascomb scowled, "I don't see how I can work if Rubin gets in little pot shots like this all the time. Oh, I'll grant you, it isn't the damned board—although I still think it's a good idea. Producers and directors nearly killed themselves getting their pictures up on it."

"I know, Tom. I think it was good too."

"It's just that it's so petty. I won't kiss his ass and he can't stand it. Rubin is a really second-rate guy who is out of his depth but thinks he's top dog. He just takes orders from Weiss, and I guess it grinds him. He hates anybody who sees through the charade."

They ate in silence.

Ben didn't share Bascomb's contempt of Rubin. Rubin was

118

not a nice man, and Ben had heard a lot of unpleasant stories about him, but he was really responsible for turning out most of Majestic's pictures, and they were tops. Rubin knew a good picture when he saw one and could fix a bad one with editing and reshooting.

Bascomb refused to leave after lunch. "I may just tie one on, Ben. Just hang around here and drink it up a little. Take a walk on the beach, maybe. Some pretty jazz babies come in here after dark. May just take somebody home with me." Tom looked at Ben solemnly. "Ben, don't worry about it. I'll find some way to get back at the bastard. We haven't lost the war, only a little skirmish. Go on back and keep a light on in the window for me." Tom sat down at the piano in the front room and began to play "Keep the Home Fires Burning."

Ben woke up suddenly, the telephone ringing. It was Don, the bartender at The-Hole-In-The-Wall.

"Sorry, Mr. Sommers. I bet I woke you up. I don't normally do this, but I think Mr. Bascomb is too drunk to drive. He's been here since you left at noon and I just think maybe you should take him home."

"Thanks, Don. I'll get there as soon as I can. Keep him there. Get his auto key out of his pocket if you have to."

As Ben turned into Sunset Boulevard, driving toward Santa Monica as fast as he thought he could, he wished that he had put up the isinglass side curtains. It had grown cold and foggy. He was a little apprehensive about how he would handle Tom when he got to the bar. They had been friends and business associates for six months, but that was hardly a lifelong friendship, and certainly not a firm basis for telling Tom that he was too drunk to drive. Considering the events of the day, it might even result in a fight.

Loud music surrounded The-Hole-In-The-Wall. The small jazz band certainly made more noise than its size would lead one to expect. The cigarette smoke inside was overwhelming. The Hole was crowded and Tom was nowhere in sight. Ben called out to Don, who came up to the near end of the bar and shouted above the music.

"Jeez, Mr. Sommers, you only missed him by twenty minutes. Honest to Christ, I couldn't keep him here. He began makin' an awful scene. I never saw him act like that before. Even when he'd been puttin' it away steady, he was always a gentleman. But not tonight. No siree. It was white of you to come out here."

119

"Thanks anyway, Don. It was swell of you to call me." Ben put a folded fiver in his palm as they shook hands.

Ben took the curves of the hilly part of Sunset more slowly heading back into town. He wondered if Tom would go home or what? He had been stupid not to ask if Tom left the Hole with a girl, but it was so crowded, Don might not have noticed anyway. There was a line of roadhouses along the coast highway, but there was no point in stopping at any of them. If Tom wanted to keep on drinking, he could just as well have stayed at the Hole. He must have gone home. Ben would stop by the court and check in on him.

Rounding a curve, the head lamps swept over a long dark roadster pushed off the road in a level spot between two trees and the side of the hill. Tom's Lagonda. It must be, there wasn't another like it in Hollywood. He swerved to a stop. He was certain he would find Tom inside, but it was empty. A chilling wave of fear began to seep down through his stomach, sending trickles of cold sweat down his sides. He saw that a fender was badly crumpled and the windshield was shattered and stained. He felt the glass. It was sticky with blood.

"I'm looking for a man who's been in an automobile accident. In the last hour or so. Named Bascomb."

The nurse behind the reception desk looked up at him.

"Are you a relative?"

"No. Not really. I work for him. I guess I'm his closest friend. Was he brought here by some people?"

"I'll see. If you'll just wait over there, I'll check on the entries. Bascomb?"

"Yes. Thomas Bascomb." Ben felt cold and wretched. He slammed one fist into the palm of his other hand.

The nurse touched his arm. "Yes, he's here. But I don't see a notation of what ward he's in. Maybe it was only a minor injury and they fixed him up in emergency and sent him on home. I'll continue checking and be back as soon as I can." She smiled a professional smile and walked soundlessly down the corridor. Within a minute or so she returned with a young intern who stood in front of Ben.

"You Bascomb's friend?" Ben nodded. "I'm afraid I have some bad news for you. Your friend was dead when he was brought in here. Died almost immediately, I suspect. Head injuries. He must have been pretty boozed up and his head went through the windshield. What's your name again?"

120

"Sommers. Ben Sommers. He's—was—my boss. We work at Majestic Studios."

"I see. Mr. Sommers, we had no real identification so we turned the body over to the coroner's office. You can go there tomorrow and identify it and have it sent to an undertaker. I'm sorry, Mr. Sommers. I know it's a real shock. Do you want to sit down?"

Ben parked his Franklin on the hill below Spring Street and walked up the hill to the Los Angeles County Court House. The old stone building squatted on the dead grass looking like a misplaced Tower of London, each of the bronze clock faces on the tower showing a different hour of the day, none correct. Ben walked through the tunnel cut into the stone retaining wall on the downhill side of the block, his footsteps echoing in the dank gloom. At the end of the tunnel he stepped into a circular cage threaded onto two steel cables. He yanked on a wooden knob and the cage started to rise jerkily. Suddenly it emerged from the darkness of its underground berth and slowly and grandly floated up into the blinding sunshine. From the outdoor elevator he could look out across the city to the Hollywood Hills, framed by the lacy ironwork of the tube in which the elevator hung.

The coroner's office was on the second floor and Ben was told to wait. An attendant in a white jacket entered, picked up a folder and smiled.

"I'm Ben Sommers. I've come to identify. . . ."

"I know, Mr. Sommers. It's all here. A Mr. Thomas Bascomb. Accident victim. Follow me, please."

Ben walked behind the white jacket, dreading what would come next. Instead of a cold storage locker, he was led into a small beautifully furnished sitting room. Easy chairs were casually placed about and the room was lighted by shaded lamps on small tables. A settee, in the center of the room, faced a draped window.

"It's very nice," observed Ben, "comfortable."

"Thanks." The attendant beamed. "Barker Brothers did it." He walked to the side of the window, pulled a cord, the draperies slowly drew aside disclosing another tastefully decorated room. Tom Bascomb had been laid out on a rose-colored chaise, his head propped on a tucked velvet pillow, a crocheted afghan thrown casually over his lower body. At the foot of the chaise stood a vase of long-stemmed wax roses. Tom lay as if napping, nude from the waist up, his face marred by massive purple bruises. Ben gasped and sat down.

121

"Is there enough light?" asked the attendant turning a knob on the wall. A floor lamp with a pink silk shade garlanded with rosebuds suddenly flared to light and the body looked, if anything, more ghastly.

"Jesus Christ. That's terrible."

The attendant pulled another cord and the draperies closed. "I take it that that means a positive identification. That is Mr. Bascomb?"

"Christ, yes. But that's the most terrible thing I've ever seen."

"I know it's a shock, Mr.—Mr. Sommers." He looked down at his folder. "That's why we try to soften the blow with our slumber boudoir."

"That's what I mean is awful. Your goddamned room. Awful. I was a reporter and looked at a lot of bodies in iceboxes. None of them ever looked half as dead as Tom does in there. You ought to have your heads examined."

"I'm sorry you're upset, Mr. Sommers." His voice took on a distant and disapproving tone. "Most people are grateful to be helped in this moment of bereavement. I'm sorry that Los Angeles County has failed you."

"How do I get him out of here?"

"Well, your undertaker can do that. I'll give you the forms. Is there a next of kin?"

"I'm the closest thing to it, I guess. The studio will handle the funeral."

"I imagine it will be beautiful. Which studio?"

"Majestic."

"Oh, it'll be wonderful. They always go whole hog."

"I don't care what you want, Mr. Rubin. I will name the next man to head the department. You just stage a class funeral."

"Mr. Weiss, I placed this call to advise how I felt."

"Mr. Rubin, I don't encourage long-distance telephone calls for two reasons. First, you can say the same thing in a wire, which is cheaper. Second, I don't have to listen to no arguments. This call is exactly the reason I don't like telephone calls. Here I am in a foolish argument with you at twenty dollars a minute. Mr. Rubin, I will send you a wire. It will instruct you to name Ben Sommers as the new press chief. It will be signed 'Regards, Weiss.' The word 'regards' is just a formality. In this instance, I won't mean it. Good-bye, Mr. Rubin. I mean what I say."

"Mr. Weiss. . . ."

The line was dead. Saul Rubin sat with his hand on the telephone for a long time. Then he picked up a heavy glass ashtray and threw it into the fireplace with all his strength. It smashed against the iron fireback and flew into a thousand pieces.

21

October 1919, Redondo Beach, California

"You must be Ben. I'm Elsie's father. Come on in, I'm glad to meet you after hearing about you. Nice to put a face with a name."

Ben looked down at his shoes and stamped his feet.

"Don't mind the sand. It gets tracked all over—one of the penalties of living out here at the beach. Nice here, though, now that the summer people have gone back to town."

Ben looked around the small bungalow. Heavy mission oak furniture was covered in sturdy brown leather, held in place by big round-headed brass tacks. On the walls were a number of hand-tinted enlargements of Kodak snapshots of the California missions, framed with small branches. Monk's cloth hung at the windows and a large vase held stalks of pampas grass and cattails.

"Very comfortable looking home, Mr. Wright."

"Sit down. Thank you. It is and it isn't. God knows where Elsie is, she's been getting dressed for an hour. The less they wear, the longer it takes to put on. You're over at Majestic, too?"

"Yes. That's where we met. On location. I'm head of press and publicity." He didn't know what else to say. Mr. Wright looked at him with a fixed smile. "It's a good place to work," he finished lamely.

Mr. Wright adjusted his sleeve garters and sat down. "Yes, I hear they pay good wages in the pictures." Absently, he handed Ben a section of the newspaper. "You can have the second section. Got the movie news in it. I daresay that's what you want." Ben had already seen it but took it anyway.

Mr. Wright unfolded the front section and began to read. Suddenly he lowered the paper and asked, "What do you think is wrong with President Wilson?"

Ben frowned thoughtfully. "I think it sounds like a stroke or something. My father died of a stroke, and this sounds the same. Wonder what they'll do? I mean, if he can't govern the country?"

"What I thought, too."

Ben turned to see what was making a soft clicking sound behind him. A pretty woman stood in the portieres that hung between the living and the dining rooms. Waving at invisible specks of dust on the beaded hangings, she smiled a lovely smile, Elsie's smile. Her bobbed hair shocked him a little. He never thought twice about girls with shingled hair, but he couldn't get used to short hair on a middle-aged woman.

"You must be Mr. Sommers. I'm Elsie's mother. Please don't get up. That's an old-fashioned gesture we don't need." She sat in a rocker, moving ever so lightly back and forth. "I think Mrs. Wilson should take over, if the President can't function, which it appears he can't." She looked smug. "And, I must say, it's about time."

Puzzled, Ben asked, "Beg pardon, Ma'am, what is? About time, I mean?"

"A woman in the White House, of course."

Mr. Wright's eyes appeared as he lowered his newspaper a few inches. "Watch it, boy. You're swimming in very deep water."

"Hush," Elsie's mother said to the newspaper. She beamed at Ben. "There's no time like the present to find out if Mr. Sommers can burn gemlike in the flame."

Ben squirmed slightly in the chair. His underwear was sticking to his skin and he wished to God that Elsie would hurry up.

Mrs. Wright continued. "I was prominent in the National Woman's Party. Picketed the White House in the fall of '17. I didn't get arrested, but it wasn't for not trying. Working for the vote, you know."

Ben did not appear to understand.

"Now I'm working at the Sanger Clinic downtown." She sighed, as if in pain. "Those poor Mexican women! You can't know what it is, Mr. Sommers, to have a dozen children. All those strict conservatives who rail against contraceptives, I don't see them down there adopting any of those extra children. They do their campaigning from a safe distance. Shameful!"

"He doesn't look Mexican, Mother." Mr. Wright looked at Ben. "Are you a conservative?"

Ben shook his head. "I don't think so." He really wasn't sure.

"I sincerely hope you use condoms, Mr. Sommers?"

Ben could feel his face falling open. There was no way for him to answer that question and stay out of trouble. Why hadn't Elsie warned him about her mother? Probably listening through some door, thinking it was a great joke.

"Leave the boy alone, Mother. That's his business, not yours."

Mrs. Wright sniffed. "If you are not interested in the young man who is about to take your daughter out for the evening, I am." She turned to Ben. "If you need one, Mr. Sommers, I'll be happy to give you one." She said to her husband, "I only want to make sure that his attitudes are correct before a mistake is made."

Ben felt that he had to defend himself. "Golly, Mrs. Wright, I hadn't really planned to do anything like that. We're just going to a picture preview out in Alhambra."

Mrs. Wright leveled him with a stare. "It's the unplanned evenings that are the most dangerous. How does Elsie feel about your limited range of social ideas?"

Ben swallowed. "I don't think she . . . that is, I don't know. We keep our conversation on light topics. You know. Gossip. Pictures. Things at the studio . . . you know." His voice trailed off.

"We've got lots to talk about, evidently. I'll try to alter some of your antediluvian concepts, so be warned." She reached across and patted his knee comfortingly.

126

Ben had only the vaguest idea of what was happening, but he realized that he was badly out of his depth.

A door opened and Elsie stood there, wearing something blue, looking more beautiful than he ever remembered seeing her. He stood up, both enchanted and relieved. Mrs. Wright kept her eye on him.

"He's really very old-fashioned, Elsie dear. Fallow ground for us to work." She sounded enthusiastic.

Elsie leaned down and kissed her mother on the forehead.

"I know, Momma. A real Southern gentleman. I think it's kind of sweet. A novelty in this house, I might add." She looked at Ben. "What's she been saying to you? You look all red and flustered."

Ben shuffled his feet and looked at the floor. Mr. Wright laid down his paper. "Better get him out of here, honey, before your mother makes mincemeat out of him. It's not really a fair fight. She's used to coming up against federal judges, hard-bitten Mexican priests. They're fair game. Ben's like a Christian in the arena. He never knew what hit him." He stood up and offered his hand. "You're a good sport, Ben. Next time you'll be prepared and when the bell rings, come out of your corner with your condom on."

Ben hurried Elsie out to the motorcar. They rode a block without speaking, then Elsie began to laugh. Ben looked at her sideways.

"Honest to God, Elsie, I don't think it's funny at all. You might have given me some little warning. I never thought I'd be discussing my love life with my girl's folks."

Laughing, Elsie said, "You really have to watch Momma. She's a terrible radical, fights everything. She was a Lucy Stoner and really very influential in getting the 19th Amendment passed here in California." She looked at him in amusement. "When you get upset your accent goes all to pieces."

"But she was sayin' things I didn't even talk about with my mother, much less yours. And I can't help where I was born."

"Good for you, probably. It's the new woman, Ben. Things are changing." Elsie snuggled up against him. "And I do think some things are changing for the better. You could put your arm around me."

"If I'm going to do that, you'll have to shift gears."

"OK, just tell me when."

The audience straggled out of the theater making notes on their preview cards, adding them to the pile on the card table in the lobby. The small group from Majestic stood silently and read the cards, passing them from one to the other.

"They continue to like Wanda and Wallie as a team," Rubin grunted.

"Yeh. They shoot sparks." Jimmie Cruze was excited.

"Did you hear the cheer go up as the name Wallace Reid flashed up on the screen?"

"Clever titles. Got lots of laughs. Titles are important."

Saul Rubin flipped through a pile of cards as if he was shuffling a poker deck. "Lotsa disappointment here, it looks like." He held the stack of cards toward them. "Look for yourself, Jimmie."

The director began to read some of them. "But it's only the 'new' Wallie they don't like."

"They expected an auto race somewhere in it." Rubin sounded disgusted. "God, couldn't you have gotten Wallie to drive fast for only a minute or two somewhere in the picture? Do we have to remold his personality into light comedian at this stage in his career? We—Majestic, that is—depend too much on his box office to fool around with him."

"After a few light comedies, the audience will accept Wallie in a variety of roles. After all, he didn't always race in pictures. They loved him as a college Joe." Cruze spoke earnestly. "I think it's a mistake to typecast an actor as versatile and able as Wallie."

"I think we can promote him in new ways, make the audience forget they ever knew a different Wallie," Ben said. "They'll accept him for whatever we tell them he is. I agree with Jimmie that audiences loved him long before the Dusty Rhodes series."

"Good idea, Ben," Rubin said, looking at him as if he never had one. "Now come up with a promotion scheme that'll do just that."

C. C. Brown's soda fountain was a narrow slot of a store almost at the end of Hollywood Boulevard. The booths were narrow, too, and Ben's knees touched Elsie's. She smiled.

"This is the best sundae in the world." She licked the thick warm chocolate from her spoon. "I'm not sure I can finish it."

"Behind that very soda fountain," he pointed with his spoon, "is where the hot fudge sundae was invented. Ought to

128

be a plaque." He smiled at her. "If there's anything I like, it's fudge."

She sighed and laid her spoon on the saucer. "Honestly, Ben, you're a bad imitation of Francis X. Bushman leering like that. Meaningful double entendres just aren't your style." She patted her lips with the napkin. "It'd be just like you to drag me all the way out here just to make some crack about wanting some fudge."

He kept his eyes on his ice cream. "How else am I going to get you into bed?" He looked up suddenly; as their eyes met he felt an unexpected flush on his cheeks.

She stared at him.

"That's what I thought," he said as he reached across the table and picked up her spoon, dipped it into her sundae and popped it into his mouth.

"Just give that back." She reached for the spoon. "Don't you think you're being just a little possessive?"

"But you're my girl. What's wrong with feeling possessive?"

"I'm not ready to be possessed, is all."

The corners of his mouth went down and she laughed at him.

"You look like you've been caught being naughty." She hesitated. "Ben, I'd like to go home with you," she sighed. "But I'd like it to be because I'd like to, not because you own me." She smiled bewitchingly. "I'm human, too."

"You mean you would?" His voice was low with wonder.

"Sure thing." She gazed at him with wide-open eyes.

He jumped up then sat down suddenly. "You haven't finished your sundae," he almost moaned.

"Thank you." She ate with a deliberate slowness, savoring each spoonful of the hardening fudge. When she finished, she took out her compact and carefully powdered her face and put on fresh lipstick. "Are you ready?"

He stared at her then burst into laughter. "I was ready months ago."

Through the mist of his orgasm, Ben heard a knocking sound. Panting, he lay and listened. There it was again. Now Elsie heard it, too. He felt her relaxed body tense up under him.

"Maybe whoever it is will go away," he whispered. "Probably has the wrong bungalow." Then he heard someone calling.

"Ben, I know you're in there." It was a girl's voice. "Your motor's out by the curb. And your light's on. Open up, honey."

"Who is it?" Elsie asked. "Who could it be at this hour?" She was frightened.

After groping in the closet for a robe, Ben walked into the living room, carefully closing the bedroom door. On the front porch, the light was burning and there stood Alma. Behind her stood a young man, not as tall as Ben but with huge shoulders.

"Hiya, Big Boy. I brought Phil along." She giggled. "He likes to watch. Doesn't do anything, just looks on, you know." She winked.

Ben was appalled and looked over his shoulder to make sure the door to the bedroom was closed.

"Alma, sweetie, I'm already busy." He was trying to speak softly. "I just forgot to turn off the light, is all. Be a good kid. Some other night." He forced himself to look at Phil. "Sorry to disappoint you." He smiled weakly.

Ben started to shut the door but Phil held it open with one straight arm.

"Now look! Alma, here, set me up for this. I been really lookin' forward to it, 'Big Boy.'"

Ben tried, but couldn't close the door. Nodding at Phil, he asked Alma, "What is he? Some sort of pansy?" He reached for Phil's arm. "Look, pal, I already said I'm busy with another girl."

Alma hit his chest with her fist. "Spoilsport." She was giddy, excited, barely in control. Drugs. She was hopped up on something.

Phil pushed forward, pressing Alma against him. Ben braced his hand against the door frame. He felt her grasp his penis.

"Oh," she trilled. "He's all sticky. Guess he's telling the truth." She giggled, turned and wiped her hand on Phil's lapel. He looked down, then slapped Alma hard across the face. Ben slammed the door and turned the bolt, leaning against it, breathing heavily. He could feel the door give every time Phil hit it.

Through the door Phil was shouting at him to come out and fight. He looked up and saw Elsie standing in the open doorway to the bedroom, white with fear. Finally Phil stopped pounding. Elsie stepped back into the darkness of the bedroom and then Ben heard her sobbing.

They rode out Santa Monica Boulevard in silence. Ben had put up the side curtains and Elsie was wrapped in a blanket to keep warm.

"I suppose it's stupid to say how sorry I am. Our first time and all that." He sighed.

Elsie shivered. "She saw me standing there, I'm sure."

"She couldn't possibly have seen you. She was looking up at me the whole time."

"It'll be a long time before I feel comfortable again. Does that happen all the time, Ben? I mean, I don't want to pry into your affairs." She sounded distant.

Ben suddenly found it difficult to speak. "I always turn the porch light off. Tonight I forgot." They drove on in silence.

"Does a steady stream of girls line up there for you?"

"Jesus, Elsie. Don't make it sound so terrible. I'm a healthy man with a healthy interest in girls. That's all. Once in a while a girl comes over. They never call first, so I set up the porch-light signal." He realized how that must sound to Elsie and grasped the steering wheel tightly.

Elsie laughed bitterly. "And I thought we were doing something special. You've got half of Hollywood in your bed. You don't need me at all." Pulling the blanket closer, she continued. "It's the most degrading, disgusting thing I ever heard of. You mean those poor girls—who need your approval to make a living—have to come by your bungalow hoping against hope the light will be on, so they can service the man who signs the checks?" She moved away from him slightly and shrank down into the blanket.

Ben felt his throat constricting. "Anything I say will only make it sound worse, honey."

"I'm not your *honey!*" She almost spit the words at him. "What kind of a job do I get, Mr. Sommers? Was I good in bed? Do I get a day's work?"

Ben wanted to close his eyes but was afraid he'd hit something.

"Oh, for Christ's sake, Elsie, you're different. I'm crazy about you. You mean something to me, besides . . . it's not the same at all."

Elsie looked across at him. "You're right. I was there because I liked you." She stared straight forward. "Idiot!" There was another uneasy silence. "You know, Momma was right. You're fallow ground. I hope you'll be worth the time it'll take for someone to work on you." Ben glanced at her. Her face was expressionless.

131

"I think I'm worth your time." She didn't respond but he went on anyway. "I think I love you, if that makes any difference. It was wonderful tonight. Different. I think that's because I love you."

"Ben, do you know what all this is doing to you?" She looked over at him, almost tenderly. "Of course you don't. Otherwise you wouldn't be doing it. It's a kind of slow corruption, that's what it is. Wearing the edge off your ability to tell right from wrong."

He kept silent while Elsie's voice grew angry again. "Just because you're a big executive, you can make a girl do anything you want. You don't even have to hope that she likes you enough to let you fumble around between her legs. It's your right to be there."

Fumble around? So that's what she thought of his lovemaking. His mouth felt dry.

"If I was a man, that would kill my ego." Her voice had a real edge to it. "I'd want to think that I was able to do something special that a girl would want, be anxious to get." She laughed bitterly again. "You could be Krazy Kat and they'd still pound on your door." There was a long silence as Ben pulled up in front of the Wright bungalow. "Just think about that, great lover," she said softly.

Elsie did not even take the trouble to say good night. She slipped out of the automobile and ran up the sandy path toward the porch light burning in the distance. She went inside, and the porch light went out.

22

October 1919, New York and Vermont

The Financial Times

KUHN, LOEB AND COMPANY UNDERWRITE $10 MILLION STOCK ISSUE FOR FAMOUS PLAYERS-LASKY—KNOWN AS PARAMOUNT PICTURES.

NEW YORK. Kuhn, Loeb and several associated bankers today underwrote a ten-million-dollar stock issue for a moving picture studio to buy theaters. The issue, both preferred and common, was listed on the exchange before noon, and by the close of business, the entire issue had been sold. Some brokers say the novelty of motion picture stocks may have helped.

With a groan Weiss smacked the financial section of the *New York Times* with his fingers and slumped back in his chair. Bessie hovered behind him with a worried look, hands moving helplessly. The girls ate silently, knowing the danger signs.

"Zukor!" Weiss said bitterly. "To think he would beat me." He stared at the notice in the newspaper. "I was sure I would be the first."

Working through Kuhn, Loeb, Paramount had become the first major movie company to put a public issue on the New York Stock Exchange. Looked down upon by brokers, film stocks had previously been sold only on the curb. Now Adolph Zukor had all the money he needed to finance the theater empire. Ten million shares had been sold the opening day. Once the shock of being upstaged had passed, Weiss began to worry about how many theaters Adolph Zukor could buy with his new millions.

"I must go to the banker this morning." Weiss sat muttering, spilling his coffee, ignoring his bagel and wonderful lox. He got up and wandered to the front of the house and stood in the parlor staring out into the street, not seeing anything, holding the lace curtain aside with one hand.

"Yes, the issue was oversubscribed the same afternoon," Falcon said with a detached air.

Weiss grasped the front of Falcon's desk with both hands. "Now I'll have to fight to catch up with Zukor again. He'll buy everything in sight."

Walter Falcon leaned back in his chair and sighed. "Mr. Weiss," there was a simple, patient note in his voice, "you continue to regard Majestic Pictures as if it were some sort of personal kingdom. Everything that happens is a personal affront to you. You must develop perspective. Objectivity."

"Everything Adolph Zukor does to me is designed to be an insult."

"But Majestic is a business. Privately held, but a business nonetheless. And it must be run like a business. Especially if you keep coming back asking for bigger loans. We must take steps to put our relationship on a more businesslike basis."

Weiss frowned. "Like how?"

Falcon settled back in his chair. This was not going to be easy, but it had to be done. "Let's talk about your stock, Mr. Weiss. We want a block of stock in exchange for the next money. We will buy into the company, not lend you the money. We will pay cash for a big enough block of stock to give us two men on the board." He looked at his note pad. "I see that there are a million shares. Nine hundred thousand Class B shares owned by you and some associates. One hundred thousand Class A, or voting shares—you and Rubin own those."

"Rubin has thirty thousand. I control the rest."

"We want to buy thirty percent. We don't even ask for controlling shares, you notice. Then we will buy up enough of the Class B to give you the money you need to continue your theater operation."

Weiss looked at Walter Falcon helplessly. The first thirty million had been bait covering the hook. He had swallowed the hook, and now they had him. No other bank would lend him money, knowing that he was locked into this one. They had him and they knew it.

"You don't understand the business and neither do any of your men. We will sink without a ripple in a year." Weiss made swimming gestures with his hands.

"Mr. Weiss, please give us more credit than that. All we wish to do is protect the investment made in your companies by this bank. I will personally see that they look only to money management. You will still determine artistic policy, such as how many times Fatty Arbuckle splits his pants in a picture."

Weiss stood up and leaned across the desk. Falcon did not lean away, as he instinctively wanted to.

"You fool," Weiss exploded, "that kind of crack shows how you still feel about us and our business. You take the money, the interest we pay you on the loan every month. Money made by Roscoe Arbuckle splitting his pants. You want to buy in, of course! Where else can you find an investment that will return nearly a million dollars for every hundred thousand invested."

Weiss paused, gathering his rage. "You go out and put a fat pink ass on film and see if you can do it. You can't. But I can. And you are willing to make a fortune out of it, but you're not willing to respect it as a legitimate business. Why didn't you pick some other example? A beautiful Spanish cathedral, with the nuns praying, or one of the other uplifting things we do? A wonderful love story?"

"I apologize. It was cheap."

"I stood in the back of my theater for years finding out just how many times Roscoe should split his pants. It's an art, and don't you forget it."

"Let's get back to the stock purchases. Maybe I can stay out of trouble there." Falcon smiled at Weiss, who showed no sign of acknowledging his apology. "We want you to go public, but on the curb, not on the exchange. It's more elegant to be listed, but the stock can be capitalized at one price and we sell it at a slightly higher one on the curb and pick up a few millions right there. It all helps the financing."

Weiss looked at him for a long while. There was no other way. As long as he retained control, he could manage. Rubin would scream. Let most of the A stock come out of his share. Weiss would retain the controlling interest.

"You can have thirty percent. I must retain a controlling interest in the voting stock. I'll sell you ten thousand of mine and twenty thousand of Rubin's. That will give you thirty thousand shares. Rubin will have to be content with ten. We can make it up to him in Class B. Keep his income the same. He'll be very unhappy, but I will take care of that."

"I suppose we will have to be satisfied with that, for the present, Mr. Weiss. For the present, then."

"I'm glad you agree. I don't like what I see happening to Sam Goldwyn and those Du Pont people."

Falcon grimaced. "He was very foolish to buy that *Caligari* fiasco. It cannot make money and if he insists on art instead of profits, the Kuhn, Loeb men wil make sure he is not in a position to make any more mistakes."

Weiss thought, let that be a lesson to me. Don't make any mistakes and try to put art on the screen. Bankers are not interested in art. He shook his head.

"Sam has wonderful taste. He buys and makes beautiful pictures. They don't always make money, but they set an industry standard."

"Well, he now has directors from Du Pont on his board."

"What happens if I feel a little artistic?"

Falcon's expression did not change. "Get yourself a date with a pretty moving picture actress. When you're feeling better, start making pictures again."

Weiss nodded. "We'll see. We'll see."

Falcon felt the subject should be changed.

"What are you buying now?"

"We just bought a large chain in the South—gives us control of New Orleans and the surrounding area. Now we go into the New England booking offices and the Back Bay chain." Weiss settled down and smiled wickedly. "You want to hear a good one? They both got contracts with First National. This will allow me to have a *secret man* on the First National Exhibitor's board. Now I can find out what they are planning, where they are expanding, buying theaters." He almost looked gleeful.

"Where will you start operations after that?"

"I plan to move across the South into Oklahoma and Texas."

"Who owns the biggest chain there?"

"It isn't always the biggest that is the best. Size of houses, locations, how swell the theaters are. The Hulsey Circuit is probably the best, all around."

Falcon sat back, warming to an idea he was about to present.

"I think the greatest weapon you can use in Texas is

136

money. Money is intimidation if it's in big enough quantities. Think about this: Your man Lynch opens a bank account with a million dollars in it. That, plus his reputation, might just work wonders."

Weiss looked up, eyes innocent as a child's. Falcon thought he would make a great poker player. "What do you know about Lynch?" Weiss asked.

"Enough to stay out of his way," Falcon chuckled. "Look, Mr. Weiss. We don't question your methods, just as you don't question ours. You think you can get results with a dynamiting here, a burning there. That's your decision. Men have done worse to make a few millions. We found out by simply putting two and two together. But then, we have more information than most people."

"The violence was not my idea."

"Of course not." Falcon sounded very understanding. "Many employees have a way of using bad judgment and letting go of details, don't they? You're hardly to blame, unless you lit the fuse yourself."

"Let's get back to the million dollars."

"Of course. Let's say we make that deposit and Lynch lets the word out that he is there to buy and to build theaters. Even in Dallas, a million dollars in a single deposit is not one of your everyday occurrences. The entire financial arena will be buzzing. Word will be all over town by nightfall. Then sit back and wait. I bet Lynch will get a hatful of offers from frightened theater owners, worried about new competition down the street, selling out while the getting is good."

Weiss looked at Falcon in admiration. It was the answer. How to continue the buying and cut out the violence.

"Mr. Falcon, for a banker, you'd make a wonderful thief."

"Mr. Weiss," Falcon replied, "for a thief, you make a wonderful partner." He stood up to see Weiss to the door.

Weiss paused. "What do you hear from your man?"

"Cotton? Not much, really. One memo on wasteful spending that I didn't pay too much attention to. But since then everything has been quite favorable. He seems to think you run quite a shipshape studio, I gather."

"He's seemed quite busy when I've been out there. Likes California, does he?" Weiss smiled.

"Seems to. But then all that orange juice and those pretty girls—what young man wouldn't? I hope he doesn't get in the way."

"Not at all, not at all," Weiss said cheerily.

"I hope he keeps his feet on the ground. A banker must

play the ant, not be the grasshopper," Falcon said as he handed Weiss his hat. "Remember my suggestion about the million dollar deposit."

"I'll try not to forget. But you know, a million here, a million there."

They both laughed heartily.

23

November 1919, Hollywood

"God almighty, you look terrible."

Virginia opened her eyes suddenly. She had fallen asleep in the bathtub and the water was cold. Henry Lehrman was standing over her.

"Oh, Pathé, don't lecture me."

She stood up in the tub, water running down her body in little rivulets. Henry stepped forward, cupped her breasts in both hands and kissed them.

"Now I can face your kitchen." She could hear his voice as he walked through the bedroom. "Honestly, Virginia, you live like a pig."

Virginia was as neglectful of her kitchen as of the rest of the bungalow. A bottle of milk had spoiled on the drainboard. Dirty dishes lay everywhere and flies buzzed around the trash pail under the sink. Cupboard doors hung open, the coffee percolator was half full of stale coffee, the strainer in the sink

139

filled with dried grounds. Disgusted, Lehrman strode back into the bedroom. Virginia stood nude in the center of the room, a towel wrapped around her dark hair.

"Honest to God, I refuse to make coffee in that mess. Get dressed and we'll go out to some coffee pot. Ginny, you'll make some lucky man a rotten wife, except in bed."

"Thanks, sweetie. I was thinking of starting with you."

Lehrman was in her closet picking out a dress. It was the director in him. He liked arranging little scenes for her to inhabit. She stood still and let him look at her.

"Who was there with you last night?"

"Maude Delmont. She called and said she'd go if I would. Saul Rubin was there. I got to talk to him. It was boring."

Henry handed her a dress he especially liked. She kissed him.

"Not so incidentally, your friend Roscoe was there. With his hands. He offered me a big part in his next Majestic picture."

"Did you say yes?"

"Are you kidding, kiddo? He is so repulsive. I just don't want any part that badly. I'll do a guy a favor to get a part, but not Roscoe Arbuckle."

"Honey, Roscoe is really a sweet guy and a great comedian. I'd like to follow him over to Majestic from Keystone, and I don't want anyone else getting ideas about directing him. Don't make it any harder for me. He likes girls like anybody else, even if he does weigh 280. Just say 'no' to him in a nice way. It's an act more than anything else. Stars are 'on' all the time."

Virginia ran her hands up and down her legs to smooth out the stockings. "I don't want him 'on' me, that's all. Just keep him away from me or I may have to belt him one. A good slap once in a while earns a girl a little respect. That's all I want from Roscoe. Respect. No laughs, no cheap feels, respect."

Dressed now, looking pale but ravishing, she sat down. "Where do you want to go?"

"Let's hit The-Hole-In-The-Wall out near Santa Monica. Hal makes a great tomato juice thing for hangovers. Be good for you."

Lehrman's custom-built touring car was spectacular, and Virginia loved to ride in it because people stared. The Rolls-Royce grille on the Packard body was unusual enough, but it also sported two windscreens, one for the driver's compart-

140

ment, the other for the rumble seat. Virginia laid her head back against the leather and closed her eyes.

Henry turned to look at her as he drove west on Sunset. The first day she walked on the set at Keystone, wearing a sunbonnet, she'd drawn men to her like flies to honey. She exuded some sort of unconscious come-on. It had attracted Roscoe too and he had been chasing her ever since. But Henry got there first. Virginia was a strange girl. She slapped producers' faces and lost out on good parts when they got fresh and then spent the night with some man because she liked him. She gave Mack Sennett crabs, for which he never forgave her; and after he spread the story around, Virginia's reputation grew even worse.

Henry had asked her to marry him several times and she'd refused. Now she was willing but he was less so. His career was rising and he thought maybe he could do a little better. Maybe Virginia had become a little too picturesque. They went out all the time and made love regularly, but marriage? He would have to think about that.

Coming down the grade into Santa Monica Henry could see Catalina Island on the horizon. He began to sing softly.

> I found my love in Avalon, beside the bay.
> I left my love in Avalon, and sailed away.
> I dream of her and Avalon
> From dusk till dawn
> And so I think I'll travel on
> To Avalon.

The first few blocks at the edge of the coast highway were filled with a scatter of flimsy beach houses and mission style bungalows. To the south lay the little town of Santa Monica, to the north, Malibu, where some of the Hollywood crowd had weekend shacks on the beach. Lehrman parked in front of The-Hole-In-The-Wall.

"Hal, we'll sit in the back room. In a quiet corner."

They found a booth at the back of the restaurant. The building had been a big beach house and still looked more like a residence than a roadhouse. A huge fireplace of misshapen clinker bricks filled one wall. Bookcases on each side were stacked with statuettes of nudes. All sizes and shapes, from saltshakers to bronzes, they stood on one toe, stroked indifferent borzois or bent over tying ribbons of ballet slippers, revealing dimpled buttocks.

141

Henry slipped into the booth, next to Virginia.

"I wish you'd called last night. I would have gone with you."

"Pathé, dear, don't get mad if I get around. I just have to be seen a bit. I want to build my own career. If I'm always with you everybody thinks you get parts for me." She took his hand and gave it a squeeze.

Henry seemed rigid. "What's the difference, I'd like to know, between your going to bed with me and getting a part, and your going to bed with some producer and getting a part?"

Virginia sat up and laid his hand on the table. "Silly," she said, "I go to bed with you because I love you, not because you get me parts."

Hal arrived with his Tomato Special, a pick-me-up made from a lot of secret ingredients. Virginia took a gulp and sighed, "That's better." They ordered omelettes.

"Henry, I hate quarreling with you about this. If I had a dollar for every girl you've made by promising her a part, I could go back to Chicago and live like the Queen of Roumania. There isn't one girl in Hollywood who hasn't been a lay for someone who promised her something. You have to get them off the train at Banning to find one who hasn't. Twenty-four hours in this town and she's been had. It's the cheapest commodity. Even oranges cost a penny apiece. The fucking is free. A girl just hopes it will pay off somehow. So don't criticize me for joining the game you men invented."

She put her arms down on the table and laid her head on them. "Tell Hal I need another Tomato Something. Who would have thought two Orange Blossoms would do this to me."

Henry stroked her hair gently. "It's the orange juice. Get you every time."

They ate without speaking and then sat close to one another, sipping coffee.

There was a sudden commotion at the front door and a large party of noisy people came in. They had already been drinking, and the girls were hanging onto the men and to each other. In the middle, loudly demanding a table, stood Fatty Arbuckle, the most instantly recognizable star in Hollywood.

Virginia drew back when she heard his voice. "Get me out of here. I can't face him today."

"Just sit back here quietly and maybe he won't see us."

Arbuckle's party sat at a big round table in the front dining room by the window, silhouetted against the bright sunlight streaming in from the western sky. The Hole was pretty crowded by now, and the patrons were delighted to see a real movie star, especially a funny one. All too often actors and actresses were not easily recognizable off screen. With Fatty there was no mistake. Fatty obliged his public and put on a show. He giggled and pinched the girls and knocked over glasses of water. After every cute stunt he would hide his mouth behind his hands and giggle. The patrons of the Hole sat back, relaxed, and enjoyed the free show.

Fatty was drizzling egg yolk on a girl's arm and licking if off when Virginia decided they should leave by the back way. Henry paid the check and stood up. Roscoe saw him.

"Pathé! Hey, Pathé? That you there in the dark? How long have you been here? Why didn't you sing out? Come on and join us. Lots of room, if you don't count me."

Virginia sank back into the booth and tried to disappear.

Fatty stood up, knocking over his chair. He hurried toward the rear booth in little mincing steps, not quite skipping. Friends always said that Roscoe was surprisingly light on his feet for such a big man. He had learned to skip in such a way that he looked light. It was a matter of short, quick movements, rather than the ponderous ones expected from such a fat man.

"Who's that with you? Peekaboo!" He slowly slid his face up and over the high back of the booth. Virginia's insides began to churn.

"Hey, it's gorgeous Ginny." He slid around the edge of the bench and sat next to her. "Why you hiding back here in the dark, sugar?"

"Hello, Roscoe. I woke up feeling rotten after that party last night. I just don't feel up to joining another party. I really want to be home in bed."

"Great, I'll go with you." Fatty snickered.

Henry sat down again. He smiled at Roscoe's remark.

"Roscoe, take it easy. She really feels terrible. She didn't want to go out. I thought she would feel better if she got out of the house. Didn't work."

"Did Hal give her one of his specials?"

"Two." Virginia shrugged her shoulders. "They didn't do all that much."

"You're really in bad shape, then. God, they always work wonders for me. Ginny, you didn't drink all that much last night. I had my eye on you."

143

"I just can't drink, Roscoe. Never could. Did you pay the check, Henry? I really want to go home."

"All taken care of. Sorry we can't join you, Roscoe. Next time." He stood up but Fatty made no effort to let Virginia get out of the booth.

"Ready to go Ginny?" Henry asked. "Why don't you let her out, Roscoe?"

"I was secretly hoping that she would try to climb over me," Fatty simpered. "Upsy-daisy." Sticking his lower lip out in a huge pout, he reluctantly got up. Virginia moved rapidly. As she squeezed past him, Fatty goosed her. Virginia pretended not to notice.

"Nice seeing you, Roscoe. Sorry we didn't get to talk much." She moved on past him and walked rapidly toward the front door. "I'll wait in the car, Pathé," she called over her shoulder. "Bye, everybody."

"Very unfriendly girl you've got, Pathé. I gave her my trained finger, and she didn't feel a thing. I hear she lets everybody in town get into her pants. What she got against fat men?"

"Roscoe, don't take it personally. She's just independent. Moody. Sometimes she's hot to go and at others, not a thing. Women. You know." He winked at Roscoe and nudged him in the ribs. The two men laughed.

"Well, I got a hot one there at the table. See, the redhead. I'll let you know if she's a natural redhead or henna." He giggled. "See you tomorrow on the lot."

Fatty danced back to his party and leaned across the table and said something to the group in a low voice. They yelped with laughter. Henry closed the front door and walked toward the car.

"I just can't stand him. I'm sitting here shivering. My grandmother used to say that someone just walked on your grave when you feel like this."

"Ginny, don't carry on. You'll be all right. You'll be home in a little while."

"Grandma was right. When I see that man, I feel like someone just walked on my grave."

24

March 1920, The Majestic Press Department

Nugget Times, Reno, Nev., March 3, 1920

**MARY PICKFORD DIVORCES OWEN MOORE
GLADYS MARY SMITH MOORE GRANTED
DECREE IN MINDEN COURTHOUSE BY
JUDGE FRANK P. LANGDEN**

MINDEN, Mar. 2. Special from our correspondent.
Almost unrecognized, with her golden curls combed
straight back in a severe style and wearing smoked
glasses, Gladys Moore, better known to her millions
of admirers as Mary Pickford, was granted a
divorce today from actor Owen Moore. Miss Pickford has been living on a small farm in nearby
Genoa for several weeks. A number of newspaper-
men have been searching for the tiny star since she
dropped from sight.

When Miss Pickford stepped into the witness box
she was still in disguise but was recognized the
instant she took off her glasses. Miss Pickford wept
on the stand as she described Moore's drunkenness
and abuse. There are no children.

Continued inside.

Ben read the story aloud from the front page of the *Los Angeles Times*. Norma, his secretary, listened, fascinated.

"This is what I like. Listen to this. 'Judge Langden is the circuit judge who presides in the Minden court every second Thursday. His wife is a great fan of Miss Pickford.' That kills me!" Ben laughed. "Copied straight off the wire from the Minden release, a little local interest. Jesus, you'd think the *Times* would at least rewrite."

The telephone rang and Norma answered it. She covered the mouthpiece with her hand.

"Mr. Weiss is up at the Executive Bungalow and would like to meet with you this morning. Are you in?"

"What are you asking for? Yes! Of course, yes! Ask what time." Ben swiveled his chair around and dropped his feet off the desk and onto the floor as if Weiss were looking at him. Norma hung up.

"Eleven A.M. Boy, aren't you the bee's knees!"

"No, just a department head, is all. Jesus, I wish I'd worn a better suit."

"Maybe he'll think you look shabby and give you a raise."

"Get out the latest press books, I got to have something to show him. And get some bathing suit pictures. He likes to look."

Norma sighed. "You're all the same."

Abe Weiss traveled to Hollywood only five or six times a year because he hated the long train ride. He liked to arrive unexpectedly, but if he was unreachable at the New York office for two consecutive days, it was assumed that he was on the train and could appear at any moment. His office was aired and fresh flowers were arranged in the vases, all the latest trade publications were lined up on the library table, and the huge table of awards and honors dusted, the bronze and gold medals polished. But compared to the elaborate gothic library which served as an office to Saul Rubin, Weiss's private office was modest and almost plain.

Weiss talked to his visitors in two different locations. If he wished to be a formal executive, he remained behind the desk. If he wanted to be genial and friendly, as he was when trying to sign a star to a new contract, he sat in a chair away from the desk, in a conversational corner in the office, next to the awards table, as he now did with Ben.

"Have you seen the *Times*, Ben?" he asked.

"Sure have, sir. You must know her pretty well." Weiss nodded. "Mary said she might stay in Nevada for at least another year. Would she throw over a great career just like that?"

"She might have to, Ben. In the United States nice women do not get divorced. Mary is the first moving picture actress to ever try it." He smiled as if at a fond memory. "Just think. She must be very certain of her queenship to risk everything.

And she must love Douglas very much. I wonder if they will marry when they can?"

"They go together all the time. I guess it's no secret."

"They've been in love for years. Be interesting to see how the women's clubs and the hard-shelled ministers and the stiff-backed priests react. Poor Mary. She'll be roasted from every pulpit in the country. Mary might just wake up and find she is box-office poison."

"Terrible risk for United Artists, I'd say," Ben observed.

"But not for Mary." Weiss leaned back in his chair. "She can retire and live like a queen. She has millions by now." He laughed ironically. "I'm telling you. I paid them to her." His expression changed and a troubled look came across his face; then he shrugged it off. "Thank God it's not our problem anymore. There are forces that will crucify a star. There are people who won't go and see a Chaplin picture. Don't like his morals. Reputation. That's what does it." He thought for a moment then smiled. "On the other hand some people don't get hurt. A little smudge enhances them. You met Olive Thomas yet?"

Ben laughed. "Yes, once on a train. I heard she was on the lot. I can hardly wait. She's my idea of a really lovely woman."

"Nice girl. She was very big in the Follies. Not so big yet in pictures, but that's because Lewis didn't know what to do with her. We know."

"What did you mean about a little smudge?"

"After Flo Ziegfeld got tired of her, he added her to his stable of girls he lent out to rich men for weekends. He called them his 'connoisseurs.' He made elaborate arrangements to have his Follies girls sampled by blue ribbon jury, so to speak. It had a reverse effect. Instead of being tarnished, the girls were enhanced and most of them married well."

"I don't understand."

"Men who weren't so rich found the former playthings of really rich men very desirable. The rich set styles, after all, and the newly rich and the not so rich copy."

"You mean they were high-class whores?"

"Far from it. You just pay a whore. These girls were ushered into Cartier or Tiffany and allowed to choose something. Whores don't usually wear Poiret gowns or are dressed by Ali Ben Haggin or Joseph Urban. It was Urban, by the way, who set Olive's trademarks—the violet scarves, violet cigarettes." He smiled. "He also forbade her to wear any

147

underwear. He dressed her in Egyptian linen gauze so fine you could read a page of the *Times* through it. She was some sight at a party, I'll tell you."

"Must have been." Ben racked his memory. She must have been wearing underwear that day on the train. Surely he'd have noticed. "Did the girls have to go with anyone? Could they say no?"

"The men were on their best behavior, as much as any man is in bed. One of the girls told me that they used to like the older men better—they were more considerate, they weren't so energetic, and gave them bigger diamonds the next day. It didn't make any difference to their future husbands. They all married well."

"I understand that Olive and Pickford have separated."

"It's too bad." Weiss nodded. "A picture-book wedding. I was Jack's best man. Mary asked me. Flo gave her away. They were married in Mary's garden behind the Willoughby Avenue house. It took an army of police to keep the crowds away. There was such an uproar that they couldn't even hear each other say, 'I do.'"

"And Jack Pickford knew that she'd been . . . out on loan, so to speak?"

"Of course." He laughed. "Everybody knew what went on. There wasn't any need for a whitewash."

"What's a whitewash?"

"Cover up some unsavory scandal. You just hope to God we never have one with one of our stars here at Majestic, Ben. You'll be painting the town and everyone in it with whitewash."

"How does it happen?"

"Lots of ways," he said offhandedly. "A nasty motor car accident and a big star kills some kid while he's drunk." He paused for a moment as if remembering incidents. "Or somebody botches an abortion. A star gets caught taking drugs." He made a helpless gesture with his hands. "A thousand ways, as many ways as there are people."

His dark eyes drilled into Ben. "It's your job, Ben, to make sure reporters print only what I want them to print and what the studio decides the public should know. Not one word more. Not even a suspicion." He bobbed his head as if speculating on Ben's ability to carry off such a difficult assignment. "It's tricky. They demand as much information as they can get. Most of the time you're delighted to give them everything you've got and hope to God they use it. In a

148

whitewash, it's your job to misdirect, give false stories, give out as little information as you can and hope they don't print anything."

"My God, Mr. Weiss," Ben leaned forward, "how do we manage all that?"

"Lie," Weiss answered blandly. "It's the only way. With a bald face. You cheat, steal, suppress evidence if you get to the scene first. Destroy clues. Pay off everybody you need to bribe. If you can buy time or silence, you pay for as much as is necessary."

Ben was vaguely troubled. Then he thought, oh, hell, I might as well ask.

"Mr. Weiss, isn't some of that criminal, or don't I understand what you're saying?"

Weiss gazed at him, unblinking. "Ben, I hope you understand, all right. You have to look at it this way: If you're going to let a little scruple stand between a million-dollar star and catastrophe, you're in the wrong business." The office was so quiet that Ben could hear the desk clock ticking.

Smiling at Ben, reassuring him that there was no implied threat in his statement, Weiss watched closely, studying his face, trying to read there what the young man was thinking. The point was very important. This young man would have to do all of these things one of these days, and Weiss wanted to make sure that Ben understood the importance of the duty that lay in his hands.

Ben realized that he was being weighed and felt the pressure. He decided that the point was not worth debating. The possibility of his having to destroy evidence was too remote to risk having an argument with the boss. Anyway, he'd face that when he got to it.

He nodded slowly, understandingly. "I guess I'd have to decide what was at stake, wouldn't I? Nothing else really matters, except for Majestic, does it?" He watched Weiss's face to gauge the effect of his statement and was relieved to see a smile.

"You understand, Ben," Weiss beamed. "I hoped you would, and I'm glad you didn't fail my hopes. Majestic does come first, always."

A shaft of sunlight fell on Saul Rubin as if some lighting man had trained the sun through the leaded glass of the oriel bay window.

"Olive Thomas will be here in a few minutes, Ben. I

wanted to introduce her to you, then you can take her back to your office and get all the dope you need to start a publicity campaign."

"I'm really looking forward to meeting her," Ben grinned.

"Everybody gets the hots when they see her. She has the goddamnedest effect on men. You'll feel your balls tingle when she walks in. See if they don't."

"Mr. Weiss filled me in on her and Flo Ziegfeld yesterday."

"He ought to know," Rubin said levelly. "He was quite dashing in his prime. Used to date Follies girls, I understand."

Their eyes met and Ben decided he'd have to think about that one.

"Did he tell you Olive was Ziegfeld's mistress between wives?"

There was a vicious undercurrent to his voice that Ben disliked. "Yes, he did."

"Well, she was no untouched flower when she went into the Follies. She'd been painted in the nude by some Peruvian, and Condé Nast ran photos of her in *Vanity Fair* as 'art' that would have gotten other magazines confiscated by the police." he smirked. "You ought to see if we can buy up some for studio use. She's a creation, Ben, like some of our stars. The man taught her to walk, talk, sit, stand, everything. She managed not to get ground up, though, like some of those country girls who found themselves taking their shoes off at Madison Square Roof so gay blades could drink champagne out of them."

"What do you mean, 'ground up'?"

Rubin put his elbows on the desk and grew confidential. "All you ever hear about is how well they married. Nobody ever talks about the divorces, the suicides, the drunks. The same thing happens when you take some brainless pretty little thing out from behind a Woolworth counter somewhere and the next thing you know she's up on the silver screen. Some of them don't survive. That's all." He was very matter-of-fact. The buzzer on his desk sounded. "She's here." He stood but did not step out from behind his desk. Olive Thomas would have to walk the full length of his office to shake his hand.

25

April 1920, The Screening Room

Bill Taylor sat in the first row of the screening room as the lights dimmed. His hands grasped the round leather arms of the chairs, fingers feeling out familiar cold brass nailheads. There was a soft whoosh in the chair next to him and he turned, disconcerted, to see the unsmiling lean face of Saul Rubin, his glasses reflecting the lights, staring straight ahead to the empty screen at the far end of the narrow room. Taylor looked back at the flat rectangle of silver that would come alive in a moment. He had always wondered about the dark scar that ran down one side, perhaps the mark of a shoe thrown in despair.

He had invited only a few carefully selected men to watch the test of the little Walenska girl. He wanted the freedom of making his own judgment in private. Now as he glanced at the rear of the theater, he could see a shadowy line of Rubin's assistants moving into the back seats. Rubin's number two secretary, Vivian, never more than a dozen feet away, hovered in the side aisle waiting for darkness. She lived in dread of missing a swiftly thrown signal. During the screening, however much she might want to watch the test, she would never take her eyes from the back of Rubin's head.

Bill was furious over what had become of the screening. Now Polly's future would be decided by official opinion. A screening room full of executives and assistants could easily become a charnel house, everyone waiting for Rubin's pronouncement. If the verdict was even doubtful, the rows of assistants would then claw the victim beyond any hope of salvation. If the screen test was not exciting enough, Polly might never get a second chance. Taylor sighed and pressed the buzzer for the operator to start the projector.

As the scratch leader appeared on the screen, Taylor heard Rubin's voice muttering in his ear. He did not turn his head.

"Droste told me you found something special. Young meat, a real chicken. You been holding out on me, Billy?"

"I wanted to make sure she was worth your time, Mr. Rubin." Taylor disapproved of Rubin's taste for little girls, but he tried not to let his voice betray his attitude.

Rubin folded his hands across his hollow frame and settled down to watch the test as the first long shots of Polly appeared, standing before a backdrop of a garden.

"Nice little tits," he muttered almost inaudibly, but making sure Taylor could hear.

Taylor paid no attention. He was leaning forward, watching the images with focused intensity. Most members of an audience sat back and relaxed. The director went to work in the dark, intent on the new face, the artist with the technician's eye looking at each tiny flicker for its message.

The screen test, as did most, started a bit uncertainly. Polly walked to the center of the screen, paused by a battered looking tree, opened a wobbly gate, and stepped through. She looks frightened, Bill thought. Why didn't I start over again so she'd be more sure of herself?

Obviously listening to his directions, her eyes darting to the spot where the director sat, Polly walked forward and back, to the left and to the right.

Taylor began to feel a growing excitement as Polly acted in her first scenes. Pay no attention to her clumsiness, he thought, the tentative movements, her uncertainty. There was a vitality that he had seen too few times.

Then it happened. A long lingering set of close-ups filled the screen. Her features were not absolutely regular, so there was interest, not symmetry. What can it be, Taylor wondered, what is that quality? He could tell what she was thinking by looking at her. He could feel her reaching out into the darkness of the theater. He glanced at Rubin, who had not moved and sat fixed, gazing at the screen.

Taylor's mind raced forward, intent on the luminous face. Heroines tumbled through his memory.

Polly Walenska was obviously a child—the stance, the walk. But that glowing face belonged to a little girl who knew too much and was unable because of lingering innocence to conceal it. She didn't know enough to care who knew and was still too ingenuous to conceal her eroticism—a child who had become a woman too soon.

Taylor recognized the last shot in the test and turned to Rubin to gauge his response. Out of the corner of his eye he saw the film continue. Puzzled, he turned back to watch. Apparently the cameraman, led by some impulse of his own, had continued to turn the crank after Taylor had called "cut." Walking his camera forward to stay in close, the cameraman had followed Polly across to a corner where she stood in the nearly empty studio, exhausted. Leaning against some unused flats, she trailed her finger idly down a length of molding gazing at something in the distance. Wistfully, she sat on a plaster stump as fears and uncertainties flickered across her face. Then someone approached and her eyes flashed in a spontaneous smile. The figure turned out to be Taylor extending his arm to shake hands with her. Then the film ran out.

The lights dimmed up to half brightness. Rubin looked at Taylor for a full minute, speculating.

"Well, where the hell did you find her? I knew you were holding out on me, you dirty bastard."

153

"I told Casting what I wanted and that it had to be an unknown, and Droste turned her up."

Rubin snorted. "Droste couldn't find his ass with both hands. It must have been one of his girls who found her. Paul can identify twenty thousand pairs of tits, but he never looks at faces. And that's a face. How old did you say she was?"

Taylor smiled. "I didn't. But she's about thirteen or so. I'm really amazed at how beautifully she photographs."

Rubin stood up and stretched, reached his hand inside his shirt and scratched his stomach. He looked down at Taylor. "Can you get a performance out of her? If so, I'd sign her to a contract. What part you got in mind for her?"

"The tomboy in *Spirit of Youth*. She'll knock them in the aisles." Taylor looked up at Rubin and smiled knowingly.

Rubin brought his face down to Taylor's. "She still a virgin, Billy?"

"How should I know, Mr. Rubin?" Taylor smiled through his annoyance at Rubin's innuendo. "She's been over to Casting. You know what happens over there."

Rubin stood up. "If she was, and Droste got to her first, I'll kill him."

He started up the aisle still talking to Taylor. "All right. I'll go along with her. Billy, it's up to you. Give me a performance. Big eyes and little tits I can get by the dozen. I want more. Legal can draw up a contract. Sommers, do a background. No more of those goddamned Hungarian countesses stranded by the war. Give her a name and a background we can play up." He stopped and turned. "What's her name?"

"Walenska. Polly Walenska. It can be changed," Taylor added.

"You're goddamned right, it can be changed. Start a list. Be in my office tomorrow afternoon with the list. We'll pick one out. Have her stop by my office. I'd like to meet our newest little star and spend some time with her." He punched open the door and a blinding shaft of sunlight stabbed into the room. The secretary grabbed up the telephone and asked for Rubin's office. A moment later she shouted into the mouthpiece.

"He's on his way." She dropped the earpiece and ran up the aisle.

At one moment during the week there were almost a hundred names on the Polly list. One faction, headed by Helen, Saul Rubin's head secretary, and supported by Ben, favored alliteration, such as Polly Powers, Polly Peters, Polly Pointer, Polly Porter.

Rubin sat at the head of the long conference table and listened to the list.

"What about Polly Piss?" he growled. "I hate all of them. Don't sound real."

Ben could not remember a morning when Rubin had been so contrary and disagreeable. They all looked at each other. No one wanted to read out the next list and come under attack.

Rubin sat drumming his fingers on the table. In the oppressive silence, Ben thought the drumming sounded like fearful heartbeats. Everyone in the room was afraid of Saul Rubin.

"I like the Irish idea," Rubin barked. "Irish is always good." He laughed. "Irish eyes and all that dreck." He sat up suddenly and looked at Helen. "What's that singer's name? You know the one. High voice. No balls. You know the one; he sings Irish songs and always makes me cry. Mack something."

"John McCormack? 'The Last Rose of Summer'?" a small voice ventured from the far end of the table.

Rubin smacked his hand, palm down, on the table. "That's it! That's great!" He jumped up and stood in triumph, now pounding his fist on the table. "Polly McCormack. I like it." He looked around the table at the stunned expressions. "I pay you people a fortune to come up with ideas. Who always has to save things? Saul Rubin does. I don't know why I even ask you for suggestions. I always have to do everything myself. I ought to dock you all a week's salary."

There was no sound in the room except for Rubin's shouting. Everyone looked at the top of the table or studied the floor.

26

June 1920, Big Bear Lake, California

The New York News, June 2, 1920

DOUG AND MARY MOBBED
POLICE RESCUE DOUG FAIRBANKS AND
MARY PICKFORD IN EUROPE'S CAPITALS

SPECIAL TO THE NEWS. Doug Fairbanks and his new bride, Mary Pickford Fairbanks, have been repeatedly trampled and mobbed by excited crowds of well-wishers. Their hotel in Paris was stormed by thousands of admirers.

In London Little Mary was almost pulled out of an open car from which they were attempting to view Kensington Gardens. The quiet interlude was ruined by mobs which pulled all the buttons off Doug's suit.

The constant press of fans and crowds eager to see their idols has made Mrs. Fairbanks nervous and on the verge of being ill. British authorities have appealed to the mobs to respect the privacy of the newlyweds.

Everyone thought *What's Your Hurry?* was a natural for Wallace Reid. Byron Morgan, who created the character of Dusty Rhodes for his *Saturday Evening Post* series, moved to the Coast to write the scenarios as well as stories. He specialized in dreaming up new thrills for the final reel of Wallie's motorcar pictures. In *Hurry* Reid would play a logging-truck driver who saves a community with a daring feat.

There was a recent awareness at the studio that Reid's drawing power had diminished a little. Disappointing scripts, some poor directors, quick and sloppy productions, all contributed; but the real truth was that Wallie was tired.

Wallie never let up. The new house was constantly full of guests who never went home. There were a dozen for dinner almost every night. Wallie loved music and played a number of instruments. Several nights a week a small orchestra met and played impromptu concerts. New pictures were shown in the projection room for those who were not musical or who did not want to swim or play billiards. There was plenty to eat and a generous supply of good liquor brought in by two bootleggers.

Already averaging eight or nine pictures each year, he had been rushed into the vacuum left by the departure of Douglas Fairbanks, so that he now had less than a week between the finish of one picture and the start of another. He asked that Sam Wood not be assigned to direct *Hurry* as he wanted to work again with Jimmie Cruze. Saul Rubin said no and Wood was determined to make Reid regret he had requested the change. Wood's inexperience had been obvious on his previous Reid picture, but now he carefully planned each scene in a taut style to keep tensions high.

After a series of disastrous attempts to get Wallie out from behind a steering wheel and make him into a Jazz Age type, *What's Your Hurry?* put him back into the driver's seat. The part of the truck driver was filled to the brim with Reid's special animal energy and the action would mount in tension and suspense. Most of the excitement was planned for the final third of the picture. A new dam, built across the top of a populated valley, threatens to break on Christmas Eve, flooding hundreds of homes. To repair the dam Wallie leads a caravan of trucks down a treacherous mountain road in a terrifying rainstorm. At one point the brakes go out on Wallie's truck and only by dint of his superb driving is he able to keep it from crashing. At the end of the picture Wallie was to drive straight up the face of the crumbling dam and thrust his truck into the hole in the earthworks, stopping the water from flooding out. For the first time in months Wallie was excited about a picture and genuinely delighted by all of its aspects.

All of the location scenes, except for the final drive into the dam, were being filmed at Big Bear Lake, high in the mountains above Los Angeles. The mountains were covered with great groves of towering spruce and pine. The lake was not as big as Tahoe but a good deal larger than Lake Arrowhead, down the mountain and closer to Los Angeles.

157

In order to get the most spectacular cross lighting among the trees, Wood shot from six in the morning until about nine. More scenes were filmed in the late afternoon when slanting rays of sunshine modeled the trees and rocks once again. This pleasant arrangement left the company free for five or six hours during the middle of the day.

The crew lived in a small tent city set up near the beach. The actors, the director, and the writer lived at the Big Bear Lodge, a rustic inn a few minutes' walk away. It was a very happy company, working on a daring adventure film each morning and afternoon, spending midday swimming and playing volley ball, napping, gossiping, flirting, sometimes making love beneath the fragrant fir trees. Lunch was set out on long picnic tables in a pine grove near the Lodge. Dinner was also served there for those who wanted it. Reid and Wood and Morgan ate at the Lodge. Some of the crew tried local restaurants in the little town of Big Bear or drove down to the resorts around Arrowhead.

Sam Wood remained a little distant with Reid. During the second week of shooting, Dorothy Reid arrived for a few days and her company made Wallie more cheerful. By the middle of the second week most of the scenes involving the logging trucks had been shot and they were well ahead of schedule.

The script called for the climactic driving scenes to be filmed in a torrential downpour. As it almost never rains in California during the summer, the rain had to be created. A series of perforated pipes and lawn sprinklers were set up on stands covering a relatively short length of the dirt road. Wood had blocked the road into sections and planned the sequence of shots for each section of the road. These scenes were shot at the same hour each day so the lighting would match when the film was cut.

First, Wood filmed a long shot of the caravan of five trucks coming down the road in the rain. Gasoline-driven pumps raised the water from the lake at the bottom of the hill to the pipes and sprinklers. They made a terrible noise and frightened away all the wildlife for hours. Two tank trucks went down the road to wet it down in advance of each shot. The mountains were so dry that all the water put out by the rain pipes soaked into the dirt road instantly, and Wood wanted nice sticky mud for the close-ups of wheels and tires. Next, a camera mounted on one of the tank trucks preceded the caravan down the same stretch of road getting medium shots of the trucks, catching the look of strain on Wallie's face as

158

the windshield wiper drove back and forth. Last, came the loving, close-up shots of details—the muscles twitching in Wallie's jaw as he wrestled the huge truck around a deadly curve, the squish of mud from under a tire, the rain glistening on the huge chain that held the giant logs on the rear of the truck giving it weight and increasing the danger.

Wallace Reid was extremely strong, but he needed all his strength and driving ability to handle the truck on some of the steeper downgrades. Out of sight, beyond the edge of the cameras' frame, stood a number of loggers watching the dudes and greenhorns do as a lark what they did for a living. They had all made offers to drive for Wallie, but he was determined to prove himself and show that he was no cream puff. By morning of the fourth day they were convinced and began to applaud when the caravan successfully negotiated a particularly difficult turn.

At midmorning Wallie's truck was supposed to lose its brakes and go careening down the mountainside. To accomplish this effect, the truck was to veer crazily from side to side while the cameras were cranked at half speed. When the film was projected at regular speed all of the action would seem to be happening much faster; the truck would appear to be totally out of control. The road was soaked again and again and rain pipes were set up in several locations, always out of camera range.

Wallie's truck slowly gained speed and began to rock from one side of the twisting road to the other. Everyone held his breath—the effect was truly terrifying. Excited shouts came up from the loggers hidden behind trees along the route. Halfway down the run a new and unexpected danger arose— the logs strapped to the truck bed began to roll dangerously from side to side and threatened to overturn the truck. The shouting loggers, realizing the danger, fell suddenly silent and the crew's elation collapsed into terror. The production crew, ordinarily seated in their canvas chairs under a sunshade, stood alert for an accident. There was nothing anyone could do. It was all up to Wallace Reid in the cab of the careening truck. With superhuman effort Reid stopped the truck safely out of camera range so as not to ruin the shot. There was a long moment of silence, only the pumps could be heard, then the release of shouting and yelling, cries of relief and congratulations.

Everyone ran for the truck. The door of the cab opened and Wallace Reid stepped down onto the road. If the cameras had been turning they would have caught a man triumphant over his fate. He stood, hands on hips, head thrown back, laughing in defiance. Beautiful, satisfying—a perfect scene. Reid was, for a moment, really the man that he represented in the hearts of millions of Americans, the perfect hero, the fearless idol. He was what everyone wanted to be in their dreams.

There was a sudden wrenching groan, a sound as if a wooden peg was being twisted in a wooden hole, and the logs on the truck shifted. The chain holding them snapped and the length of chain whipped out so that the end link hit Wallie on the back of his skull. If he had been standing a foot further away it would have whisked past. He fell to the muddy road slowly, turning slightly as he fell, like a marionette whose strings had been cut. The logs did not fall. They shuddered, they lay still, the broken length of chain dangling, swaying, glistening wet in the mountain sunshine.

Reid lay on the ground, his eyes closed. One of the loggers reached him first, tore his shirt open, knelt down in the mud and pressed his ear to Wallie's chest.

"He's alive! He's breathing. Just out." He sat back on his legs. "Thank God."

Sam Wood's face was greyish white. "Call a doctor. There's a telephone at the Lodge. There must be a doctor up here somewhere."

One of the loggers picked up the hanging chain and looked at it.

"There isn't even blood on it. Just nicked him, I bet. Look you can see him breathe."

Another logger sprang into action. "There's some planks over a ditch up the road. We'll get 'em and carry him down. Jest a minute."

Three of the men hurried up the road to fetch the planks. The rest of the crew and the company stood and looked on helplessly. One of the crew held a sun reflector so that it cast a shadow on Reid's face. The men came back with planks and lifted him tenderly onto them to carry him to the Lodge.

Part of the way down the road, Wallie's eyes fluttered, opened, then shut again. There were murmurs from those who walked alongside. The men carrying the makeshift stretcher had to walk slowly so the planks would not split apart and let their burden fall to the ground. At the Lodge they lifted him to a tabletop from the dining room, then carried him upstairs to his room. They undressed him, dropping the muddy clothes on the floor, and put him under a sheet. Then, leaving the door open so they could hear him if he called, they stood uneasily in the hallway, waiting.

After about a half hour Wallie stirred and muttered and finally opened his eyes. It didn't look to Wood as if Reid could focus them, but he grinned and asked what happened.

"Log chain snapped. Flicked you on the back of your head, just as pretty as you please. How do you feel?" Wood grinned back at him.

"Kinda dizzy. I guess I'll be all right. How did the shot go? Is the run good?"

"The shot will be great. Best you've ever done. A few close-ups and it's in the can. You just lie back and take it easy." Wood patted Reid's shoulder. "The doctor's on his way."

"Oh, Christ. I don't need a Doc. How'd I get down here?"

"The loggers carried you. On a plank."

"Tell them thanks."

"You can tell them yourself. Hey, men. Wallie's awake."

They looked in the doorway, embarrassed and apprehensive about what they might see. Wallie waved his arm at them, then closed his eyes in pain. The movement was too much. The men, reassured, slowly walked downstairs.

The doctor drove up about a half hour later. He examined Reid and, after giving him a shot of morphine for the pain, talked to Wood.

"I don't think it's too serious. But he really ought to be looked at by a specialist to make sure he doesn't have a fractured skull. I don't think he has, but I don't like the way his eyes look. Can't be too careful; he'll sleep for a while after that shot. I'll give him another one in a few hours. He ought to have another when the ambulance gets here to take him down the mountain, at any rate. It's a long drive on an unpaved road. I'm not really worried, though. I think he'll be all right."

The ambulance arrived in the middle of the afternoon, and after the doctor gave Wallie another shot, he was driven to the hospital in Los Angeles.

Sam Wood visited Wallie at the Sister of Angels Hospital to tell him that the rushes were very exciting and the downhill shots would make it the picture of the year.

Wallie was progressing very well, up on his feet but still in pain where the chain had clipped him. Later in the week his vision cleared and he went home to recuperate. After resting two weeks he drove himself to the studio to finish interior shots and some missing close-ups. There remained only the climactic shots of Wallie driving the truck into the hole in the dam. The top of the dam had been built on the back lot against a gigantic canvas sky. Wallie's costume, carefully picked up from the floor of the Lodge, was dusted off and put back into service.

One of the loggers drove the truck down from Big Bear for the final scenes and to use for some close-ups of Wallie behind the wheel. He and Wallie had lunch at the commissary and Wallie fixed him up with a couple of girls for the night. It was an experience he talked about for months.

What's Your Hurry? was released in late August and received very good reviews. The *Chicago Tribune* said it was the best Reid picture yet, and *The New York Times* said it ended with genuine thrills.

Wallie continued to have headaches and finally had to see Dr. Stein at the Hospital Bungalow for more shots so he could start on his next picture, *Always Audacious.* The morphine shots seemed to help and Wallie appeared to be his old self. But he decided to rest before starting on *The Love Special,* another racing picture. His headaches were now intermittent and he could work some days, not on others. Dr. Stein told him not to worry, when his head ached too much, he could just run over for a shot.

27

July 1920, The Alexandria Hotel

Variety, July 10, 1920

MOVIE PALACE BATTLE DRAWS BIG GUNS —WEISS AIMS AT HITS

Abe Weiss, who has been spending all his time and cash building and buying picture houses out in the stix, returned to Gotham to tend to his B'way houses threatened by strong competition from a new source. When the new Capitol closed near bankruptcy in June, Majestic was left with the top B'way show-cases all to itself. But the purchase of the Capitol by Joe Godsol, using DuPont coin, has put a new bulb in the socket. Godsol has also saved the Goldwyn Studio from shuttering with an infusion of Delaware cash. Purchase of the Capitol will give Goldwyn its first B'way showcase and Weiss renewed competition.

The battle of the Majors at the Capitol has been won by Roxy (S. L. Rothafel), the former manager, Major Bowes, is sulking but still on the premises. Fight was over show policies and Roxy's win is reflected in new $1.00 top tab and no reservation in force today. Roxy claimed the Capitol was suffering from too much art and not enough show biz.

Weiss says Majestic will counter with bigger hits from its West Coast studio.

"Who's calling?"

"Jack Pickford, her husband."

The maid looked at the telephone, startled, as if it were alive.

"There's a man on the 'phone Miz Thomas. Say he your husband. Name Pickford. You want me to get rid of him?"

"No, Velva, I'll talk to him."

Olive looked at the telephone for a long moment, picked it up and slowly put the receiver to her ear. She took a deep breath.

"Hello, Jack."

"Hiya, sweetheart. How've ya been?"

"I'm just fine, Jack. Very busy. I've finished my last picture for Selznick and I've already started over at Majestic, so I've been seeing the publicity people and talking to Billy Taylor about my first picture." There was a pause.

"How have you been?" she asked. "How long are you in town for?"

"Fine. Majestic is a good outfit, Mary was always happy there. I've decided to move back. New York is dead. I'm fine. Reading scenarios, keeping busy. Around." He was silent for a moment.

"Olive? I've just got to see you. We have to talk." There was another long pause.

Olive's mind was racing, trying to think up some plausible excuse.

"Please, Olive. Please." He broke the tension with a sudden laugh. "If I was there, I'd get down on my knees and beg."

"Don't, Jack. That's why I don't think it's smart for us to see each other. I can't take another scene. There have already been too many."

She thought about it for a minute. "I suppose we could have dinner. Some public place. I don't want to be alone with you. You understand, Jack?"

"The dining room at the Alexandria public enough for you?" He sounded eager.

"That'll be fine." She stopped, then added, "Jack, if you're drunk or high, I'll leave. You understand?"

"I'll be okay. I haven't had a drink in weeks. No dope either. I'm really trying, Olive. It's for you."

"I'm glad you are. I'm—I'm looking forward to seeing you."

"Look beautiful for me?"

"I'll try. Jack? Please don't spoil it for me." She could hear him laugh.

"See you tonight. Eight. Under the swan in the dining room."

Olive stood by the table for a long time. Velva watched

her. "You all right, Miss Thomas? You need to lie down or something?"

"No, I'll be fine. Velva, I'll be having dinner out. Tell cook. I'll need Arthur and the car at seven-thirty. I'll wear something white, one of my old linen things. And a violet scarf."

She sat down suddenly and laid her head on her arms. Velva watched her anxiously.

They had been married too young, Olive thought, Jack only twenty, she a year older. The marriage had lasted only a few months and they hadn't seen each other since. She wondered why Jack was so anxious to see her again. And why had she said yes? Their marriage had ended so bitterly, the two of them shrieking insults. Jack falling down drunk or unconscious from drugs. The nights that she locked herself into the bathroom so he wouldn't attack her. She didn't want it to start all over again.

Outside the Alexandria Hotel she sat in the darkness of her limousine gathering courage. Picking up her scarf, she paused in the door of the Packard, "I may want to leave in a hurry, Arthur. Please wait where I can find you easily."

"I understand, Ma'am."

She stood for a few seconds between the columns of the dining room, out of habit, making an entrance. Heads turned, recognizing her. Jack, seeing her there, stood up on the other side of the room, under the mural of the swan with a crown on its head which he laughingly referred to as 'Mary.' He smiled as he heard the buzz of recognition, speculation, from the other guests. Their meeting in a public place would be the subject of at least one column in the morning papers.

Without a word Jack embraced Olive and kissed her on the cheek. She sat down and looked at him, hoping not to find traces of drinking and drugs. He looked better than he had in a long while.

He smiled, white teeth brilliant against his deeply tanned skin. "My, it's nice to see you. I simply love to look at you, that's all."

She laughed and put her hand on his. "Oh, Jack, you're silly. I've seen you with girls prettier than I."

A waiter began to serve. Jack had ordered in advance, all her favorite foods, artichokes, Pacific Northwest salmon, tiny tomatoes.

"You look thin, Jack. I bet you still don't come home to dinner, or else whoever she is doesn't know how to cook."

165

"I've got a surprise for you. There isn't anyone."

"That is a surprise. I didn't think you ever spent a night alone."

"I often think of how you used to wait for me to come home and eat with you," he said sadly. "I didn't know how lucky I was."

"I miss you, too, Jack. It's strange, but sometimes I think, if we hadn't been so young and stubborn, we might have made it work. On one level, at any rate—companionship." She looked down at her plate. "When we weren't fighting, I loved being with you."

Jack leaned forward with an excited look. "Olive, that's why I wanted to see you. To have us meet and talk. I can't live without you. It's ruining my life. I'm ruining your life. I can't help loving you any more than I can stop breathing. Any more than you can keep from being repelled by me." His voice faltered.

She looked up at him. "Repelled? Jack, I was never repelled, just sort of left untouched, repelled is too strong." She lowered her voice and looked around to make sure that they were not being overheard. "It's just that I—I can't stand being touched anymore. Maybe it's all those men Flo pushed off on me. To teach me to like it." Her voice almost faded away. "Each one was more repulsive than the last." The color was draining from her face. "Sometimes I think I'm crazy, should be put away. In some sanitarium—in a padded cell, maybe." She laughed.

"Oh, for Christ's sake! That's nonsense, Olive. And you know it. Besides, who is normal in this town? I'm certainly not. How normal is it for a young kid to have two or three girls a night when he's still in high school? That's what I had. Like some fucking sultan. I was the Queen's little baby brother and everyone gave me all the candy I wanted." He sat back and looked at her. "Olive, I'm really a nobody. I'm not an actor, not a star. Every time I was broke I could get a part in a picture because my name was Pickford."

"I wonder if your mother has ever realized how she sacrificed you and Lotte for Mary's success?"

"No. She doesn't think of it that way. We all share Mary's success, money, position, the works. Only it doesn't work out, does it? Jesus, I've got to stop kidding myself." A tear formed in the corner of his eye and he brushed it away quickly. Olive took his hand. "I don't have anything," he continued. "I don't have a name, I use my sister's. I don't have a wife, she's afraid of me. I can have any girl I want in this whole goddamned town, and I don't want any of them. I only want you and you don't want me."

"Please, Jack, if you start crying, I'll have to leave."

He grabbed at her hand. "Don't. Please, don't. I'll be all right in a minute. I'm sorry. I didn't mean to act up. Olive, I just need to talk to you. Just to see you, be near you. I'll control myself, I'll do it, you'll see."

"Jack, I love you. That's what makes it so dreadful to have you talk like this. I hate to see you unhappy, wasting your life. But I don't think we can make it work."

"Look. We can get a big house. Separate bedrooms. Separate wings, if that will make you feel better. But I have to see you, talk to you. I haven't had a drink in three months. No cocaine for longer than that." He held out his hands. "Look. No shakes. Olive, look at me." She raised her eyes from his hands to his face as his voice fell to a whisper. "Olive I must be with you. I'm no good without you. I might as well kill myself. I'd rather be with you on your terms than be dead on my terms. And that's what's going to happen. I'll be dead in a year if you don't take me back. I simply won't make it."

They had only picked at the food. The waiters looked on helplessly, put a new dish on the table, then waited a decent interval and removed it.

"I won't touch you. I won't even ask you. If I need a woman, I'll go out and get one. Always have, anyway. I won't bother you."

Olive looked at him, her eyes brimming with tears. "Jack, getting together again was the furthest thing from my mind. I do love you. I find myself wondering what you're doing, where you are, who is with you? I never see anyone else, I never go out. But I'm afraid of you, I'm afraid you'll touch me. I'm not normal, and I can't help it. I thought I'd get used to it after we were married. But it got worse. Sometimes I had to keep from screaming."

He looked down. "I'm sorry. It just seemed so natural for me to make love to you."

Olive leaned across the table and took his hand. "Jack, it isn't you. It's me. This isn't getting us anywhere." She wrapped the long violet scarf about her throat. "Let me go home."

He looked at her, a pleading look. "Tomorrow night, here, again. Please let me talk to you. See how good I've been? You can't punish a good boy." She could see the

167

desperation in his eyes. "Please? Olive, dearest?" His voice was so urgent it frightened her.

Her voice was resigned. "All right, Jack, tomorrow night."

Big city theaters were operated by men like Grauman and Roxy, born showmen. But for every Grauman there were thousands of small-town merchants of film who were no more imaginative than the corner druggist. Majestic came to their aid with elaborate press books, guides to successful advertising and promotion.

Ben's press book for *What's Your Hurry?* looked like an eight-page newspaper printed on expensive paper—a catalogue of photos, ads, and stories that could be cut out and given to the local newspaper; lobby displays and colored posters that could be tacked onto telephone poles.

Ben had been looking for an excuse to visit Wallie Reid, so he took two press books for *What's Your Hurry?* out to show him. Reid's new home, white Spanish stucco with a red tile roof, was barely finished and stood in the middle of a dry, dusty field. Behind the house, snuggled into the hill, was Beverly Hills's first swimming pool. Water spouted into the pool from an animal head on the retaining wall. The open side of the garden was still unfinished, but a barren pergola supported newly planted tendrils of wisteria.

Wallie lay in the sun on a chaise longue, an awning shielding his closed eyes. Dorothy woke him and then left them alone.

"Hiya, Ben. How's tricks?"

"Just great, Wallie. Gosh, I'm sorry to hear that you're still having trouble. What does the doctor say?"

"Not much. You know, I got a bad back up in Oregon on *Valley of the Giants* a couple of years ago. That was tolerable, I could still work most days. But the headaches really got me down. Doctors don't know all that much, if you ask me. I know almost as much. You know I went to medical school? Almost was a doctor. That would have been something. Deny the women of American the chance to look at this kisser." He laughed. "Maybe I should have, at that. Do some good in the world instead of getting rich by making funny faces into a camera." He struggled to sit up. "Let's look at the book."

After a few minutes Wallie looked as if he might drowse off at any moment. Ben took the press book and read some of the news story plants out loud, emphasizing the melodramatic elements of Wallie's heroism. He watched Wallie's reaction.

Reid smiled obligingly, but there was no animation, no pep in the actor for whom the word had been invented.

While Wallie idly looked at the photos Ben wandered about in the new garden. Walking past the swimming pool, he realized Reid's eyes were drooping shut, then opening with a sudden start as he awakened. Ben knelt down and put his hand in the water. It was very warm. He noticed Dorothy Reid standing at the French windows in the library, watching them. The atmosphere was strange, almost sinister—not quite that of a sanitarium, but certainly not the outgoing happy home that he remembered. He found himself unable to translate what he felt about the house into words, but he was uneasy.

Wallie noticed him kneeling by the water and called out. "Hey, Ben, come on over and use the pool any time. Nobody much comes around anymore so it's not used very much. Don't go to that crummy Biminy Baths—unless, of course, it's more than swimming you want." He winked broadly.

Ben laughed. "I been getting all I need without picking 'em up under water." He sat beside the chaise. "Elsie was really shocked when she heard I swam there. Christ, I didn't even know it was a pickup joint until she told me and I began to look around. The girls there certainly aren't very aggressive."

"Either that or you're unconscious. I wish I could give you some of my admirers. Take that back. Now that we live out here, there aren't so many of them. God almighty, when we lived in town, sometimes there'd be four or five girls sleeping on the front steps, waiting for me to walk over them on my way to the studio every morning. Honest to God, hanging on my legs, lifting their skirts to show me their boxes. Dorothy got to the point where she stopped looking out to wave good-bye. I fought them off." He sighed. "Every man dreams of all the ass he can use, but I tell ya, there comes a point. . . ." They both laughed. "Oh, the problems of fame," Wallie finished. They sat silently for a long while, comfortable and relaxed. "Well, anyway, I mean it Ben. Swim any time." Wistfully, he said, "It's a little lonesome out here, not going into the studio every day. No parties anymore."

"But you'll be back soon," Ben interrupted cheerfully.

"Sure. They're really pushing to get me back in harness again. Honest to God, Rubin calls every day. Don't hardly know what to say to him." He paused. "I guess they miss the grosses from the Dusty Rhodes pictures. They're like owning your own mint."

"I'm anxious to get started on the campaign for *The Affairs of Anatole* next month. It's a big one, Wallie. DeMille, Swanson, the works."

"Jesus, I'd better be on my feet by then. How about a drink?"

"Sure thing. Something with a lot of ice."

Wallie grinned. "I got some new gin from the bootlegger that's pretty good. At least it won't grow hair in your mouth." He rang the bell and a maid took their orders. Wallie settled back on the chaise and asked, "Any good gossip?"

"Not much. Since Tom died, I stay mostly in the office—don't get out much on the stages. That's where you hear it. Or in the dressing rooms."

"I was sorry about Tom. He was a nice guy. Decent man."

They didn't say much after that. Ben sipped his drink and Wallie dozed. The late afternoon sun gradually slipped down behind the west wing of the house, putting them into shadow. Dorothy silently appeared, putting her finger to her lips, and tucked a soft blanket over Wallie. He opened his eyes slightly, reached out for her hand, held it gently for a moment, smiled, then closed his eyes again. Ben watched silently.

He would have liked to look around the new house, but he hadn't been invited and he didn't want to ask. For nearly two hours Wallie didn't stir on the chaise. At a few minutes after six Ben touched him on the shoulder and said good-bye. Wallie slowly got up and they shook hands. He seemed unsteady on his legs and didn't offer to show Ben to the house. Ben left him standing in the garden, drink in hand, swaying slightly.

Dorothy Reid was in the front hall waiting for him.

"Oh, Ben thank you so much for coming to see him. It meant so much."

"Don't be silly, what are friends for? Besides, I wanted to show him the press books. He had some good laughs."

"I'm sure it did him a world of good." She hesitated. "I know now how many of his so-called friends were only fair-weather." She smiled ruefully. "When the free liquor and dancing and the music stopped, we found out who our true-blue friends really were. There aren't very many of them." Ben took her hand.

"That's always the way, Dorothy. When Wallie's feeling better, just remember." Ben picked up his Panama hat.

She laughed. "I will. It's Wallie who won't. Anybody who

170

waltzes in off the street is OK by him." She sighed. "He's impossible," she said fondly.

"I'll come by more often. I didn't realize how sick he'd been. I don't think anyone at Majestic does either."

Dorothy stood on her tiptoes and kissed Ben on the cheek. "Come back soon, Ben." She looked up at him fondly. "It was almost like old times to hear him laughing out there." She paused. "Don't say anything about how he's feeling at Majestic, Ben. Wallie is so proud. He's terribly anxious to get back to work and is so looking forward to working with Mr. DeMille again." She pressed his hand. "Let's not say anything at all." She smiled again. "Promise?"

"If you and Wallie don't want me to say anything, I sure won't. I'll come out again real soon." He opened the front door.

"Thank you, Ben." Her voice was calm, even casual, but he felt the tension and the struggle for control that lay beneath.

28

September 1920, New York and Paris

The New York Herald, Aug. 27, 1920

HOTEL READIES FOR BIG GUEST!
WALDORF SHORES UP

NEW YORK. Big things are doing at The Waldorf-Astoria. The biggest thing of all is Roscoe "Fatty" Arbuckle, due to check in today as part of a nation-wide promotion trip for Majestic Studios. A special bed has been placed in a room on the tenth floor in readiness. The bed has steel slats instead of the regulation wood. Delicate antique chairs were removed from the suite and replaced with big overstuffed pieces this morning.

An icebox in the pantry has been stocked with a wide variety of rich foods and gastronomic specialties. *The Round-Up*, Arbuckle's newest picture, opens this weekend at several area theaters.

Jack and Olive decided to celebrate their reconciliation with a honeymoon trip to Paris. It began with a luxurious train trip across the country: Jack and his valet, Clifford; Olive and her maid, Velva; and Ben Sommers to handle the press. Ben was puzzled that the newlyweds had separate bedrooms, even though they had been married before.

At the press conference in New York Jack announced that his new Goldwyn picture, *The Man Who Had Everything*, would open at the Capitol the following day. He kissed Olive and said that he did, indeed, have everything. Olive Thomas Pickford looked radiant and happy. Jack, his hair shining with brilliantine in the new South American style, acted subtly possessive of his wife. The reporters were touched and murmured appreciatively. Olive told the crowd of reporters in the ballroom that she would start a new picture for Majestic to be directed by William Desmond Taylor. There was applause. Jack and Olive held hands and posed for pictures, the smoke from flash powder hanging in a layer above the floor. Olive showed a few women reporters some of her lingerie while they took notes. The biggest question, asked repeatedly, was whether or not she would bob her hair. Still uncertain, Olive said she would be guided by what Jack thought. They smiled at each other.

Tugs pulling hawsers backed the *Imperator* slowly out of its berth on the Hudson River side of Manhattan. The ship, taken from the German government after the war as part of reparations, thrust an ugly figurehead into the clear morning air of New York—an imperial eagle, holding a sphere girdled by a spiked ring with German script on it. Some wags attributed the pained expression on the eagle's face to its having just laid the spiked egg.

Ben was disappointed that there were only a thousand or so fans at the dock to see the ship leave. Maybe people had to work or something. He had even tried to persuade the Cunard Line officials to delay the sailing until six P.M. in the hope of a larger crowd.

In their suite on board the *Imperator* Ben wished them luck as the gong sounded the final warning.

"Anything else I can do for you?" he asked at the door. "I'll get the pictures to the papers. I hope you're not too exhausted. You've both been just great."

"No, thanks, Ben. It's been swell having you along to handle things for us. You took care of that crowd at the Waldorf like a master." They shook hands. Olive caught hold of his arm and kissed him tenderly.

"You're a good friend, Ben," she said to him. "I'll buy you something naughty in Paris. A postcard or something." She winked and laughed and kissed him again. Ben blushed. Olive was so ravishing, so full of life and beauty. He wished he could hold the minute forever. A blast of the ship's whistle brought him back to reality.

"I'd better get the hell out of here or you'll have company in Paris." He ran toward the stairs. At the end of the corridor he turned to wave, but the door to the suite was closed.

Ben stayed on in New York for a week. He had been preparing a national promotion for Majestic Week ever since the day in Saul Rubin's office when Abe Weiss had heard and approved the idea. Now Majestic Week was here, starting in every city and town across the country on Labor Day weekend.

The distribution of a movie followed a fairly rigid pattern. A picture opened in a big downtown palace, then after several weeks it gradually worked its way down until it reached third- and fourth-run houses out in the neighborhoods.

Majestic Week was an attempt to break the pattern. Ben had sold Abe Weiss on the idea of opening a few carefully selected pictures in as many theaters as possible. Over the big holiday weekend anyone in the United States who wanted to see a movie was forced to see a Majestic picture and along with it a reel of coming attractions showing scenes from every Majestic picture in production and others being considered for production during the coming season. Some of the scenes were fakes that Ben had created especially for the attractions reel because filming on many of the pictures had not yet started.

In Hollywood, on Labor Day, a big parade was scheduled to march from the studio gates to the Majestic Million Dollar Theatre. Stars would ride on floats depicting various pictures in the schedule. Hollywood Boulevard was to be cleared of traffic for three hours. In New York, the three biggest theaters on Broadway would run a Majestic picture, and another picture was scheduled to play over a hundred neighborhood houses—from Greenport, Long Island, to Rhinebeck, far up the Hudson River.

The picture selected for first-run release was *The Round-Up*, Roscoe Arbuckle's first full-length feature. Up to now Roscoe, like Charlie Chaplin, had always made two-reel shorts. Then Charlie Chaplin made a big hit with a feature and Roscoe, the second most popular comedian in the world, was anxious to try the same format. Roscoe would not be outdone by Chaplin if he could help it.

The Round-Up proved to be a strange picture in which Arbuckle played an almost straight dramatic role as a sheriff. Occasionally he fell down, and once he split his pants to get a laugh. But it was the ending of the picture that caused great controversy at Majestic. After losing the girl to the handsome leading man, Fatty broke down and wept, leaning pathetically on a corral fence. The closing title read, "Nobody loves a fat man!"

Rubin's opinion was that it was suicide for Arbuckle. But

previews at outlying theaters showed that the unusual ending was taken by audiences as a great joke and drew huge laughs and applause. Rubin, against his better judgement, stopped arguing the point with Arbuckle and the ending was kept intact.

On the Sunday of Majestic Week full-page ads in every newspaper in the major cities listed each theater and the Majestic picture being shown. Banner headlines read, "It's Majestic Week! Celebrate by Going! Everybody's Going!" The budget for advertising alone was unequaled in moving picture history. Industry gossip had it that Ben Sommers must have an inside track to Abe Weiss to spend money like this.

That morning Ben met with his boss. Abe Weiss smiled across the desk at him. "You certainly got the industry talking."

Ben was gleeful. "It's exciting, isn't it? Nobody's saying anything but 'Majestic! Majestic this! Majestic that!' Goddamn! I love it."

"That's the spirit. Keep it up. With all the new theaters I got, we've got to keep the spirit up."

Ben took his watch out of his pocket and looked at it.

"The parade in Hollywood is just starting right this minute —boy, I wish we were there to see it. Beautiful floats, beautiful girls. The works."

"Ben, I want you to add something to the big ads. I'm trying to keep up the pressure on theater owners to get them to play each and every Majestic picture. Put a list of the entire production schedule in the ad. Use a caption like this: 'Save this list. Refer to it during the year and show it to your theater owner. Insist that he order these pictures from Majestic so you can see them. Don't be disappointed!' " Weiss sat back smiling.

Ben smiled back. "That's a little risky. But if a picture never gets made, I guess no one will really remember. Puts the owners behind the eight ball, doesn't it?"

"Exactly where I want them."

"I'll put it in a box with a dotted line around it. Little caption, 'Cut out and save'!" Weiss nodded approval. "I wish you could see all of the promotion stunts I got planned for the downtown theaters tomorrow. Roscoe is going to arrive on a papier-mâché horse pulled by forty police motorcycles. Big piece in the *News* on the steel reinforcements inside the horse to support his weight. He'll be surrounded by an honor guard of cowgirls on horseback."

"Cute. Ought to be good for some photos. Keep Roscoe

away from the girls, though. Don't laugh. He has a little streak. Don't let that shy smile deceive you. What else you got going?"

"A lot of different things. Some of Mae Murray's costumes in Bergdorf's windows all week. The extreme ones with feathers and jewels. You know the sort of crap she wears."

Weiss's eyes took on a distant look. "I know better than you think. When she was a Follies girl I took her out to supper once. The evening was a great disappointment. She was sewn into her goddamned skirt and I couldn't get it off. I got into her another time, though. It wasn't worth it."

Ben smiled. "The really beautiful ones never are."

Weiss nodded. "Picture stars more than most. How can you enjoy a girl if all she thinks about is how she looks?" He grew serious. "So tell me, what about Jack and Olive? Will it last? I don't want a messy scandal and a divorce. There are enough scandals to whitewash each year without one with the name Pickford on it."

Ben tried to sort out his thoughts. "I don't really know. They just don't seem happy. Olive is the mystery. Jack is just a spoiled, willful Hollywood brat. Indulges himself all the time. Anything he wants he grabs. They had separate bedrooms on the train, which I thought was odd. But then, who knows what goes on in a man's bedroom? I know this, Jack is crazy about her."

"Well, keep an eye out. I don't want any divorces. Every goddamned rabbi, priest, and minister in the country will jump down on Majestic. Mary could get away with marrying Doug. Like a fairy tale come true. But nobody else. With everybody else it's a sin. Watch out."

"I'll try to keep an eye out." Ben wondered what he could do about it even if he found out Jack and Olive were about to divorce each other.

Weiss stood up. "I'd like you to come to the house while you're in town. My wife keeps a kosher kitchen. She is a good cook. You like Jewish food?"

"Why, sure. That's very nice of you, Mr. Weiss. I'm honored." Ben sounded a little uncertain.

Weiss smiled at him.

"Tomorrow night, then. You can ride down with me in the motor."

29

September 1920, Paris and Hollywood

The New York Times, Sept. 6, 1920

OLIVE PICKFORD PARIS FASHION PLATE

Olive Thomas Pickford went on a fashion spree this week in Paris that has the entire City of Light talking. She spent one whole day at the House of Madelaine et Madelaine choosing model after model. A bottle green directoire suit with braided skirt is topped off by a bicorne hat that makes the beautiful star look as if she stepped out of a portrait of the Reign of Terror. Over the suit Miss Thomas will wear a coat of black monkey fur on chiffon, from the House of Chanel.

Olive's husband, handsome Jack Pickford, takes a great interest in what his wife wears and goes shopping with her.

By the end of the first week in Paris the strains began to show. Jack brought girls into his bedroom. He casually displayed a gold cocaine spoon. He was careful not to appear drunk, but Olive knew that he was not always sober.

On Friday afternoon of the first week Jack found Olive alone in her bedroom. She had given Velva the afternoon off to shop and see Paris. They had been invited to the American Embassy for dinner, and Olive was lying down before dressing, but she stood up quickly as Jack entered her room. He did not approach her, but carefully kept himself between her and the door. She could feel panic rising. He was carrying a bottle of champagne and two glasses.

"Olive, can we talk?"

"Of course, Jack. That's why I came back, remember? So

177

we could talk. Sit down. Please, sit down. It makes me nervous to have you circling the room."

He looked at the chairs. "I'd rather stand. I'm too high to sit down."

"You're breaking one promise after another. I was crazy to do this. It's like a bad dream, only I don't wake up. Please don't come any closer, Jack. You're frightening me."

"I don't mean to. I don't want to frighten you. Olive, I love you. That's why all of this is happening. I love you. And you won't let me do the one thing I'm driven to do."

"Jack—this trip was a mistake. It's my fault, I shouldn't have listened to you. As soon as Velva comes back I'll have her pack my trunks and go to the Athénée. I'll take the first boat back to New York. If I'm not around to remind you, you'll soon forget. There are plenty of girls you can take to bed, Jack. You don't need me."

"Oh God, I do. I'll go out of my mind if I don't have you. Just once. Please, Olive, I can't hurt you. Just once."

Olive sighed, and walked to the window, then turned to him. "Give me some of your champagne." He held out a glass to her, then filled it, hands shaking. She turned away from him and drained it in one gulp. "More."

Jack filled her glass again and then again.

"Olive, don't. You don't really need that much. I'll be gentle."

She could see that he was excited. "It's been more than a year since the last time on the floor of our bedroom. You were far from gentle and I don't think either of us has changed all that much. But we can try. I'll try." She threw the bed cover back and began to undress.

Clifford, who had been standing outside in the salon, closed the door quietly and stood there for the next hour.

At five-thirty Velva let herself into the apartment and found him standing there.

"What are you doing there? Let me on by."

He grinned at her. "Don't go in. They're in there together. It's a honeymoon, remember."

"It's about time somebody remember. All those dolls you been finding for his bed. It's a wonder he ain't broke her heart. How long that been going on?"

"'Bout an hour. It's pretty quiet now."

"Well, they got a dinner engagement. She got to get ready. It all take time."

"They got time for this. The embassy people will wait."

Velva sat down. As the light faded neither made any move

178

to light the lamps. Just after six the door opened and Jack walked out completely naked.

"She wants you, Velva. We've got to get ready." Clifford followed him across the salon to his bedroom and closed the door after them.

Velva found her mistress huddled on the rumpled bed. Her expression was remote, she seemed almost in shock.

"You all right, honey? He hurt you? Look at Velva. It don't look good to me."

Helping Olive up, Velva guided her feet across the floor into the tub. Then she began to wash her gently with the sponge. Velva looked into Olive's face. Her eyes were closed, but tears were running down her cheeks. Velva tried to wipe them away with the sponge but more followed.

"Some honeymoon," she muttered.

Dinner at the American Embassy was quiet. Everyone was slightly in awe of the two movie stars and conversation was forced. Jack was surprised by how much champagne Olive was drinking. She flirted quite openly with the diplomats at the table, borrowing a cigarette from this one, a light from another. The conversation was mostly about the reluctance of the United States to join the League of Nations, which was to hold its first meeting in Geneva. One of the Frenchmen said that the U.S. was not needed; even without the participation of the United States, the League had already been able to curb white slave traffic.

Olive was incredulous. Surely white slaves were the inventions of Hollywood scenario writers. Everyone laughed. Across the table a young officer attached to the embassy leaned toward Olive and spoke quite seriously.

"Oh, there are white slavers in Paris, all right."

"You mean pimps?" Olive smiled and sipped her champagne.

"No. There are dives in Montmartre where actual gangs capture women for shipment to the harems of Algiers and Morocco. Men, too. Castrated blond men are very popular as harem guards."

Olive looked at him. "You're safe. You've got dark hair. And I assume everything else." She glanced around the table. Everyone snickered.

Lieutenant Andrews reddened. "You think I'm joking. Tell her, Bill. Mr. Gresham here has been on several cases with the local gendarmes."

Gresham nodded seriously. "Most Americans have no idea

how really lowdown Paris is. They go to a few of the safe spots and watch apache dancers smack each other around. Or sit in a bar with a lot of prostitutes that no pasha would touch with a ten-foot pole. They think they've seen it all."

Jack grinned at Olive at the mention of apache dancers.

She looked alive and excited. "Jack, we must see Montmartre. Let's go tonight. I'd like to do something really wicked."

He turned to Lieutenant Andrews. "How about it? Can you show us some really interesting night spots and give us a little something to talk about when we get home? Good old Hollywood is pretty hard to beat when it comes to depravity, but there it doesn't happen in dance halls. Only in offices. Show us how it's done French style." He winked at the officer.

Lieutenant Andrews lowered his voice. "I don't think we want to take the ladies, sir. It's pretty rough. If you want to go with a group of men from the embassy, we got some places we regularly take visiting congressmen who want to get . . ." He broke off and coughed. "Excuse me, Ma'am," he said to Olive.

"Get a lay, Lieutenant?" she asked, with a bewitching smile. "We do that in Hollywood, too. Don't be embarrassed. The motion picture industry is oiled by sex. Just ask any big exhibitor from Kansas City how many girls First National or Metro sent to his hotel room last time he was in town buying pictures."

Lieutenant Andrews looked down at the tablecloth. "Well, that may be the way it is in Hollywood, but I know a hell of a lot of Kansas farm boys who thought they'd seen everything there was to see back home in the barnyard and then got the surprise of their lives here in Paris. I got a surprise or two myself."

He looked Olive in the eye. "I could arrange a small party, a few cars, and we could hit a few spots. Not the really rough ones, you know. Just some of the more colorful shows. Kind of dirty, but high-class. Not where I'd go if there were just men."

Jack, slightly drunk, nudged Andrews in the ribs. "I don't know. Maybe she might pick up some ideas," he whispered.

Olive winked at him. "I can hardly wait."

Lieutenant Andrews looked at Jack. "You wouldn't want your wife doing some of the things we're going to be seeing. Whores, yes. That's what we have them for. But not for your wife."

"How do you know I wouldn't? She might even like it. I know I would."

Lieutenant Andrews glanced at Olive, now surrounded by young men, then back at Jack, who was laughing at his discomfort. He pushed through the crowd to make arrangements for the motorcars.

"Jesus Christ! Hollywood," he muttered through his teeth.

30

September 1920, The Majestic Lot

The Los Angeles Examiner, Sept. 1, 1920

DOUG'S OLD PAL PINES AND DIES

**THERE IS NO LAUGHTER HERE TODAY,
GRIM DEATH HAS STOLEN AWAY,
YET, HE WAS BUT A DOG.**

Sorrow cloaks itself about the home of Douglas Fairbanks today for Death's shadows stole softly in the changing colors of the setting sun last evening to claim Rex from the Fairbanks household.

Pals for seven long years, Rex grieved as his Master left on a honeymoon that the faithful dog could not understand. Rex missed his Master's hand and would take food from no one else. So the loyal friend pined away. He lasted just long enough to die, contented, in his Master's arms.

Doug, the whole world feels for your sadness.

It was Helen on the telephone. "Mr. Rubin would like to have Miss McCormack sign her contract in his office. Can she be here at eleven o'clock tomorrow morning?"

"Sure thing." The assistant director walked back to the stage where the cast of *Spirit of Youth* was rehearsing.

"Polly," he called out. "Go over to Rubin's office tomorrow at eleven. Your contract is ready for signing." There were congratulations from a number of members of the cast. Extras looked at her with an undisguised mixture of envy and hatred. Bill Taylor took her to one side.

"First thing tomorrow, get yourself right over to Grace in

Wardrobe. Tell her where you're going and what for. She'll know what to do."

Wardrobe, in a loft above the dressing rooms, was an endless room filled with long pipes hung from the ceiling by wires. Jammed onto the pipes were hundreds of costumes that over the years had been made or bought for films. Some of them had been reused a dozen times. They were not in any special order. Grace carried a catalogue in her head and knew what every garment was, where it came from, who had worn it in what picture and in what year. She looked up at Polly.

"What's the matter? Doesn't Taylor like those classy rags I fixed up for you?"

"No, Ma'am, they're fine. I'm here for something else. Mr. Taylor said to tell you I'm going up to Mr. Rubin's office to sign my contract. He said you'd know what to do."

"Oh, he did, did he?"

Grace sighed as she rummaged down a line of costumes, pulling up an occasional dress, then returning it. "Maybe. No, the color is too drab. Well, suppose. No, it'll make her look too . . . now, here's one." She let out a small cry. "This is it! Just right!" She held up a dress made of cream-colored lace with a wide blue satin sash.

"Here, this may fit and if it does, it will be perfect. Mary Pickford wore it in *Poor Little Rich Girl* back in '17. I had it laundered and it's been here just waiting for the right part."

Polly put the dress on. It was rather out of style, with a skirt that was mostly ruffle hanging low on her hips. The skirt was a little short, but otherwise it fit reasonably well. It made her look like an old-fashioned doll.

"We'll put some long white stockings on you and you can carry a flower. I wish you could carry a teddy bear, but I suppose that would be overdoing it. You look lovely, dear."

Polly agreed. The dress was beautiful, lined with a pale pink silk that showed slightly through the openings in the lace to give it a faint blush tint.

"In case there's a photographer, you'll look grand," Grace said. "But I rather think Mr. Rubin wants to see you alone," she added softly. She started to mend the lace on the collar and pulled on the buttons to make sure they were secure.

Finally Polly said, "I really gotta go." She hugged Grace.

"Good luck, dear," Grace called down the stairs after her.

The secretary stood in the doorway. "Mr. Cotton is still waiting, Mr. Rubin, and little Polly McCormack is on her way."

"Tell Cotton to put it in a report. Show the girl in when she gets here."

A few minutes later Rubin looked up, as if surprised, when Helen led Polly into the office. He stood up and smiled at her. "Well, don't we look pretty! Who fixed you up? Grace? I'd know that frock anywhere. Mary wore it. Grace is trying to bring you luck."

"I know," said Polly, standing in front of the desk.

"Luck like Mary's we could all use. You should be so lucky. I should be so lucky. Polly, I have your contract right here. Let me explain it to you." He got up carrying a sheaf of papers and crossed the room to a settee that stood by the fireplace. "Sit here beside me. At the end of every six months we can sit down and have a talk and decide if we want to continue together. We don't have to talk about that now, though."

Polly looked puzzled. "You mean I can leave at the end of six months if I'm unhappy?"

"No, darling. It's the other way around. We can decide that it just is not good to continue, that it's hurting your career. You don't have any escape clauses. We do the deciding. As far as you are concerned, you are set for seven wonderful years." He smiled at her. "Think of the girls all over this great land of ours that would give their souls to be in your pretty shoes."

"I know. I'm very lucky. I'll try not to disappoint you."

"I know you won't, darling. I know you won't. Now you can sign the contract with my fountain pen. I'll call in Helen to witness it, and we'll take a nice picture for the trade press."

He leaned forward and pressed a button.

While Rubin held the leather pad steady Polly signed two copies of the contract. Rubin smiled as the photographer snapped away. "That's our business. Pictures. Wonderful, clean entertainment that nobody can criticize. Everything for the family! Bring the kiddies!" After the photographer left he turned to her as if he had just had a brilliant idea. "Polly, would you like to stay and eat lunch with me here in my big office?"

"I guess so. Will Mr. Taylor be worried if I don't come back?"

"Bill knows that what we're doing is important to the studio."

Helen smiled at Polly. "I'll call him and tell him you've been invited to stay." She turned to Rubin. "In about an hour?"

"That will be just fine," he answered.

"Well," he said, bending down and putting his arm around Polly's shoulders. "We have an hour to ourselves. Want to look around? I have a little apartment back here that is a secret place. Come look at it." He took her hand and opened a door in the paneling. "See? Here's where I keep extra outfits so I can get dressed in case I must stay late and go directly to some party or a dinner. See? Suits, shirts, hats. Everything. I even keep some ladies' clothes in case one of the girls needs something. Here." He opened a drawer and showed her a velvet-lined tray of evening bags. They were all different. Some were beaded, some gilt metal mesh, some studded with pearls and inlaid with glittering stones. Polly drew in her breath.

"Want one? You are a little young to be going out on dates, but you never know. Better be prepared. Take one. Any one you like."

Polly had never seen anything like them. She knew they were expensive and regretted that she didn't know enough to pick the most expensive one. She slowly passed her hands over the row of bags and lifted a gold one with a blue stone and two pearls for a clasp out of the drawer as if it were very fragile and would break. She pressed it to her throat. The gold mesh felt nice and cool.

"Thank you," she whispered, staring at the bag as she held it at arm's length and it caught the light. "Thank you."

Rubin took her hand and they walked past a bathroom door. "See? Here's my private bathroom." It had a skylight and the light coming down from the ceiling made the room look like an underwater grotto. He opened another door and reached inside a dark room. He switched on a light. It was a luxurious bedroom. There didn't seem to be any windows.

Rubin shut the door behind them and walked to the center of the room. "Now, darling, it's your turn to be nice to me. You just pretend this is a lollipop and we'll both enjoy it." Polly dropped the bag on the floor and stepped on it as she walked numbly forward and got down on her knees.

31

September 1920, Montmartre, Paris

Chicago Tribune, Sept. 5, 1920

THERE'S GOLD IN THEM THAR PICTURES
SALARIES KEEP CLIMBING IN HOLLYWOOD
STUDIOS

HOLLYWOOD. A.P. The astronomical salaries paid to Hollywood stars, directors, and writers keep climbing. Alla Nazimova has just signed again with Metro for $13,000 a week. William S. Hart, back in the saddle after a year off, will be paid $2,224,000 for nine pictures at Paramount.

Writers are currently paid $1,000 to $2,500 every week, and directors can receive as much as $50,000 for directing a single picture.

If you wonder if the salaries are worth it, consider this: The studios spend over a half million dollars a year just answering fan mail!

One of the embassy wives, whose name Jack Pickford didn't catch, started to giggle and turn red when she saw the Negro doorman of *Abbazade*. He stood, naked except for transparent gauze harem trousers, at the entrance to the large dance hall, decorated in the Persian style.

Bill Gresham whispered to Jack, "If that's too much for her, wait till she gets inside."

"*Bon soir, Mesdames et Messieurs.* Ah, Lieutenant Andrews. How kind of you to return and bring your friends. You are fortunate to arrive at the hour of the performance in the *Théâtre du Miroir.*"

Andrews turned to the group and asked, "Want to see the

circus? Let me warn you, it's pretty dirty. Live sex. That sort thing."

They were led down a flight of stone steps into a large octagonal room. The walls and ceilings were lined with old mirrors. The floor was covered with Turkish carpets and a large number of men and women reclined on them against huge cushions. In the center of the room was a raised platform covered in red velour.

Olive sat on the floor, back against a cushion, between Jack and Lieutenant Andrews.

"Now what happens?" she asked in a low voice.

"Wait and see. Lots of very unusual things. I hope you won't be shocked, Miss Thomas. It's very erotic."

Olive smiled at him. "I certainly hope so. I'm disappointed in Paris so far."

The lights began to dim and they settled back on the cushions expectantly. Jack felt for Olive's hand in the darkness and gave it an affectionate squeeze. Below them, under the floor, a low rumbling started and they could feel the floor vibrate. In front of them in the darkness something was happening.

Slowly the lights in the room began to glow and in the semidarkness they could see the pale form of a nude woman rising out of the center of the platform. As she rose into view, she revolved slowly, gazing at her reflection in a hand mirror.

"It works by clockwork," whispered the lieutenant.

"But *she* must be real. She *is* real, isn't she?" insisted Jack.

"She's real all right. Just wait."

The woman continued to be borne up until it appeared she was standing on the top of a low column. As she turned slowly they heard a strange chattering sound. From small holes concealed by the joints between the mirrors on the ceiling small fluttering shapes were being lowered on slender rods. Suddenly they were caught in the lights and Olive could see that they were brilliantly colored butterflies of enameled metal. The effect was lovely, the woman reflected dozens of times in the walls and ceiling, surrounded by her nimbus of flickering insects. The butterflies began to approach her, swaying lightly, suspended from the willowy rods, they began to caress her with their antennae and wings. The woman began to stretch and move very languorously, welcoming the butterflies to her body. One of them would rest lightly on her

187

breast then rise and fall again, just brushing her nipple, then light on her arm. They moved in gentle waves of color and motion. Kissing, nestling, fondling, touching her like excited fingers. She tried to gather them into herself. They nuzzled in her pubic hair, lightly whirring to rest; then, their wings still making the strange clicking and clattering sound, they would move off just as she tried to enfold them between her thighs. It was an enchanting sight and, reflected in the veined mirrors, cast a magical spell over the guests. The muted sounds of a music box could be heard, playing some Third Empire waltz.

As the swarm of butterflies slowly disappeared into the ceiling, the woman returned to her looking glass and the lights went out. When they came back up, nude girls were serving glasses of champagne and bright-colored liqueurs.

Silver tree branches began to unfold with a soft tinkling sound from concealed ports in the mirrored walls. After a moment the ceiling was a shimmering mass of glistening branches and soft green silk leaves trembling in the lights. Reflected in the mirrored walls and ceiling, the room became a wonderful woodland bower. The audience whispered with pleasure.

Jack leaned across Olive and said to Lieutenant Andrews, "To hell with the sex, the special effects alone are worth the price of admission."

The lights went down again, and a spotlight picked out a tall young man dressed in a Greek chiton as he walked through the audience carrying silver thunderbolts. He loosened his shoulder strap and the garment dropped to the floor. He stood naked for a second, then stepped into the pool of water that had appeared in the top of the platform. Using some underwater stairway, he walked down into the water and disappeared, leaving only widening circles.

A lovely girl glided in and sat on the edge of the platform and began to rub her body with a golden dildo. There were murmurs of approval from the audience. From the surface of the water rose the magnificent head and arching neck of a white swan. Slowly the entire bird emerged from the water and cocked its head, almost smiling, a clever and beautiful puppet. The huge bird winked at the audience and swam across the surface of the little pond to the girl, who seemed surprised as she dropped her dildo.

"Leda," someone whispered in recognition. There was a scattering of applause. The swan began to nuzzle the girl with its gilded bill, she returned the affection, and soon they fell into a passionate embrace. Leda lay on the edge of the pool and the swan's bill and head entered her. The long feathered neck glistened with drops of moisture as it penetrated deeper and deeper. With a shuddering moan she encircled the swan with her legs and pulled it on top of her where it lay, passions spent. The spectators gasped their delight.

As Leda walked into the darkness, the swan submerged and an instant later the young god Zeus walked up out of the water sporting a remarkable erection. He picked up his chiton, walked into the darkness toying with his thunderbolts. There were shouts of approval.

In the darkness there were more mechanical noises and the silver branches folded away into the walls. When the lights came back up, the nude girls were refilling their glasses. Some couples had begun to pet.

Olive turned to the lieutenant. "Is this here every night?"

"Yes. There's a performance every morning at two. The program changes. I've seen the butterflies before but never that swan thing. It was created for the World's Fair in '93. To entertain visiting royalty. It's all worked by the son of the man who built it."

Olive sighed. "It's simply beautiful. In most public exhibitions you only see the nasty side of sex. This is refreshing, a work of art, really." Olive sipped her champagne and leaned back as the lights went out.

When they came up, a huge papier-mâché penis projected from each wall making a gigantic formalized phallic ceiling that was repeated over and over in the mirrors.

Onto the center of the platform pranced a centaur. His sculptured body was supported by the legs of two men, one of whom also formed the human torso that grew out of the shoulders of the horse. The horse's buttocks and spectacular genitals belonged to the man in the rear, evidently bent over, hidden in the body of the animal.

The centaur began to dance with the music. The effect was not comic as such horses so often were on the vaudeville stage, but overwhelmingly sexual. A nude girl approached the centaur and began to tease him. The two engaged in an erotic ballet of astonishing gymnastics. A stone bench arose on the platform and the girl lay back on it and invited the beast to mount her.

As the creature thrust its great member into her the audience began to shout encouragement. The music boxes had been replaced by the throbbing of some North African instrument. The coordination between the front figure of the centaur and the rear was superb, and a great shout emerged from the throat of the creature when it reached its orgasm.

At the same moment an ejaculation spurted out of each of the eight huge penises suspended over their heads—confetti. There was a scream of appreciation as the symbolic sperm floated down over everyone. The members of the audience, laughing and applauding, threw handfuls of confetti at each other.

The performers stepped out of costume and, standing naked on the stage, bowed to the applause. The lights came up as all of the performers in each of the previous romances took curtain calls. Standing next to Leutenant Andrews, Jack smacked one fist into the other hand.

"Nothin' like this in Kansas City," he said loudly. "You were right. Hollywood, either." He grinned impishly. "I felt kinda sorry for the guy in the horse costume. For years the back position has been a joke in show business. This is the one time when the guy in the rear gets all the breaks." They both laughed. "What happens now?" he asked.

"It stops being quite so artistic." Lieutenant Andrews leaned closer and lowered his voice. "We ought to go. That's the end of the main show and I don't think we want the ladies to see the next part."

"Wait a damn minute!" Jack was outraged. "Just what does happen?"

"They send in a few more girls and some men from the room upstairs, and members of the audience here can join in for a gang shag. That's what." Andrews stood with his hands on his hips looking directly at Jack. "Usually only a few visiting congressmen want to take part."

Jack grinned gleefully. "Well, you can go upstairs and dance with the girls if you want. I never seen anything like this. I'd kinda like to help out. I think I might just lay claim to that swan's territory." He sat down deliberately on a cushion and started to take off his shoes. Amid whispering, two of the couples from the embassy left. The lights began to dim, and tiny light bulbs were lowered from the ceiling, creating the effect of a starry sky.

Laughing, Jack said, "Fucking under the stars. Well, I'll be damned. This cost extra?" His voice was becoming thick from the brandy.

"Yeh," said Bill Gresham. "It costs a fair amount. We usually don't stay for this part with embassy guests."

"Look, it's on me," said Jack. "Get that girl with the drinks over here. The one with the big tits. Let's have a few drinks and see what develops." He laughed, took off his jacket, untied the black bow tie and loosened his collar button. "Sit down, Olive, honey. This may be fun."

She sat down next to him. "Jack, I don't want to join in. Please, I couldn't endure it. If you want to, I'll stay and watch. But don't ask me to do anything." The music began to pound insistently.

On the platform one of the performers was undressing a woman guest who had walked up to him unsteadily. Several men stood naked in the audience, uncertain how to start.

Jack stood up suddenly. "Goddamn. Hey, Lieutenant, you want some of that fancy ass up there? Don't be shy. This is Paris, remember? I'll stand for all the treats you can handle."

Lieutenant Andrews stood up. "OK, Mr. Pickford. I will if you will. You got a big mouth. Let's see if the rest of you can stand up to it." He stepped out of his trousers.

Jack, laughing, began to undress. "You're on. Follow the leader."

Lieutenant Andrews took his arm. "I'd like to start with your beautiful wife, Mr. Pickford. Follow the leader."

Jack looked at him for an instant, then continued undressing.

"Don't bother. I'd like to have her myself once in a while. Trouble is, she can't stand men. You're welcome to her." He stood for a minute looking at Olive's bloodless face, then turned. "Last one in is a nigger baby," he shouted as he ran up onto the stage.

Lieutenant Andrews looked at Olive with dismay.

"I'm truly sorry, Mrs. Pickford. Jesus Christ! I don't know what to say. I'm sorry." He was almost ill with embarrassment.

Olive looked across the room at Jack standing on the platform with the girl who had played Leda. He was beginning to get an erection.

Olive turned to the lieutenant. "You still want me, Lieutenant? I'm willing if you are." She began to undress, looking at him steadily.

Her body was as lovely as her face. They lay down on the carpet and he began to kiss her passionately. At that moment Jack ran back to get his billfold out of his tuxedo jacket. Olive opened her eyes and looked up to see him standing over them, watching. She closed her eyes.

32

September 1920, New York and Hollywood

> "And the publicity mills of Hollywood grind out
> a continuing plea, 'Don't judge the barrel by one
> rotten apple.' Well, I can only remember the words
> of Job in the Holy Book, 'Who can bring a clean
> thing out of an unclean? Not one.' It is impossible
> to say that the loose morals of the men and women
> who make the movies don't taint the products they
> produce."
>
> Sermon delivered by Reverend E. J. Clarke
> First Presbyterian Church, Menlo Park, California

The stagehand pulled on the set of ropes and the pulleys
tightened. The huge green fan at the rear of the stage opened
wide, paused, then folded back down into the floor again. The
crew applauded.

"Wonderful. Perfect." The director, in corduroy jodhpurs
and leather leggings, turned to them. "The effect is one of a
gigantic Jananese fan that unfolds as the music and dances
change. Every time it opens the mood will be different. How
long before the cast is in costume and ready for places?" he
asked the assistant director.

"Mr. DeMille, I just checked again. They're having trouble
with that heavy cloak of Miss Swanson's. It keeps snagging
on the beading of her dress. Grace is working on it, though.
Says not too long."

"We'll wait. It's cheaper to wait now than to ruin a take
with a bad gesture." DeMille started to sit down and a chair
bearer, standing at the ready, rushed forward. DeMille never
looked behind him; he expected the chair to be there, and it
was.

Wallace Reid, dressed in a pleated white shirt and formal
white tie, strolled over to sit by the director. He wore no
jacket because of the heat. A makeup assistant hovered with a
square of wadded-up cheesecloth, patting the beads of perspi-

ration away as they appeared. Wallie waved him away and sat beside DeMille.

"Fabulous set, Mr. DeMille. You've done it again. Knock 'em dead in Iowa City. Never seen anything like this, I'll bet."

DeMille laughed. "Never saw anything like it in Vienna, either. This is one of the things I love about pictures. We create our own reality. When *The Affairs of Anatole* is released, half the world will believe this is what rooftop cafes in Vienna look like." He looked smug. "We're the greatest single influence on society in the world today. Possibly we're the most influential single element since Gutenberg invented movable type."

Cyrus Cotton approached, nodded at DeMille and listened. He shook hands with Reid as DeMille introduced him.

"He's one of our bankers," DeMille explained drily.

Cotton nodded and sat down without being invited.

Reid watched DeMille with amusement.

"How do you know that pictures carry such an influence?" Cotton asked. "What makes you think you're so influential?"

"Because of the fan mail, the word we get from retailers, the fads we start and then watch sweep the country. Tell him about your shirt collars, Wallie."

"I liked the collars on my polo shirts and had a tailor run up some regular shirts with polo collars. Christ, you'd thought that Majestic had personally shot an arrow right into the heart of the Arrow Shirt Company. You know, I was one of the original models for the Arrow Collar Man ads. Well, they sent a deputation out here to plead with me to go back to stiff collars. Seems shirt sales dropped overnight. No one would buy stiff collars anymore. Except maybe bankers." Cotton flushed. "No offense, Mr. Cotton. I just advised them to make soft collars and they did."

"Don't underestimate our powers, Mr. Cotton," DeMille wagged his finger in the banker's face. "Millions of young men on their first date will open the door for their girls just the way Wallie holds it for Gloria today."

Reid interrupted. "Door, hell. They'll watch how I hold Gloria."

DeMille frowned. "It's the small things too. How Gloria will light her cigarette, use the silver at the table. People copy our flower arrangements. Americans are becoming an urban, sophisticated nation. But there are no traditions to follow, as there are in England, for example. There, if you get rich, you hire a butler who knows how everything is done. Here, we're making it up in Hollywood and the nation is following suit." He seemed very pleased. "We're showing all those millions who are leaving the farms how to behave in polite society."

Reid grinned. "And impolite, as well. Naughtiness is still more attractive than goodness, Mr. DeMille."

"Don't I know it," DeMille said.

The Klieg lights snapped on one by one and DeMille looked through the view finder on the camera positioned for the master shot.

"I can only see one chandelier." DeMille stepped back and looked up at the grid of pipes that crisscrossed the space below the glass ceiling. "The others are cut off in this shot. I can't see them."

There was dead silence while everyone waited. DeMille grew more agitated.

"I need to see all three chandeliers. We'll have to rehang those two."

"Everybody break for lunch," the assistant director called through his red megaphone. "Back in two hours."

The cast and crew straggled off the set, the extras jubilant —the delay meant an extra day's work for them.

Cyrus Cotton tapped DeMille on the shoulder.

"I really must protest this wanton extravagance, Mr. De-Mille. Surely seeing all three chandeliers is not important enough to justify all this costly delay."

DeMille looked at him as if he had suddenly become an insect. He spoke slowly. "They may not be important to you, but they are vital to me." He started to walk away, then thought better of it and walked back toward Cotton jabbing a finger. "All over the world millions of men and women are waiting for my next picture. They will stand in line to see it. They will pay hundreds of thousands—maybe millions—of dollars in admissions to see *The Affairs of Anatole*. There is one thing they can be assured of when they see the words 'A Cecil B. DeMille Production' above the title. And that one thing is that they are guaranteed they will see more than one chandelier in every scene." He looked up at the crew, standing frozen like statues, listening to the drama being played out at the foot of the ladder.

"Make that four chandeliers. Four, not three. I don't care how long it takes to find the fourth one." He whirled back to Cotton, pointing. "Get that man off my set. Off! Off!" DeMille turned on his heel and stormed off to his portable office in the corner of the studio.

When the door had slammed behind him Wallie hooted at the expression on Cotton's face.

"That's your little lesson in movie making for today." He walked away, roaring with laughter.

Ben sat back in a huge, old-fashioned chair, keenly aware that he was the only one at the studio whom Abe Weiss would invite to his home for dinner.

After opening the windows of his study Weiss stood in front of the empty fireplace lighting his cigar. After puffing for a moment, he looked at Ben and said, "You keep up with the theater-buying program?"

"Yes, sir, I do."

"What do you make of it from a public relations point of view?"

"Well, I'm afraid the public will begin to distrust you the way they do the steel and railroad tycoons."

Ben could see the glowing tip of Weiss's cigar bob up and down as he laughed. "You must learn one thing, Ben. Americans love millionaires and especially big businessmen. How can you hate what you want to be yourself? It's in the blood. The American Dream. The American Way. One of the first things that happened after I came here and learned good English so I could follow what was going on, was the breaking up of the trusts. You may not remember, but they were big ones: Rockefeller and oil, Havemeyer's sugar, Harriman's hold on the railroads. The muckraking newspapers called them 'malefactors of great wealth.' "

A soft breeze rustled the lace curtains. Weiss continued, a dark figure standing in the twilight.

"Well, the muckrakers shouted to their hearts' content and finally the government lawyers obliged with some lawsuits. The trusts were busted up. I remember in particular the Harriman companies being compared to an 'Iron Octopus' strangling the country. So they cut off all the arms of the octopus and each arm became a new company, still feeding its profits to the Harrimans. Legal, profitable. One thing never happened, though. Not one of the so-called 'evil millionaires' ever so much as set foot in jail or even got slapped. They were inconvenienced, but they still spent their summers in Newport and Tuxedo Park; they wintered in Warm Springs.

"So I decided as long as I didn't buy up competing companies and only enlarged one company, the government and the people wouldn't care if I dominated the moving picture business or not. It's been easy."

"You make it sound very easy, Mr. Weiss, but I'm sure it wasn't."

Weiss shrugged. "Hard work. But then I like hard work. And I learned. Ben, boy, always learn from every man you talk to. Don't try to teach nobody nothing. Learn from everybody, though. Even the men who would destroy you. Don't knock a man over until you find out how much he knows. If he is smart enough to be a threat, either you have to hire him or kill him."

"How many theaters do you want?" Ben asked. "I mean, how many is enough?"

The glowing tip of the cigar brightened and dimmed. "Until I dominate the industry. Whatever that takes." Weiss was silent for a moment. "Ben, I want Majestic to be the greatest entertainment company in history. The biggest, the best, not just the most profitable. Any fool can make profits. I want to set the style. Make everyone else follow what Abe Weiss decides is best. Profits will follow all right." He paused for a moment, then jabbed his cigar at Ben. "We got 400 theaters now, and pretty soon nobody'll be able to catch up. Not Loew, not Zukor, not Fox. I'll leave First National in the dust, too. What it comes down to is owning the distribution exchanges, the theaters, everything on our own. So nobody cuts into the profits but a Majestic subsidiary. I don't split with anybody. It's mine, all down the line."

"And you're not worried about antitrust, no matter how big you get?"

"Not as long as I don't buy up the competition. We form our own. It's all one big happy company, not a piling on of former competitors that I bought up to take away the competition. The competition is still fierce. Uncle Sam can't complain until I put the competition out of business."

The room was completely dark and they sat comfortably silent in the warm fall night.

"It must be very satisfying to know that you not only have a profitable business that you have developed, but that you are a part of making works of art that will live forever," Ben ventured.

"Who told you that?" There was a note of derision in Weiss's voice.

"DeMille. At the press conference for *Anatole*."

There was a laugh spluttering in the darkness. "Don't believe everything Cecil tells you." Then his voice became more serious. "I suppose there is some truth to it. I don't like to think that we turn out crap. It's like making a fur cape or a fine man's suit. You like to think that you're turning out a high-class, quality item." He thought for a moment. "I guess there are some great pictures being made now and then. Maybe some works of art. I'd have to think about it."

Bessie Weiss stood in the darkness with a tray. She had been listening to the voices, low and earnest. She could scarcely recall Abe this relaxed and at ease. Talking of what he loved best, his real life. For years she had worried that he had no one at home to talk to and longed for a son for him. But God was not willing. Now this nice young *shaigetz*. If only he was a nice Jewish boy instead.

"How does cold lemonade sound to you two?" Bessie asked as ice tinkled in the glasses. She set the tray down and turned on a lamp.

33

September 1920, New York

ABE WEISS MAJESTIC NEW YORK STOP COTTON
MISSING STOP THROWN OFF SET BY DEMILLE FOR
INTERFERENCE WITH SET DESIGN STOP YOU KNOW
DEMILLE STOP CHECK WITH BANK STOP MAYBE THEY
HAVE HEARD STOP DEMILLE SWEARS HE WAS NOT
ABUSIVE ENOUGH TO CAUSE RASH ACT STOP AM PUZ-
ZLED STOP REGARDS RUBIN

SAUL RUBIN MAJESTIC HOLLYWOOD STOP BANK IN
DARK ABOUT COTTON STOP ANY SIGNS OF FOUL PLAY
STOP MAYBE ON DRUNK AND NEEDS TIME TO SOBER
UP STOP CHECK BORDER OFFICIALS AT TIJUANA STOP
REGARDS WEISS

Roscoe Arbuckle squinted dreamily through his glass at the
two girls sitting at the bar. He leaned across the table and
winked elaborately at Ben.

"Play your cards right and you won't have to sleep alone,
Benny-Boy. They look oh-so-lonesome." He drew out the
syllables.

"Roscoe, I'm so tired I couldn't get it up for the Queen of
Roumania. This has been one hell of a week. All you had to
do was to ride that damned horse up Broadway. I feel like I
pulled it." He sipped his whiskey.

"Don't downplay that! I was really scared up on that thing.
I thought I'd wet my pants. Hanging on for dear life and
trying to smile and look like a funny fat man all at the same
time. Dear God, it was not fun, believe you me."

"I believe you, all right. You had a kind of frozen look on
your face when you hove up in front of the Rivoli." Ben
finished his drink. "I never want to see another Majestic
picture or talk to another theater manager as long as I
live."

"Don't let Abe Weiss hear you say that," Roscoe giggled.

"Roscoe, you stay here and pick up the girls. There's enough of you for both of them. I'm walking back to The Waldorf and get to bed. I feel like I've been through a wringer." He patted Arbuckle on the shoulder as he stood. "You've been a real joy to work with, Roscoe, I mean it. Many thanks for all your cooperation. See you tomorrow."

Roscoe jogged toward the bar on his tiptoes as Ben left the "21" speakeasy to walk back toward the hotel. It had been a long day coordinating all the advertising for Majestic Week and visiting the local theaters to make sure everything was working well.

The phone rang and Ben sat up in bed in the dark hotel room. He sat there groggy, half asleep, waiting to see if it wouldn't stop. There must be some mistake. The ringing continued. It was four thirty A.M.

"I'm terribly sorry to wake you, Mr. Sommers, but you have a cable from Paris and I took the responsibility on myself to call you. It sounded important. Shall I read it to you, or send it up?"

"Read it."

TERRIBLE ACCIDENT STOP OLIVE THOMAS IN AMERICAN HOSPITAL WITH MERCURIAL POISONING STOP NURSES AROUND THE CLOCK ATTEMPTS TO REACH SISTER MARY UNSUCCESSFUL STOP PLEASE YOU TRY TELEPHONE STOP WILL CABLE DETAILS AS OLIVE IMPROVES STOP REGARDS JACK PICKFORD

"Oh, my God." A spasm of nausea hit him. He tried to think. "What time is it in Paris?"

"They're seven hours ahead of us, sir. I just gave the cable to the boy. It'll be there as soon as he can get upstairs. It must be about eleven-thirty in the morning in Paris. Do you want to send an answer?"

"I'll let you know in a few minutes," he said dully. He was having trouble putting words together. "What about . . . oh, hell, tell me. Does long distance work at this hour of the morning?"

"Only to some cities. Big ones. Is this Olive Thomas the movie star?"

"Yes. Tell me, is Los Angeles one of the cities?"

"Golly, that's too bad. I always liked her."

"What about Los Angeles?"

"Yes, you can call. I'll place the call if you wish. It takes a little while to get through to an operator."

"I'll let you know."

He sat down and read the cable. He reread it several times, actually hoping that it would say something different. How the hell did you get mercurial poisoning? He looked at his watch again. His hands shook as he lifted the receiver off the hook and asked the operator to get him Bellevue Hospital.

After a long wait Ben reached a sleepy Dr. Straus who answered his question.

"How serious depends on how much poison your friend got."

"I don't know. I just got a cable. Tell me what it is."

"Well, it must have been an accident. I can't imagine anyone taking it deliberately. Very poisonous. Here we keep it in the form of Mercuric Chloride or Bichloride of Mercury. It's a very powerful disinfectant and germicide. But, God, you have to be careful how you use it. We use it on kids for ringworm. Blue tablets that you drop into water and soak the afflicted parts. It kills everything it touches—really dead. More poisonous than arsenic or strychnine. More like cyanide."

"Why do you think it must have been an accident?"

"Because it's a terrible way to die. Very, very corrosive and will eat away flesh if it's too strong. Slow and painful. It's too ugly."

His stomach knotted as he visualized the lovely Olive with a mass of scars around her mouth.

"If that's all, I got rounds to go on," the doctor said.

"Thank you. You've been very helpful."

Ben sat by the telephone in the darkness for a long time remembering her on the train coming east.

By six A.M. he had sent a cable to Jack in Paris asking for more details and one to the American Embassy asking for all they knew. Then he sent a cable to the assistant manager of the Majestic Exchange in Paris whom he'd met a few months earlier on a studio tour.

At seven, Ben called Abe Weiss. There was a long silence after he broke the news. "Poor Mary," Weiss murmured, "she worries so about Jack. What a terrible thing. Terrible. That beautiful girl. Flo will be all broken up. He really loved her. Was it accidental?"

"The cable from Jacks says 'accident,' Mr. Weiss."

"Then there's no problem there. She hadn't started shooting yet, had she?"

"No. Billy Taylor is still rewriting the scenario. They start on October first. Or were to start."

"Good. Rubin can substitute a star and we won't lose a picture from the schedule. Terrible. I guess Selznick will cash in on the publicity. Too bad we didn't get one picture in the can. Of course, if she recovers, the publicity will be like money in the bank. Terrible."

Ben felt a chill enveloping him. He seemed to be shaking inside but he forced himself to speak.

"Mr. Weiss, I suggest that we play up the accidental angle. Make it look like a tragedy of two young star-crossed lovers whose devotion to each other is being tested in the flames of fate."

Ben listened to himself and honestly didn't know where the words came from. Surely it wasn't he talking that way about Olive. He ought to have his head examined. The business was getting to him.

Weiss was speaking again and Ben had not heard what he said.

"I'm sorry. Please say that again, Mr. Weiss. I was distracted for a minute."

"I said, your story sounds good. But don't waste too much time on it. We don't have a picture and only Selznick will benefit. He'll rerelease every picture of hers that he can. Let him *schlepp* around to the papers."

"I'll keep you informed, Mr. Weiss."

"Terrible thing." Weiss hung up.

Ben looked at all the morning papers while he tried to eat breakfast. Nothing. Evidently the story was still a secret. Later in the morning a collect cable arrived from O'Neill, the manager of the Paris Exchange.

OLIVE PICKFORD VERY SERIOUS STOP ATTEMPTED SUICIDE IS POSSIBLE STOP NEAR DEATH STOP HUSBAND AT SIDE AT ALL TIMES STOP NASTY RUMORS DRUNKEN NIGHT ON TOWN STOP WILL FOLLOW WITH ANY DETAILS CAN DIG UP STOP BEST O'NEILL

The call to Mary Pickford was answered by her maid, who said Miss Pickford couldn't be reached. Ben then called the entertainment editor of *The Los Angeles Examiner*. Hearst would have a scoop and get out an extra, as the story had still not moved on the wire services. The scoop for Hearst served two purposes. Marion Davies and Olive had been friends since their Follies days. And the editor at *The Examiner* would be eternally grateful to Ben for the story. It wouldn't hurt having her owe him one.

Flo Ziegfeld wept on the telephone as Ben gave him the details. Maybe Abe Weiss was right and he had really loved her. Why had he married Billie Burke, then? Ben suddenly realized he didn't understand why anyone did anything.

The New York evening papers carried a brave statement from Jack in Paris. There was no mention that Olive might not live. The following morning Ben instructed O'Neill to hire a private detective and cables began to arrive hourly. Hideous details were carefully spelled out in them. Ben reported to Abe Weiss.

The bichloride of mercury was so corrosive that Olive's mouth and vocal cords had been eaten away. She had not uttered a sound since Jack had heard her strangled cry, "I've taken poison. I'm sorry for everything. Help!"

Jack and Olive had spent a sordid night carousing in the nightclubs of Montmartre. There was police speculation of orgies, drugs, and things too immoral to put in cables. Ben told Abe Weiss that he had instructed the Majestic office in Paris to try to whitewash all they could. The American Embassy was maintaining an official silence.

"Hide what you can, Ben," Weiss said. "Just make sure there were no Majestic people in that party. I don't want to see their names in the *Times* if they were there. Pay them off. Get them out of sight."

"There don't seem to have been any, Mr. Weiss. The party that went on to Montmartre was put together by some embassy men. Our people were at the dinner but they didn't go on to the orgy."

Ben heard a strange gargle on the telephone. It was Weiss spluttering. "Don't use that word. Even with friends on the telephone. That's all the *Daily News* or the *Graphic* have to hear, much less Hearst. Has he called you, by the way?"

"No, but *The L.A. Examiner* is carrying some pretty lurid stories. Based mostly on what they hope happened. They'll do anything to sell a paper," Ben said with a deep sigh.

"All we can do is keep Majestic out of it. She wasn't really ours, remember. Hadn't started shooting." Weiss sounded hesitant. "I guess she will die?"

"My source at the hospital says it's a matter of a day at the most. She went blind this morning."

"Terrible. Terrible."

202

Olive Thomas Pickford died on September 10th. The front page of *The New York Times* carried a headline announcing:

POLICE SEEK EVIDENCE OF DRUG AND CHAMPAGNE
ORGIES, REFUSE TO RELEASE BODY.

Subsequent stories told of a wild night on Montmartre and how Jack and Olive had led a group from the American Embassy on a tour of night spots and cafes. Majestic was nowhere mentioned.

Most of the witnesses were embassy employees, and the State Department was working hard to keep things quiet. Lt. Andrews and Bill Gresham were immediately reassigned to remote outposts and disappeared from Paris in a few hours. Two embassy guests, Al Paulson and Robert Chase, both of Los Angeles and not government employees, gave sensational interviews. When asked if they had participated in "orgies," they both looked at their shoes. *The Los Angeles Examiner* speculated on the expressions on their faces.

Reporters from American newspapers interviewed the proprietor of "The Dead Rat," where Olive had given herself to customers on the sidewalk tables about six in the morning, while passersby cheered and shouted advice.

Los Angeles newspapers were filled with melodramatic accounts of "gilded tango palaces and clandestine resorts where gold is the key to the most inconceivable debaucheries." Across the nation "shameful nightlife orgies of a modern Babylon" were denounced from pulpits. It took only two weeks for the Women's Clubs of America to prevent Selznick from rereleasing any of Olive's features. They organized a boycott of any theater who tried to defy the ban. Photos of staunch ladies wearing ribbons suffrage-style across their bosoms, backs pressed against box-office windows, defying customers to purchase tickets, ran in all of the local papers. In Indianapolis the Women's Club stormed a large theater and barricaded themselves in the projection booth and were thus able to prevent a showing of *Follies Girl* and the corrupting of the minds and hearts of the good citizens of that city.

After a week of ineffectual investigations, the Paris police released Olive's body. It was accompanied home by her heartbroken husband. The burial was private and simple. Jack Pickford hoped he would be the only one there and he nearly was. Ben rode out with him, and when the rented limousine reached Woodlawn Cemetery, two reporters, Velva, and an elderly woman who had been wardrobe mistress at the Follies were waiting in the early fall sunshine.

Olive's last resting place was marked by a simple stone:

OLIVE THOMAS PICKFORD
1898–1920
LOVING WIFE OF JOHN PICKFORD
My Happiness Lies Here

34

October 1920,
South Alvarado Street, Los Angeles

Moving Picture Daily, October 13, 1920

LYNCH TAKES ATLANTA LIKE
SHERMAN DID

ATLANTA, Oct. 13. Word that the Lynch Amusement Company has completed negotiations for Wells' theaters in this city, Savannah, Augusta, and Knoxville, Tenn. was released today by the Wells organization. The purchase price was said to be in the $1,000,000 range. Rumors that the Lynch Company is a front for Majestic Pictures have been denied. The truth will be out if the houses, now allied with the First National circuit, start showing Majestic photoplays.

Neither Jake Wells nor Amos Lynch was available for comment.

Bill Taylor lived in the rear bungalow in a very expensive court on Alvarado Street just a block above Westlake Park. The house was double, two front doors next to each other. Ben looked at the name plate by the first door. It read *Edna Purviance.* Charlie Chaplin's star and girl friend! Taylor must live next door. He stepped over a low wall. There, an engraved calling card had been trimmed to fit the brass holder by the bell. *William Desmond Taylor, Esq.* Ben pushed the bell.

The door was opened by a Negro butler. It was a surprise, since the half of the house that Taylor lived in was not large enough and certainly not fancy enough to need a butler. Taylor evidently liked to live in style.

"Hello. I'm Ben Sommers. Mr. Taylor asked me to stop by for a drink."

"Of course, sir. Won't you step in and wait? He'll be down in a moment."

The main floor of the bungalow consisted of two large rooms separated by low bookcases and two pillars. At the rear a dining table stood in the center surrounded by chairs. Ben sat on a sofa that took up most of the wall. Across from him was a piano, covered with a colorful silk oriental shawl. The room was furnished with what appeared to be antiques, and the walls were hung with dozens of paintings. Little bronze statues and pieces of carved jade stood here and there. In the corner was an Atwater Kent radio on a stand, its battery jars on a shelf underneath, filled with dangerous looking green acid. Ben went over to look at it.

"There's not much to listen to, I'm afraid," Taylor said as he entered. "But what there is, is rather fun. It doesn't start until after dark. You must come over in the evening and play with it." Taylor extended his hand. "You must have had a rum time of it in New York, handling all that tricky rot about Olive. Now the vile stories start."

Ben nodded. "I can't believe all the things they said she did on that last night," he said somberly.

"It's terribly sad. I only met her once, a few weeks ago after she signed her new contract, but I certainly liked her and, my God, she was lovely. Prettiest girl I've ever seen, I'll warrant."

The butler served them whiskey. Ben's glass had ice in it. Taylor's didn't.

Ben, disappointed that Taylor didn't feel more deeply, glanced at the floor and changed the subject. "This is the most unusual room I've ever been in." He looked about. "Tell me about some of your things."

Taylor laughed lightly, rather relieved. He hadn't realized Sommers was such a gloomy young man. "I suppose it is unusual for Hollywood. It's more like a typical London flat. Just a few things I've collected in my travels. We British pick up things here and there as we wend our way through the far-flung outposts of the empire." He smiled at Ben and sipped his drink. "I'll show you about if you like."

Ben began to feel more at ease. "Yes, I'd like to see everything. I just live in a plain old apartment. This looks so—so sort of theatrical."

"Well, that's deliberate. I've created a setting for my life. A place where I can feel at home and relax and enjoy my

206

friends and my things." He rearranged some small bronze figurines on the table beside him, putting them into a conversational grouping. He stopped and looked sharply at Ben. "Good God, man, you can't just live in a blank room, anonymous, just as you don't drive just any motorcar. You express yourself. Your apartment should express your personality too. There is nothing accidental about anything in my life. I make deliberate choices down to the smallest details."

Ben followed him into the dining room.

"They're all my leading ladies." Taylor gestured to the side wall of the room, which was covered from wainscoat to ceiling with framed photographs of beautiful women, all inscribed to him.

Ben studied the inscriptions as Taylor rummaged through the bookcases in the living room.

"You mean you've directed all these actresses in pictures?"

"Every one of them." He chuckled softly. "Isn't that a rogues' gallery? God, I love them." Something in his voice made Ben look at him. He was standing, book in hand, gazing off into the distance. "Every last one of them," he said, almost to himself. He was suddenly aware of Ben watching him and busily began to pull books off the shelf. "How much time have you spent on the stages?"

"Just enough to learn how it's done."

Taylor nodded in approval. "Good. But you probably haven't noticed, then. You have to experience it day by day. A picture company becomes a complex layering of love affairs. You read Freud?"

"No," Ben shook his head. "What is it?"

"Freud is a he, old sport. Sigmund Freud. Viennese doctor who decided that men's heads could get sick as well as their physical bodies. So he devised ways to look into their minds. He maintains that sex is the motivation for most actions." Looking at the shelves, he shook his head. "But you'll have to borrow that book another time. Mabel Normand has mine at the moment. I thought it might help her."

"Sennett's Mabel Normand? Do you know her?"

He placed a little pile of books on the piano and sat down.

"Mabel is a deeply troubled woman really, who never got beyond grade school and who doesn't realize the potential of her mind, which is brilliant. She makes hundreds of thousands of dollars a year and is miserable and doesn't know why. She literally has no life outside that studio stage." He sipped his whiskey.

"Oh, she has a few friends, but they're no better off than she is. What do they do?" He raised his glass as if proposing a toast. "Drink, fornicate, take drugs, drive fast cars, buy expensive trinkets, take sleeping pills, and try to forget that they don't know how to live. It's a ghastly circle. They all feed on each other. And there's an outer circle of leeches that feeds on them." He shook his head sadly.

Ben looked down at his drink. "Boy, I never thought of it that way before." He laughed lightly. "I wouldn't dare. I'm only supposed to write good things. I have to believe it's the American-dream-come-true to be a movie star." He stopped suddenly. They sat silent. "What did you mean when you said a company was layers of love affairs?"

Taylor sighed. "Oh, I fall in love with each lovely actress in every picture. They fall in love with me and with their leading men. The better the actress, the more likely she is to fall in love with one of us. It's more real if it's real, you understand?"

Ben wasn't sure he did, but he nodded anyway.

"Wait till you see the performance young Polly gives me in *Spirit*. You won't believe it. It's absolutely genuine. Wonderful!"

"Hey, that's great. I'm working on a full campaign for her. We'll have a big publicity bash at The Ambassador and introduce her to the press. I'm glad she's doing a good job—makes it easier when there's something there."

"Oh, there's something there all right." Taylor settled back comfortably and looked at Ben speculatively. "How's the job going?"

"Pretty well. I just work."

Taylor nodded in silent agreement. "That's the attitude all right."

The doorbell rang and Henry went to answer it. He led a young woman back into the room.

"Miss Normand is here," he announced in a formal tone as he walked past to the kitchen, where he seemed to spend all his time.

"Mabel, dearest! Come meet a new friend. We mentioned you just a while ago. Mabel, Ben Sommers. Ben does the publicity and press at Majestic. We were just talking about Olive Thomas."

Mabel kissed Taylor lightly on the cheek. "You weren't saying bad things about *me*?" She kissed Ben as well.

Taylor laughed. "Only that you don't return books promptly."

208

"I heard all about Olive. I was better before I heard. I guess the real story isn't coming out. Well, maybe it's better that way. Henry," she called out, "get me a gin rickey, please. I'm dying."

"What do you mean, the real story?" Ben was disturbed.

Mabel stepped out of her shoes and curled up in the big armchair with her feet tucked under her. She was wearing a filmy printed chiffon dress that he could see through.

"Oh, my God. They were completely incompatible. They used to have terrible fights. Mostly over sex." She added lightly, "Everybody knew. I could never understand what made them get back together again." She held up her glass and studied Ben through it.

Ben looked at Taylor and put his empty glass on the table. "I really must go. Thanks for the drinks."

"I'm sorry you must run. Please come again when we can talk further. Take these books with you. This is Lady Mendl's on interior design. Maybe you'll see something to do to your plain-Jane apartment."

Taylor closed the door behind him.

"What an intense young man," Mabel said.

"Yes. He needs a father, or perhaps an uncle. Well, he's not cultured, but he's bright enough. Another addition to my salon." He laughed and stretched his arms toward Mabel. They embraced, kissed, and then she snuggled into his arms and they stood together quietly in the darkening room.

"Oh, Billy, you're such a comfort. Just like an island for me in a terrifying sea." She stepped back and looked up at him, eyes wide. "I need your strength and calmness. Everyone else here is as crazy as I am." She raised one hand to her forehead in a theatrical gesture and the chiffon sleeve slid back revealing a graceful arm. Then she let it drop suddenly.

Taylor took her hand and led her to the sofa. "You're not crazy, dearest." He kissed her eyelids. "Silly," he whispered. "Henry will get us some supper. Can you stay?" He kissed the tips of her fingers, then the palm of her hand.

"Billy, dearest, I need to stay. Of course. That's why I came."

"All night?"

"If you wish." She laid her head against his chest and closed her eyes.

"I wish, you know I wish."

He held her close and looked down on her hair.

Cut and print.

35

October 1920, The Majestic Commissary

Finishing her beef stew, Polly was about to wipe the bowl
with a piece of bread when she caught Taylor's eye. She
paused.

"Not nice?"

"No, Polly. A well-bred young moving picture star does
not wipe her plate with a roll. Order a second serving if
you're still hungry."

Ben found her ingenuousness charming, and he smiled as
he picked up the press release he'd been working on and
began to read aloud, exaggerating his Southern drawl.

"You were left as a foundling on the steps of a home near
Boston. Your foster parents are not wealthy but are very
proud." Polly listened raptly, her chin on her fists. "The shawl

in which you were wrapped was edged in Irish lace. In addition, it was embroidered with a crest, the crest of the McCormack family."

Polly giggled. "Hush," Ben said. "Listen. Your booties were knitted from the softest wool—wool from a kind of sheep raised only in County Kerry."

"Ben," Taylor interrupted, "I see you in a new light. I'd no idea you were such an accomplished liar." He snorted sternly, then winked at Polly. She giggled again.

Ben continued lamely. "However, you won't reveal your foster parents' name because your leaving home was a very great hurt to them. You will only tell the world who they are when you have achieved stardom."

Polly took a deep breath and sat up straighter. "It's almost true," she whispered.

"For the first time I wish the commissary served liquor," Taylor muttered. "I need a drink."

"Then you can return home, head held proudly, and tell them why you left their warm hearth for the hot studio lights in the Entertainment Capital of the World. You have followed your star, met your destiny, and plucky tyke that you are, found fame." Ben exhaled loudly. "Like it?" He sat back looking pleased with himself.

Polly sighed softly. "I think it's perfectly grand."

"Who made up that rot? Surely not you?"

Ben couldn't tell if Taylor was serious or not. He bridled. "Well, it's better than having her a countess or something."

"Especially with a name like McCormack!"

"Well, what are we going to say? That she got lost in Chicago when her mother was sending her to a sister in Minnesota?"

"Wisconsin," said Polly.

"They're both the same," Ben said irritably. "That she decided on a whim to come to Hollywood after seeing her first movie?"

"But that's what really happened," Polly said cheerfully.

"Who is going to sit in a beauty parlor and read about you in *Moving Picture World* or *Photoplay* if all you did was to get lost in Chicago? We have to give them some mystery."

"Well, it's partly true. I did leave home and decide to be in the movies." She giggled again. "But ma would be surprised about the baby in the snow." She lowered her voice. "She had me the regular way." She laughed heartily at her joke, then became serious. "There are some parts you don't know about, though."

211

"No one needs to know everything, Polly," Taylor said hurriedly. Sometimes he worried about her. She had already hinted at things that disturbed him.

"Ben is correct about mystery," he went on. "Always keep something of yourself a mystery, dear. It will add to your allure." He smiled at her, then turned to Ben.

"Our real problem is that Polly has been seeing too many photoplays and copied too many mature actresses. I want her to stay a young girl."

Polly looked at his stern face. Did that mean she could never be glamorous like Gloria Swanson?

"I think we'll cut her hair," Taylor said thoughtfully. "Bobbed hair is becoming all the rage, and it'll help that tomboy quality I'm after—spirited, full of pep and energy. A lot of laughs. Do you understand, Polly?"

"I'll do anything." She sat forward in her chair and crumpled her napkin in one hand, squeezing until he could see the tendons in her forearm straining. "Just ask me, I'll do it. Somebody said I walked clumsy in the test. You should have seen me before I started walking up and down those stairs at the Million Dollar." She put both arms on the table and leaned toward Taylor. "I only saw my first movie a year ago. I knew that night where I had to go and what I had to do." Taylor stared at her. She had begun to sound like dialogue for a scenario.

Then he smiled. "Then take that preposterous background Ben has created and memorize it. Get yourself off to Wardrobe," he said, looking at his watch. "They want to fit costumes this afternoon." Polly jumped up, kissed him on the cheek and ran out.

Taylor seemed pleased.

"Except for her wiping her plate, that's the first time I've seen anything like a normal reaction out of her. Sometimes she's frightening—like a windup toy. You point her in one direction, and she just goes forward until she smashes into the wall."

"She'll be fourteen in a few weeks," Ben said. "We really ought to do something. Maybe I'll take her out to dinner. If I can think of a place a kid her age would like."

212

36

January 1921, The Tour

Harrison's Reports
A weekly Guide to Moving Pictures
for the Theater Exhibitor

January 9, 1921   Vol. III No. 15

EDITORIAL

There is new hope for the small theater owner. Majestic Pictures is about to be challenged by the feisty new Motion Picture Theatre Owners of America led by Sidney S. Cohen of the Cohen Theatre Co. of New York. Cohen's objective is the end of Majestic's stranglehold on the exhibitors of America.

Abe Weiss is a great industry leader and one of our real pioneers. He had vision and the will to build, when others only took profits. He created stars and established a great chain of first-run houses in which to display the truly artistic photoplays he mounted them in. He spent to improve production values so the audiences of America could laugh and cry and be entertained on a scale unparalleled in history.

But Majestic was not content. Weiss has long wanted to—yes, we will say it—create a monopoly. Majestic now owns more than 500 theaters! Besides the houses, it has the top box-office draws. This kind of showmanship and skill should be honored.

But Abe Weiss does not get honors. His very name and the names of his henchmen bring fear and trembling to every theater owner. Now he is about to feel the wrath of his fellow exhibitors. The word boycott is being freely bandied about at meetings. Watch out, Abe. It is not too late to mend your ways. Think about it.

The train shed at the Southern Pacific station was a madhouse. Girls from the studio dressed in green taffeta were handing out special dollar bills with "Fatty" Arbuckle's picture on them. It was the beginning of a cross-country press tour to promote Roscoe's third full-length feature, *Brewster's Millions*. The tour had been scheduled to give audiences in eleven cities an opportunity to see Roscoe on stage on the opening day of the local engagement of the picture.

Ben took Roscoe inside the Pullman car Majestic had engaged for the tour. The car had a central lounge and everyone was assigned bedroom suites at either end. A porter distributed their luggage, and a bartender unpacked cases of liquor. Ben tapped Roscoe on the shoulder.

"Roscoe, do you think it's smart to unlimber the hooch while we're still inside the city limits? And where did the bartender come from, anyway?"

"He's mine," Rosco said. "He's got a berth in the next car so he can stay close in case of an emergency—like a glass getting empty." Roscoe studied Ben's face and giggled. "Don't worry, Benny. I'm paying. We got plenty of ice and all's right with the world."

"Well, I must say it hadn't worried me all that much."

Arbuckle looked at him seriously. "You really oughta think about it more. Bad ice can be a killer." He snickered and stood up. "I'm ready for my first drink, bartender. Say, what's your name, anyway?"

"Alessandro."

"OK, Al. I've been on the wagon for three weeks. In training, so to speak. Do your stuff."

Al obliged.

The party had grown—Roscoe had invited a group of friends without Ben's knowledge. "They'll have to make their own sleeping arrangements, Roscoe. My upper is filled with boxes of fake dollar bills."

Sitting around drinking were some pals from Roscoe's Sennett days. Ben recognized Tom Forman, the cowboy star who had appeared with Arbuckle in *The Round-Up*; Lew Cody, a handsome leading man; Lowell Sherman, noted for his portrayal of lounge lizards and one of Roscoe's best friends. There were four girls who didn't seem to have any names at all, outside of Cutie, Sweetie, Sugar, and Honeybuns. One of the men from Sennett was playing jazz on the piano. Ben was sure the piano hadn't come with the car. Arbuckle cheerfully admitted he had rented it.

"How is the goddamned piano going to get back to Los Angeles, Roscoe?"

"If it doesn't, I'll just have to buy it, I guess."

Ben shrugged. Roscoe could afford it. He frequently joked with reporters that he was the only major star making less than ten thousand dollars a week. He made eight.

By the time the train got to the mountains and made the Tchachapi Loop, the serious drinking was under way.

There seemed to be two Arbuckles. In private, at home or at the studio, he was Roscoe. As soon as he gathered an audience, he became Fatty, as if he had stepped into another self. In an elevator he was Roscoe as long as there were no strangers present. But if someone got on and recognized him, he became Fatty instantly.

Everyone had a good time for the next two days. No one got out of line in the lounge; occasionally one of the girls would disappear for a while. Roscoe didn't seem to get mixed up with any of the girls, but he turned out to be a thoughtful host.

Early one morning Cutie knocked at Ben's door. Roscoe had sent her, it seemed, because he thought Ben was acting too much like a camp counselor.

"Roscoe only wants to make sure that everyone has a real good time. He thought you might need an eye-opener," she told Ben as she opened her kimono and then let it slide to the floor.

Two or three times a day waiters would wheel in carts of food—roasts, steaks, a whole turkey, cold crab and lobsters, salmon in aspic. The function of the food seemed to be to absorb some of the liquor. By the time they reached Omaha, Ben figured they had finished off five cases of whiskey and two of gin. Roscoe was certain someone was stealing it, but Al solemnly assured him they were drinking it all.

"There's only about 450 miles to Chicago and about fourteen cases. That's plenty," Al said soothingly.

In Chicago, the Arbuckle-Majestic party took over the entire eleventh floor of the Palmer House. The party still included all the original participants, including Al the bartender. The girls continued to circulate among the men.

The personal appearances along the way had gone over well. Roscoe had been a vaudeville headliner for many years so he was experienced on the stage. During his vaudeville career he had sung sentimental ballads in a high sweet tenor, and now he added a song to the routine he performed at each showing of the picture. It was a sensation. He would frequently come off into the wings, eyes filled with tears, moved by the waves of love and laughter surging up over the footlights to engulf him. Frequently uncertain of the reaction of strangers to his girth, Roscoe was delighted when audiences loved him.

One noon in the Palmer House dining room a waiter placed a triple-decker club sandwich on white toast in front of Roscoe and stepped back. Fatty bounced to his feet, picked up the sandwich, put it on top of the waiter's head. The waiter stood still, visible apprehension growing on his face. The word around the hotel was that Roscoe was a big spender and the waiter did not want to antagonize him.

Fatty raised his hand and smacked it down on top of the sandwich. Mayonnaise and juice from the tomato slices ran down the man's face. Chicken slices flew in all directions, and finally, a strip of bacon balanced itself over the waiter's ear for a second before it fell to his shoulder, where it teetered for another long second and then fell to the floor. Ben later told Saul Rubin that it was truly funny if you didn't look at the waiter's face. Fatty wiped his hands on his napkin, kissed the waiter on both cheeks, and sat down laughing his high-pitched giggle.

The crowd in the dining room roared along with him. Ben promised himself that he would never eat in public with Roscoe Arbuckle again. The waiter shook his head and the mashed sandwich fell off in pieces, sliding down his face and landing on the floor. Calmly, he picked up the water pitcher and emptied it over Fatty's head. There was a wonderful moment of silence, then the crowd cheered and howled with laughter. This was like pie throwing—first one, then the other. Now what?

Arbuckle, however, was stunned. This was clearly not in his scenario. The waiter fled while the crowd laughed and applauded in appreciation. Roscoe sat and sulked. He was wet and now the waiter was gone and he had no food. While the headwaiter searched for another sandwich, the first waiter returned with a policeman and had Roscoe Arbuckle arrested.

The hotel management tried to interfere, but the offended waiter insisted on full revenge. Several Chicago policemen assisted a screaming Arbuckle down the stairs and out the State Street entrance into a Black Maria waiting at the curb. It required the rest of the afternoon for Majestic's Chicago attorney to bail out Roscoe. Long lines of patrons in front of the Majestic Theatre in the Loop staged a small riot when it was announced Fatty would not appear that day.

Although Al and the girls continued to try to liven things up, the rest of the tour seemed like drudgery.

Jack Pickford looked down at the grave. Despite the slush underfoot, it was a brilliant winter day with a blue sky and sunshine that cast long shadows. As he stood there trying to remember Olive, a long black Marmon drew up next to the limousine that had carried him from Manhattan. A deliciously pretty blonde woman stepped out as the chauffeur stood at attention. She walked rapidly to a low mound of dirt that Jack had not remembered from his last visit. A new widow, dressed in black.

The earth was still mounded on Olive's grave, too. He wondered how long it would be until it lay as flat as the grass that surrounded it. The blonde seemed familiar, but he couldn't place her. She looked across at him and nodded. He sat on a stone bench and watched her. She wiped her eyes. He wished he could place her. Must be someone who had seen him at a party or knew him from his pictures.

She walked toward him. "Hello," she said, extending her hand. "I'm Marilyn Miller. My husband is over there." She jerked her head toward the grave decorated with red carnations. "What a lousy way to spend a Sunday."

"I'm Jack Pickford, but I guess you know that. I remember you now. We've met at parties."

"Well, I knew Olive from the Follies. She was a nice kid."

"Thanks. I'd forgotten you were in the Follies, too. Olive didn't talk much about her days in New York."

"Yeh. Flo could really lay them out if he wanted to. You heading back to town?"

"Sure. You need a ride?"

"No, but you could buy a girl a drink. I feel like I've been through a knothole. We could go to Jack and Charlie's or some place. I really don't want to go home alone."

"Be glad to! Never turned down a blonde in my life." Pickford smiled at her and offered her his arm.

"I've heard that about you."

"Tell me what else you've heard."

They walked back to the drive where the two limousines waited. One returned to Manhattan empty.

Years before, Saul Rubin had decided that if he listened to every piece of Hollywood gossip and tried to run it down, he would have no time for anything else. But when a number of disturbing stories began to accumulate about a single star of his, Rubin worried. Right now some of the most persistent stories concerned Wallace Reid.

"Wallie Reid could hardly stand up on the set today. He just sort of swayed, as if a high wind would topple him over."

"I hear Wallie Reid's all out of control. Jimmie Cruze had to rethink an entire scene in *Charm School* because Reid couldn't hold a paper out at arm's length. Hands shaking too much."

Saul Rubin asked Reid to have lunch with him in his private dining room. Wallie looked thinner, Rubin thought, but acted cheerful.

"It's been a long time. How's tricks?" He squeezed Rubin's hand in his powerful grip

"Things are fine, Wallie. Business has picked up a little. Recession scare is over now that Harding is almost in the White House."

Wallie smiled. "I only pay attention to my own grosses. I guess I ought to read *Hollywood Reporter* from cover to cover."

The waiter placed a fruit cup before each of them. Wallie lit a cigarette. "Nice to see you, Mr. Reid," the waiter said. He looked at the fruit, then at the cigarette. "Would you rather have something else?"

Reid looked startled. He smiled and hurriedly said, "No, no, Alfonso. This is fine." He smiled at Rubin and picked up his fork.

Rubin watched Wallie carefully as they talked. He ate practically nothing. "Fruit's good for you, Wallie. Aren't you the guy who used to drink orange juice by the quart?"

"I'm doing fine, Mr. Rubin. I'm just fine."

"Are you glad to be back with Jimmie on a picture again?" Rubin asked.

"Sure am. We're a good team. Jimmie did my best pictures, I think. He understands action. Although I certainly liked working with DeMille on *Anatole*."

Wallie became animated and leaned toward Rubin as the waiter picked up the fruit he had hardly touched. "Tell me about *Forever*. What chance do I stand to get the part?"

"A very good one—if you don't lose any more weight. You're supposed to be a hero, not a skeleton."

Wallie sat back. "I still have bad days, Mr. Rubin. But I'll be in shape soon. I've hired a trainer. Work out every day."

The waiter placed a steak in front of Reid. Rubin smiled.

"I remembered how you love steak. Go ahead. Start. Wallie, we have something serious to talk about." The waiter passed vegetables. Reid helped himself and slowly began to eat his steak, as though with difficulty.

"Wallie, there are some unattractive rumors floating around about you. I thought rather than worry about them, I'd just nip them in the bud and ask you directly."

Wallie cut another piece of steak and put it in his mouth.

Rubin was keeping his voice light, inconsequential. "At first everybody thought you were drinking too much. Nasty little scenes on the set. Bad temper, tantrums. Not the sweet guy, Wallie Reid, who is worshipped by the crews. But recently the stories have taken a different turn."

Reid stopped eating and watched Rubin intently.

"Eat, Wallie, eat. Got to get your weight back up." Rubin looked up from his plate suddenly. "Drugs, Wallie. Drugs is what the rumors said. Of course, I paid no attention."

Reid opened his mouth to speak but no sound came out. Then he managed to say, "Of course," in a strangled way.

Rubin laid down his fork and knife. He leaned forward and in an intense voice said, "Wallace Reid, you are an honorable man. We've known each other for years. I know you would not lie to me. Are you on drugs?"

The fork fell from Reid's hand and clattered on the plate. He held up his hand, a solemn look on his face, eyes almost filled with tears.

"Honest to God. On my children's lives," his voice quavered with emotion, "I'm not on drugs."

"I believe you, Wallie."

"Mr. Rubin, you know me. I'm strong. Jesus, I'm strong. I had a little trouble for a while. I got used to being on painkillers for my headaches. It took some doing to get off them. I still hurt from time to time and it makes me jumpy. But I whipped it. Simple as that." He held out his hand. It was steady. "Look," he said.

"I believe you, Wallie."

Reid sighed with relief. "I know you do."

"Now finish your steak. I want to see you eat all of it." Rubin smiled happily. "Tell me about the kids," he said, cheerfully. "No, don't talk, just eat."

"I'm calling because I don't want it written down in a cable, that's why, Mr. Weiss. I had Wallie Reid to lunch and asked him directly if he was on drugs. He looked me right in the eye and said 'no.' "

"How do you know he wasn't lying?" Weiss said slowly. "Addicts will do anything to protect themselves."

"I'm sure he wasn't. I think he *was* on drugs, though. But he shrugged it off. That boy has character, Mr. Weiss."

"I hope he has a lot of it, Mr. Rubin. And I hope you are not a fool. He's worth a million dollars a year in profits. Gets more valuable every year. Makes fifty million women wet their pants every two months like clockwork. We can't afford for him not to have character, Mr. Rubin."

"I had a thought," Rubin said hurriedly. "Maybe it's not drugs. Maybe a cancer or something. I made him promise to see Dr. Stein. He said he'd drop by the Hospital Bungalow this afternoon and get a complete physical. If there is anything wrong, Stein will find it."

"Thank you for the cheerful long distance. You move so happily from addiction to a cancer. Finding that he is not an addict, but has a cancer, is a real solution to our problem." Weiss hung up.

37

March 1921, New York and Dallas

"I think it is safe for Lynch to come out from under cover. Send him a wire." Weiss smiled at Charles Grossman. "It's time to put Falcon's million dollar deposit to work."

"Hulsey has applied to his bank for a new loan. Wants to build a new picture house in Dallas."

Weiss sat up straight. "When did you find that out?"

"Just this morning. Our man in Dallas. This wire just came in. I brought it to you first."

"Hulsey has been one of my objectives all along." Weiss rubbed his hands in glee. "Just think, all of Texas and Oklahoma in one deal." His voice trailed off as a new idea presented itself. "If we don't announce any takeover of the Hulsey properties, just let him keep managing them in exchange for not bankrupting him, we could have another

221

secret member on the First National board. Oh, word would get out somehow. But wouldn't it drive Tom Talley crazy, not knowing?"

"Hulsey will cooperate," Grossman said. "He has a regular revolving credit from the bank for about a half a million. The bank will call that in. Then we can name our own terms. I'll send the wire."

Lynch and the twelve men who traveled with him registered into a small hotel on the south side of Dallas. Lynch signed the register as representative of The Texas Theatre and Amusement Co.

Lynch made no particular effort to stay out of sight. Several of his men fanned out across the two states and asked a number of theater owners if their houses were for sale. When told they were not, Lynch's men thanked the owners politely and left town in the big black touring cars that had become such a fearful sight parked in front of one theater after another all over the South.

Some of the owners, especially those in small towns, began to carry guns. No one could patronize a picture house in Dallas without passing an armed guard.

Amos Lynch filed incorporation papers for his new company. On the same day Edward Hulsey tried to extend his loan to build a big first-run house in the center of Dallas. Business wasn't all that good, but the rumors about Lynch helped make up his mind. That morning a Federal Reserve order for a million dollars was deposited in the account of The Texas Theatre and Amusement Company.

Hulsey strolled into the bank and asked to extend his loan for another two hundred thousand dollars. He was turned down for the first time in twenty years. Two days later all of Hulsey's notes were called in by the bank. He found it impossible to raise the cash anywhere to pay them off. Selling the theaters was the only way to stave off bankruptcy and ruin. After a few days of sparring through newspaper advertisements, Hulsey sought out Lynch in his hotel room.

It was hot and flies buzzed. The pretty Mexican woman who opened the door disappeared. Lynch lay in sweat-soaked B.V.D.s on an unmade bed, smoking a cigar and fanning himself.

Hulsey, in a white suit, stood in the center of the room. "You Lynch?"

"The one and same."

222

"Can I sit down?"

"If you want to."

"What do you offer me for the entire chain?"

"You get right down to brass tacks, don't ya? Don't worry none. I'll pay ya what it's worth. I'm not here to fuck nobody but the girls."

Hulsey laughed. "Not much. If you weren't here, I wouldn't be here."

"You gotta meet certain terms. You get paid a fair price, but you gotta meet those terms. I may own The Texas Theatre Company, but it's a front for an investor. I act for him."

Hulsey smiled. "Everybody knows that Abe Weiss and Majestic are behind you. It's common knowledge."

"You said it. I didn't. Anyway, no one's proved it yet. You keep your nose clean and play your cards right, and you could end up a pretty rich man."

"I was a rich man," Hulsey said bitterly.

"Then stay that way. You continue to operate the theaters as if nothing had happened. No word leaks out. You get paid for managing and get a fair price for the chain. Pretty good deal?"

Hulsey looked at Lynch with distaste. "I agree to meet your terms. Now let's talk money. How much do you offer?"

Within three days the papers were drawn up and The Texas Theatre Company was the new owner of the Hulsey chain. Although rumors spread, Hulsey kept the secret. Lynch and his men left town and rumors intensified.

Weiss chuckled at the idea of Hulsey sitting in at confidential meetings of the First National board. When they talked by telephone, he found Hulsey less bitter than he expected.

Weiss now had so many representatives at First National meetings that Tom Talley found it unwise to discuss anything at all. Unable to stand the uncertainty about Hulsey, Talley asked him directly at an exhibitors' convention.

"Ed, the word I get is that you sold out to Majestic. What's the real story? It won't go any further, but I got to have a yes or a no from you."

Hulsey laughed to show he had taken no offense. "Golly, Tom, I just can't understand your asking a question like that. Have you noticed that I've lost interest in First National projects or anything?"

"You're not answering my question."

"Maybe I don't intend to. One way or the other. Kind of

223

insulting to ask a man you've done business with for years if he sold out. You ever been in that position?"

"You know I haven't."

"Well, siree, don't put me in it, or you'll regret it. Even if we are friends."

"Oh, Christ, Ed. I'm half crazy with Weiss buying up franchised theaters. I don't know which way to turn. We had him on the run there for a while. Now I think *he's* chasing *us*. He's got this whole industry by the balls. I can't keep my legs together anymore from hurtin'. First National is the only thing in this industry that's keeping him from owning the motion picture business lock, stock, and barrel. Don't you help him wreck it. He wants it all his own. And he's nearly got it. We gotta stand up to him or he'll run us out of business."

Hulsey said gently, "You don't know how right you are, Tom. Give him a chance and you're lost. If you lose your theaters, the ones you spent your whole life building up, you'll never quite get over it."

Talley looked up quickly at the sad note he detected in Ed's voice. Hulsey walked away and Talley watched him with a speculative eye. He had said it. Without saying it, exactly, he'd said it. He had sold out. Jesus, if a fighter like Hulsey had sold out, the pressure must have been terrible. Talley wondered if Ed still had both his balls. It must have taken something terrible to make him sell to Weiss.

Moses Klein looked at Abe Weiss. He laid the newspaper on his desk. "Yes, I read it on the train. They're going to get us yet."

"Us? I never made a dirty or degenerate picture yet. No mother or father ever had to put a hand over the eyes of the youngest child in a Majestic house. Even babes in arms can attend and not be upset. What do you mean, us?"

"Mr. Weiss, I meant the industry. Censorship. It's on the way."

"But why? A few *schmucks* making cheap pictures on Poverty Row, that's why. They get a little dirty and the sermons start pouring from the pulpits. The Women's Clubs rise up in arms. Why don't they go to a Majestic house and see how clean and upstanding we are?"

"Why should they? They like to campaign against dirt."

"So what's new?" Weiss asked. "Pictures got the only censorship now. Name me a state where a board watches out for magazines or newspapers or even the legitimate stage, yet? There was never official government censorship of any kind in the United States of America until pictures came along. They've been considered sinful since peep-show days. I remember when nickelodeons were sinful because they were dark! More girls been ruined by pictures than by books now, I'll bet."

"I know, Mr. Weiss. I know. You got censorship already in some states. I could name a dozen. Maryland, Pennsylvania, New York, Illinois. You got red-light districts running full tilt, young boys half price until five o'clock in some towns, and your pictures can't play there. Immoral influence!"

Weiss threw the newspaper in the basket and sighed. "You should be at an exchange when the prints come back. In every town they cut a different scene. No one knows what to censor out. You know sin. I know sin. Only the censors can't tell." He laughed bitterly.

Klein grew serious. "It's no laughing matter. We could be out of business one of these days."

"Not if we're smart, Mr. Klein. I've been thinking. We should throw them some kind of a bone. Like a barking dog. Keep them quiet by letting them chew on something." He pressed the tips of his fingers together. "I don't quite know what it is yet. But unless we clean house publicly, say we're going to be good, grass may be growing on the stages at Majestic."

"You sound alarmed, Mr. Weiss. No picture has been banned outright yet." He sighed. "But that may be only a matter of time."

Weiss closed his eyes for a moment. "We have to look like we've cleaned up. Not that we're doing anything dirty. It just looks like that sometimes. I must talk to Ben Sommers. Too many whispers of sensation in the advertising. Pictures sold on sizzle. 'Drenched in passions too bold to be described.' It's that kind of bullshit that gives us a bad name. Cecil gets a little ripe once in a while, too. But his passions are really quite tame.

"Middle-aged clubwomen, whose husbands wouldn't know a bold passion if it bit them, read the lobby displays and the fat is in the fire."

"Maybe we ought to listen to Charles Pettijohn."

"Pettijohn is a political hack."

"Hack or not, he has some powerful friends. I see him moving right along in Washington all the time," Klein said.

He opened his hands for emphasis. "Mr. Weiss, Pettijohn's idea of a czar in charge of cleanup is a good one. Look what Judge Landis did for baseball after the White Sox scandals last year."

"The moving picture industry is not a baseball game," Weiss growled. He turned and stared moodily out of the window. "I'll think about it."

Charles Pettijohn was waiting in the lobby of Delmonico's when Weiss and Klein arrived. The men shook hands and walked up the stairs to Weiss's table, as a number of motion picture executives stopped eating to watch the procession across the main dining room.

Pettijohn turned to Weiss.

"Word of this meeting will be all over New York by midafternoon."

Weiss nodded in agreement. "That's why we're eating here."

After their order was taken, Weiss sat back and looked at Pettijohn. "I heard a lot about you from Mr. Klein here and from Lewis Selznick."

"Yes, a friend of mine, Will Hays, who is well connected in Washington, helped a friend of Mr. Selznick's get through some red tape on Ellis Island with a minimum of trouble."

"So I heard."

Moses Klein laughed. "Well connected. That's a modest way to describe the Postmaster General. Tell us your idea, Mr. Pettijohn."

Pettijohn leaned toward Weiss and lowered his voice. "The Republicans have never forgotten that Ince's picture, *Civilization*, was a major factor in getting Wilson reelected for his second term. I'm a Democrat and I was delighted, but many of my best friends are Republicans." He laughed. "That's the political equivalent of saying some of my best friends are Jews, I suppose. But it's true. You know about the extensive use of motion pictures in getting President Harding into the White House. Will Hays was in charge of that. Hays was the man who thought of your newsreels and got the President to pose for them during the campaign. Cox ignored them and he lost. So Harding gave Will the Post Office. I must say, he's getting it back in shape, too.

"I would like to see the industry approach Will Hays with an offer. Get him to be the 'moving picture czar' and clean up the industry. He can only do good. He is above reproach, well connected in Washington," he smiled and nodded at Klein, "and can improve the appearance of the entire industry."

"Would he leave a high government post for us?"

"You offer him enough money and he would."

"What's enough money?"

"A hundred thousand dollars a year. Firm contract, one the industry can't cancel."

They ate silently for a long time.

"How would Hays operate?" Weiss finally asked.

"Form an industry organization. His salary would be paid by all the production companies. He would represent you in Washington and counter unfortunate publicity and any attempts to institute greater censorship from women's club movements and the like."

Weiss stood up, signaling that lunch was finished. He and Pettijohn shook hands. "Thank you for meeting with us. I will give your suggestion some thought and let you know what I think of it."

"Are you inclined to be favorable at this moment?"

"I never give snap judgements."

"I understand. Thanks for lunch."

Weiss watched Pettijohn get into a taxicab and then started to walk. "I'll see you back at the office in one hour, Mr. Klein. I want to think."

He started down Fifth Avenue walking briskly in the spring sunshine.

38

April 1921, New York and Hollywood

Photoplay

MAJESTIC STUDIOS LIKE SMALL CITY

Nothing was lacking as far as this reporter was concerned, even to a bouquet of lovely gladiolus on the librarian's desk in the Library Bungalow, as in any big city library.

The busiest place, though, was the Fan Mail Bungalow, a cute Normandy style cottage with low eaves and a rippled shingle roof to emphasize the quaintness of the architecture. Inside it was anything but quaint. It was all business as a dozen girls attempted to cope with the ten thousand letters that arrive each week.

The Four Horsemen of the Apocalypse opened at the Lyric Theatre on March 6th, 1921. Instead of the usual polite applause from the invited audience, there were roars of approval. During the following days women were said to faint in the aisles as they watched an unknown actor, Rudolph Valentino, slink into a cabaret, take a cigarette from between his lips, grind it out beneath the heel of his gaucho boot, then stalk Alice Terry like a beast of prey. Women took to screaming during the notorious tango scene.

By the third day word spread throughout the industry that a sensational new star had appeared. Metro rushed Valentino into *Camille* with Alla Nazimova, then into *Eugenie Grandet*, again with Alice Terry. There was only a week between pictures for costume fittings. Valentino, already separated from his lesbian wife, Jean Acker, was served with divorce papers. He was furious; the marriage had never been consummated, and she had charged him with desertion and neglect, demanding three hundred dollars a month and attorney's fees. Valentino, who was broke, asked Richard Rowland, president of Metro, for a fifty-dollar raise from the four hundred dollars a week he received. Roland told him he was only beginning his career and couldn't expect more.

Meanwhile, in New York, three thousand people a day were standing in line to see *The Four Horsemen*. Within three weeks of its opening, Metro foresaw that, with the possible exception of United Artists' *The Three Musketeers* with Douglas Fairbanks, it had the top money-making picture of the year. *The New York Times Sunday Magazine* featured a glowing essay on the film as its cover story, illustrated by stills of Rudolph Valentino.

Desperate about his financial plight, Valentino grew unruly on the set of *Eugenie Grandet*. He refused to appear on time, sulked in his dressing room, took exception to the costumes. He had also fallen in love with a designer named Natasha Rambova and wanted all the more to be free of his wife. He remembered a note of congratulations he'd received from Saul Rubin at Majestic, put on his best suit, and took the Pacific Electric car to Majestic Way.

Saul Rubin looked up from his desk to see Valentino standing in the doorway and Helen behind him protesting that he had no appointment.

"Will you see me? I will wait if necessary."

Rubin waved her out. "Please sit down, Mr. Valentino. Can I get you a drink?"

"Please. I am agitated. Thanks for your kind letter. You are the only one thoughtful enough to write in all Hollywood." Weiss, who had been alerted to Valentino's situation, had ordered Rubin to write the note.

Rubin acknowledged the thanks with a graceful nod. "I meant every word of it. It is a very good performance in a very good film. That woman writer, June Mathis, was right about the book, about what she did with it, and most of all, about you."

"She is a wonderful lady. She understands me." He leaned forward anxiously. "Am I worth four hundred and fifty dollars a week to you? They will not give me more at Metro, and I need the money badly."

Hoping against hope, Rubin asked about his contract with Metro.

"I have not a contract. I work from picture to picture. I ask fifty dollar more for the next picture. Rowland say no."

He sagged down in the chair and looked at Rubin through eyes blurred with strain.

Rubin stood up, mentally rubbing his hands together. "How does five hundred dollars a week sound to you? To start with, of course."

The following week fan mail figures showed that Valentino was drawing more mail than all the other Metro stars together. The April issue of *Photoplay* printed its first photo of Rudy and women battled on the streets for copies. The issue sold out nationally in four days, and the page was ripped out of the magazine in beauty parlors and public libraries.

Rowland, tired of stories of Valentino's temper, decided that the raise he'd asked for might make his new star more tractable. He told Rudy that Metro had reconsidered his raise. He could have the four hundred and fifty. All smiles, Valentino told Rowland that he now worked for Majestic at five hundred. A five-year contract.

Rubin hired June Mathis the following week. She informed him that Majestic already owned the rights to a property that would be ideal for Rudy. It was a romance written by an English spinster, Ethel Maude Hull. Though it had been considered too risqué to film, Mathis assured Rubin that she could adapt *The Sheik* for Valentino in a way that would be both electrifying and safe.

With misgivings, Rubin finally approved.

"Oh, Ben! It's Tom's Lagonda. How did you get it?"

"I bought it from his estate. I almost bought the Marmon, too. But I decided that was silly. What do I need with a great big boat like that?"

"You're pretty extravagant as it is." She stepped back to admire the low roadster. "But it's nice. Can you afford it?"

"Well, I'm making more than a thousand dollars a week now. The new bungalow is only a bit more expensive than the old one. I don't have a passel of servants, just the cleaning lady and laundry. I just keep salting it away in the bank." He glanced at her. "And there's no one to spend it on." There was a pause. He ran his hand over the leather seat. "Say, remember that guy Cotton? The banker from New York?"

"I think the inside is really beautiful. I miss Tom. He was a very nice man. I feel close to him in here."

Ben was silent for a minute. "I miss him, too. He was one of the few men I enjoyed talking to." There was another pause. Ben slipped into the driver's seat and closed the door. "You know, I really miss your company, too."

"You said something about that man Cotton."

Ben sighed. "Yeh. It's funny what this place can do to you. I saw him at Tom Ince's party last Saturday and hardly recognized him. He's gone native. He's in real estate now, making a bundle. Good, huh?"

"The rich get richer."

"Elsie, I have to drive over to Universal and interview a young guy. They're giving me an assistant. He's supposed to be very good in publicity. He handled all von Stroheim's pictures for Laemmle. It was his idea to put the line through the S in Stroheim and make it into a dollar sign." He took her hand. "Please come."

She sighed. "Well, I have to be back later this afternoon."

"I'll get you back in time," he said quickly.

Beginning at the top of Highland Avenue, Cuhuenga Pass wound up through the Hollywood Hills to the San Fernando Valley to the north. The paving stopped at the first grade, and the road became a rocky shelf, one lane wide, cut into the canyon wall halfway up on the western side. Opposite, on the eastern wall, a similar shelf held the Pacific Electric car tracks.

"Sensible people take the electric cars," shouted Elsie. "This is awful."

At the bottom of the trail on the Valley side, they drove toward a tall grove of trees, dark against the ruddy hills in the distance. A large sign informed them that they were approaching the Universal Film Manufacturing Company.

"Looks like a phony Spanish mission," Elsie said.

Broad white plaster walls were supported by tile-roofed buttresses. Above the walls they could see a number of towers with arched openings where mission bells should have hung. On each side of the road stood a double row of towering old eucalyptus trees. The air was filled with their spicy scent mixed with the smell of horses.

"I guess they don't call this the 'Home of the Westerns' for nothing," said Ben. "Look at that."

In front of them a rodeo was in progress. A horse thundered past, and the cowboy dropped a red bandana on the ground. He reined up quickly and hanging onto the side of his horse, neatly picked up the bandana from the ground with two fingers as he rode past. He waved it in a salute to Elsie, who stood up and applauded him.

"A pretty trick for a pretty lady," said a voice above her. A tall man on horseback had ridden up behind them and was sitting next to the roadster. As Elsie looked up at him in surprise, he smiled at her. She met his gaze, then lowered her eyes. There was something unmistakable about the way he was looking at her.

"Quite a show goin' on," Ben shouted over his shoulder.

"Oh, this is nothin'. Jes' a little cuttin' up." The cowboy leaned down so he could be heard as a horse galloped past. "My name's Kennard. Kelso Kennard. I got me a little spread over there a ways."

"You ride in pictures, Mr. Kennard?" Ben asked.

"Once in a while. Mostly I jes' ride over to see what's excitin'."

Elsie wondered if his teeth were really so white or if it was only the contrast between them and his deeply tanned face.

Ben turned off the engine. "Is it like this every day?"

"Oh, this here's quiet. No castin' goin' on today. So everybody comes over jes' to practice ropin' and chew the fat and amuse the ladies." He grinned. The ladies were sitting in the shade dressed as Mexican maidens or pioneer mothers.

While he and Ben watched the riders, Elsie stared at Kennard. He was tall and lean, with black hair that curled around his ears, much longer than was fashionable. His angular face was deeply creased, and his eyes were the most intense blue she had ever looked into. Elsie could hardly take her eyes off him. He was far too rugged to be really good-looking. Not like a leading man, she thought, but terribly attractive anyway. He saw that she was looking at him and his eyes flickered. She felt herself blushing and was furious for reacting like a schoolgirl.

Ben reached up his hand. "Name's Sommers. This is Elsie Wright. We work over at Majestic. Drove out here to take a look."

There was a sudden commotion over by the studio gates, where a grey-haired man rode up on a beautiful palomino. Everyone was excited and hats were thrown into the air. Someone shot at one of the hats, sending it spinning. Kelso skillfully kept his horse steady when it wanted to rear. He stood up in the stirrups and Elsie noticed the spectacular silver mountings on his saddle. Maybe he was a star after all. But then wouldn't she have known about him?

"Who's that?" she asked.

"Why that's Wyatt. Wyatt Earp. He comes by every once in a while. Some of the boys grew up in Tombstone and remember him from when they was small. They talk about olden times." He tipped his hat to Elsie. "I'll jus' mosey over and pay my respects."

She knew that he was still looking at her and sat down suddenly.

"Who's Wyatt Earp?" she asked, trying to detain him but not looking at him.

Kelso reined up his horse. "Earp? You never heard of Wyatt Earp? Miss Wright, he was jus' about the greatest peace officer in the West. Wyatt is famous, ma'am."

She let herself blush, relieved to have an excuse.

"I'm sorry. I just never heard of him. Not up on peace officers, I guess."

"Wyatt's good for the movies," Kelso continued, "because he was there. He can tell those greenhorn dudes that direct the pictures how it was. I'll jus' go over and say howdy, now. Glad to have met you, ma'am," he said, raising his white hat. "You, too," he shouted at Ben as he rode away.

A hundred feet in front of the car he stopped and twirled his lariat in a flat circle, parallel to the ground. The beautiful roan pony stepped in and out of the ring of rope, lifting his feet high, stepping lightly. When he finished he turned toward the Lagonda where Ben and Elsie stood clapping. The pony bowed toward them and stamped his feet.

"What a character! Kinda nice fellow, though." Ben said as he sat down and started the engine. He grinned sideways at her. "You caught his eye." The Lagonda started toward the gates, moving slowly through the crowd. Everyone waved as the car crept past, and the cowboys doffed their Stetsons.

The streets inside Universal City were lined with big old pepper trees with their clusters of dry red berries and feathery foliage touching the pavement in many places. It seemed more like a friendly little town than a picture studio. Ben parked in front of what had been a big farmhouse. There were awnings at the windows and a row of hickory rockers lined up on the wide porch.

"I've never met Uncle Carl Laemmle, but it looks like somebody named Uncle Carl runs it, doesn't it?" Ben asked.

"I'll wait out here. I don't want to sit inside on a day like this." Elsie found a bench in the shade of the pepper trees, leaned back and closed her eyes.

"He just abandon you here?" the deep voice woke her up. It was the cowboy. His spurs tinkled as he moved toward her.

233

"Oh! Hello." Elsie was suddenly alert. "You seem to be everywhere."

"Well, they use my ranch for picture makin' so I'm on good terms with the people hereabouts. Can I sit down, ma'am?" he asked, sitting down.

"A ranch?" She studied his face. "Are you really a cowboy? Or are you just an actor?"

"I'm real. It's better bein' real than bein' in pictures. What pictures you been in, ma'am?" His eyes glanced quickly over all of her.

"Oh, I'm not an actress," she said modestly, moving away from him slightly. "I've just become a writer. I write titles. Do you work here?"

"Oh, I get around. I do lots of tricks with Thunder, over there. Work at Fox some with Tom Mix. I made some action pictures at Majestic a while back with Wallie Reid. I work around."

He leaned closer. She put out her hand and pushed him away.

"You have to let up a little if you expect me to stay and chat with you," Elsie said uneasily. "You're pressing too hard."

Kennard looked down at the hat he clutched in both hands. "I apologize, Miss Wright. That's the name, isn't it?"

"Yes, Elsie Wright."

"I . . . I didn't mean to force my attentions on you." He sat silently turning the hat in his hands then grinned at her. "That's a dadburned lie. I did too. The minute you drove off I hightailed it in here lookin' for where you'd got to." The creases in his face deepened as he smiled. "I never saw anyone I thought was so pretty. You knocked me off my feet."

"Well, I didn't mean to."

"Oh, I'm glad you did. Made my day, that's what it did. You're better than seein' Wyatt."

Elsie burst out laughing.

Ben came out onto the porch of the office bungalow and stopped short. The couple sitting so cosily on the bench in the shade of the pepper tree was Elsie and that damned cowboy. Son of a bitch! There he was talking away, and Elsie was laughing like a fool.

"Ready to go?" he asked as he walked up to them.

"Just a minute, Ben, wait till Kelso finishes his story."

Kelso said to Elsie, "It'll keep. Some other time."

"Do you think there'll be one?" Elsie asked.

"Oh, we'll see each other at a party or something. I go to a lot of Hollywood parties. Or else I'll look you up at Majestic. I get into town every so often."

"I'm glad I wasn't gone any longer," Ben said airily. "You move in fast, don't you, cowboy?"

Kelso smiled coolly. "The lady didn't tell me your brand was on her."

Elsie stood up, her eyes like green ice. "This is ridiculous!" She turned toward Kelso. "Brand, indeed!" she snapped disgustedly. To Ben, "And if a brand was on me," she said turning, "it wouldn't be yours!" Then in a softer voice she added, "I'm sorry, Kelso, I hope we do see each other real soon."

Ben snapped his fingers. "That's where I've seen you before. It's been bothering me. At the billiard table at Wallie Reid's house."

"Probably," he answered reservedly. "I worked on a few pictures with him."

"See you around sometime." Grasping her arm firmly, Ben steered Elsie back to the automobile. She looked back over her shoulder at Kelso, who tipped his hat, then after putting it back on, brushed his hand up against the brim on one side, setting it at a cocky angle. He winked at her as if they shared a secret.

The ride back to Los Angeles was silent, and Ben felt that something had gone wrong, but he didn't want to risk a quarrel. Every so often something happened that defied reason. Now, why had that tall ugly cowpoke been so interesting to her? She didn't have to be polite to every tinhorn extra and stunt man in the business. Women were crazy, honest to God. Harder to handle even than a motorcar on this road he decided as he swerved around a sharp curve. When he couldn't stand the silence a minute longer he asked, "Are you going to say something?"

"There's nothing to say. You've said it all." She calmly gazed straight ahead.

"You still want to go to Bill Taylor's with me?"

"Of course I want to go to Bill's. I wouldn't miss it for the world." Then she smiled angelically, which made Ben feel more uneasy than ever.

Two limousines were parked on Alvarado just below the bungalow court, and Ben parked behind them. He helped Elsie out and said hello to Taylor's chauffeur, Courtnay, who was lounging against a fender smoking a cigarette, talking to another driver. Courtnay stood up straight and tipped his cap, trying to hold the smoke behind him. Ben tried to put a guiding hand around her shoulder as they went up the walk, but she sidestepped it.

He touched the bell. Ben had described Taylor's place to her, and he wanted her to see it, but it would be too bad if she was going to act strange and standoffish.

"Mr. Taylor's expecting you, Sir. Miss," said Henry at the door. He nodded at Elsie. "Can I get you something to drink?"

"Usual for me, Henry. What about you, Elsie?"

"Nothing yet, thanks. Let me look around first."

As they entered, Bill Taylor rose from an armchair where he had been sitting. Opposite, on the sofa next to an older woman, sat Mary May Maxwell dressed like a little child with a short ruffled skirt, long white stockings, black Mary Janes, a pale blue ribbon in her long blonde corkscrew curls.

"This must be Elsie." Taylor turned to Ben with an admiring smile. "You dog, you. You said she was lovely, but I had no idea." Elsie warmed to him as he took her hand. "My dear, meet two good friends. This is the talented Mary May Maxwell, and this is her wonderful mother, Carlotta Sheldon."

Mrs. Sheldon nodded sternly, her mouth a grim line, as Ben shook hands with Mary.

"Hiya, Mary. *Don't Call Me Little Girl* looks wonderful. I just approved the stills. Some of them are the best ever."

Mary smiled. "Thank you, Ben." He thought he had never seen a prettier girl—like a pink rosebud or a valentine.

Taylor was talking to Mrs. Sheldon, who was regarding Ben with a suspicious stare. "Miss Wright worked with me as a script girl but now has moved up to our title department. She is writing some of the best titles we get. Mr. Sommers—Ben—is in charge of promotion and publicity."

"Why, I told you about Ben, Momma," Mary said. "He's the man who gets my picture in all of the papers and magazines." She smiled sweetly up at him, then lowered her eyelashes ever so slightly.

Mrs. Sheldon tried to smile at him. She paid no attention to Elsie. "I'm thrilled, Mr. Sommers. Mary, you naughty little girl." Mrs. Sheldon waggled a fat finger toward her daughter. "Why haven't you asked Mr. Sommers to tea?" Mrs. Sheldon attempted her smile again with somewhat better results. Practice makes perfect, Ben thought. Why does she insist on talking to Mary as if she were twelve years old? Everybody knows that she's twenty.

Mrs. Sheldon patted the air beside the armchair as she sat down. "Draw up that chair, Mr. Sommers. Do sit beside me. Let's make up for lost time." She called out toward the kitchen door. "Henry, after you've given Mr. Sommers his drink, I'd like a teentsy bit more sherry."

Bill sat down in the center of the sofa with Mary on one side and Elsie on the other. Mrs. Sheldon shot a wary glance at him but then evidently decided there was safety in numbers. While being talked at by Mrs. Sheldon, Ben watched Taylor murmur flatteries at both women, one after the other, walking a high wire with skill and nonchalance. As he turned to Elsie, he casually placed his arm along the back of the sofa and his fingers lightly caressed Mary's shoulder.

Ben wondered if Mrs. Sheldon was conscious of the adoration her daughter was showing toward Bill—open, even rapturous. Maybe that's why the mother came along as chaperone. If he were Mary's mother he wouldn't leave the moonstruck daughter alone with Taylor for one minute. He wondered if Mrs. Sheldon had seen any of the suggestive messages on the photographs of women in the dining room. Then, catching a furtive glance she darted at Bill, a sudden thought crossed his mind. Maybe Mrs. Sheldon knows all about Taylor from personal experience.

Carlotta Sheldon tapped Bill on the knee. "Bill, dearest, we must be going. Mary has lines to learn. And an early call. She is a growing girl and she needs her rest. Don't you, dear?" Mary hurriedly nodded.

As they were saying good-bye, Carlotta turned to Bill.

"I don't like to pry into your affairs, Bill, dearest, but I feel that I must speak out."

"What's wrong, Carlotta?"

"It's your man. Really, Bill, I'm just as tolerant as the next person, but don't you think Henry has gone too far?"

Taylor smiled brightly. "Oh, do you think so?"

"Well," she sniffed, "he *is* a pansy and he answers the doorbell with a crochet hook in his hand. It looks bad for your reputation, Bill, a single man, unmarried, living alone."

Taylor patted her hand. "Thank you for worrying about me, dear. I assure you that my reputation is such that no one who knows me believes that my tastes are similar to Henry's. You've been in show business for so long, I'd have thought that you would have grown used to eccentrics by now." He took her arm and forcibly turned her toward the walk. "I

237

know I have. Besides, I think it must be very difficult for a Negro to be homosexual—it's two strikes against a man. That's too many, I think. Henry is kind, not a cruel bone in his body. His tastes are not his own fault, as neither are yours or mine. We must not be too hasty to judge—first stone and all that rot, remember?"

She sighed, "Well, as you say. But ask him to leave his crocheting in the kitchen, please."

"I'll mention it to him. It's just that he feels so wonderfully at home with you, Carlotta, dear. It's the effect you have on people. They dare to be themselves with you. It's a rare talent." He let go of her arm and kissed her hand.

She stood on her toes and kissed him back, on the mouth. "You're outrageous, but I love you anyway. What a way you have." She stepped into the limousine, and Mary climbed in beside her. Mary's eyes drank in Bill's face as the motorcar turned away from the curb, and her fingertips, hidden from her mother's sight, fluttered good-bye.

Taylor sank down in the armchair and gulped his drink. Ben had shown Elsie all of the art objects and antiques in the bungalow, and now they were laughing over the inscriptions on the photographs.

"I hope you're broad-minded, Elsie." Taylor laughed as he saw her reading the inscriptions.

"You have to be to work in a movie studio."

"I suppose I shouldn't really hang them in such a public spot. But I think anyone who is going to be offended, I don't really want here anyway."

"We must go, Ben. My family expects me home for dinner." She turned to Bill, and with a trace of a mischievous smile she said, "Maybe you can straighten him out."

Taylor looked at her intently, then as she turned, glanced at Ben questioningly. Ben made a helpless gesture with his hands.

Taylor took Elsie's hands and looked at her seriously.

"He's a very nice young man, unusual in this day and age. You could do worse, I'll warrant. Don't be hard on him, my dear. It's not easy to come here and be submerged in all of this fantasy world without any preparation for it. Help him. He needs you."

Elsie looked at Bill for a long time. Then she kissed him on the cheek. "You're a good friend. A truly good friend."

The barber chair was lowered back gently and Wallace Reid opened his eyes and smiled up at Herbie.

"Hiya, Herbie. How's tricks?"

"Just great, Wallie, now that you're back regular. God, I missed you. Are you feeling better?"

"Tip-top. Tip-top." Wallie closed his mouth so Herbie wouldn't get it full of lather as he shaved him. He didn't know if he could endure lying still during the shave. His nerves were jumping, and he could feel points of pain and prickles in his arms and legs that made it hard for him to lie still.

"Boy, are you a bundle of nerves this morning. You'll be lucky if I don't cut your throat. Honestly, Wallie, lie still. Please."

Reid suddenly jerked off the bib and sat up. Herbie, startled, looked at him as if he had gone out of his mind.

"Goddamn it. I've shaved once this morning. Isn't once good enough for you?" Trembling, he stood up and glared at Herbie. "Just slap some makeup on my kisser and let me the hell out of here. Get this muck off my face." He seized a towel and wiped the lather off his face and threw the towel on the floor.

"I can't make you up unless you're shaved. You are getting so thin I have to put makeup all over your face. What are you yelling at me for? You stay up all night and drink yourself into a stupor, then when your nerves are shot you come and abuse me. Well, put on your own makeup. I can't make you look like Wallace Reid anymore. I've been trying every trick I know, but you look worse in every picture. I don't even go and watch the rushes, I'd just sit there in the dark and cry. I won't be a part of it. You're killing yourself. If you want to do it, fine, it's your life. But don't come in here and expect me to patch you up, because I won't."

Reid didn't know what to say. He reached out to pat Herbie on the shoulder, but thought better of it. He looked through the makeup laid out on the shelf and took a few jars and tubes to use on himself in his dressing room. He started out doing his own makeup in the old days before Herbie had come to Majestic. He'd have to do it again. Maybe a pill would stop his jitters. He'd take one as soon as he got back to the dressing room.

"I'm sorry, Herbie. My nerves are all shot to hell."

Herbie gave no sign that he had heard.

39

July 1921, Whitewash

Los Angeles Times, July, 1921

THOMAS TALLEY SELLS THEATER CHAIN IN SURPRISE MOVE
EXTENSIVE CHAIN SOLD TO SOL LESSOR

HOLLYWOOD. In a surprise move Thomas Talley sold his large chain of theaters to Sol Lessor today. Talley has been a major theater owner since he ripped out the shooting gallery of his arcade to show "flickers" in 1904.

Originally a cowboy who gave up the open range to open a shooting gallery, Talley had become a major industry figure because of his pioneering in First National, a gigantic theater chain, which also produces a large number of photoplays to be exhibited in the theaters of members.

No price was given, but it was believed to be in the several millions. Talley will retire to his extensive ranch and raise cattle.

The phone rang at a few minutes after six in the morning. "This is Abe Weiss." A wave of anxiety rolled through Ben's stomach. Weiss almost never phoned, and when he did his secretary announced him.

"Good morning, Mr. Weiss. How are you?"

"I don't have any time for idle chitchat," he snapped. "Listen carefully, as I won't repeat." Ben sat up straighter, straining to hear over the long-distance crackle on the line.

"Go ahead, I'm listening," he said, picking up a pencil.

He heard Weiss clear his throat. "Tomorrow or the next

day, but probably tomorrow, an unfortunate story will break in the Boston newspapers. I will try to get it killed here in New York, and our Boston exchange manager is already paying off whoever he can. We hope at least to get it played down. I want you to try and get it killed in Los Angeles and San Francisco. Especially in the Hearst papers. If that son of a bitch, Hearst, plays it up big, we're in awful trouble."

There was an ironic laugh. "I tell you confidentially that this couldn't come at a worse time, Ben. I'm talking to a high government official—asking him to become a czar of the industry to clean up the morals."

"I understand. It could be embarrassing." Ben paused, then asked, "Do you want to tell me the story?"

He could hear Weiss sigh. "Four years ago—it was March of '17—a lot of us went up to Boston for an industry tribute dinner. You know the kind of crap we do for the exhibitors." There was a silence, then he cleared his throat painfully. "Roscoe Arbuckle arranged a little party at a roadhouse in Wodburn afterward. There were a dozen or so of us. It got out of hand a little, and the police were called. No one was held or anything like that, but it would have looked very bad to our wives, and several of us were asking for big bank loans, so we paid off. Easy to do in Boston," he grunted. "Up to then, not too bad. Just hijinks. A little harmless whoopee." His voice sank lower. "But they have been blackmailing us." There was a long pause. "We been paying the district attorney of Middlesex County a hundred thousand dollars a year ever since."

Ben whistled softly. He put his pencil down. No notes.

"The new state attorney general found out and wants to get the Middlesex D.A. out of office because of it and is blowing the whistle on him. Now we don't look so good," he said angrily. "We're trying to hush it up, and now the attorney general wants to go to court and haul out all of our dirty linen and hang it in public."

Ben took a sip of coffee. "Who's involved? Just Majestic men?"

"Good God, no. All the biggest names. Besides me there's Saul Rubin, Marcus Loew, Zukor and Lasky of Paramount. Joe Green, Hiram Abrams of United Artists, Larry Klein, Joe Levenson, Harry Asher, Ed Golden. Some of us left early, but a few stayed all night." He cleared his throat again and seemed to have trouble speaking.

"Be square with me, Mr. Weiss," Ben said carefully.

"Something must have happened to make you pay all that money all these years."

"Nothing by the time I left," Weiss answered quickly. "But who would believe that? We're all rich men and at the time it seemed easier not to have to tell our wives." There was a long silence.

"Ben, you've met Bessie. She's a lovely woman and I wouldn't hurt her for the world. I told her last night." He drew in a deep breath and exhaled it very slowly. "She's very forgiving. Blamed herself. You're not married so you don't know, but sacrifice is very hard to live with. A few of us may end up divorced, God forbid"

"I'm terribly sorry, Mr. Weiss." Ben thought for a minute. "How much money can I spend?"

"Anything you want, Ben," he said eagerly. "The sky's the limit. Just ask and you'll get. Remember, the stock issue is going out and I don't want to be answering a lot of questions down at the bank. They wouldn't understand, anyway. Some of the wives are a lost cause. But maybe we can save the industry. Rubin may wish to give you more details." His voice distinctly chilled. "He stayed all night."

"I understand. We'll do everything we can."

Weiss hung up abruptly.

Ben sat for a few minutes overwhelmed by what he had to do. He remembered the conversation he'd had with Weiss about whitewashing a scandal. Well, here it was. It must have been more than a little whoopee. He decided to call his new assistant. A girl answered, and Ben felt like a prying father.

"Get Peter to the 'phone," he said.

"Hello?" Peter sounded sleepy.

"Answer your own goddamned telephone from now on. All I need is another scandal."

"Jeez, what's the matter, boss?" Peter sounded suddenly alert and a little scared.

"Peter, there's an emergency and I need your help. Get down to the office. See you in thirty minutes."

Ben closed the office door. Peter looked serious.

"I'm sorry about. . . ."

Ben cut him off. "Don't worry. It could happen to anybody. Peter, we have a whitewash job to do on an extremely delicate matter for Mr. Weiss."

"Mr. Weiss?"

"Yes."

"Golly."

Ben explained the situation to Peter. "Who do you know well enough on the staff of each paper to bribe into toning down any articles that are written?"

Peter looked doubtful. "If it was on the entertainment pages, I could do it in a minute. Do it all the time. Booze here, a little cocaine, a few bucks in the right places; hell, Ben, you know what we do. On cityside, I just don't know. Just start out and see what anyone wants to quash it, that's all."

"We got until tomorrow. That's when the hearings start. That gives us a little time."

Peter brightened. "That means the story won't break until the day after in Boston. The papers here won't get it until the day after that." He shrugged and grinned. "That gives us three whole days."

Ben narrowed his eyes, trying to remember. "There used to be two guys on the city desk at the *Times* who were always kidding me about getting them a date with a movie star."

Peter nodded. "Still there." He suddenly seemed to catch on and grinned brightly. "Hey, anything goes? Girls, the works?"

"Christ, yes. That's what I've been saying. This is important to all of us. Give anybody anything they want to kill the stories." He underlined each word for Peter. "Last thing, if they want girls, we have a suite set up at the Alexandria." He paused, considering, then continued. "It's designed for compromising fucking. You can threaten them with the film afterward."

A slow smile crept across Robinson's face. "Golly, you mean business, don't you?"

Ben closed his eyes, trying to be patient. "That's what I've been trying to tell you. You don't fool around when you're working for Abe Weiss." Ben lowered his voice. "Not when he's in trouble."

"How do I make arrangements? With a room like that, I could stop the German army."

"It's Room 914. The manager keeps the keys and controls the action. Paul Droste'll get the girls for you."

Peter stood up, eyes gleaming. "I'll make it pay off, Ben. You'll see. The city desks won't know what hit them."

"For God's sake, be careful. I don't want another scandal coming out of trying to whitewash this one."

Rubin sat back looking at Ben speculatively. Then he examined his fingernails carefully. Without looking up he asked, "Exactly what did Mr. Weiss tell you?"

Ben wished the man would look him in the eyes. "Not all that much, really. He said he left early, but that you stayed and to ask you for the details." He tried to sound light but wanted Rubin to realize the implied threat from Weiss.

A cynical smile spread across Rubin's face. He looked up.

"That's what they all said when the trouble started. If everyone left early, why did we all pay so much for so long, I ask you?"

Rubin's desk was placed in a great Tudor bay window of diamond-paned glass. Shafts of sunlight bathed his face. Suddenly he stood up and drew the draperies closed.

"I suppose you have to know." He held up his hands. "What the hell, it's between us men, OK? I'm told you get a lot of nookie yourself, so you won't be shocked by a few details?"

Ben shook his head. "Hardly. I'm not trying to pry into your private affairs, Mr. Rubin. It's just that I have to know what it is I'm trying to whitewash."

Rubin nodded. "I suppose." He turned his chair sideways and glanced at Ben sheepishly. "In the winter of 1916 I signed Roscoe Arbuckle to a long-term contract. We started him off on a cross-country public appearance tour of twenty-eight cities. A nightmare. Well, you know. You just been through it."

Ben nodded and blew out his breath.

"Only that time it was beyond belief. He got sick, lost weight, for God's sake. Nearly lost his leg from an infection, a real mess. He could hardly stand up, needed crutches on the train." He stood up and demonstrated Arbuckle's swaying figure. Ben laughed at the imitation; it was very good.

"Oh, it was wonderful. Hardly the image of the jolly fat man we were trying for." Rubin shook his head slowly, then continued, his manner less confident.

"When we got to the final city, Boston, the local exhibitors decided to use the occasion for an industry-wide tribute—a big banquet at the Copley Plaza." He closed his eyes as if remembering painful details. "The weather was foul—freezing rain. Roscoe was still on crutches and feeling mean. We were all tired and irritable as hell. The banquet was a pain in the ass and nobody wanted to go."

He stood up, put his hands in his pockets, nervously

touching his genitals. "So there sat several hundred exhibitors, all dying to be seen with the big picture moguls, their wives all dressed fit to kill and out of the house for the evening. And every politician in Boston." He seemed to be looking past Ben to the head table of long ago.

"Roscoe said we all needed a little break and set up a party for us to go to afterward. At the roadhouse he knew, a whorehouse, really, but nobody knew that at the time. In Woburn. He did it as a joke." He laughed humorlessly.

"Joke?" Ben asked, puzzled.

Rubin nodded, then stood up, walked behind his desk, occasionally leaning forward to straighten papers that were already precisely aligned. "Yeh. A joke on Woburn. Several years earlier, the town fathers had decided to ban the showing of all moving pictures in Woburn. Protect morals and all that crap." He put his hands on the desk and spread his fingers wide. "Of course they did nothing about the biggest and most interesting whorehouse in the whole Boston area. Pinkie O'Donnell's, running full tilt on the edge of town. The town fathers of Woburn could—and did—fuck to their hearts' content at Pinkie's." He smiled thinly. "But their kids were protected from the debauchery of the silver screen." The smile melted. "Funny joke. I got to hand it to Roscoe. He can really think them up."

Ben watched Rubin quietly. He was struck by his caustic tone. He hadn't sensed any bitterness against Arbuckle in Weiss, but it certainly showed in Rubin.

"There were sixteen of us in four cars. We gave each of the drivers a couple of free pops with the girls to while the time away," he said gleefully. "All we asked was that they stay sober enough to get us back to the hotel." He leaned back in his chair and looked expansive. "You'd have thought it was Christmas. All nice Irish, good Catholics, and good family men, all of them."

He looked at Ben to make sure he hadn't missed the point. "Well, they served a little supper. Chicken." He laughed at the unintentional double entendre. "The champagne started to flow and so did our juices." He paused thoughtfully. "Everything got a little out of hand." He slapped his thigh in a burst of laughter. "God, I wished DeMille was there. All that tame crap he stages and calls them orgies. Goddamn! We could have showed him a thing or two." He gazed toward the window, smiling, is if remembering certain details, then faced Ben, who smiled back at him.

"I've never been to an orgy."

"You ought to try it once. Everybody should. Actually, it was just a nice dirty party—no one even went upstairs. We just did it on the table and the floor. In the middle of the food."

His voice took on a confidential man-to-man tone. "The girls stuffed chicken breasts up their cunts for starters. Ever eat chicken that way?" Rubin laughed. Ben shook his head and Rubin smiled in a superior way. "Sure beats a knife and fork." He sighed. "I just threw my tuxedo away afterward." With a swift movement of his fingers he dismissed the dress suit. "It wasn't worth cleaning.

"Abrams paid the check. Over a thousand dollars." There was a certain pride in the way he said it. "It was daylight when we staggered out. I didn't even know the cops had been there. I was sore for days." He laughed and added, "Funny thing. Abrams wasn't even in the picture business then. He was Baseball Commissioner."

Rubin laughed. "It was 1917," he sighed. "Things were different then." He sat down, very serious again. "You know, when I first came out here, if you didn't take the girl sitting next to you at dinner upstairs for a fast one between courses, everyone thought you were a pansy. Or at least strange.

"Times are changing," he said to himself softly. "A month later the extortion started." He picked up an ivory letter opener and slapped it against his palm, emphasizing his sentences. "I always thought Pinkie got paid off to talk. A couple of the men had gotten rough, and one of them beat up one of the girls for fun, but the cops didn't do anything that night."

"Who got the money you paid?"

"The District Attorney. We also keep James Curley in cigars. And every tinhorn Irish politician in Boston has been financed by us for five years now. Curley personally helped make the arrangements."

"Who with? Mr. Weiss?"

"Not on your life! Our team of attorneys had a series of meetings with their attorneys in a hotel room like a goddamned contract negotiation with Doug Fairbanks." He shook his head in wonder. "They got no shame in Boston."

Rubin scowled, his face darkening with anger. "Then the D.A. referred to us—I can remember his exact words—as 'a bunch of debauched and licentious Jews!'" He glared at Ben. "You're a Gentile, you wouldn't understand."

246

Ben held up his hands as if to stop him. "But I do," he said softly. "Hypocritical bastard!"

"Pinkie told me he was a regular himself." He exhaled sharply. "The crowning touch was when he talked about 'deviated sexual practices'—I suppose that refers to the chicken eating." He snorted. "I bet everything known to man has been done in Woburn. Pinkie and her girls didn't learn anything new from us." With a slight smile he added, "They showed me a couple of tricks that were new to me."

Ben wondered what they could possibly be, but hesitated to ask.

"Buy a few girls some chicken dinner and some champagne and get a little harmless nautch, and you're buying your way out for years. Damned expensive chicken." Rubin sat glaring at Ben.

Ben waited for him to continue, but that was evidently all he intended to tell. "We have a choice, Mr. Rubin. We can try and convince everyone that there has been a terrible mistake made. I don't think that will wash. My advice is to try and kill the story wherever we can. Then our line will be that it was just a little drunken roadhouse fun blown all out of proportion. Millions of traveling men do it all the time. Let it all blow over. It was just good clean fun."

Rubin nodded a bit wryly. "Do you think you can handle the papers?"

"We're sure as hell going to try. There's only one danger, and Mr. Weiss hit it on the head."

"What's that."

"Not a what. Who. Hearst." Ben let the name sink in. "I've decided to call him up and ask him to play the story down."

"You've got as much chance as a snowball in hell."

"All I can do is try. If the Hearst papers don't pick it up, the story will die in a few days. Nobody else handles Hollywood scandals the way Hearst does. Except for the tabloids. And who cares about them? There's always a new murder to fill the front pages. They got a short memory."

Rubin brightened slightly. "Maybe I'll get rid of you yet. If Hearst says no, you'll be out on your ass, Sommers." A crafty look darted through his eyes. "Mr. Weiss know what you're up to?"

"Mr. Rubin, he said for me to handle it any way I see fit," Ben said calmly. "Spend any money, buy up anybody. I don't know what Hearst will want for his cooperation, but I'll give it a try."

Rubin laughed gleefully. "You're too wet behind the ears to know what you're doing. I wouldn't lift a hand to stop you."

"Or help either, I guess. Even if it's your career."

"You're right there. I told Weiss to get somebody with some experience in this job. But no, he wanted you."

Ben got up slowly and walked to the door. "Then I guess I have to repay his faith in me, don't I?"

"It's the least you can do." Rubin smiled unpleasantly.

The old biplane landed and taxied to a stop while Ben waited in the middle of the field, glad of the goggles that protected his eyes from the blowing dust. The pilot, William Wellman, walked toward him, looking straight out of a war film—leather jacket, helmet, long white scarf, gloves.

"Hiya, Bill. That thing fly? Looks plenty rickety to me."

"You should see some of the wrecks I flew over France. This one's practically new. I fly it up and down the coast all the time. As long as we're in sight of land we'll be OK. This plane's already been to San Simeon," he said as they walked toward the fragile plane.

"It has? How'd you get to know Hearst?"

"Through Marion Davies. She has a beach house just up from Doug Fairbanks' place. I used to buzz him from the air, land on the beach for a drink and some grub, tell a few war stories. I saw her wave at me one day and I landed there." Ben settled uneasily into the rear cockpit. Wellman strapped him in. "Marion's really a swell gal, for all the gossip."

"I'm glad you've been up the coast before. At least you know where San Simeon is. The deal is twenty-five dollars and gas. OK?"

Wellman straightened up, the wheel chock dangling from his hand. "The price is OK, but I just hope you know what you're doing. The old man values his privacy."

"I called him and he said to come on up. I figured you don't turn down an invitation like that more than once."

Ben had never flown before, and he gripped the edges of the cockpit with both hands as they took off. They flew quite low over the rugged country and followed the coastline. At Santa Barbara the hills jutted out into the Pacific, and they flew toward Morro Rock in the distance, its base shrouded in mist rising from the surrounding sea.

William Randolph Hearst had been building San Simeon for three years. As they flew over the crest of the mountain Ben could see three large white houses arranged in a semicircle on the ocean side of the hill. They had red tile roofs and, except for their huge size, did not look out of the ordinary. But beyond the crest of the hill, a forest of scaffolding surrounded what seemed to be a a gigantic Spanish cathedral under construction. Full-grown oak trees in wooden boxes were being hauled by teams of horses. Heaps of stone and hundreds of crates were scattered across the entire top of the mountain. To one side, what seemed to be a marble swimming pool was partly completed. The adjoining mountain top was girdled by rows of stone columns set in a circle a mile or so in diameter.

Wellman zoomed toward the houses and waggled the plane's wings to attract attention. Small figures ran out of one of the buildings and waved them toward the ocean. Soon a large black car was driving down the twisting road toward the beach and the landing strip with its red wind sock on a pole.

Wellman landed the plane neatly on the bumpy dirt strip. Half a mile up the coast they could see a freighter being unloaded at a long pier that ran out into the Pacific. Two large warehouses stood near the end of the pier, which was crowded with boxes, crates, racks of lumber, piles of cut stone.

After a long wait, the automobile appeared on the hill and drove out onto the strip.

It took over a half hour to wind their way up the graveled road to La Cuesta Encantata. Along the hilly road they saw zebras and gazelles. The driver explained that Hearst was "trying them out to see if they would naturalize in California."

Three finished Mediterranean houses fronted on what would undoubtedly be a plaza some day. The partly finished main house was crawling with workmen. Huge steam cranes lifted buckets of concrete to the tops of forms. It looked as if someone had contracted for a city. A secretary waited for them at the door of the center house.

Ben stepped into a spacious room with an elaborate renaissance ceiling and a fireplace you could stand in. Three wide plate-glass windows looked out at the blue ocean miles away at the foot of the mountains.

"This is La Casa del Mar. House of the Sea. Because of the views. Mr. Hearst is on the telephone but will be able to see you in a few minutes. Please wander around and look." She pointed to a door. "You may want to wash. Your face is smudged."

Ben laughed. "Thank you. It's the open plane." The bathroom was luxurious, but it was the main room that astonished Ben. Carved stones with code numbers painted on them stood by the chairs. Oriental rugs were piled three deep. Hangings and tapestries were thrown over the sofa.

"Will all of this go into that building I saw across the way?"

"All of this and more. Did you see those two warehouses down by the bay?" Ben nodded. "They're filled and ships keep bringing more. Agents buy a column, a facade, a doorway, a ceiling. Then it is measured, and Julia Morgan, the architect, designs it into one of the rooms." She lowered her voice. "It's an amazing project, and Mr. Hearst's an amazing man." She straightened suddenly, and Ben became aware of Hearst, a silent hulking figure, standing at the side of the room watching them. He was wearing corduroy trousers, a faded blue work shirt, high boots with puttees. He noticed Ben looking down at the puttees, thrust out his hand and smiled.

"You probably thought only film directors wore these. They're for the rattlesnakes. We're disturbing them with all the earth moving." He motioned Ben to sit down on one of the sofas. The huge man sat in a thronelike armchair opposite, put the tips of his fingers together, and waited.

"Mr. Hearst, I'm here to ask you to do a favor for Abe Weiss. He didn't authorize me to come and he doesn't know I'm here." Ben took a deep breath. "I'm going to ask you to soft-pedal a story." Hearst's eyebrows shot up. "The story will move on the wires in the next two days, as soon as certain hearings start in Boston."

As Ben told the story, Hearst shook his head slowly in disbelief and looked pained. Partway through the account he got up and walked over to a painting and examined it closely. Ben hesitated, and Hearst, without turning around, waved a hand for him to continue. After Ben finished, there was a long silence and he could hear muffled construction sounds.

"I simply can't understand it. I thought Abe Weiss was a very smart man." Hearst blew a fleck of dust off the surface of the canvas and turned to Ben. "These men control the industry that uses more beautiful young women than any other. Men who could have any girl in the country at their feet. Probably have had!" He closed his eyes and shuddered involuntarily. "To pay cheap whores, then submit to blackmail!" The pained look deepened.

Ben stroked the Persian cat beside him. "I think they found

themselves in a situation and it got out of hand. Now they're in a bad spot and you can help."

The cat got up, stretched, then curled up in Ben's lap.

"He likes you," Hearst said approvingly. "What do you think I can do?"

"Just don't go after it. I'm not asking you to ignore the story or kill it. You can't do that." Ben watched the publisher's face for some clue to what he was thinking.

"I wouldn't do that under any circumstances," Hearst snapped. He waved his arm. "Despite all this, I'm still a newspaperman with a tendency to go for the jugular." He smiled grimly. "I just wouldn't do it. That's all." Ben was afraid for a moment that the interview was at an end but the man remained seated.

"I didn't think you would, and I have too much respect to ask for that," he said quickly.

Hearst seemed to relax a bit. "I might be accused of being 'creative' with the news, but I never ignore a good story," he said with a sardonic smile.

"What we're hoping is that you'll play down the more sensational aspects of the story," Ben said carefully. "You know, words and expressions: 'house of ill repute' rather than 'roadhouse,' 'orgy' rather than 'party'—words like that." Ben's voice took on an admiring tone. "You know better than I what I'm talking about. It's the little things that determine the way the story is handled, the attitudes it creates." Hearst nodded impassively.

"You might also want to view it as a four-year-old story. Stale news."

Hearst's eyebrows rose alarmingly and Ben quickly took another tack. "Mr. Hearst, it's not just marriages that are threatened. The entire industry is threatened. Half the executives in the picture business were there. This could rock the industry, which is in a delicate, if not precarious, financial position right now. Attendance is off from last year. Majestic is about to float a stock issue. Paramount has gone public as well. Negotiations are in progress to buy Metro. Their officers were all there. They're all in it together."

"Why should I?" Hearst's voice was very quiet, dangerous.

Ben tried to look straight at him. "Because you're a decent man. And so, basically, are they. Out of respect for some men who are not evil, who are pioneers who created the country's great entertainment industry."

There was a long silence. The small pale eyes grew more baleful, if anything; the long nose wrinkled. Then Hearst burst out laughing. "You're absolutely unbelievable, Mr. Sommers! Your straight face—I could almost hear the sobbing of violins in the background." He laughed for another moment, wiping his eyes, and finally blew his nose. "That's wonderful. The best laugh I've had in days. You must come more often." The laughter quieted. "Those sharks. The way they cut each other up! They'd punch sprocket holes in their mothers if they thought anyone would pay to see them projected. There are broken lives strewn across every studio in Hollywood and in most of the theaters, too. Decency and respect, my ass!"

Scared that he had failed, Ben sat wondering what to do next.

All traces of humor had vanished from the long face. "All right. You've moved my 'decent' heart. I'll play it down as much as possible." Ben let out his breath slowly, controlling every muscle to remain impassive. Hearst sat thinking and a crafty look stole into his eyes. His voice lowered and became silken. He smiled again but it was a different smile. "Now you owe me a card. I'll call for it one of these days, and when I do, you better be ready with what I need, or I'll crucify you. Repayment tenfold are my regular terms. That's the only deal I ever make." He pulled his head down into his shoulders and seemed to be getting ready to spring on Ben. "If I think you're holding back on me, I'll drag all of this out and let the buzzards feast."

He grasped the arms of his chair in powerful hands and leaned forward, almost spitting the words. "All right. I'll tell you why I'm doing it. Cosmopolitan Productions has just moved to the Majestic lot. I don't want my production company, and especially Miss Davies' name, sullied by lousy publicity." He sat back and relaxed slightly. "Marion has suffered enough without being tarred by this, too," he said quietly.

He looked out of the window at the horizon for a long time. When his gaze returned to Ben, he said indignantly, "You tell Abe . . . no, by God, I'll tell him to his face next time I'm in New York! . . . when he wants his ashes hauled, to do it in private. Jesus Christ! The stupidity! An orgy! Extortion!" Then his cold smile spread across his face again. "I hope it cost them plenty. What do they do with their money, anyway? Fuck it away." He breathed deeply and sat up. "At least I'm creating a great work of art up here." He looked around the room with a pleased expression. "You should come back for a weekend sometime when it's finished."

Considering the number of prominent men involved, the story got little attention. Even *The New York Times*, considered unapproachable, placed the breaking story on page fifteen. It ran only three columns, and a one column follow-up the next day. After that the story simply disappeared. Few papers bothered to carry the rest of the story a week later— as a result of the hearing before the Massachusetts Supreme Court. The District Attorney was fired. Everyone forgot the incident except William Randolph Hearst.

40

September 1921, Los Angeles

Los Angeles Record

HULL NOVEL, "THE SHEIK," TO BE FILMED

Ethel Maude Hull's novel of flaming desert passions, *The Sheik,* long considered too risqué to be made into a moving picture, has been adapted for the silver screen by June Mathis for the new star, Rudolph Valentino, it was announced yesterday by Majestic Pictures president, Saul Rubin.

Mathis, one of the most respected scenario writers in the business, is the person credited with discovering and developing Valentino for the leading role in the *Four Horsemen* still playing at leading theaters.

"Look, Ginny, I desperately need some sort of boost in my career right now. Roscoe didn't take me to Majestic with him from Keystone. I've only directed three pictures this year. I figure a little gift to Wallace Reid might just do the trick."

"And what do you think is 'just a little gift'?"

"I don't know, exactly. That's why I asked you along. Women know all these things. I'd just kinda like to look. Come on in and see if something doesn't catch your eye. Please?"

Henry and Virginia were sitting in the front seat of his touring car parked on Spring Street. Virginia was seething. Henry had not taken her out on a date for weeks. He turned up several evenings a week to spend the night, but outside of that she never saw him anymore. When he'd invited her today to go to a jeweler's to pick out a surprise, Virginia had thought he was going to buy her an engagement ring at last.

She tried to control her anger. "Pathé, I love you and I really have thought all along that you loved me too. We're practically an old married couple. I want an engagement ring *today*."

"Ginny, you know I can't marry you until things get better. It's not fair of you to keep asking."

"Oh, for Christ's sake. Don't feed me that. I'm making twelve hundred a week. I can't spend it all. We can certainly live on that until things pick up for you. It's just a lull. Henry, I'm asking for the last time. Marry me. Now." She pounded her fist on the walnut dashboard. "Damn it all! What's wrong? You find your way into my bed regularly enough—or is that really all you want?"

"For God's sake, Virginia, don't talk like that. I do care about you. You mean the whole world to me. But this is just not the right time for us to get married."

He slumped behind the wheel. He really didn't want to marry her. Bad reputation. Almost a joke. But Virginia was undoubtedly the best piece he'd ever had and somehow he had to string her along.

"Please, come into the store and help me pick something out for Wallie. Then I'll take you home and we'll talk it all out. This is no place for us to settle the most important question of our lives, is it?" Reluctantly, Virginia agreed.

"This is very nice for a gentleman," the salesman said as he laid the gold ring on the red velvet pad. It was set with a golden tiger's eye carved with a heraldic crest.

Henry toyed with the ring, putting it first on one finger, then another. He held out his hand letting the light catch the stone. Turning to Virginia he asked, "Think Wallie will like it, honey?"

"I couldn't care less. I'm bored. Get it if you want."

The jeweler smiled unctuously. "Perhaps the gentleman could help the lady pass the time more pleasurably if he would allow me to show her some things more to her taste."

"No thanks."

Virginia looked away furiously, and the jeweler made a helpless gesture toward her.

Henry stood up and held out the ring to the jeweler. "I'll take it. Please wrap it and I'll enclose a card."

When the jeweler was out of earshot, Virginia snapped, "You've got a nerve, Henry."

"Lay off, honey. I'm nearly broke. This is an investment in my future. I can't afford to buy you a ring just now."

255

"But you can afford a thousand-dollar trinket for Wallace Reid?"

"Maybe he'll let me direct his next picture. Jesus, he *made* Jim Cruze, who's built his career on Reid pictures. I need that chance. Don't force me into anything hasty, Virginia."

"Hasty, my rear end." She tried to make up her mind what to do next. She was frantic at the thought of losing Henry but also realized he was using her. Everybody in town knew they went together, and she had burned all her bridges with other men for him.

She decided what she had to say. "Pathé, I won't fight with you here. Don't call me this weekend. I've got to think—sort things out in my mind—without you directing me in a scene. This is one I am going to play by myself. I'll call you next week." Virginia stood still for a long moment, looking at him as though trying to grasp him once and for all. Then she turned and walked rapidly out of the shop. He made no attempt to go after her.

As she unlocked the door to her bungalow Viriginia heard the telephone ringing. It was her agent, Al Senmacher, who asked her if she wanted to drive to San Francisco for the Labor Day weekend. His friend, Maude Delmont, knew people there, and Al was sure they would get invited to a party or two. Virginia immediately said yes and began to pack a small bag.

41

September 1921, San Francisco

Roscoe Arbuckle needed a rest. His full-length features for
Majestic had proved so successful that Saul Rubin rushed him
into three more at breakneck speed. Only a few days for
the last-minute costume fittings were scheduled between the
end of one film and the beginning of the next. Final shots for
the third one were made just before the Labor Day weekend,
and Arbuckle decided to take a vacation trip to San Francisco.

Reserving a suite at the Hotel St. Francis, he gathered up
Lowell Sherman, his actor friend, and Fred Fischbach, a producer pal of long acquaintance. They had a leisurely drive
to San Francisco in Roscoe's new twenty-five thousand dollar
Pierce-Arrow. The touring car, called by Roscoe his "gasoline
palace," contained a fitted bar and, beneath the rear seat,
a toilet.

The three men arrived in San Francisco in time to have a late supper with some showgirls Lowell knew. They danced in the St. Francis's Mural Room, and as the girls had to get back to Tait's, the club where they appeared, Roscoe and his friends were in bed by one.

The St. Francis was his favorite place to unwind and make whoopee. He was considered a choice guest and was always given his favorite suite.

The suite, 1219, 1220, and 1221, consisted of a spacious corner parlor, two sides overlooking Powell Street and Union Square, and on either side, a bedroom and bath. Lowell Sherman had scheduled a stream of girls through his room, so he took the bedroom on the left for himself, while Roscoe and Fred Fischbach shared the room on the right. Roscoe had a double bed moved in; Fred slept in the remaining twin.

On Sunday Mae Taub dropped by, a friend of Bebe Daniels, the beautiful star at Majestic, who was one of Roscoe's best friends. There was a flurry of excitement up on the roof as a motorcyclist rode his machine across a wire stretched between two flag poles on different wings of the hotel. Suspended from the cycle was a hanging chair and in the chair sat a lovely young girl. Roscoe and Mae leaned out of the window and watched, Mae shrieking with anxiety. A photographer for the *San Francisco Examiner,* standing on the roof, heard her, recognized Arbuckle and snapped a photo.

Monday morning, eating breakfast at the Palace and waiting for Maude and Virginia to come down from their room, Al Senmacher saw the picture on an inside page. Al knew Roscoe from Sennett days and called him at the St. Francis. Roscoe said he was having a big party that afternoon, and Al and his lady friends should drop by for a drink before they started back to Los Angeles.

Virginia and Maude walked through the columned lobby of the St. Francis and found the elevators.

"Honey, I don't know who's giving it. Al just said to go on up, it was a surprise, they are expecting us. He'll catch up as soon as he parks the motor."

The door to 1220 stood open and a waiter wheeled a table inside. The two women, uncertain, stood and watched.

"There's more liquor in there than could float a battleship," the waiter remarked. "Good stuff, too. Won't send you blind." He grinned.

Maude took Virginia's arm. "Come on, honey. Sounds like my kind of party." Walking through the open door, Maude stopped suddenly and said, "Well, I'll be damned. Roscoe Arbuckle. It's Roscoe Arbuckle!"

Virginia froze, then took a step backward thinking she would simply back out of the door before she was seen. She backed, instead, against the wall next to the door, and in an instant the door was blocked by the waiter wheeling in another table.

Arbuckle was seated in a large armchair with a drink in his hand waiting for the waiter to serve him breakfast. Lowell and Fred stood talking to two pretty girls who were introduced as Zey Prevon and Alice Blake, dancers at Tait's Club. Maude took Virginia by the hand and sat her on the sofa in front of the open window. Virginia could hear the click of the Powell Street cables quite clearly.

Roscoe came over and sat down beside her. She felt the sofa give under his weight. "Gee, Virginia, honey, it's good to see you. Whatcha doing in 'Frisco? Are you alone? Where's Pathé? He with Al?" He smiled at her sweetly.

Maude leaned over and whispered, "They've had a dreadful quarrel and Henry took off for New York. The engagement is off and Virginia doesn't know if she'll ever see him again."

"Gosh, I thought Henry had better sense than to go off and leave a good-lookin' chicken like you, toots."

"He was never good enough for you, Ginny," Lowell called over to her. "And I hear you're pretty good, too." He winked at her. "Kick up your heels and have a fling. Life is too short. Lots of fish in the sea."

"What happened, Ginny?" Roscoe was being solicitous.

"It's a very long story, Roscoe. Go eat your breakfast. Your eggs will get cold."

Al Senmacher knocked and walked in. Roscoe jumped up, and he and Al shook hands, laughed, and slapped each other on the back.

"How's tricks, Roscoe?"

"Don't know. Haven't had one yet today." He giggled and turned to one of the girls. "Zey, tootsie, get Daddy a scotch and White Rock. It's early, so go light . . . on the White Rock." He turned back toward Al. "Zey and her friend are showgirls at Tait's. We'll go by there and see the show tonight after dinner. Stick around. Gonna be a swell party."

Zey had called down for a Victrola and some dance records, and a bellboy arrived with the machine and set it up on a table. There were two leather albums of records. Zey

259

selected one and put it on the turntable. Fred wound up the crank and the sounds of "Stop It" filled the room. Everyone danced.

> Don't do it! Don't make that clarinet moan.
> Don't do it! Don't tease that saxophone.
> Pounding rhythms, jazzin' blues,
> Dancin' mommas right out of their shoes.

"Swell party, Roscoe," Alice shouted over the music as she and Al danced by.

> Don't do it! Don't make my head spin around.
> Don't do it!
> Hot poppas, jazz mommas,
> Dying for more of that sound.

"Roscoe always gives swell parties," Fred said, lifting the tone arm. "Tell them about the dog wedding, Roscoe."

Roscoe sat back in the armchair and sipped his scotch. "Well, the bitch next door to my place on West Adams Street come in heat. My neighbor said he was going to breed her. I said, shockedlike, 'Without a proper wedding? Let me give the bride a wedding so I can give her away.' So I went shopping and bought a bridal veil, white gloves, the whole shebang. A florist did up a bridal bouquet."

Lowell Sherman interrupted. "It was just beautiful. White orchids, the works. I cried. Doesn't everybody cry at weddings?"

Roscoe, shaking and laughing almost helplessly, continued. "Nothing too good for the neighbor's dog, I always say. Well, I got in a caterer and he put up a tent and I invited about a hundred people. I couldn't get a preacher, Saul Rubin refused to play rabbi," he winked, and there was more laughter, "so finally Mack did it. Turned his collar backward and everything. It was a great party."

"You skipped the best part," shouted Lowell. "After the ceremony, everyone started to eat and drink and forgot about the bride and groom. We looked around, and there was the groom humping the bride under the table with the wedding cake on it!"

Roscoe was laughing so hard he was red in the face. "I didn't forget. There are ladies present, you dodo. Really, it was funny, the little dogs on top of the cake so sedate, holding paws. And under the table . . ." He couldn't continue. Fred started the Victrola again.

Alice put on another record, Irving Berlin's "All By Myself," and after a few seconds Roscoe jumped up and said, "It's one of my favorites. Start it again." Alice set the needle back to the beginning and, standing by the Victrola, Roscoe sang along with the girl on the record, in his clear tenor.

The harmonies were perfect and the moment was charming. At the end everyone applauded.

Dancing started again. Roscoe said to Virginia, "What are you drinking, toots?"

"Just orange juice, Roscoe, thanks."

Maude got up and moved toward him. "Slosh a little joy juice on her drink, Roscoe. She's giving everybody the blues. Really low because of Henry."

Roscoe waved the gin bottle in the air. "Never hurt a flea, just makes him frisky." Maude carried the drink to Virginia.

Couples kept coming and going. Strangers walking along the hall on the twelfth floor dropped in, helped themselves to a drink and wandered along. Someone was always on the telephone, everyone was talking, laughing, eating and drinking, mostly drinking.

"Watch out for Lowell, Maudie," Roscoe called to her above the din. "He's got the hottest pants in Hollywood, and that's saying something."

"I think I can handle him—if I want to." She smiled and looked up at Sherman bending over her, his arm around her shoulder. "Show me some of your class, big boy."

"I'll let you look all you want if you'll show me yours, too."

"Oh, oh. The party's getting rough," Roscoe shouted. "No naughty stuff, you two. Go into the bedroom if you want to talk dirty so we don't have to hear." Another record on the Victrola drowned out Lowell's answer to Roscoe, but Maude doubled over laughing.

Roscoe, tapping his feet, began to dance in the center of the floor. He grabbed Al and Fred and started to line them up as a chorus line. He looked around and shouted for Lowell to join them.

"Now where did he go, all of a sudden?"

Alice shrieked that Maude was too hot in her dress and had gone to change and Lowell had volunteered to undo the snaps. Roscoe made a face with eyes wide open and mouth compressed into a pink rosebud.

261

"Oh, oh. Naughty, naughty."

Fred laughed. "He's going to be busy for a few minutes, Roscoe."

Lowell and Maude had locked the bedroom door, which cut the available bathrooms down to one. The noise was deafening but it was exactly how Roscoe wanted it. There was a steady stream of people in and out, music, laughter, liquor, pretty girls, good food, all the things he worked for and lived for.

Maude stood uneasily in the door to 1221 and waved the too long sleeves of Sherman's yellow pajamas. Roscoe walked toward her, wavering slightly, beginning to look slightly drunk.

"Hey, you two, how was it?"

"Not bad." Maude laughed. "You ought to give him a try."

"He's not my type," Roscoe laughed. "I got my eye on someone else." He walked back to the drink table.

Al grabbed Maude's arm and spoke sharply to her. "Jesus, Maude, you're making a fool of yourself. Pull yourself together. I thought we'd drive back this afternoon. It's three o'clock already."

"Al, sweetie, don't be dumb. This is too good to leave. We can always go home tomorrow." She hiccuped slightly. "Where's Virginia?"

"I dunno. She was here a minute ago. She's around somewhere. Maybe taking a pee."

Zey Prevon danced by and said, "She went in the bedroom with Roscoe."

Maude looked at Al. "Oh, Jesus. She's scared of him. Told me he was waiting to get her."

"What the hell you talking about?" Al said.

"She doesn't like him. Wonder why she went in there with him?"

"Maybe she went to use the toilet and he followed her in."

"Then maybe we ought to look in on them."

"Aw, come on, Maude. Christ, leave them alone. Nobody watched you and the Sherman guy jazzing it up."

"That's different. I'm not a rich movie star." She waved the long yellow sleeve around indicating the room and the people. "Catch Roscoe in the act and he might be good for a favor once in a while."

Al was sharp. "That's stupid. He's a friend and a swell guy. Leave 'em alone."

Maude sniffed. "Well! He might be a friend of yours. I never met him before today. Be a dear and get me another gin and orange."

"You've had enough already. Change your clothes. As soon as Virginia gets through, we're getting out of here." Al tried to push Maude back into the bedroom. She wriggled away from his grasp and, bumping into dancing couples, wavered across the floor. Everyone was drunk and nobody paid attention as she began to pound on the door.

> Jazzin' your feet,
> Snappy beat,
> Makes you feel giddy and strange.

There was a scream, difficult to hear because of the Victrola. Maude suddenly felt frightened and pounded again.

> Jazzin' your soul,
> Out of control,
> Makes your head feel all aflame.

Maude whirled around and screamed. "Turn that damn thing off. Something terrible's happening in there." Then she pounded on the door again.

> Don't do it! Don't make that clarinet moan.
> It's too exciting.

Maude wailed, "Let me in. Let me in. What are you doing to her in there?" The urgency in her voice telegraphed itself to the guests.

> Don't do it!
> Don't make my head spin around
> Don't do it!

Alice, dancing with Fred, stopped and said, "Hush up, everybody. What's wrong, Maude?"

The vocalist on the record started to sing again.

> Snap your fingers,
> Jazz your shoes,
> Shimmy away all of your blues.

Someone picked up the arm of the Victrola. There was a sudden silence. From behind the closed door came another scream.

"My God," someone whispered, "what do you suppose he's doing to her?"

Dollie giggled. "You get three hundred pounds bouncing up and down on you and you'd scream, too." Still giggling, she looked around at all their faces. No one was laughing with her.

Fred Fischbach walked over to the door and opened it. Inside was another door without a knob. "Damn. It's a double door. Can only be opened from in there." He pointed helplessly. Maude kicked at the door with the pointed toe of her shoe but she was so drunk that she nearly lost her balance, and one of the men grabbed her to keep her from falling down.

Fred continued to pound. Suddenly, the door was flung open and Roscoe stood, soaked with sweat, still dressed in his blue pajamas.

"Get her the hell out of here. She's making too much noise." He lurched toward the table and, hands shaking, poured himself another drink.

Maude stumbled into the bedroom. The shades had not been drawn and daylight streamed through the window. The bed was a tumbled mess and Virginia lay on it moaning. She was fully clothed, and she had vomited on the pillows, and it had run down the side of the mattress and onto the carpet.

"Oh, Jesus Christ!" Fred muttered softly.

Virginia sat up suddenly and began to tear at her clothing as if in great pain and began to scream.

"I'm hurt. I'm dying. I know I'm dying." She tore at her clothing, scattering it in all directions. Maude and Zey tried to help her out of her clothing.

Roscoe returned with his drink and ripped a sleeve off her blouse. "If you want your clothes off, I'll help," he giggled.

Zey slapped his hands. "Oh, Roscoe! Stop that. She's really hurt."

Arbuckle, from the door, turned and said, "Oh, she's just putting it on. Leave her alone and she'll sober up."

"Get out of here, Roscoe. Let us handle her. Fred, hold her

264

upside down by her legs. I read somewhere it helps if the blood runs to your head." Maude was taking charge.

Fred obliged by grasping the nude girl by the ankles and hoisting her into the air over the bed. Virginia fainted.

Zey said, "Put her down. Maude fill the tub with cold water. I've got some bicarbonate of soda. That ought to help. And the cold water will bring her around."

"I just think she's too drunk," someone said from the parlor door.

Fred lowered her into the cold water, wetting the sleeves of his coat. Virginia moaned. She vomited the bicarbonate. Fred lifted her out of the dirty water and placed her back on the bed.

"Ice. Let's try ice." Alice Blake brought in a tub of ice from the parlor. The girls put pieces of ice in towels and lay them on Virginia's abdomen, which was where the pains seemed most intense.

Virginia screamed as the ice lay on her. Roscoe took a piece of ice and shoved it between her legs.

"That ought to make her come to."

Maude yelled at him to get out. Roscoe, standing by the open window, looked out to see if anyone was watching from the windows in the opposite wing. He turned and shouted at Maude.

"Shut up or I'll throw you out the window!"

Finally someone called the manager of the hotel and he rushed upstairs. Maude was changing back into her dress so the party wouldn't look like an orgy. The manager suggested putting Virginia in a room down the hall, and Fred carried her there and put her to bed. Maude followed and fell asleep on the other bed. The manager called a doctor, who finally arrived at Virginia's room just before five o'clock. After talking to Virginia, the doctor decided that she'd had too much to drink and should be allowed to sleep it off. Maude was annoyed at having been awakened.

The party in Roscoe's suite was going full tilt about seven P.M. when the house detective dropped in. He had been to see Virginia and wanted to get some details from guests in the event she filed a complaint or a suit.

A few minutes later the house doctor called on her because she was again in great pain. Dr. Beardslee found that he was unable to examine Virginia's abdomen because the slightest touch was excruciating. He gave her an injection of morphine so he could continue his examination. Maude told him that Virginia had been attacked by Fatty Arbuckle.

Virginia, through a veil of drug and pain, denied that Arbuckle had touched her. Maude said that Virginia was out of her head and the doctor should not pay attention to her ravings. She had definitely been attacked. Maude then went back to the party.

Roscoe and Lowell had dinner in the Mural Room with some of the girls and then danced to the orchestra there. When they returned to the suite, the party was still in full swing. Maude became abusive because Roscoe had not taken her to dinner, and Fred called the house detective to get her out of the room. The detective took Maude back to the room where Virginia was lying unconscious. He ordered dinner from room service and they used the other bed to make love.

Virginia began to moan at four in the morning and the detective left, calling the house doctor as he went. Dr. Beardslee gave her another shot. Maude was dissatisfied with the doctor's treatment of Virginia and called in another doctor.

Tuesday afternoon Roscoe Arbuckle checked out of the Hotel St. Francis and drove his car aboard the steamer *Harvard*. The boat trip back to Los Angeles was uneventful. On Thursday morning the doctor decided Virginia was very ill and checked her into the Wakefield Sanitarium on Sutter Street, where she died of peritonitis on Friday afternoon.

42

September 1921,
The Northern Theatre, Minneapolis

**THE UNITED WOMEN'S CLUBS OF AMERICA
FILM LIST**

Your club has decided to help you stamp out the
pervading evil that is submerging the United States
in a tidal wave of smut. As the Bible tells us, "A
good tree cannot bring forth evil fruit, neither can a
corrupt tree bring forth good fruit." (Matthew
7:18.) It's up to your club members to stop the
showings of the following pictures if your theater
manager tries to ruin the lives of your family by
exposing them to this filth. Don't allow your family
to eat of the fruit from that corrupt tree, the
neighborhood theater.

Within a year the membership of the Motion Picture
Theatre Owners of America had grown to twelve thousand.
Organizer Sidney Cohen moved back and forth across the
country; his main target was the menace of Abe Weiss and
Majestic. Weiss became the common enemy, bringing everyone together. Each independent considered himself next to be
attacked by Weiss's agents, Black or Lynch. The financial
pressure that had driven Hulsey to sell out became common
knowledge. The M.P.T.O.A. announced a national convention
to be held in Minneapolis to organize a boycott against
Majestic.

"It looks terrible," Charles Grossman admitted while Abe
Weiss finished reading the latest editorial in *Motion Picture
World* denouncing Majestic policies.

"You've got to protect yourself, Mr. Weiss," added Greenglass.

"What else? I'll go to Minneapolis and do what I can."

"It won't be easy," Grossman said. "Even though it's been kept quiet, everybody knows that Black and Lynch work for us. Everyone knows what we've done."

Weiss stood up. "And I'm not ashamed of any of it." He pounded on the desk with a clenched fist. "It wasn't all that illegal. Most of it, anyway. Mostly pressure." He thought for a minute, smiled and said, "Well, it was and it wasn't. Most men can't take pressure. Besides, what are we supposed to do now? Give it all back? Lynch is almost through, only a few stragglers to clean up. Then he'll retire and manage the Singer Circuit. It's a lot of water over the dam."

"You could just lay low until it blows over."

"Mr. Greenglass, I need every one of those twelve thousand theaters that will be represented there in Minneapolis to show my pictures. I can't buy them all out. Besides, I'm beginning to wonder now about owning so many small houses. Mr. Grossman thinks they cost too much to operate, the little two-holers in out-of-the-way towns. We added up the number of houses and number of seats. We can gross more showing one print to three thousand seats than by showing a hundred prints to a lot of little houses."

Moses Klein suggested, "Why don't you ride the special train with the exhibitors? Disarm them. Charm them."

Over the Labor Day weekend, Minneapolis was filled with theater men. Hotels had to double up, and the parlors reserved for meetings were abandoned in favor of the biggest picture palace in town, The Northern Theatre. Weiss sat in the darkness under the balcony for two days listening to Majestic being vilified. Then he sought out Sidney Cohen in the lobby.

"I'm Abe Weiss of Majestic. Can we talk for a minute?"

Cohen, who was talking to Senator James J. Walker of New York, looked Weiss up and down. So this was the enemy. "I heard you were here."

"Mr. Cohen, I want an opportunity to defend myself in there."

"Why on my time? Hold your own convention."

Weiss held up his hand. "I thought this was the United States of America. Everyone gets a chance to be heard and to defend themselves."

Walker cleared his throat. "Give it to him, Sid. If you don't, he'll be able to cry foul till the cows come home. And he's right. He should have a chance to defend himself. Interesting to hear what he's got to say."

Weiss nodded at him. "Thank you, Senator."

Cohen began to look eager. "This afternoon at three. Just after the men from Georgia get through. They will be talking about the Lynch Company." He stepped back looking pleased.

"I'll be there. Thank you," Weiss said, giving Cohen a withering look as he turned to leave.

"Jesus, he's got the balls of a bandit," Walker said. "I can hardly wait."

"Spread the word," Cohen said. "We want a full house."

Most of the three thousand men in The Northern Theatre had never seen Abe Weiss in person. To most he was a sinister figure who operated out of New York, pulling strings that led to dynamited theaters and maimed victims.

There was a sullen silence as Weiss walked down the aisle to the stage. From the rear of the house a hissing started, growing into a blaring, swelling tumult of boos, catcalls, whistles. Obscenities were shouted from all over the auditorium.

Weiss, standing beside the lectern because he was too short to stand behind it, was silent as the uproar enveloped him. He held up his hand for quiet, but they quieted down reluctantly, not wanting to waste their opportunity to let him know how they felt.

Finally there was a silence of sorts, but the theater never became totally quiet. Resentful mutterings and angry whispers continued as an abusive accompaniment to Weiss's speech. He drew a deep breath and started to speak, hoping his voice would not betray the anxiety he felt. Anxiety and anger.

"I've been sitting at the back there, listening for two days."

Someone shouted, "You ain't heard nothin' yet." Laughter.

"I felt it was time you heard another side of the story."

More laughter and, from the balcony, a long shrill whistle.

"My name is Abe Weiss and I'm forty-six years old. I came to this country in 1893 with twelve dollars in my pocket.

269

After a few years I decided the picture business looked good, and I been in it ever since. You all know the rest. But maybe some of you have forgotten some of the things I've done. My commitment to the industry, you could say. I'd like to remind you.

"I'm doing the work I was born to do. I never stood up in front of an association like this one before. I stay in the background and let my work speak for me. But I am one hell of a fighter, and I will not stand by and listen to some of the lies I have heard said here in the two days just past. You got some answers coming.

"Some of what you said is true. I'm sorry certain things happened. Men get overzealous and then get out of control. I learned a lesson.

"There is another side of me. You should know that, too. I have always had great dreams. Not every man in the picture business has great dreams. They dream power, revenge, money, women, fame—you know what they dream. My dream, gentlemen, was of a great industry—when there was nothing but a few flea-bitten nickelodeons and one-reel pictures.

"I helped weld this industry together. Who do you think brought this business out of chaos and made it a business? Who recognized the vital relationship between production and distribution? I did. I built the first distribution arm for a studio. I saw that the theaters had to have regular distribution, so I formed Majestic. Then I recognized that we had to have better pictures than we were getting. So I went to the studio with the reputation for turning out the best and suggested a merger. It worked. I straightened out the exchanges and the bookers by insisting that they handle Majestic properties a certain way. On time. Correct playdates. The right picture, even. Some of them balked. Sometimes they lost Majestic. When they got straightened out, we came back. Sometimes we bought the exchange and fired the men who wouldn't cooperate.

"Who regulated production so you could depend on a new picture—a high-class picture with a good story you weren't ashamed to take your mother to, filled with stars guaranteed to thrill the audience—a new picture like that every week? I did.

"Gentlemen, unless you got a good picture you can leave your doors open twenty-four hours a day and hang a sign in the box office, FREE. And you won't get one man, woman, or child to come in and laugh and cry.

270

"Who gave you the first five-reel picture, over the insults and threats of the Patents Trust? Who now even remembers *Mary, Queen of Scots* with Eleanora Duse? Only eight years and already it's ancient history.

"Innovations. I do not use that word lightly. And no one else did them. I did. You think everyone went along with me on these? Saying thanks as they reaped in more *shekels?* No. I had to do it all myself. Maybe I stepped on a few toes here and there. Stepped a little harder, maybe, than I had to, once in a while. Otherwise a new industry would never have developed.

"There is not one other man who has worked so hard to protect in every way this industry from the greed of the men who work in it.

"Are you still in business? Do you still have profits? Even when the rentals go up? Still profits. You bet.

"Do you still get two high-class pictures each week from Majestic? You're damned right you do.

"Show me how I've hurt this industry. This year, more theaters than ever. More patrons, more pictures. Sure, it makes me rich. But you're getting rich, too.

"You sat here and criticized Majestic for buying theaters. You know we couldn't survive without first-run situations. Look at Metro before Marcus Loew rescued them with his theaters. They had a year's backlog of unplayed pictures. This is a dynamic business and the word is competition. If we don't get it, they will. We had to have those theaters and we paid millions for them. I'm not ashamed of any business deal I ever made, and I do not cheat the men I do business with. Any man who ever booked a Majestic picture got his money's worth.

"You criticized Majestic for raising the rentals on Mary Pickford's pictures. I was paying her plenty and she was packing your houses. Put Mary's name up in lights and it's a stampede, right? So what happens? First National steals her. First National is owned by exhibitors and what do they do? Charge more than I ever did.

"Quality. That's what I've been after. I took the moving picture out of the storefronts and put it on Broadway. With *Mary, Queen of Scots* we exhibited for the first time in a first-class theater on an equal level with the legitimate stage. You weren't ashamed to tell your girl's father you were in the picture business anymore.

"And writers. Until I came along producers were paying thirty dollars for scenarios. I hired famous writers of note,

271

famous Broadway producers to bring class to the screen. I hired playwrights and novelists to work their wonders.

"Little by little I fought to give pictures some dignity. To wipe away the contempt and scorn people had in their voices when they said the word 'movie.' A slum tradition. Entertainment for unwashed immigrants, farm workers looking for a Saturday night spree, ironworkers settling down in a dark place to kiss their girls.

"I spent more money than any man who ever lived who wasn't a king or a pharaoh. I paid Broadway prices for Broadway talent. I promoted and advertised more than anyone else. I paid a young girl ten thousand dollars a week and got it back tenfold. You got rich on her, too. I walked on the edge of disaster for ten years. Who else helped me make something out of this industry? No one. I did what I did without any help from anyone in this hall . . . in Hollywood . . . in New York. Oh, some talented men and women made great pictures. But no one else looked at the totality—from top to bottom—and the organization necessary to make it work.

"I'm not ashamed of anything I've done. I'm proud!"

He stopped for a second as his voice broke. He wiped a tear away with one finger, then continued.

"I've heard the word 'boycott' thrown around. Don't try it, my friends. It won't work, because if I have to I can whip you all. I will make pictures the likes of which the world can only imagine. The greatest ever made. Unless you sign up for the output of my studio, you will watch the lines forming down the street. I am determined to beat the competition at all costs.

"I would hate not to have you as part of the Majestic family. I need as many of you as I can get. The Majestic houses alone will not support the kind of pictures, the kind of high-class operation, I intend to keep going. But I didn't come here to beg for support. You are going to support me because you know the kind of quality I stand for, and you will be better off with my product.

"Now. This is what you've wanted to hear. Majestic will no longer buy independently-owned houses in small towns. We will buy only big houses, chains, circuits, and booking agencies. We will continue to build great picture palaces. You no longer have anything to fear from Majestic or me. I intend to let bygones be bygones. I promise to continue to produce the greatest pictures that skill, taste, artistry, and money can make. Those of you who decide to show Majestic pictures will never be sorry."

There was silence as he left the stage and walked up the aisle to the lobby. Sidney Cohen was waiting for him there.

"I've got to hand it to you, Mr. Weiss. You're a master."

"And you know it's all true."

Cohen extended his hand, but Weiss ignored it.

"I still think you're a dangerous man, Mr. Weiss. A danger to the industry and a danger to every independent theater owner. You can only operate on a scale where you control everything. That, to my way of thinking, is dangerous. But I think your claws are clipped. You'll have to watch your step. We're on to you. On to you and watching."

September 1921, San Francisco—Friday

A woman's voice on the telephone asked when the autopsy would be conducted. Deputy Coroner Brown sat up in his chair, suddenly alert.

"What autopsy? Who is this?"

"The Wakefield Sanitarium." There was a conversation in the background, muffled as the woman partly covered the mouthpiece with her hand. "Oh, never mind. I got the information here. Thank you." The line hummed as she hung up.

Brown's cheerful face grew serious as he sat on the edge of his swivel chair and wondered what was going on at the Wakefield Sanitarium. "What was that all about?" he said, half aloud. Why should somebody at the Wakefield be asking about an autopsy? He looked at the schedule. No autopsies had been scheduled since late morning, the last one at the City

Morgue. Brown looked up the number for the Wakefield and Central connected him. The voice answering was the same woman who had called.

"This is Deputy Coroner Brown. You just called and asked me about an autopsy. I want to know why."

"I'm sorry but you must be mistaken. No one here called, sir."

"Aw, come on now. I recognize your voice."

"I'm sorry. That is all the information I can give you." She hung up abruptly.

Within five minutes Brown was in a city car driving up Sutter Street to the Sanitarium. The girl whose voice he recognized sat behind a reception desk. She refused to give him any further information.

"Who is the doctor in charge here?"

"Dr. Rumwell. But he won't be able to help you. He's very busy."

"So am I. But I'll wait." He leaned across the desk. "If you want to stay out of trouble, sweetie, don't tell him I'm here. Just point him out to me when he comes through. Understand?"

She nodded, eyes wide.

Brown picked up a copy of *Munsey's* magazine and sat down to wait in a bay window overlooking the street. After a few minutes two doctors walked down the stairs. One of them was carrying a tray loaded with specimen jars.

The girl spoke loudly. "This man's here to see you, Dr. Rumwell. He's from the coroner's office." She smiled at Brown.

Rumwell cast a withering look at her. "I'm very busy. Can't you make an appointment?"

"I can see you've been busy." Brown nodded at the tray. "That's what I want to see you about. I've heard of illegal abortions, Doctor, but illegal autopsies? Never."

Dr. Rumwell's face grew pale.

"No one reported a death," Brown went on. "No permissions came from our office for an autopsy." He stood waiting while the doctor decided what to do.

"Follow me to my office, please."

Brown sat down in the office while Rumwell stood by the window and tried to explain.

"We tried to call your office all afternoon and couldn't get through." He cleared his throat. "We really tried," he said lamely.

"Your receptionist had no trouble getting through. I had no trouble calling back. Nice try, anyway. Who died? Those the guts?"

"An actress. Virginia Rappe. Ruptured bladder. She was drinking heavily at a party."

"Why don't you tell me all about it?"

Rumwell cleared his throat again. "I don't really know what happened. The girl died about one-thirty today. Peritonitis. I was only called in to do the autopsy. She was admitted on Thursday. Nothing anyone could do, evidently." He looked very uncomfortable.

"I think you'd better come downtown with me, Doctor. Bring your jars. My car is outside."

Two reporters, one from the *Call-Bulletin*, the other from the *San Francisco Examiner*, watched Brown and a man they couldn't identify carry the tray of bottles into the coroner's laboratory. Within an hour they were on the trail of Virginia Rappe. That led to the Hotel St. Francis where, because of fear of federal liquor agents, they got nowhere. Except that the Wakefield Sanitarium was inadvertently mentioned.

At the Wakefield Sanitarium, the reporters found a nurse, Jean Jamison, who had cared for Virginia during the final moments of her life. Nurse Jamison told them that the dead girl's best friends, Maude Delmont and Sidi Spreckles, might still be in town. She intimated that there was dirty work involved and a whitewash might be in progress.

Maude Delmont, thrilled to be at the center of some excitement and looking for ways to get her name in the papers, told her lurid version of the party, which she now called an orgy. The San Francisco police, finally learning the details from the press, began to investigate. But a reporter from the *San Francisco Examiner* called the Los Angeles office of the Hearst papers first.

LOS ANGELES—Friday

The crowd of reporters surged past the butler and then, not knowing where to look, stood in the foyer.

"He must be around somewhere." The reporter stood on tiptoes.

"Hey, Fatty," shouted another.

"Just a moment! Just a moment! You can't come in here like this. This is a private home."

"Where's Arbuckle? We know he's here. Come on!" The man sounded threatening.

"Mr. Arbuckle is in his study. Now all of you get out of here. This is disgraceful!"

One of the reporters shoved his face at the butler. "You're goddamned right it is! You get Arbuckle and his fat ass out here! Just because he thinks he's a big star doesn't make him God!" He turned the butler toward the hall and gave him a shove. "Get him out here or else!"

There was a yell of discovery at the rear of the hallway and the reporters ran toward it. Several photographers ranged through the principal rooms, snapping pictures of the opulent furnishings, exploding flash powder in little blasts, filling the lower floor with smoke. The reporters stopped at an open door.

Roscoe Arbuckle stood by a leather armchair with a scenario in one hand. There was a strange half smile on his face. In moments of stress he always fell back on his silly Fatty smile, his trademark. But the smile would not quite come.

When he saw the notebooks Roscoe recognized that these men were reporters and relaxed slightly.

"What's going on, fellas?" He tried his smile again.

"As if you didn't know, Fatty, you old rascal." There was laughter all around.

A voice from the rear of the group. "Mr. Arbuckle, did you know the dead girl well?"

Another voice: "Who was at the orgy? Come on, give us some names, Fatty."

"Is it true that you used a Coke bottle on her? What's wrong with your dick, Fatty?" There was a gasp. The question everyone had wanted to ask had come out.

"Was she agreeable to your making love to you, Mr. Arbuckle, or did you just rape her?" Someone laughed.

Stunned, Roscoe tried to pull himself together with anger. "I don't know what you're talking about. If you don't clear out, I'll have to call the police."

"Yeh, you do that, Fatty. I understand they'd like to talk to you in 'Frisco. Just pick up the telephone." The reporter laughed in a nasty way.

One man stepped forward and held up his hand.

"Just a minute, fellas. Maybe Fatty hasn't heard yet." He turned to Roscoe and spoke softly. "Mr. Arbuckle, an actress friend of yours named Virginia Rappe died in 'Frisco earlier today. Seems she was at some sort of drunken orgy at the St. Francis last weekend. Your orgy. Before she died, she accused you of raping her, and we'd like to hear what you have to say."

Roscoe was clearly shocked. "I don't know what happened," he said. "This is the first I heard. I knew Virginia slightly. She was in town and came over to the room. She had a few drinks and went into the bedroom and began to scream and tear at her clothing. We all thought she was drunk." He giggled. "You know how some girls are."

No one laughed. Roscoe went back to being serious. "There was this friend of hers, a Maude somebody, with her. I rented another room for her to sleep it off. The other girls put her in a tub of cold water to sober her up. A doctor saw her and said she was fine, so Lowell and I went downstairs and had dinner. We came back on the *Harvard* Tuesday night. No one called me from San Francisco so I had no idea Virginia was sick." He stopped and looked puzzled. "You say she's *dead?*"

"Died this afternoon of peritonitis."

"God, it's a terrible thing to hear. Especially like this. How'd you fellas hear?"

"Our 'Frisco office called. They know all about it up there."

"Mr. Arbuckle, Lowell who?"

"Lowell Sherman. He's an old friend."

Everybody wrote it down.

Roscoe stepped forward. "Now why don't you clear out so I can make a few calls and find out what's happening. I've told you all I know."

Reluctantly, the reporters straggled out. It was clear they suspected that Roscoe knew more than he was saying.

A few minutes later the phone rang. "Roscoe? This is Joe Schenck. Have you heard about the mess in San Francisco?"

Joe Schenck was the producer who had made Roscoe a star after he left Keystone and Sennett. Schenck had then sold his contract with Arbuckle to Majestic for several million dollars.

"I just heard. There was a mob of reporters forced their way in here. They told me. Joe, I never did anything to that girl."

"Roscoe, it's going to get worse. Look, this is what you have to do. Go away somewhere, somewhere they won't think of looking for you. Who's a good friend who would hide you away?"

Roscoe thought a minute. "Sid Grauman. I could go up to his office. Upstairs in the Million Dollar. Nobody'd think of looking there. It's got a little bedroom and an icebox. Booze.

Everything. I could spend the night." He could even get a girl to stay with him there. It was beginning to seem like fun.

"Roscoe, listen to me. No booze. I want you sober. OK? I have the number of the telephone. Don't take that big white boat of yours. It's too easily spotted on the street. Take a cab. I'll be in touch. Roscoe. You still there?"

"Yeh. I'm here. Joe, I can't believe this is happening. It'll be all right, won't it, Joe?"

"I hope so, Roscoe. Go slowly, don't panic. I'll make a few calls and get back to you."

"Thanks, Joe, you're a real pal."

Roscoe called Grauman and then went upstairs to change and pack. The telephone rang again. It was Ben Sommers from Majestic. Sommers offered to pick him up and drive him to the Million Dollar. He sounded grave, and again Roscoe felt frightened as well as confused.

A few moments before, Ben Sommers had received a phone call. A man's voice asked him to hold for Mr. William Randolph Hearst.

"Ben Sommers? This is Bill Hearst."

"Good evening, Mr. Hearst. Are you in town?"

"No, I'm up at San Simeon. Coming down tomorrow, though."

"What can I do for you?" Ben said in his most deferential voice.

"Cut the crap. Tell me about Roscoe Arbuckle."

"What about him?"

"Don't play games." Hearst laughed. "But maybe you haven't heard yet. He killed some trollop, an actress actually, in the St. Francis in San Francisco. On Labor Day."

Ben nearly dropped the phone.

"She actually didn't die until early this afternoon in some hospital up there. Arbuckle is going to be in a lot of trouble. Seems he went after her with a Coke bottle and ripped her up inside. Some of my local *Examiner* people got onto it and are running faster than the police there. They've interviewed a nurse who heard the dying girl accuse Arbuckle, and some woman friend who was actually at the party and practically saw it happen."

"Oh, my God." Ben felt sick.

"I'm calling to remind you of our last meeting. I told you I had played a card for you and some day I'd call it back. Today's the day."

"I remember, Mr. Hearst." A chill settled into Ben's stomach.

"I intend to go all out on this story. It'll sell a million papers a day. When my people run into a stone wall, as they did at the St. Francis, I expect some help from you. Do you understand?"

"I'll help all I can. But you understand, this is the first I've heard about it."

"I understand. Keep in touch, Sommers. I'll be at the beach house when I'm in Los Angeles. My office can connect you. You going to San Francisco?"

"Mr. Hearst, I don't know what I'm going to do. This is a real shock. I've got to find Roscoe. I have to talk to Saul Rubin and ask him how he wants it handled."

"Just don't try to whitewash it. I want this story. I want to milk it for everything I can get out of it. Don't give me the runaround, Sommers. I'll want to know where you are and what you're doing."

"I promise you, Mr. Hearst." The line went dead. Ben sat for a minute deciding what to do. The first thing was to find Roscoe. The butler answered the telephone and said that Mr. Arbuckle was changing his clothes and was going out. Ben shouted at the man to get Arbuckle to the phone.

"Roscoe, that butler of yours is a fool. Don't tell him a thing. You don't want anyone to follow you. Where are you going?"

"To Sid Grauman's office. Joe Schenck suggested it."

"Good. I'll pick you up in twenty minutes."

"Mr. Weiss? Ben Sommers. I have some potentially bad news."

"I'm sorry to hear that. What has happened there?"

"Roscoe Arbuckle has gotten himself into trouble. How bad the trouble is nobody knows yet. A girl died under mysterious circumstances in San Francisco at a party given by Roscoe. Roscoe may have raped her and hurt her. I won't know more until I talk to him. I'm picking him up in a few minutes. We're hiding him out in Sid Grauman's office at the Million Dollar." There was a long silence.

"How many unreleased pictures of his do we have in the vault?"

"Three, and *Gasoline Gus* just opened here."

"I don't like it. I got a bad feeling about the whole thing. Whitewash, if you can. Any chance of a hush-up?"

"No. Bill Hearst has already called. He says if it's true, he is going to nail Roscoe up. He implied that he had protected Majestic once already this year."

"That bastard."

"He's right. If Roscoe is guilty, no amount of hushing it up will succeed. Not in a rape and murder. I don't think anyone knows what's going to happen yet. I'll keep you informed."

"Thanks. For what, I can't guess."

Roscoe sat silently in the front seat of the inconspicuous car that Ben had borrowed from a neighbor. Ben watched him out of the corner of his eye when he could. The round face was impassive. Otherwise he acted as if nothing much had happened.

Ben parked in the side lot at the Million Dollar and they entered using the stage door. A small elevator took them to the fifth floor where Sid Grauman had his office. Although Majestic now owned the theater, Grauman was maintaining offices and a small apartment upstairs until his new theater, the Egyptian, was finished on Hollywood Boulevard. The elevator was small for both Roscoe and Ben.

Grauman's office was empty and Roscoe, who seemed to know his way, led Ben to the side where a door opened into a lavish parlor. One side of the room was draped in a luxurious brocade. When Roscoe pulled on a cord these draperies opened and they were looking through plate-glass windows at the dimly lighted gold and white auditorium spread below. From the screen the gigantic face of Fatty Arbuckle looked out at the audience. *Gasoline Gus,* Roscoe's newest Majestic picture, had opened the previous weekend as part of Majestic Week and was playing to a packed house.

"Watch this," he giggled. "It's a good scene." Gasoline Gus looked down into the opening of an oil well. The greedy villain, played by Charles Ogle, pushed Fatty to one side and was caught in the face by gushing oil.

"It's not a cream pie," Roscoe roared, tears forming in his eyes, "but almost as good."

"Roscoe, we need to talk. Can we close the curtains? I need your full attention." Reluctantly Roscoe pulled the cord. Muffled laughter could be heard through the glass at frequent intervals.

Roscoe couldn't take his eyes from the draperies.

"They love me, all right. They just love me. It always amazes me to find out how much they love me."

"Roscoe, tell me what happened at the St. Francis."

And Roscoe did. A simplified version, to be sure, but Ben

was satisfied with Roscoe's explanations. Just then the door opened, and several men looked in at them for a moment. Roscoe stood up and smiled.

"Hello, Joe. Thanks for coming. Ben, this is Joe Schenck, a good friend, long time." Roscoe shook his hand and said hello to one of the other men in the party. "This is Frank Dominguez, my lawyer. Frank, Ben has just been advising me to get a lawyer. I told him I didn't need one." The third man in the door was Al Senmacher.

"Al, you were there. Tell them I didn't do nothin'."

Al smiled in an embarrassed sort of way. "I wasn't watching you every minute, Roscoe. I didn't see you do nothing to Virginia—not while I was looking at you, anyway." He seemed unwilling to look at Roscoe while he spoke. Ben's heart sank. If this eyewitness friend of long standing wouldn't clear him, who would?

Schenck sat down behind the desk and asked the operator to get the San Francisco police on the telephone. Then he sat and waited. No one spoke.

When the telephone rang Roscoe stood up. Schenck motioned to him to pick up the receiver. "Just give your name and ask to speak to the chief. Don't say anything else. If they want you to come up for questioning, just say you will be there as soon as you can get there. Don't volunteer anything." Schenck's voice sounded very stern, as if he were speaking to a naughty child, rather than to a friend of many years or to a celebrity whose career he had controlled and from whom he had become very rich.

"This is Roscoe Arbuckle calling from Los Angeles. Can I speak to the chief, please?" There was a long wait. Roscoe covered the mouthpiece with his hand and smiled a bright smile. "Wait till Sid gets the bill." Finally Roscoe was speaking to someone on the other end of the line. "Yes, sir. I'll start driving tonight. Be there tomorrow. I understand. No trouble. See you tomorrow." Roscoe hung up and grinned at them. Then he sighed a huge, theatrical sigh of relief and held his head with both hands, holding them so this fat cheeks and mouth were pushed forward in a look of cherubic innocence. "He just wants to ask me a few questions for the record. No problems. Well, gang, who wants to drive back to 'Frisco, lovely city by the Golden Gate? Don't all speak at once."

"I'll go with you. You must have legal representation," Dominguez said quietly.

"I better go, too," Ben said. "Somebody has to look out for

282

your reputation and the reputation of Majestic. I suspect the newspapers will have a field day."

"Al, you better go up, you might be needed in the event of an inquest or something." Schenck spoke quietly. He turned to Roscoe. "Don't drive all the way yourself, you shouldn't be all tired out when you get there. I want you on your best behavior. Very polite. No jokes. No funning. A girl is dead—try to remember that. The police may not think that's funny."

Roscoe looked at him strangely. "I don't think it's funny either, Joe. And I'm surprised you would think that I would." He looked at the unsmiling faces surrounding him in a half circle. "I guess it's true. Nobody loves a fat man."

44

September 1921, San Francisco—Saturday

Variety

DEMILLE AGAINST CENSORSHIP
SPEAKS OUT AT WOMAN'S CLUB

Los Angeles. In a speech here at the Ebell Club
(Tues. 6) Cecil DeMille allied the film industry
with books and newspapers in needing the First
Amendment.

"If a motion picture offends any private group,
they have every right to urge their members to stay
away. That is their liberty. But the right to produce
without prior censorship is ours. A censor can
extend his definition of righteousness to include
political, economic, scientific, or religious views.

"Grant him that power, and he can logically apply it to plays, books, newspapers, or speeches.
When we fight censorship, what we're defending is
every person's right to freedom of speech."

Reaction to the speech was not especially enthusiastic. The Ebell Club has been a prime mover
behind the censorship movement.

"The more the merrier," laughed Roscoe as they climbed
into the white Pierce-Arrow. "Only it ain't going to be very
scenic, driving through the night." By the time they'd stopped
for everyone's overnight bags, it was three A.M. Ben drove
first, then they all took turns, sleeping as best they could. It
was warm driving up through the valley, so they were more
comfortable with the canvas top down. There was not much
conversation; everyone was preoccupied with what might be

happening in San Francisco. When they stopped for gasoline in Fresno, the headline of the local newspaper struck them like a blow.

FILM STAR DEAD AFTER ORGY

Ben, standing in the gasoline station waiting for the sleepy attendant to finish filling the tank, felt a sense of doom hanging over the trip. Bill Hearst's smugness disturbed him, too—the voice of a man who had everyone where he wanted them, particularly Fatty and Ben himself.

As they pulled out into the empty highway, Ben turned to Roscoe and said, "Even if this blows over and we head back tomorrow, you'll have to live like a saint."

"What d'ya mean, even if? I tell you nothing happened." He was thoughtful for a few miles. "Hell, I can't live like a saint. All I'm in the game for is to have a great old time. For God's sake, who lives like a goddamned saint? There ain't a man alive who hasn't sinned a little here and there. That's what makes life exciting. Knowing that everybody is not exactly what they paint themselves to be."

On the ferryboat going from the Oakland Mole to the Ferry Building, Roscoe stood outside in the chilly, damp air on the upper deck. When he came back into the cabin, just before docking, Ben was struck by the sadness in his face.

The big white touring car parked in front of the Hotel St. Francis at a little after eight o'clock on Saturday night. Al Senmacher went in to register them while Roscoe handed the car keys to the doorman. A bellboy began to unload the small bags they had hurriedly packed. Al came out of the hotel, face flushed.

"They don't want us. The manager nearly fainted when I mentioned your name, Roscoe. He said they had no rooms. How do ya like that?"

Roscoe looked down at the pavement, then up at the hotel. "I spent plenty in there. Thousands and thousands of dollars. Well," he grinned, "there's other hotels where my money is good." They piled back into the motorcar and Al headed around Union Square and down Stockton to Market Street. He was going to try the Palace.

They were not welcome there, either. As the four of them stood on the sidewalk trying to decide where to try next, a crowd gathered around the spectacular white automobile and it was spotted by a reporter. Using a public telephone in the hotel lobby, Frank Dominguez called a San Francisco attorney, Charles Brennan, who arrived a few minutes later by taxicab. A crowd of reporters shouted questions at Arbuckle, who refused to answer them on the advice of Dominguez. Ben, sitting with Roscoe in the automobile, was frightened by the lynch attitude of the reporters.

Brennan made arrangements for them to stay in a small hotel on Post Street, and they were about to drive off when a group of police officers arrived, who told them Roscoe was to go immediately to the Hall of Justice on Kearny Street for questioning.

While the rest of the party waited in a corridor, Roscoe Arbuckle was questioned by batteries of detectives and two assistant district attorneys. He was not allowed to have either Brennan or Dominguez with him during the questioning. Although Arbuckle refused to answer any questions or make any statements, he was alone with the assistant district attorney and the police for three hours.

Ben was talking to a group of nearly twenty reporters when he saw Roscoe move wearily out of the room where he had been kept since their arrival. He looked exhausted and close to tears. Dominguez sat down beside him on a bench and they whispered together, while Brennan stood close to them and listened.

Suddenly Assistant District Attorney U'Ren burst out of the room where he had been questioning Arbuckle and said loudly, "Roscoe Arbuckle, you are under arrest and are charged with murder."

U'Ren stepped back against the wall and folded his arms across his chest. He was joined by the captain of detectives. The crowd of reporters swarmed about the two men. Ignored, Arbuckle paid little attention to what was happening. He was too exhausted. Dominguez and Brennan were too stunned to intercede.

U'Ren explained to the reporters that Arbuckle had been charged under a section of the penal code that made death as a result of rape a murder. Roscoe Arbuckle began to cry. First he covered his eyes with his hands to hide the tears. Then he moved his hands to cover his ears so he couldn't hear what the captain of detectives, Matheson, was saying.

"Neither I nor Mr. U'Ren nor Chief of Police O'Brien feel that any man, whether he be Fatty Arbuckle or anyone else, can come into San Francisco and commit that kind of crime. The evidence shows that an attack was made on Virginia

Rappe. San Francisco is tired of being the garbage can of Hollywood."

A detective led Roscoe Arbuckle upstairs where he was formally charged with murder and booked. He was then placed in a cell, as there was no possibility of bail on a murder charge.

On Sunday, Arbuckle's good friend, Sid Grauman, withdrew *Gasoline Gus* from his theaters. On Monday two smaller theaters in Los Angeles changed bills and substituted other films for the Arbuckle pictures then playing. In San Francisco, all of Roscoe's films were immediately withdrawn.

The cancellation of *Gasoline Gus* caused a great deal of harm to Arbuckle's reputation in Hollywood itself. Because Grauman and Arbuckle had been such good friends for so many years, everyone assumed that Sid Grauman knew the real facts in the case. If Sid Grauman withdrew Roscoe's picture, he must be guilty.

The New York American, Sept. 11, 1921

DEAD GIRL'S FIANCÉ CALLS PRISONER BEAST
"CAN'T FACE ARBUCKLE, I'D KILL HIM,"
HE SAYS
SPECIAL HEARST PAPER CORRESPONDENT

New York, Sept. 11, 1921. Henry Lehrman, motion picture director and producer, today discussed the death of Miss Virginia Rappe, his fiancée. Lehrman has directed "Fatty" Arbuckle. At present he is directing Owen Moore in a Selznick film.

During the interview Lehrman nervously fingered a pair of platinum cuff buttons given him by the dead actress. The buttons bore the inscription: *"To Henry, my first and last sacred love. Virginia."*

Lehrman said, "My prayer is that justice be done. I don't want to go to the coast now; I could not face Arbuckle. I would kill him."

Lehrman raised his hollow and weary face to a large photograph of Miss Rappe. It showed her girlish face silhouetted against a big picture hat hanging from two velvet cords about her neck. He read from the affidavit of Mrs. Jean Jamison, the nurse: "She said she blamed Arbuckle for her injuries and wanted him punished for it."

Lehrman continued: "That is just like Virginia. She had the most remarkable determination. She would rise from the dead to defend her person from indignity.

"I had a talk over the long-distance telephone with Sidi Spreckles, who was with her when she died. 'Don't tell Henry,' she kept repeating. That means one thing to me. She lost the battle she made to defend herself. She didn't want me to know. She knew what I would do.

"Arbuckle is a beast. I directed him in photoplays for a year and a half. I finally had to tell him if he didn't keep out of women's dressing rooms, I would see to it that he was through. He once boasted to me that he had torn the clothing from an unwilling girl and outraged her."

Lehrman looked around the room. On the table were such books as H. G. Wells' *Outline of History;* on the walls were Japanese prints. He continued: "That's what comes from taking vulgarians from the gutter and giving them enormous salaries and making idols of them. Arbuckle came into pictures nine years ago. He was a barboy in a San Francisco saloon. Not a bartender, a barboy, one of those who wash the glasses and clean the cuspidors.

"Such people don't know how to get a kick out of life, except in a beastly way. They are a disgrace in the film business. They are the ones who resort to cocaine and the opium needle and who participate in orgies that surpass the orgies of degenerate Rome. They should be swept out of the picture business.

"I'm no saint but I've never attended one of those parties and Virginia certainly wouldn't. Her friends were like Charlie Chaplin and other decent people.

"Arbuckle was large, but he was incredibly strong. I remember once in Mexico he bested several well-known athletes. I have a telegram from Dr. Rumwell saying that Virginia's bladder was ruptured. Doctors here in New York say that only crushing external forces could have done that to her. Last time I directed Arbuckle, he weighed 310 pounds.

"Virginia always had a violent physical aversion to Arbuckle. One time when he attended a party her attitude definitely dampened things. I took her aside and asked her to be nice to him, after all, we had to work together. She replied, 'He's coarse and vulgar. He nauseates me. He is cheap and thinks he is funny.'

"I can see now in my mind's eye how she must have fought him like a tiger. I remember once when there was a report of a terrible assault case in the newspapers, she said, 'If anyone tried to do that to me, I would fight to the death.'

"Well, she's dead.

"Nobody can put me off. Arbuckle is rich and has powerful friends and much influence and money will be used to save him. But he will have me to reckon with, even if he succeeds in buying his freedom.

"God," prayed Lehrman, "give justice!"

"There's no way to keep Lehrman quiet, I suppose?" asked Nathan Greenglass. "No pressure we can apply?"

Weiss shrugged his shoulders. "He doesn't work for me. He works for Selznick. I suppose I could ask Lewis to shut him up. But why should I? It would only get out, and I don't want it to look like Majestic is applying any pressure or trying to buy Roscoe's freedom in any way. That *schmuck* U'Ren keeps implying that big money will cheat the public out of justice if the good people of California don't watch out. I'd like to get him free, God knows. There's three or four million dollars' profits in those unreleased pictures. But I don't want to pour oil on the fire. Lehrman'll never work again if I can help it, but I'll see to that later when things have cooled off."

The secretary interrupted. "It's Clarence Darrow on your telephone, Mr. Weiss."

As he picked up the receiver, Greenglass lifted the separate earpiece to listen. Weiss swiveled his chair so his back was to the group of associates sitting around the desk.

"Thank you for calling back, Mr. Darrow." There was a long silence, so intense that the men could hear each other breathe. "I'm very sorry to hear that. We hoped you would say yes." Moses Klein looked up at Greenglass standing by the desk. Their eyes met for a second and Klein looked down at the black headline on *The New York American* lying on his lap. He shook his head sadly.

"I certainly understand, Mr. Darrow," Weiss continued.

"No, you couldn't risk that. Well, you did your best. No, Mr. Rogers is too ill to take the case. I agree he would do a fine job. Thank you, Mr. Darrow. We'll need it."

Weiss sat looking at the phone for a minute, then turned slowly to the others.

"There is a standing warrant out for Darrow in California if he ever practices law there again. He once perjured himself to win a case. If he took the case, he'd be arrested in an hour. He'd like to take it. For one thing, he knows Majestic is good for a big fee. For another, he thinks Roscoe is innocent and will be railroaded." Weiss looked surprised. "Do you think that is possible?" he asked. "It never occurred to me for one minute that he was innocent. Nobody is ever innocent in this business." He shrugged. "But he could be, I guess."

Moses Klein was shocked. "Mr. Weiss, everyone is innocent until a jury says they're guilty. That's the way things are."

Weiss smiled at him gently. "You think what you think, and I'll think what I think. I've been to parties with Roscoe. He isn't so innocent as that fat baby face would make you think."

Greenglass said, "The fat face will kill him. Everyone thinks he flopped down on that girl and crushed her. Nobody will ever look at him again and smile at the good-natured, roly-poly, lovable fat man. He has become an obese monster, a fat killer, a slobbering rapist."

Weiss stared at him as the words sank in. "But his pictures were always so clean. Never a bit of smut or dirt."

"That doesn't make any difference," Klein said. "Look at what's happening. The exhibitors are canceling the pictures themselves before the censors let out a peep. Look at Majestic stock. Down fifteen points in a week. And still dropping. Majestic never made a dirty picture in its entire history. Now look."

Weiss spoke slowly. "No, it's more than that. It's Hollywood itself people don't trust. It isn't Roscoe's fault. He did what every man would like to do. He liked girls. Everybody does. He liked good times. Who doesn't? He liked to take a drink, to eat a good meal. Just like everybody. But if you put all those nice things together with eight or nine thousand dollars a week for a man who was a plumber's assistant ten or twelve years ago, they become vices as far as the public is concerned. Nice things backfired on him."

"It's liberal times, since the war," Greenglass added. "The young people are rebelling against old ways. You should hear my father talk and ask questions. I might as well work in a whorehouse as for Majestic. They're the same." Weiss's eyebrows went up. "No, Mr. Weiss, I mean it. Everything's upside down. Short skirts, bobbed hair, petting parties, drinking, girls smoking, jazz, tangoes. People think the kids learn it at the movies. They don't learn it at home, for God's sake."

Weiss looked into the distance. "And they're right," he said. "Movie people are like royalty, above all rules. Look at Mary and Doug. Divorced. Since when did nice people get divorces? Look at the publicity stories. Taking a bath used to be a private business. Now we release photos of Gloria Swanson's bathtub. A bathtub isn't dirty exactly, but it makes people think of nudity and sex."

"People get jealous, too," said Greenglass. "Who is worth ten thousand a week? They confuse the romantic stories we film with the real lives of the stars. And the stars do, too. I wonder sometimes how they separate reality from make-believe. How does that stop at six o'clock? How does a man adjust when he knows there are women everywhere who are dying to pull his pants off and stroke his *gid?* No wonder, no wonder," he mused.

Moses Klein held up the newspaper. "Whatever it is, this time it's out of control." He read off the headlines: "New Girl Tells of Revel at Arbuckle Party. . . . Guests Tell of Kicking at Locked Door. . . . Torn Silk Undergarments of Dead Girl Found in San Francisco. . . . Arbuckle Witnesses Guarded, Intimidation Feared." He shook his head. "It's hopeless."

Weiss nodded in agreement. "Ben Sommers tells me that free-lance writers are storming the studio gates trying to get material on the scandal that they can sell in articles to some magazine or paper. The dirtier the better."

"My wife hides the papers from the kids. She said she didn't know some of those words," Grossman said, laughing.

"What about the wife?" Klein asked, nodding at the newspaper.

"Sommers offered her five thousand if she would go and stand by Roscoe in court. She agreed. Said she would have gone without the money." They all laughed.

"We laugh," Weiss said, "but it's like a funeral." He paused a long while. "I guess we will have to dump Roscoe. He's beyond help. Just let him go. Withdraw the pictures and consider it the price of continuing business." He snapped his fingers in the air. "Three million gone, just like that." He took a deep breath. "Send Sommers a wire and tell him to wrap it up. We give up." His voice took on a tone of resignation. "We'll have to figure out some way to wash our hands of Roscoe publicly so we get the most beneficial public relations from the move. Make it look like we're cleaning house or something."

Klein nodded enthusiastically. "The most important thing is to save the studio." He paused as if a stray thought had suddenly entered his mind. "Maybe now is the time to talk to Pettijohn and his friend Hays?"

Weiss's eyes brightened. "His first job could be to get rid of Roscoe for us. Let it look like the industry is reacting in righteous indignation. It's an idea, Mr. Klein. It's an idea."

45

October 1921,
Majestic Studios and South Alvarado Avenue

MISTER EXHIBITOR!
SCREEN BIOGRAPHIES A NEW MAJESTIC SERVICE

Mary May Maxwell

Miss Maxwell, born in Rockville, Md. in 1902, made her professional debut at the age of 5. The child's success was instantaneous. While Miss Maxwell was still in her teens, she was established as the highest paid actress of her age on the stage or the screen.

In 1919, she signed a three-year contract with Majestic Pictures for which she will receive over a million dollars. That contract will undoubtedly be extended for a much larger sum.

Her genius for the theater has never wavered. She began her career as a star, and a star—but of greater magnitude—she remains. Hers is a story of unadulterated success, absolutely unique, from beginning to end.

*   *   *

Present the above biography to your local news editor, and ask him to run it in the newspaper when you next program a Maxwell picture. Remind him of your regular advertising budget if he is unwilling to run it as editorial material.

Rubin turned to Ben, who was seated across the empty, gleaming desk. He was trying to keep his voice light and inconsequential.

"You've become very friendly with Bill Taylor, I understand."

"Yes. I spend an evening or two there during the week. He has a very nice radio and we listen." Ben wondered where all this was leading.

"He goes out a lot, I suppose?"

"I really don't know, Mr. Rubin. I don't keep track of him." Ben let his irritation sound in his voice.

"I only wondered if he and Mary May Maxwell were still going around together. They both work here, and as president I have a little right to know."

"For Christ's sake, that's all common gossip. Why don't you ask Bill? He'll tell you right off."

Rubin shot him a withering glance. "If I could do that, or be sure of gossip, would I be trying to find out from you, dumbskull?"

"Why can't you?"

"Look, Ben, I need your help. It's very confidential and can't go beyond these four walls. Abe Weiss don't even know I'm asking."

"I never talk, Mr. Rubin. I know a lot of secrets, if you'll stop for a minute and think." He was indignant.

"OK, OK, no need to be upset. Look, Ben, Majestic has a great many very emotional people working here—artists, really. They have a tendency to act like willful children. It's my job to try and keep order so they can all work together with a minimum of steam. Understand?"

Ben nodded and allowed himself to relax slightly. Rubin became expansive as he decided to take Ben into his confidence.

"Mary May Maxwell's mother is the closest thing to a barracuda this side of the Catalina Channel. All these other stage mothers who push and shove and would kill to get their kids ahead are amateurs compared to her." He shook his head as if in amazement. "In twenty years in this business I've never seen anyone as greedy and grasping. Well, Ma Sheldon found out her baby bank book had been dallying around with Bill Taylor in ways no little girl should. You know Mary adores Bill. It's clear as a bell on her face."

"I know." Ben was reserved. "I've seen it."

"Well, Ma Sheldon went through the roof. So Mary and Bill had to sneak around." He smiled nastily. "They say love will find a way. As I hear it, love did. Up at Lake Arrowhead, out at Malibu. You know. Bill had a good thing going. A tender young thing in love will do almost anything and, as I hear it, Bill enjoys almost everything." He winked broadly. "Gossip only! But I hear these things." He exuded self-assurance.

Ben relaxed back into the chair gradually. He was becoming interested.

"Then it hit me personal," Rubin continued. "Mrs. Sheldon climbed on a train and dropped in on Mr. Weiss in his New York office one morning. Complained about the sophisticated son-of-a-bitch, man-of-the-world director who was getting all that nice squab. She demanded that Taylor be denounced publicly," he nodded energetically as if in answer to the disbelief on Ben's face. "Yes, as a cad and seducer. Furthermore, that he never be allowed to direct her innocent baby in a picture again." He closed his eyes, a perfect picture of despair. "I tell you, I nearly hit the ceiling when Weiss agreed to her terms. Could have knocked me over with a feather. It's not like him to sell out." He acted as if it was still hard to believe. "Impossible to run a studio like that! Impossible!" The outrage was vivid in his voice.

Ben whistled in surprise. "So that's what happened. I always wondered. Up to a certain point all her pictures were so successful—big hits. It was then that you stopped assigning Bill to Mary's pictures." He leaned back smiling. "I thought you'd lost your mind."

Something occurred to him and he sat forward.

"You know, Mr. Rubin, when I first came to the studio and people were filling me in on who was who and all the gossip, I heard that Mrs. Sheldon was madly in love with the director of Mary's pictures and he was giving it to both of them." He shuddered. "But when I met Bill I couldn't imagine it. He has better taste than that."

A slow smile spread across Rubin's face. "Maybe it was a smoke screen. Once with the mother for every dozen or so times with the little girl." He shrugged expressively. "Throw her off the scent."

"You know, Mr. Rubin, as friendly as I've become with Bill, I really know very little about him. He never talks about himself or his friends. He is just here now—no past, no memories, nothing. I've always thought of him as being slightly mysterious."

Rubin leaned forward as if to confide in Ben. "Bill surrounds himself with an aura of mystery, all right. There was a very queer situation back a couple of years—a valet, I think, disappeared with a lot of money and jewelry. Bill refused to prosecute. Word spread that the man was really his brother." He sat back. "You won't find out anything about Bill that he doesn't want you to know. Ben, that's why I need your help," he said appealingly.

Ben could now see why. "I've only seen two girls there. Once Mary and her mother, and Mabel Normand another time. She seemed very attracted to him."

Rubin grunted. "A lot of women are. Ben, there are only a few of us mature sophisticated men in Hollywood. Oh, there are thousands of good-looking, callow, vapid types, whose only asset is a beautiful profile. Bill treats women in an old-world way. He knocks my wife dead—turns on that British charm like a goddamn faucet."

Laughing, Ben said, "I've seen him at work. He bats those pale grey eyes and juices up the old accent, and visions of a country house surrounded by a thousand acres of lawn make the girls giddy. They just naturally fall on the bed and the lord of the manor grabs 'em." His voice was tinged with awe. "You ought to see the inscriptions on some of the photos on his dining-room wall. I tell you, I wouldn't take my mother there for dinner."

"Whatever he's got, he knows how to use it on young actresses. They fall for him and give him the performance of their lives."

Ben asked cautiously, "What do you want me to do if I should find out that Bill and Mary are still seeing each other?" He was still reserving his option of saying nothing, but Rubin didn't have to know that.

Rubin responded warmly, gracious to his fingertips. "Nothing, nothing, Ben. Just let me know, is all. Mr. Weiss has a way of finding out little things then turning them into darts to throw at our operations here. I'd kinda like to be prepared, is all."

Ben considered the situation for a moment. Rubin stared at him intently. I guess it can't hurt Bill, Ben thought, and it might help Majestic.

"OK, I guess there's nothing wrong in it."

Rubin stood up from behind his desk and extended his hand in a hearty handshake.

"Nothing wrong and everything right," he beamed.

After finishing Henry's beautifully served candlelight supper, Bill and Ben fiddled with the Atwater Kent radio. Bill snapped it off at eight P.M., when KNX had to relinquish its time to the next station.

"The light classics are the only music worth listening to, as far as I'm concerned," Bill said fastening a cigarette into a long ivory holder and lighting it. "I only like jazz for dancing."

The room glowed with a warm light from the pink silk shaded lamps. Ben felt relaxed and comfortable. "Gee, it's exciting, though. To think that some band is playing that music all the way over in Los Angeles somewhere, and we're out here in Westlake and can hear them perfectly. It must be five miles."

Henry placed snifters of brandy on the tables beside them. "Are you all set for the party on Saturday next?"

"Guess so." Ben took a sip. "I went out and bought a new tux and everything. Elsie's coming with me and she's got a wild dress from Grace. She won't tell me what it is." He grinned. "I hope it's not some tiger skin and feathers thing left over from a DeMille picture." They both laughed. "Although from what I hear, that might fit into Hollyhock House perfectly. Is this Barnsdall dame pretty rich?"

Taylor flicked the ash off the end of his cigarette. "She's the heiress to God knows how many million dollars in oil money, and she wants to turn Hollywood into the art capital of the world, no less. Make it the new Paris of the West."

"What's wrong with the old one?"

"Nothing. She spent a lot of time there. But now she's built that big house and wants to live here. She's an interesting woman, Ben—a genuine eccentric. Avant-garde theater in Chicago, Gordon Craig in London, friends with Isadora Duncan, spent two seasons with the Art Theatre in Moscow and got mixed up with the Bolsheviks, financed Reinhardt for a season in Berlin. She was *intime* with everybody in Paris who wrote, composed, sculpted, or painted. Now she's taken aim on Hollywood."

"God almighty. Can it be done, an art capital?"

Taylor rubbed one finger idly around the rim of his glass. "I don't really think so. Culture takes a certain climate that just doesn't seem to exist in California." He thought for a minute. "It's still a gold rush out here."

"Aw come on, Bill. I know it's not London. But it's a little better than that."

"Not much. The only art that's appreciated in Hollywood is the art of deal making."

"Well, I think there's more culture in Hollywood than you

give them credit for. Gee, Bill, there's some pretty fancy places up in the hills." Ben didn't know why he was being defensive.

"Oh, come off it, Ben. You don't even know the meaning of the word. How many old masters are hanging on the walls around here? The most anyone has is an oil portrait of themselves in their most spectacular film role. Most of the art you see out here is painted on the inside of abalone shells."

Ben felt less and less that he knew what he was talking about. "Bill, you're the most cultured man I've ever met, and you live and work here."

Taylor bowed in mock humility. "Thank you. That's a real compliment." He smiled gently. "But I'm pretty much of a minority of one. Actually, I am invited out to talk 'cultured.'" He said the word in a flat accent. "I wish I could pronounce it the way they do, with a K. I'm supposed to uphold the honor of the West, so the guests from the East won't think we're all idiots." He set his glass on the table. "They'd be smarter to invite some actress with spectacular breasts and a beautiful ass, which is what the intellectuals really come to see." He took up his glass again. "They can hear good talk in Cambridge or New Haven."

They both smirked. "Don't forget, Ben, the aristocracy of Hollywood was a rabble of immigrant furriers and second-hand clothes dealers just twenty years ago. Movie royalty, after all," he continued, "was touring crummy vaudeville theaters or selling merchandise in a five-and-ten five years ago." He raised his glass in a salute. "The queen herself, Mary Pickford, washed out her own undies in hotel room washbasins just ten years ago." He took a cigarette out of a Chinese lacquered box and tapped it on the edge of the table with long fingers. "One can count on the fingers of one hand the men in Hollywood who have been to college, my God, even finished high school." He peered around the lamp at Ben. "You're highly educated, Ben, one of the few. They admire education and achievement, so they hire it." He sat back smugly.

"But at least they respect culture when they see it," Ben said with a frown. He felt as if a bit of Taylor's attack was directed at him.

"Ah," said Taylor triumphantly, pointing the cigarette holder at him. "Famous writers. Famous playwrights." He laughed derisively. "Goldwyn hired Maeterlinck, brought him all the way from Paris, with a huge publicity campaign. Art was making it big in Hollywood. Then they turned his script over to some director who'd never finished high school and got into the business as a stunt man." His eyes bore in on Ben. "This town is full of men and women who are shaping the taste of America and who never went beyond eighth grade." He sat back, disgusted. "Cultural capital, my foot. Poor Aline."

Ben, puzzled because he felt at home and comfortable in Hollywood, was disturbed by Taylor's haughty criticisms.

"But, Bill, I read in *Photoplay* that there's this Negro poet, Lindsay something, who says the movies are the only real American art."

"And I say he's looney. Ben, don't you see? That's the syndrome." He emphasized each word. "The poet's name is *Vachel* Lindsay, and he's not a Negro, and you didn't actually read his book, you read about him in *Photoplay*." He made a skewering motion at Ben with his cigarette holder and fell back into his chair laughing.

Ben's confusion turned to embarrassment. He felt as if he had been beaten handily in a particularly complicated pinochle hand. He didn't really agree, but he could see Taylor's point. After all, what did he know about culture? He took a gulp of his drink and watched Bill stroll over to the piano and untangle the long fringe hanging from the shawl that was draped across it.

"Who's your date for this cultural party we're going to, Bill?"

Taylor didn't answer immediately but continued to comb the fringe with his fingers. "I was going to explain that," he said with elaborate casualness. "It's a bit complicated." He paused, searching for a way to start. "I hope you'll go along with a bit of deception for my sake." He paused again and looked for a reaction from Ben, who gave no response.

"I had an affair with Mary May Maxwell a while back," he said lightly, a man of affairs bantering with a friend. "Then she became too demanding, and I tried to break it off." He laughed in a self-deprecating sort of way. "Demanding is not the word, exactly. I'm past fifty and can only manage it a couple of times a day—if you understand my meaning."

Ben smiled. "I'd say you've managed to hold up pretty well."

Taylor acknowledged the double entendre with a gracious nod.

"I tried to get Mary to agree to a pact where we'd stop seeing each other until she was twenty-one." He sighed hopelessly. "But she wouldn't hear of it, sends a steady stream of notes." He strode across the room to the small desk in front of the windows. He jerked open a drawer and held up a handful of letters. That end of the room was in partial darkness, but Ben could still make out the large monogram, three entwined Ms. "Letters. Little gifts." He twisted his features into an unattractive grimace.

"Yes," laughed Ben, "I'd stay out of her way."

"Yes, indeed! Just try." His voice dropped. "I made a real mistake there," he added, almost to himself. He stood in the center of the room, hands on hips. "The sole object of Carlotta Sheldon's life is to squeeze as much money out of that poor girl as she can before Mary is twenty-one and comes into control of her own fortune." He wagged a finger. "Which is considerable, mind you. I really tried to back off, Ben. That woman frightens the hell out of me."

For an instant, Ben was tempted to ask about the rumors connecting Bill and Mrs. Sheldon, but he decided not to.

"Mary is really very persuasive."

"And very pretty," Ben added softly.

Taylor sighed deeply. "You're right. Now she wants to meet me at Aline Barnsdall's party next Saturday night."

Ben snapped to attention. "I thought we were going together."

"We are. You see, it must seem to Mrs. Sheldon that Mary is going out with an approved young man. A 'safe' date, so to speak."

"What do you want me to do?" Ben tried to keep his voice light and casual, but now the whole enterprise seemed risky.

"There is a young man, Arthur Cox, who is kept on a short leash by his father. The father will allow him to attend the Barnsdall party because Barnsdall Oil is a big depositor in the family bank. And so, it happens, is Mary May Maxwell. Mary's mother knows how strict old Cox is about young Arthur, so she thinks her Mary will be safe with him. Besides, you'll be along, and you're safe." Bill laughed. "Don't take that as an insult."

He sat on the piano bench and raised the lid covering the keys.

"You and Elsie will pick up Arthur and Mary. I will arrive at Hollyhock House with two agreeable girls for Arthur. One of his little vices that his father doesn't know about. Arthur and the two girls will repair to one of Aline's many bedrooms and proceed to unleash Arthur's libido." He played a quick run of notes. "I only hope we can keep the threads of this plot separate."

"My God," Ben laughed. "It could only happen in Hollywood."

"Or in a French farce." The telephone rang in the dining room and Taylor looked up.

"It's Mr. Woolwine, Mr. Taylor. Do you want to talk to him?"

Bill looked at Ben for an instant then said, "I'll take it."

Henry had not turned on the lights in the dining room and Ben could hear Bill's voice coming from the darkened archway. He fiddled with the radio dials trying not to eavesdrop. Suddenly he realized that Woolwine could only be Thomas Lee Woolwine, the District Attorney of Los Angeles. Bill's voice rose.

"Well, someone is selling her drugs, I tell you. Cocaine. Out in the open! And I mean to find out who that someone is if you won't." There was a long silence. Taylor's outburst had been so emotional that Ben felt like an intruder.

"Well, what does constitute sufficient evidence?" Another silence. "If it were bootleg hooch, I'll wager you'd snap into action. A bottle of gin in the hand is worth a pound of cocaine in the bush."

Another long silence.

Ben winced at the mention of buying cocaine. He'd been buying it regularly in Chinatown for one of the editors on the *Los Angeles Times* entertainment page. A paper of dust insured good placement for Majestic stories.

Taylor was almost shouting. "But whoever it is knows Hollywood people. Gets to parties. For all I know, works at a studio. He has an 'in,' I'll wager. I suppose you'll wait until there's an industry full of addicts. That, Mr. Woolwine, will be too late and I will most emphatically say, 'I told you so.' Publicly!" Ben heard the receiver slammed down into its cradle. Taylor stood in the archway like a ghost against the darkness, breathing heavily, his face white with fury. It was the first time that Ben had ever seen the urbane surface ruffled.

"I know you couldn't help but overhear, Ben. Please do me the favor of forgetting what you heard." As if to gain a moment to collect himself, he walked slowly to the piano and slowly lowered the lid on the keys. "Henry gets cross if they get dusty," he said softly.

Ben was rooted to the spot by the radio. "Bill, I did hear. I'd never say anything anyway."

Bill sank into his chair. "Someone is bringing drugs into Los Angeles from Mexico. I've traced the pusher to Chinatown, but there the trail stops." Ben felt like a traitor at the mention of Chinatown. "They've found a gold mine among the movie crowd." He hesitated for a moment, then continued as if he had considered and decided that Ben should know. "I know a very prominent actress who is slipping into addiction, and I'm trying desperately to get her off the stuff." He shook his head sadly. "It's a losing battle. That ennui we spoke of, the emptiness of soul—it's a perfect setting for drugs." Ben saw a quick spark of light reflected in Bill's eye. "But I'm going to nail that man if it's the last thing I ever do, by God!"

Ben closed his eyes. A few minutes ago his only worry had been whether to tell Rubin all he had learned about Bill and Mary Maxwell and their shabby little affair. Now this. He wondered who *this* star was. She must be at Majestic. Jesus Christ! He wished he didn't know.

"I didn't realize it was so dangerous." Ben smiled weakly.

"The Devil's powder. And it's no joke," Taylor snapped. "These people are playing for keeps. They're out to make the slide from cocaine to morphine or heroin as easy and delightful as possible." His voice dropped to a whisper. "And once they go on heroin, they're gone for good, beyond any mortal help."

Ben gulped. "Bill, if there's anything I could ever do, I mean, give you any help . . ." He broke off, not knowing what else to say. "I mean just ask."

"Thanks, Ben. I just might, one of these days. They know me and they know I'm after them. I've been to Chinatown and asked too many questions." An embarrassed grin crossed his face. "I was more clumsy than any bumbling hero in a Saturday serial. They had me spotted within a half hour." He looked down at the floor. "I was lucky to get out." He didn't elaborate, and Ben was afraid to ask any more. He stood up.

"I really got to go, Bill. See you next Saturday night," he laughed. "If I can remember who it is I'm supposed to go with."

Bill gripped his hand. "I am indebted to you, Ben."

Ben shook his head, embarrassed. "Sure, Bill, anything for a friend," he said automatically. But as he said the words he was swept with a guilty feeling that he was spying. Could it really hurt to tell Rubin? Or could it even help Majestic? Jesus, he hated decisions like this.

302

46

October 1921, Hollyhock House

Arthur Cox, younger than Ben had expected him to be, sat in the rear seat, looking vacantly out of the window. Glancing at him in the rearview mirror, Ben decided he was glad he was not Arthur's father.

"Get out much?" Ben asked pleasantly.

"Hardly at all. My old man's afraid that I'll knock up some gumdrop and she'll take him for all his money."

Ben glanced at Elsie, who responded with a raised eyebrow.

"You look very young, if you don't mind my saying so," Elsie remarked.

"I'm eighteen. That's old enough. I've gotten three girls pregnant so far."

"Congratulations. Safe for little Mary," Elsie said softly.

They drove along Wilshire without further conversation and Ben turned onto Freemont, then into the circular drive at number 56, the huge house bought by Mrs. Sheldon with

Mary's first big check from Majestic. Two stone lions guarded the front terrace.

A butler in formal livery opened the door and stood with a questioning look.

Mrs. Sheldon's voice sang out. "It's all right, Wilson. It's Mr. Cox to pick up Mary." Her imposing form appeared behind the butler.

"Oh, Mr. Sommers, you're here too. How pleasant."

"We decided to go in one motor. How have you been?"

"Well, thank you. How's your father, Arthur?" she asked, still looking at Ben. She expected no answer, and Arthur remained silent. Mary appeared at her mother's side, then took Ben's arm and snuggled up to him. He could feel Mrs. Sheldon's eyes burrowing into him. Mary nodded at her date, but Arthur seemed not to notice.

"I'm relieved to see that my baby treasure is in the care of someone responsible," she said, looking at Ben.

"We'll take good care of both ladies, Mrs. Sheldon." Ben tried to sound reassuring.

"I so dread letting her out of my sight. One of these days she will grow up and be gone forever." This was followed by a sigh and the fluttering of a chiffon handkerchief.

Ben felt Mary's tug on his arm. He glanced down at her but she was staring at her mother with a fixed smile on her pretty face, showing no sign that she had given him a signal.

"We really ought to get going," Ben said. "I suspect it will be a very interesting evening."

Mrs. Sheldon nodded, leaned forward and kissed Mary on the cheek. Ben was overwhelmed by cologne. "Yes, I daresay. I don't like all of the odd people she invites, but Miss Barnsdall asked for Mary especially. She is a major influence in the experimental theater and has worked with some of the best people. We theater folk must be friendly and support each other." She tried to sound gracious and pulled her lips back from her teeth in what passed for a smile.

As Ben slipped into the front seat behind the wheel, he felt Mary lean forward. "For God's sake, let's get the hell out of here," she whispered urgently in his ear.

Olive Hill had been planted with a grove of olive trees a generation before, and now they formed a gnarled forest of silvery grey-green that shimmered in every breath of air. Ben drove up the winding drive slowly. Across the top of the hill stretched the vast house Frank Lloyd Wright had designed for Aline Barnsdall to live in. Very romantic—part Indian pueblo, part Aztec temple—from the outside Hollyhock House resembled an exotic fortress, its templelike slanting roofs, pink in the fading light, punctuated by shadowy sculptured pylons, stone stalks of hollyhock standing against the deepening sky.

"It looks for all the world like the sort of thing DeMille would have designed as a setting for a revel—you know the kind of thing he does. To show how depraved the rich are," Ben said.

Mary laughed and Elsie said, "It's just wonderful. Imagine living in that. What an experience."

"Jeez, I think it's awful. Doesn't even look like a house. It's creepy. But then she's creepy too. My father hates her politics. He loves her money, though," Arthur hastened to add.

They walked from the motor courtyard under a floating canopy supported by a pierced wall. The ports in the wall were placed so that shafts of the setting sun illuminated stone hollyhocks as if picked out by tiny pink spotlights. At the door Japanese maids in kimonos bowed greetings and took the coats and wraps. Before them stretched a long gallery crowded with people. Somewhere in the distance a string quartet could be heard playing acerbic modern music.

William Desmond Taylor was waiting with a very pretty girl on each arm. He thrust them toward Arthur, and they immediately attached themselves to him, smiling and nuzzling.

"Here's your harem, Arthur," Taylor said. "Go play eeney, meeney, miney, moe. Catch up with you later if you're still on your feet."

"Where's the booze?" Arthur asked.

"Out there, by the music." Taylor pointed toward the courtyard.

Mary threw her arms around Taylor's neck and kissed him ardently. He tried to unclasp her arms but finally gave up and embraced her until she stood back and looked at him, breathing rapidly.

"We have so much to talk about, love," she murmured.

Taylor nodded gravely. "First, respects to our hostess, then we can talk."

Where the long gallery intersected with the huge living room, stood Aline Barnsdall. She was wearing a magnificent

Japanese kimono, its waist wrapped with a brocade obi—a gift from the architect of her house.

Taylor bowed slightly. "Aline, these are my friends and associates from Majestic."

"I think your house is very beautiful," Elsie said.

Aline Barnsdall glowed with pleasure. "Why, thank you. It was hell to get built. Nobody knew how to pour the concrete. And Mr. Wright, while a great architect, is a son of a bitch to get along with. I fired his contractor, hired my own, and then he sent his son up here to keep watch over us both! How would you like to get a two-thousand-word telegram, collect," she winked, "from Tokyo, that starts out, 'Have splendid idea for garden pool stop' then goes on for 22 pages describing it in detail? He's just lucky I'm rich. It's not just a house," she said, looking around with genuine affection, "but a way of life. It's inspirational just to wake up here in the morning—and great fun for a party."

"You sound lucky to have survived to enjoy it," Ben said.

"You're damned right. Just wait until we get going on the theater, the art gallery, and the residences for actors and writers. We'll come to blows." She snorted and gave a bellow of a laugh. "And I'm bigger than he is. Going to be one hell of a fight." She looked toward newly arriving guests. "Stay right here. Alla has arrived with her Italian and his girl friend. I'll introduce you." She walked past them calling out gaily, and they turned to look at the new arrivals.

Alla Nazimova walked toward them in a shimmering silver sheath, fingernails lacquered black, hair frizzed out in a pale blonde puff, mouth framed in black lipstick. Elsie gasped.

"She looks like a goddamned dandelion," Taylor remarked and Mary smothered a laugh.

Aline walked forward with them. "You must meet Madame Nazimova. You probably know Rudy. He's on the Majestic lot now. This is his fiancée, Natasha Rambova." An exquisite creature wearing a Spanish flamenco dress nodded icily. Everything matched, from the tiny paillettes pasted on her eyelids to the orange tassel hanging from her cigarette holder. She exuded a kind of glacial coldness that only underlined the perfection of her features.

"Hello, Rudy," Elsie smiled. She nodded at Rambova, about whom she had only heard. Rambova did not acknowledge her.

Valentino took Elsie's hand, turned it over and kissed the open palm. His tongue flicked across her skin with extraordinary speed and Elsie let out a gasp of astonishment. Rambova shot him a look of disapproval.

Smiling, Valentino said, "But Natasha, *cara,* she is an old friend. Elsie writes the titles for my pictures," he explained, looking wounded.

Elsie looked at Natasha for a moment, took a deep breath and said, "You bet. The studio thought the titles for *The Sheik* were among the best that have been done in a long time." Let that sink in, you bitch, she thought.

Nazimova allowed a long tragic sigh to escape. "The picture was trash. Garbage. Only I understand the soul of an artist. You were a fool to leave me at Metro. Greatness wasted like that," she added sadly. She gently placed her arm around Natasha. "You wait until Rambova takes personal artistic charge of his pictures. The screen will explode with his glory," she said imperiously.

Rambova beamed at Nazimova and Valentino. Taylor caught Ben's eye and looked heavenward. Natasha pulled at Valentino's arm.

"There are important people in the arts here tonight, Rudy, dearest. I want you to meet artists. You can talk shop any time." Valentino looked back apologetically, shrugging as they walked off.

"She's become so abrasive and possessive, Alla," Aline said, when they were out of earshot, "but he seems very attracted to her."

"He is like a piece of clay to be modeled in her sensitive hands, Aline. She is not interested in him as a woman in a man, but as a medium in which to display her artistry. A face and a body like that come along only once in a lifetime." Nazimova fitted a long black Russian cigarette into the longest holder Ben had ever seen. She fumbled in her bag, then held up a black match. "You must do it," she said to Ben, "my arm is not long enough."

He took the match, looked about helplessly for an instant, then struck it on the bottom of his shoe.

Nazimova smiled. "How quaint," she said, exhaling a dense cloud of smoke. "So American." She took his arm.

Taylor coughed to keep from laughing.

"I thought *The Red Lantern* was great, Madame Nazimova," Ben said. "A really good picture."

She smiled up at him. "Thank you. Come, we shall find a drink, and you can tell me how wonderful I was. Have you seen me in *Camille?*"

Turning as she talked, she cleverly used Ben's dark back

307

and shoulder as a background, posing theatrically. "I love your party, Aline, dear. I will show it to the young man." Ben looked helplessly back at Elsie. Aline Barnsdall glared after them.

"Do you mind if I wander about and look at your house?" Elsie said quickly.

"Be at home, dear." Aline took one of Elsie's hands and squeezed in a familiar way that surprised her. "Maybe later I can escape and we can find a secluded corner and talk about it." Her smile promised friendship.

"Thank you for making this possible," Mary said to Aline as she leaned up and kissed Bill Taylor on the cheek, leaving a pink smudge.

"Enjoy yourself, Billy," Aline called after them as they wandered off.

Elsie walked into the living room and stood in front of a great fireplace, trying to understand the abstract sculpture towering over it. The hearth at her feet was surrounded by a pool of flowing water.

"It's a goldanged stream, all right. Water runs right under the house." The deep voice was behind her.

Turning, she looked up into the face of Kelso Kennard.

"Why, Kelso. What a surprise! I almost don't recognize you without your ten-gallon Stetson. What are you doing here? I mean, it's not quite the place I'd expect to find a cowboy." Elsie realized that she was being clumsy and stammered, "I mean . . ."

"Too classy for a cowhand, you mean?"

"No. Yes. You know what I mean. This is a funny place to find a title writer from Majestic Pictures, much less you. Well, look around. Movie stars and artists. The lunatic fringe of politics." She smiled at him.

He looked down at her and smiled, the creases in his face growing deeper.

"I'll forgive you. I'm dry as dust. Let's go find the hooch."

"The bar is outside, through there," she pointed.

The closely clipped lawn of the courtyard lay at exactly the same level as the floor of the house. She looked up. "It's not like going outside at all, is it? It's more like walking from one room to another, but this room has stars for a ceiling."

Kelso nudged her. "Look at those labels. I haven't seen Haig Pinch for a year or more."

She laughed. "She probably gets it right off the boat."

"If I know Aline, she owns the boat." He walked to the end of the courtyard. "Look here, Miss Wright, see this here pool? I'll tell you a funny story on this house, if you don't think it's too vulgar."

"Tell me." She sipped her Orange Blossom. "It can't be that bad."

"Remember that pond, then follow me." He pointed to the perfect circle of water at the far end of the courtyard. They walked back through the living room and he pointed at the pool surrounding the hearth. "And that one." He continued walking until they stood on a wide terrace on the western side of the house looking over flower boxes down into a square pool sunk in gently receding squares of lawn. She noticed that the design of squares continued under water on the bottom of the pool, but nothing else. She looked up questioningly.

"It's all the same water. It flows from way back there, past the fireplace, and ends up out down there." He lowered his voice and bent closer. "Last party I was here, some clowns started taking leaks." He stopped. "I mean, peeing into the round pool, then trying to follow the yellow stream out to here." He laughed heartily. "I hope you're not offended. Little rough cowhand humor." He finished lamely and looked at her.

She tried to keep a straight face, then couldn't. She laughed with him. "It must have been funny. Did it really happen?"

He raised his hand. "Swear to God. Aline was sure it would kill the fish." He started to laugh again. "It didn't, but she was fit to be tied."

She put her hand on his arm. "Now you can clear up a mystery."

"Sure thing. What's troubling you?"

"You haven't told me who you are."

"All right, don't shoot. I started out as a cowboy, all right. Years ago in the valley. I sold all that land to old Carl Laemmle for his studio and bought more. Now the ranch is pretty big." He grinned proudly. "Good spread, too. Covers a good part of the valley. Universal rents my box canyons for locations."

"How big is big?"

He smiled broadly. "Let's just say, big. More than a thousand acres, between the valley and over the ridge toward Ojai."

"You must be wealthy. That's a lot."

"Be worth more if there was more water. But I'm working on that now, may just buy me a river. Up north. Every time I drill for water I hit more danged oil. That's how I met Aline. We're partners in a little oil venture and she invites me to her parties to lend a little folksy atmosphere. She likes to shock the upstanding folks. Long as I clean the . . . manure off my boots before I come traipsin' in."

Elsie sat back on the edge of the flower box, impressed. There was more to Kelso than cowboy charm.

"Aline has a good head on her. Just talk to her about oil sometime. She'll make your head spin. She supervised the construction of this house." His outstretched hand defined the expanse of the house. "Can read a blueprint like a contractor."

His voice softened. "But there's also a time for a man to be a man and a woman to be a woman." He looked at her, a smile playing about his lips.

Elsie looked at him closely in the dim light. He was serious. She couldn't believe it, but he was serious. Although she just couldn't take him seriously—it was happening too fast for that.

"I'm about to kiss you. You can run away or stay and let it happen." His eyes dared her to stay.

Elsie hated what she was about to do, but she wouldn't have walked away for anything. "I'll stay," she whispered. "I'm curious. How does a cowboy kiss?"

He laughed. "That's a straight line for a dirty joke if I ever heard one. Like any man, only better," he said laughing, as he drew her toward him.

"I'll take the kiss, but don't tell me the punch line."

They kissed, but both were still laughing, and it was only fun.

Elsie decided to cut the scene off. "You can tell me something. Why did you seek me out? There are lots of prettier girls here tonight."

" 'Cause you're different, honey. I spotted that the first day we met over at Universal. You're not after anything. Everybody out here is after something. I get sick and tired of all those cheap grasping dames—running from man to man grabbing all they can. Throwing you over if you're not a big director. Makes a guy sick."

Elsie smiled up at him and took his arm. "All I want from you is another drink." She stopped at the door to the living room. Ben was walking away rapidly. Had he been watching them? She looked up at Kelso. "I'll have to explain. I have to catch him."

He grabbed her arm and stopped her. "What're you going to tell him? You serious about him? 'Cause if you are, I'll back off. I know better than to invade another man's territory."

She wrenched loose of his grasp. "If I kiss someone it's because I want to. Ben's my date, Kelso. And I wouldn't hurt him for the world." More softly she added, "I wouldn't hurt you either."

"Just because you came with him doesn't mean you have to go home with him—or does it?" He looked at her questioningly.

"Kelso, I'm not sure. I'd have to think about that. We're not engaged, if that's what you mean. That's the best way to put it."

"You go out with other men?"

"No, not really."

He nodded toward where they had seen Ben disappear. "He go out with other girls?"

Elsie exploded with exasperation. "Go out? He doesn't have to. Kelso, he's a picture executive and the girls just fall into his bed. He stays home!"

"He must be pretty good."

She stared at him steadily, unsmiling. "He is."

"I apologize, Elsie. That wasn't very nice. But I had to know where you stood. I've thought of you a lot since that afternoon at Universal. I found out who you were, but I didn't have the nerve to approach you, cold like." He looked down, and for the first time she realized that he was wearing patent leather riding boots with his dinner suit. "I'm just a cowboy, after all. But now that I've got my courage up, I don't intend to let some two-bit Don Juan take you away from me."

"But, Kelso, he's my friend."

"What's sauce for the goose is sauce for the gander, my old daddy used to say. We could leave together now. If you say no, I'll never mention it again. I'll court you and go the long way around. I like you too much to risk anything. But I wouldn't be a man if I didn't press just a little. And these are modern times, and a girl can do what she wants with the man she wants to do it with." He studied her face.

She stepped back, putting more distance between them. "I'm not sure, Kelso. I'd like to go with you, but I'm not certain it's because I want to go or because I'd only be getting back at Ben." She smiled ruefully. "Because he makes me so darned mad. If I went with you, I'd want it to be because I wanted you for your own sake."

"I'll go get you another Orange Blossom and wait with it right here." Then he winked at her. "I won't be too offended if you come home with me just to make him mad. I'd realize you were just getting back at him. But I might just recover from the shame."

47

October 1921, Hollyhock House

Publicity is a Law of Nature. If you had to start
over again, you would be forced to depend on
publicity to advertise your existence.

If motion picture publicity is to achieve useful
results it must be truthful. Truth may be interesting
or not, according to the manner in which it is
presented. Because of its nature, motion picture
publicity is picturesque.

> *Excerpts from a speech delivered by Majestic pub-
> licist, Ben Sommers, to a Los Angeles Chamber of
> Commerce dinner, Oct. 3, 1921.*

By the time Saul Rubin's sky blue Pierce-Arrow limousine
reached the motor courtyard of Hollyhock House, the sharp-
eyed reporter who had recognized Polly McCormack in the
backseat was calling the story in to *The Examiner*. While
Polly's wrap was being taken by one of the Japanese maids,
the story moved from the rewrite man to the entertainment
desk where it was approved. As Aline Barnsdall stood in
the gallery watching the approach of Rubin and some child, a
linotype operator was handed the gossip item to set into
molten metal.

"Aline, thank you for asking me. I'd like you to meet my
newest discovery, the rising star in Majestic's sky, and special
friend, Polly McCormack."

Polly curtsied and held out her hand. "Pleased to meet
you."

Aline stared at her with interest. "How old are you, dear?"
Polly looked up at Rubin. She didn't know how old she was
supposed to be tonight.

"Fourteen, Aline. But she looks older in that dress, don't
you think?"

Aline nodded. "I thought so. Really, Saul, one would think

it was Babylon or something. You grow more depraved, and openly so, by the year."

He smiled at her. "Aline, my mother said never to fight with the hostess. But you're nobody to call the kettle black. Your own tastes are widely known and talked about, but while people wink and whisper, nobody throws it back in your face. Don't be so uncharitable."

"Saul, the difference is that I follow my art. You follow some pretty base urges."

Rubin smiled at her. "The French say it well," he said, "something about 'Check sanz goout.' It translates roughly to, 'Your art, my ass.' I'm sure you've heard of it. Come on, Polly. Let's circulate." He moved off into the living room pointing out various stars and introducing her to them.

"Don't mind the whispers, Polly," he said. "You have to get used to being stared at if you're going to be a star." He stopped suddenly as William Taylor and Mary May Maxwell emerged from a door that he suspected led to the bedrooms. Taylor looked shocked when he saw him. He bowed slightly and smiled at Polly.

"Good evening, Mr. Rubin. Hello, Polly, dear."

"Hi, Mr. Taylor. Funny meeting you here."

Mary looked at Polly, then at Taylor. "Who is this dear child?" she asked.

Rubin leaned down and said to Polly, "The bar is out there. Go get yourself a ginger ale."

"Do they have liquor?"

"Of course."

"Then I'll have an Angel's Tit." She ran off.

Rubin turned to Bill and Mary. "You two must be out of your minds. This is idiocy. Does your mother know you're here with Bill?" Mary didn't answer. "I thought so. My God, if you're going to throw Bill in her face, at least do it in private. Why pick a public affair? It'll be all over the papers in the morning."

"Calm down, Rubin," Taylor snapped. "We arrived separately, no reporter has seen us together, and we will leave separately." He indicated the room full of people. "They all know already. It's hardly a secret. Now really!"

Polly came back and stood by Rubin, sucking on a straw embedded in a glass filled with vivid pink ice.

"I just saw some real Russians," she announced to Rubin, tugging on his sleeve. "Talking Russian. They're certainly funny looking. And smelled." She wrinkled up her nose and took another noisy sip of her Angel's Tit.

Rubin turned her away. "Go back and bother them some more. I'm busy." Polly looked up at him, then stepped back, took a loud sip of her drink, and eyed him speculatively, as though she suddenly had aged ten years. She stayed there.

"Momma trusts Ben. She won't be suspicious. After all, Bill and I do work at the same studio every day," Mary added.

Rubin's voice was pleading. "For God's sake, for your own sake," he took a deep breath, "for Majestic's sake, be careful. Mary, your mother has already demanded that Bill be taken off your pictures."

He jumped as Cyrus Cotton slapped him on the back.

Taylor pulled Mary into the library and shut the doors. "Did you know your mother had made that idiotic demand?"

"Of course not. I'm as shocked as you are. I told Mr. Rubin last time he assigned a director to me that I wanted you." She stopped suddenly. "Momma was there." Mary began to weep. "She must have been laughing inside."

Taylor thought for a moment. "That's the reason she made that trip to New York," he said slowly. "When you stayed with me. She asked Abe Weiss to take me off. And he said yes."

She was now sobbing so hard that she had to gulp for air to speak. "Why does she do this to me? I do everything she wants. I dress in these stupid little-girl clothes for her. I act like a child. I work and work and turn every last cent over to her. She doesn't even give me pocket money. And what does she do? Separate me from the man I love!" She sank down on a sofa.

He put his arm around her. "Don't cry, dearest. You'll look terrible and what will people think?" He kissed her cheek, wet with tears.

"I don't give a damn what they think!" She straightened up and dabbed at her eyes with a handkerchief. "Just you wait. I'll be 21 next year. Then watch my smoke! Just watch." She set her jaw. Bill knew that look.

"Ben, please talk to me." Elsie found him sitting on the steps leading down to the circular pool. The music had resumed and she found it difficult to speak over it. "Please, let's find a quiet place where we can talk."

"Nothing to talk about." He didn't look up at her.

"Yes, I think there is. You have to understand, that's all." She pulled up on his hand but he remained limp and uncooperative. He looked up at her, eyes slightly blurry. She took the glass out of his hand and poured the whiskey on the lawn.

"Miss Barnsdall won't like it if you kill her grass," he said. "She loves that grass. Look how it's clipped."

"Ben, talk sense. I want to explain about Kelso."

"Nothing to explain." Slowly he got to his feet and faced her. "It's his turn tonight, I guess. I've had my turn." He threw a pebble into the pool. It made a soft plop. "I don't know if I still have a chance with you or not, is all."

"Oh, Ben, I'm not sure that you ever had me, really. I'm not sure that I want to be had by anybody. I want to be my own, not somebody's. Why can't anybody understand that?"

He looked at her without understanding. "Elsie, listen to me, now. I've listened to you. I said I thought I loved you, but I wasn't sure. Then tonight, when I saw that big hick putting his hands all over you, like somebody out on the town on a Saturday night, I just couldn't take it." He looked sheepish. "At first, I wanted to bust him one. But he looks tough, and I've had a few drinks. I couldn't risk falling down like a fool in front of you."

"Oh, Ben, that's idiotic. I don't want two grown men I both like fighting over me. I'm glad you showed some sense. Please, can we go somewhere? We've got to get away from that music."

"OK. Let's walk out on the lawn. God knows there's acres of it. God knows. I said that, didn't I?" He grasped her arm and they wandered past the wings of the house, around to the side, where they sat on a flight of steps that led down to a pavilion of some sort.

"Ben I didn't lead Kelso on, it just happened. He's very aggressive, is all. And flattering. He's attractive and it's nice to be paid attention to."

"Well, I didn't want to go off with that creepy Madame. Jesus, I learned more about modern art than any man needs to know, for God's sake."

"Did she try to kiss you?" She was laughing.

"With those black lips? That'd be like being kissed by a lizard." He shuddered. "Besides, she was giving the *girls* the eye, not me."

She set her glass on one of the steps and sat down, hugging her knees up to her chin. "Ben, it won't work if you want me to be something I can't be," she said thoughtfully. "I won't change that much, fond of you as I am. I can't spend my life living for you alone. I have to live for me, too."

Ben stood up and walked down the stairs to the pavilion. She looked at him in the darkness. All she could see was his face, dim above a luminous shirtfront.

"Ben, you don't even begin to understand me and what I need from you." She stood up and accidentally knocked over her glass. She didn't look down. "Let's stop seeing each other for a while. Not even at the studio. No lunches or dinners or preview dates, the way we have been. Give us time to think things over."

They stood and looked at each other silently.

"OK to our new arangement?" she asked, finally.

He turned his back and the dim blur of his face vanished in the darkness. "What can I say?" His voice floated up to her. "You made up all the rules. If I have any hopes at all, I've got to play by your rules, don't I?"

She kicked the glass off the step in exasperation. It rolled silently down the grass. "Yes, for once," she snapped. "I'll get someone to take me home." She started up the steps then turned. "Don't drink so much that Arthur has to drive. Mrs. Sheldon might not take kindly to that." At the top of the steps she disappeared into the darkness.

Saul Rubin noticed Ben wavering slightly in the terrace doorway and hurried over to him.

Grasping him roughly by the shoulder, he snapped, "Ben, you didn't come clean with me about Mary Maxwell and Bill Taylor. Did you bring them here?"

"Just Mary. Bill got here under his own steam. Hiya, Saul," Ben said recklessly. He looked at Rubin with watery eyes.

"Then you knew that they were meeting here?"

"Sure. That's why they both came."

Rubin looked at him with disgust. "You idiot. You know that situation. Now you've put the studio in the position of being in on the deception. It's intolerable."

"So what's new? You're nobody to talk about deception, Mr. Rubin. Majestic deceives all the time." His voice was rising and people were beginning to realize that a quarrel was in progress. "You had me spying on Bill for Majestic. So why shouldn't I turn around and do a little favor for a friend? For God's sake, you can't have it both ways. I've compromised myself all over the lot for you. Ma Sheldon's an old battle-ax anyway. It was fun lying to her. And Mary's a sweet kid who needs help."

Rubin saw it was hopeless.

"You're drunk. We'll finish this on Monday."

Ben realized that Rubin was right. He'd already gone too far—better get out while he still could. He tried to walk without wavering, straight past Rubin, turn to the left, down the gallery—to hell with his topcoat, get it some other time—out the front door, ask for the Franklin. The attendant looked worried.

"You sure you're feeling well enough to drive, Mister?"

Ben handed him a crumpled bill. "I'll be just fine."

He drove as straight down Hollywood Boulevard as possible, feeling very satisfied with himself. He had told Rubin off, but it was Weiss who had hired him and liked him. He wouldn't come off too badly, he thought. And to hell with Elsie. All he had to do was to snap on the porch light and all his worries were over.

Elsie found Kelso talking to Buster Keaton and Barbara La Marr. Everyone seemed to know him. He noticed Elsie and excused himself. They walked out on the terrace.

"Did you find your friend?"

"Yes." She looked up at him. "We quarreled over you."

"I'm sorry."

"Oh, it's not your fault. It's been coming for a long time." She seemed to be making up her mind. He watched her intently. "I need a favor, Kelso. I need someone to get me and Mary Maxwell home. Will you take us?"

"Sure. You better sit down. You look pale as a ghost. I'll find Mary and tell her."

"Arthur Cox, too."

He returned shortly with Mary and Arthur in tow. Arthur looked drunk but happy, and Mary's eyes were bloodshot from weeping. They found Aline Barnsdall still standing in the gallery.

"You look as if you haven't moved all evening, Aline," Kelso remarked as he kissed her on the cheek. "Too bad you couldn't enjoy your own party. It was interestin' as usual. But next time let's have a dance band. That stuff," he inclined his head toward the sound of the quartet, "is too much like the bawlin' of a sick calf."

Aline laughed. "I'll tell Mr. Stravinsky the next time I see him," she said tapping him with her fan reprovingly. She turned to Elsie. "Be careful of Kelso, my dear, he's dangerous."

Elsie smiled up at him, but his eyes didn't move from Aline's face. "I'm finding that out," she said, almost to herself. As she turned to take Mary's hand she saw Bill Taylor standing at the end of the hall looking after them, his face filled with sadness.

Kelso stood looking at Aline's bland smile for a long moment, then, putting on his white Stetson, he hurried after the girls.

48

November 1921, Banksia Place

"Is the veal tender enough, sir?"

"It's fine, Alfonso. Please tell the cook."

Saul Rubin, having a late supper in his private dining room, riffled through a stack of papers. His telephone rang. It was his secretary, Helen.

"Mr. Rubin, when I hang up it will be Dick Brockman. I'm sorry to interrupt your supper. He says it's an emergency." There was a click and Rubin heard Brockman say, "Hello."

"Yes, Dick. What is it?"

"I'm at Wallie Reid's bungalow with Dr. Stein. Reid's over here in sort of a coma. He's been acting up all day. Real mean on the set of *World's Champion*."

"Thank you, Dick. I'll be right there."

As he hurriedly passed her desk toward the front door Helen pushed a buzzer and by the time Rubin reached the

320

Pierce-Arrow the door was standing open, the motor purring. He wondered what the hell had gone wrong now.

Dick Brockman, a bespectacled man in a sweater, answered the door. He pointed toward the bedroom. "He's in there, Mr. Rubin. Looks terrible. Be prepared."

Wallace Reid, naked, was slumped in a chair, his head lolling to one side, eyes slightly open. Rubin thought, as he leaned over to look into the blank face, that Reid stirred, somehow aware of him, but he couldn't be sure. He stared at the man in the chair, aghast at how thin he had grown in just a few weeks. All his bones seemed to lie just below the surface of the skin.

Dr. Stein opened the door and walked in. "I called your office and the secretary said you were here. What's wrong with him?"

"We don't know. Just got here. But, my God, look at him." Rubin turned to them. "How long has this been going on? I screened *Anatole* for friends at the house just a week ago and he looked fine. Now he looks like some war prisoner." Rubin grasped Dr. Stein's arm. "And don't keep telling me he is fine. Look at the man. I've seen healthier looking corpses."

Occasionally Reid's eyes followed the movements of the doctor standing before him with his stethoscope, but he didn't seem to see them. Rubin nodded to the valet. "We'll take over, Oscar. Thank you for calling Dr. Stein. I've got my motorcar outside and I'll see that Mr. Reid gets home safely. Why don't you just get him decent and straighten things up, then go home yourself."

Oscar put a dressing gown around the sagging shoulders and tied the sash across Reid's stomach. Then he brought a small bottle from his pocket, took out an eye dropper and put drops in each of Reid's eyes.

"When he gets this way he forgets to blink and his eyes dry out. You have to watch out for it."

Rubin looked at the valet and tilted his head to one side in a questioning look. "What do you mean, 'when he gets this way'? How often does he get this way?"

"Not very often, Mr. Rubin. It kinda builds up. Every once in a while he takes too many pills. Usually I just stay with him until he snaps out of it. Tonight he looked really funny. I got scared, so I called the Doc."

"What pills does he take?" Rubin said sharply.

"I don't know. He has a lot of them, various kinds. The Doc gives him some, and some he gets from someone off the

321

lot." He began to look nervous. "I really don't know nothin', Mr. Rubin. Honest."

"Thank you, Oscar. Put some clothes out so we can dress him. Then you can go. Please don't mention this to anyone."

"Sure thing, Mr. Rubin. I keep all of Mr. Reid's secrets."

Rubin and Dr. Stein exchanged glances, and the doctor went on examining the limp body of the most popular matinee idol on the American screen. He looked puzzled and turned to Rubin.

"He's been drugged with something, maybe morphine."

Rubin's voice was hard. "Did he do it to himself or did someone else?"

Stein stood up. "I think he must do it to himself. I've been giving him a little morphine regularly for his headaches, but never enough to make him like this."

Rubin grabbed Stein's arm and the doctor dropped his stethoscope on the floor. "How much? Enough to make him crave it?"

The doctor sounded impatient. "Of course not. And I don't think he could have become addicted. I gave him very little. Only a shot or a tablet when he couldn't go on because of the pain or fatigue. It hasn't been more than a few grains a week. But of course, if he's getting more from the outside, I can't answer for it."

Rubin began to shout at Stein. "Look! That bag of bones is the idol of America, the all-American Athlete, the secret dream lover of millions of women. The Pep King, for God's sake! My God, look at him! You've been seeing him regularly for his aches and pains. Why didn't you say something? Notice something? Do I have to see everything around here? How can I be in New York holding Abe Weiss's hand and looking over your shoulder at the same time? What the hell do you think you're doing?"

"Doing? I've kept your star from having headaches. The man has paralyzing headaches." He emphasized every word.

"Aspirin is for headaches," Rubin shouted.

"Look, Reid is almost a doctor," Stein said as calmly as he could. "He went to medical school. He told me so. He said he could handle a little each day. Knew exactly what his tolerance was. Don't you shout at me. I haven't done anything wrong." He lowered his voice to a whisper. "At least I don't think so. There's so much we don't know about these drugs. So much." As he continued to examine Reid he talked to himself in a monotone.

Rubin stood by the door and smoked one cigarette after another, helping himself from a lacquered box on the table.

"I can't tell more without blood and urine tests, but I'm sure it's morphine," Dr. Stein muttered. "I pray to God I didn't do that."

Rubin ground out his cigarette on the floor and walked over to Stein, took him by the lapels and pulled the frightened doctor's face close to his.

"Now what do we do? I used to have a star worth millions on a very heavy schedule making eight pictures a year. Now, what do I have? A dope fiend. You had a hand in doing it. Now undo it!"

The doctor brushed Rubin's hands off his suit and stepped away. Looking over at Reid's motionless figure, he thought for a minute. "I don't know if it would work, but we might give it a try." He walked back and forth while he spoke. "We could just keep him on the edge. Give him just a big enough dose every morning so he is alert and not completely knocked out, like that. Get a male nurse, keep him under observation all the time. Put him someplace at night." He stopped and looked thoughtful. "There might even be a perfect place, now that I think of it. They specialize in dipsomaniacs—drunks. Padded rooms, bars on the windows, everything. I'll call Dr. Hoffman and see if they'll take an addict."

After a short phone conversation, Dr. Stein's eyes met Rubin's. The doctor nodded and smiled. Brockman, who had been waiting outside with the chauffeur, helped get Reid dressed, and they carried him out to the waiting limousine. The long grey motorcar moved through the twilight streets of the studio lot, avoiding those places where workers gathered on their way home. They turned east on Hollywood Boulevard, then north, and were soon twisting up into the hills.

Rubin tried to remember back to his lunch with Reid when he asked Wallie about the rumors. He turned to Brockman who was holding Reid up on the rear seat.

"Would Reid lie to me about being on dope?"

"No, I don't think Wallie Reid ever told a lie in his life. If you asked him on a day he hadn't taken any he would say that. If you got him on a day he was high, I think he would have told you that he was. He's a wonderful guy. Crappy thing to happen. Criminal."

"Mr. Brockman, how many shooting days left on *Champion?*"

"Twelve, maybe fourteen, depending on whether or not he acts up." He nodded toward the slumped form beside him.

323

"We've even been rewriting some scenes that he just couldn't get through. Everybody on the lot knows."

Everybody but me, thought Rubin. Weiss would be merciless. What a fool I was to believe that *schmuck*, Reid. Now I have to keep him from killing himself at all costs.

As he let the production schedule run through his mind Rubin stared out of the automobile window, not seeing anything. It might work. Two weeks wasn't so long. Keep him on a prescribed dose. It might just work.

They wound through a series of small roads into the hills. Banksia Place, named for the roses they passed in the darkness, was a short street at the top of the first low range of Hollywood Hills, at the edge of Griffith Park, a vast undeveloped wilderness. At the end of the road two massive stone gateposts stood at either side of the iron gates. The only shape Rubin could make out was the line of the tops of a grove of eucalyptus trees, black against the evening sky. He stirred uneasily as they stopped at the gates. Everything seemed dark and deserted. Surely after the telephone call they were expected?

A man appeared out of the darkness, opened the gates, and waved them through.

At the end of the drive, against the blackness of the trees, stood the lighter grey silhouette of a huge old house with shingled towers and wide porches. It was completely dark. The limousine stopped beneath a porte cochere as a door opened at the back of the porch and a shaft of light illuminated an orderly built like a bouncer, standing beside a wheelchair on the porch in the darkness. An elderly lanky man stood in the doorway against the light and watched as they struggled to get Reid out of the rear seat. The orderly stepped forward, scooped Reid up in his arms and deposited him gently in the wooden chair, then wheeled the chair across the porch and through the lighted doorway.

"Thank you, Max," the other man said. "Please come in, gentlemen." He stepped to one side and looked at Reid's face as he was wheeled past, then held out his hand to Rubin. "I'm Dr. Hoffman. How have you been, Dr. Stein?"

"Better."

Dr. Hoffman led them down long corridors with thick carpets, past dozens of closed doors. There was no one to be seen. They turned into a brightly-lit surgery.

Max lifted Wallie onto the examining table and Dr. Hoffman went to work doing a blood test. They waited silently, uneasily. Finally Dr. Hoffman looked up from his slides.

"It's morphine, all right. He's had a very heavy dose, probably taken orally. No syringe marks. He'll be like this for hours. I don't think he can be gotten out to work tomorrow, if that's what you had in mind."

He led them back to an office near the front door. It had once been a library but most of its shelves were empty, except for a few medical books. The room had a dismal, disused look. Dr. Hoffman indicated chairs surrounding a dusty table and they sat down.

"How long is Mr. Reid to stay with us?"

"As long as he needs treatment. On his feet and behaving himself, acting before the cameras, he is worth millions to Majestic. As he is back there on that table, he might as well be dead."

"I understand. You want me to get him back on his feet and functioning."

Dr. Stein explained the shooting schedule and how he thought Wallie could be brought to the studio each morning and then returned each night to Banksia Place.

"You don't want to cure him? You merely desire a holding action?" Hoffman looked surprised.

"Yes," said Rubin.

"That's dangerous. But it can be done. We maintain an executive of a local oil company in that way. We keep him sober and able to function. It's harder with drugs, but possible."

"If you can get him to the studio cooperative enough so he won't tear down the sets like he did today, I'll be happy," said Rubin. "When *Champion* is finished we'll have time to think about cures."

"You must understand then that Reid will always be on the edge of craving and will be unreliable. He could go beserk without warning."

"How do we handle that?" Rubin asked impatiently.

"Max will live with him twenty-four hours a day. Sleep in the same room, go with him to the bathroom, attend to every detail. You can pick up Mr. Reid and Max every morning whenever you arrange. Max is very strong—you saw the size of him—he can easily control Reid in his present condition. He is trained to give sedatives, also stimulants in the events more alertness is needed. Above all, he is a trained observer. Mr. Reid will not be able to take any drugs except those we prescribe. I also suggest that you pad the dressing-room walls and have little furniture around so that Mr. Reid can't hurt himself in the event the drug wears off before the next dose is called for." Dr. Hoffman spread his fingers and smiled. "Personally, I will try to get a little weight back on him. Force feeding, if necessary. I was shocked when his face moved into the light. My wife and I have always so enjoyed his pictures. What a handsome man he was. . . . Well, we will do our utmost to get him back into fighting trim." He started to rise, then, on second thought, held out his hands. "I really do wish you would consider a cure. It might take several months, and it is hard and painful. But you would get your man back in A-1 condition."

Rubin looked up and smiled. "We'll consider it. I personally will look into the production schedule and see if a cure can be fitted into it. We must keep him working, or the exhibitors will set up such a howl that you will hear it behind your stone walls. Please ask the orderly to wear street clothes. I want to avoid unnecessary gossip. Thank you."

Dr. Hoffman stood on the steps and watched them drive away. Then, shaking his head, he went inside. When he closed the door Banksia Sanitarium was once more sealed in darkness.

The day's mail lay on a small silver plate on the desk. William Desmond Taylor picked up his ivory-handled letter opener and began to slit the envelopes. He laid bills on one pile, letters to be read and answered on another.

Then he spotted one that gave him pause. At the top of the notepaper was an engraved butterfly with the three initials *MMM* entwined in its wings. He looked at the letter. It was in code.

"Oh, for God's sake! Why doesn't she grow up?"

He got out the code sheet and began to uncode the damned thing after taking a gulp of his whiskey. Little square—I. Square open on the right with a dot in the opening—L. Taylor sighed. It had been a grave mistake to seduce her. Light that little fire in some women and there was no putting it out. Now the retribution for his sins was to have to decipher these mawkish love notes. He finished one drink and asked Henry for another. He continued deciphering it.

I LOVE YOU—OH, I LOVE YOU. IT IS SO CRUEL THAT WE CANNOT BE TOGETHER AT THIS MOMENT. I BURN FOR YOUR KISSES AS I'M SURE YOU LONG FOR MINE. THE HOURS THAT I AM OUT OF YOUR ARMS ARE AN ETERNITY. NOW I KNOW WHY GOD PUT MAN ON EARTH. YOU ARE GOD'S GIFT TO ME. GOD LOVE YOU AS I DO.

326

Taylor put the note down on the table and looked at Mary's photograph. One of these nights there'd be a knock on the door and there she'd be. Then what would he do? He smiled at the image of Mary in the little pink nightgown he'd given her. What any man would do, that's what.

He picked up the note and stepped to the bookcase. Selecting a volume of the complete poems of Byron, he slipped the note between the pages. He noticed that another note was showing at the forward edges. He tucked it in and replaced the volume on the shelf.

49

November 1921, The Country Club, Culver City, California

The Christian Advocate

A MODERN BABYLON IN THE WEST SPREADS ITS CORRUPTION

HOLLYWOOD. The basest sins of modern times are being enjoyed in this capital of the unspeakable. The sin-soaked cities of the Old Testament, destroyed by an avenging Lord, cannot hold a candle to what happens here in Southern California on a nightly basis. The beasts that cavort amongst the bodies of innocent girls are the men who make the moving pictures that hold your children in thrall every Saturday afternoon. It is a contagion that must be destroyed. Every God-fearing man and woman in America must join this Modern Day Crusade!

Ben parked the Lagonda under some old lemon trees near a rundown farmhouse. No lights showed but they could hear jazz throbbing from inside.

"Looks like a dump," Polly said. "Why here?"

"As far as I know, it's never been raided. I think there's a payoff somewhere. It's a good place to bring a rising young motion picture star who happens to be a minor and not risk getting the both of us arrested." They crossed the grass and as Ben held the door open for her the music surrounded them.

Polly snapped her fingers and swung her hips. A white-aproned Italian waiter greeted Ben by name and showed them to a table at the edge of the linoleum dance floor. Around the ceiling hung small cylindrical paper lanterns decorated with Mount Vesuvius belching smoke.

"I'll have a Gin Rickey and the lady will have a ginger ale."

Polly kicked him under the table. "Make that a Bee's Knees, waiter, please." She gave him a charming wink.

Ben leaned forward. "Polly, I don't approve of your drinking. No fifteen-year-old should be drinking that junk."

"What's so bad? I don't drink enough to get soused, and besides Mr. Rubin always gives me a drink or two when I'm over at his place."

"The least you could do is not slurp down that goo. You should learn to enjoy good liquor if you're going to drink. Besides, I thought you only liked Angel's Tits."

Polly looked up, a pink foam mustache on her upper lip. "I heard about Bee's Knees from one of the girls. It's good. It's a dance step, too. The latest thing. I'll show you later." She was again moving her body in time to the music.

He watched her, amused. "You've become a real jazz baby, honey," he said admiring the movement of her pert breasts under her silk blouse.

"The booze helps. I think maybe I ought to get jazzed up for you and you'll like me better." She snapped her fingers in time to the music. "I saw how you nosed up to that reporter dame at lunch. I figured if I got a little high, you might tumble."

He stared at her. "Polly, that stuff is purely professional. I need to be nice to her to get her to print all that material on you." He lined up the silver in neat rows on either side of his plate. "I like you because you're you, not because you're a jazz baby." He put his hand on hers.

She looked up at him from beneath her eyelashes in a way she had learned made men fidget. As did Ben. He pressed her hand and she gently opened two of her fingers around his middle one. He quickly withdrew it.

"I heard that you had as many girl friends as a man can use. Older girls. I wondered why you never showed an interest in me. I guess I'm still too much of a kid for you."

He grinned at her. "Let's not talk about the girls, OK?"

"Do you go to bed with all of them?"

Where had she learned to ask such questions? "Polly, a man and a girl can have a lot in common and do things together. They don't have to go to bed. That's only part of a good relationship." He wished that Elsie could hear him. She wouldn't believe it.

"I wish I knew how they did it," Polly mused. She looked up at him brightly. "All anybody ever wants to do with me is to drag me off to a bedroom."

He shook his head. "Those pigs, Rubin and Droste. It makes me sick the way they take advantage of a child."

Polly shrugged and sucked a long strand of spaghetti into her mouth with a snap. "I don't care as long as it gets me somewhere."

Ben leaned forward and tried to sound fatherly, partly to contain his own excitement. "What it'll get you is either a baby or a social disease."

The waiter brought the next course. But for once Polly was not interested in her food. She caught his hand with hers and he put down his fork. "Ben, you're almost the only person I can talk to."

It sounded like a title from a movie but the expression on her face was genuinely sad. "Sure kid," he said.

"Ben, I know that letting Mr. Rubin do it to me won't get me any more parts. If it did, every girl in Hollywood would have her name up in lights." Her voice was as matter-of-fact as if she were talking about using cosmetics. "I bet there've been a lot of girls in that back bedroom and most of them are not working at Majestic. The guys call them one-picture lays." Her eyes twinkled. "But I decided that as long as he wanted me and I had the opportunity, he'd never forget me. And he hasn't."

She took a mouthful of food and chewed thoughtfully. "So far." She became gleeful. "I keep whispering to him that he was the first, that I'm only a little girl and he is ruining me." She took a gulp of her drink. "It drives *him* absolutely crazy."

"Jesus Christ! How do you think these things up? You're not like any little girl I ever met before."

"Maybe you been missing something." Her eyes darted back to his face. "I think up a lot of things. Besides, you never knew a girl before who wanted anything as much as I do and was so close to getting it."

"But, good God, Polly, there's a lot of girls working in the movies who didn't have to do what you're doing."

She looked at him. "Not many. And besides, I ain't got the time." She was managing to eat and talk at the same time. "Everybody has their own way and mine is mine." She

330

thought for a moment. "I think success in pictures is as much who you are as what you can do. Well, I'm inside those gates and Rubin knows who I am."

She mopped up some sauce with a piece of bread, glancing up at him to see if he was going to scold her. "Ben," she said softly, "I've decided something." He looked at her closely. "I'm going to be an actress, not just a star. I got a pretty face, and my tits are coming right along, like Mr. Droste says, but that isn't enough anymore. I want to be what I know I can be."

"And what are you, Polly?"

She lifted her head proudly, turning it to show her best profile.

"Polly McCormack, the young motion picture actress." She reached across the table and grabbed his hand again. "Oh, Ben, I know I can do it. I can feel myself being a star. I never felt that before. A few months ago it was just something incredible, a dream come true. I was always scared I was going to wake up. But now, I can feel it all the way through me. I am Polly McCormack now."

The band started up with a fast jazz tune and she turned at the sound to watch. Ben, fascinated by her intensity, was struck by the purity of her profile, which still had the delicate lines of a child's. At the same time, her bearing was so smart, quick, adaptable. She was a perfect example of the survival of the fittest in Hollywood.

She turned toward him and asked, "Hey, can we dance?"

"Sure. What've you learned this week?"

"A whole lot of new steps. I ask all the girls to teach me between takes."

"I can remember when you couldn't put one foot in front of the other," he marveled.

Polly snuggled against him, humming softly, occasionally opening her eyes to watch the glittering spots of light flash off the mirrored ball. Blurs of light sped across tables, faces, gowns, flashing on silver and goblets, occasionally colliding with diamonds, scattering jewels across everyone. She wanted it to go on like this forever.

Back at the table Polly demanded dessert. Ben gently reminded her that she must not get fat, or the shots wouldn't match in the picture.

"Damn!" She tapped her spoon on the knife and made a ringing sound. "One reason I want to be a star is to eat all I want."

"Better think up a new reason—jewelry, men, anything."

Polly smiled at him. "Dancing with you," she said softly, "being with you. Like this. That's my reason."

Ben looked at her, enchanted.

"You're nice, Ben." Their eyes met. "Nobody treats me like you do. Oh, the crews are OK. They all treat me like a kid sister." She hunched her shoulders together and stretched her arms down. "It's kinda cute," she smiled. "They don't even swear if they know I'm around." She put her elbow on the table and cupped her chin in her hand, her eyes promising, inviting. "But you make me feel like a woman."

Ben, taken aback, thought for a moment. "Do I?" he ventured. "It's because I like you, that's why." He moved his chair slightly closer to hers. "At first it was strictly business. You know, show you the ropes, get you seen in a few nice places, show you how to act in public, use a butter knife, that sort of thing. Then I just began to have a good time with you." He indicated the room with a wave of his hand. "This isn't company business, this is Ben Sommers' business," he said smiling.

"If you like me so much why don't you take me home with you?"

"It's because you're only fifteen and I'm scared to death."

A girl vocalist appeared at the front of the platform and began to sing.

> Though April showers may come your way;
> They bring the flowers that bloom in May.

Polly started to protest and he placed his hand on her lips. "Some men get a kick out of having young girls. I don't." He grinned. "At least not until now. I never had the temptation or the opportunity." He was suddenly aware of her knee pressing against his leg.

> So if it's raining, have no regrets,
> Because it isn't raining rain, you know,
> It's raining violets.

"Besides, I didn't want you to think I'd force myself on you, to take advantage of my position."

"You *are* different," she said softly, her expressive eyes inviting him in.

> And when you see clouds—up on the hills
> You will see crowds—of daffodils.

"Jesus."

She giggled. "OK. Let's dance."

At the edge of the dance floor she leaned her head against his chest. "What did you put on your hair that smells so good?"

She looked up at him, eyes excited. "The girl in the beauty salon did it. She said it would knock you off your feet. Does it?"

She giggled happily again and buried her face against his shirtfront.

"Come on, let's dance," he sighed. Around them couples were singing softly to each other as the band played.

"When they take their break," she whispered, eyes luminous, "let's go to your house. You can show me what it's like to get treated really nice, OK?"

He cleared his throat.

"Then you can tell me how I rate against your other girls." Her voice was a low murmur. She looked up at him with a soft, full smile, then extended the tip of her tongue.

His eyes, which had been dreamily unfocused, saw everything very sharply. Damn! Every time he began to feel warm and sentimental, she snapped him back into reality. Always some little thing—calculating, shrewd.

They began to waltz slowly to "Three O'Clock in the Morning," their bodies accommodating, fitting together intimately. He closed his eyes.

The man standing over him came gradually into focus, then went out again. Wallie shook his head and a sharp pain darted across the base of his skull. His mouth was dry and tasted terrible.

"What's happening to me? Where am I?" His tongue felt fastened down.

"My name is Max, Mr. Reid. It's time to get up and get dressed and go for a walk. Your dinner will be ready soon." He was cheerful but businesslike.

"I'm not hungry."

"But you will be. After you've had a nice shower and a walk."

"Who the hell are _you?_"

"Mr. Reid, I'm your attendant. You don't have any choice except to decide how nicely you'll do what you're told. This is the Banksia Sanitarium, and you're inside."

Wallie sat up on the edge of the bed and looked around. He was in a small, plain room, the walls covered with quilts. He felt terribly weak.

333

"A sanitarium, did you say?"

"Yes. It's a very nice place. You'll get to like it here. We'll take good care of you. Now, let's get your pajamas off and I'll get you to the shower. You'll feel better afterward. Then dinner, and you can meet Dr. Hoffman."

Reid stood up, and Max undressed him and helped him into the bathroom. Half an hour later he sat in Dr. Hoffman's office. Freshly shaved, he looked more alert, his eyes clearer, his hands almost steady.

"Good evening, Mr. Reid. You're looking better already. Let me explain your situation." He quickly outlined the custodial plan he had agreed to with Rubin. "We are aware of your addiction to morphine. You will be supplied with a carefully measured amount of the drug so you don't go into a near-fatal coma as you did two nights ago. We will treat your addiction so that it does not get worse, while enabling you to continue working. Do you understand?"

Reid leaned back in his chair and laughed heartily. It was the first time in months anything had really struck him as funny.

"Majestic must be paying a fortune for all this. They're scared, aren't they? Rubin is afraid he'll lose his big box-office draw." He gradually stopped laughing. "How did I get here? Does my wife know?"

The doctor's voice was so soothing it was irritating. "Mrs. Reid has been informed that you are ill and in a sanitarium. Mr. Rubin brought you here from your bungalow. Does your wife know about your addiction?"

Wallie sounded angry. "Let's get this straight. I'm no hophead. It just gets a little out of control every now and then when I'm tired. Like last night." He looked uncertain. *"It was last night, wasn't it?"*

"Two nights ago. You've lost a couple of days."

Wallie sighed deeply.

"Mr. Reid," the doctor continued in his even monotone, "your addiction is now out of control, and you may as well admit it."

Wallie closed his eyes. The doctor waited.

"I didn't think it would get the best of me, but it has. No, Dottie doesn't know. She just thinks I'm hitting the bottle. I rinse my mouth out with gin and breathe on everybody. I have the rep of being a big he-man, so heavy drinking goes with the picture."

· Dr. Hoffman nodded. "I suggest you call Mrs. Reid and tell her where you are. Tell her you went on a binge and are spending a few days here drying out. You will call her every day."

Wallie looked slightly embarrassed. "I'm going to need some stuff. I can't get through a day without it. God knows I've tried. I get pretty awful by the middle of the afternoon, just go out of my mind."

"Max will have a supply of morphine tablets. He will give you the correct amount on a regular schedule." Reid smiled with relief.

"Rubin thinks of everything, doesn't he?" He stared at his shoes for a minute trying to recover his dignity. "Well, when do we start?"

Dr. Hoffman pushed a button on the desk and Max stepped inside the door, neatly dressed in dark trousers and a white jacket, looking like a muscular medical student.

"When you go to the studio tomorrow morning, Max will wear a conservative dark blue suit, carry a medical bag, and look like your personal physician. Look at me, please, Mr. Reid. I want to be sure you know exactly what I'm saying and that you understand your position completely." Startled by the change in his voice, Wallie turned from surveying Max and looked intently at the doctor.

"How successful we are in keeping you on your feet depends on cooperation from you. Do not try to lose or outwit Max. You can't. Your dressing room at the studio has been remodeled. A team of carpenters have worked for the past two days to make it safe for you. Mr. Rubin telephoned to say they have discovered the caches of morphine you had squirreled away, so don't bother to look for them. The room has been padded so you won't hurt yourself in the event you lose control. And if you cooperate with Max, it will make everything easier." His voice became unctuous again. "Now, please, for the sake of your fans—and I am one of them—eat a little something. Get some meat back on your bones." He stood up. "There is a gymnasium and swimming pool. Max will be glad to share any activities you care to enjoy. After dinner, there is a radio and a pool table. Tomorrow you will work all day at the studio. Have a pleasant evening."

Reid looked at him and then, without a word, turned and followed Max outside. They began to walk along a gravel path that led to the trees behind the building. After a few minutes of silence, he turned to Max.

"If I wanted to, really wanted to, could I get rid of my habit?" Wallie's voice was choked with sorrow. "I mean, is there any chance?"

"Of course, there is, Mr. Reid. And we could help you. It is very difficult and painful and, I won't kid you, sometimes men die from the shock. But it certainly can be done." He paused. "If you're man enough."

Wallie flashed his famous brave grin. "That was right to the jaw, I must say. Well, I'm a better man than you are, Gunga Din. Or something to that effect. Maybe I'll just try. Maybe I will." He began to trot lightly across the path. After a few hundred feet he stopped and stood panting from the exertion.

Max said softly, "I'll help you all I can. I really want to see you lick this. It'll take all the grit you've got. But I think you can do it." After a few minutes' rest they walked on slowly.

50

November 1921, Ben's Bungalow

The Rolling Prairie Press-Democrat

WALLIE REID UP-AN-ATTEM EARLY IN THE A.M.

HOLLYWOOD. After a short vacation, Wallie Reid is getting ready for a new kind of screen role—that of a prize fighter! Wallie will play an English commoner who becomes a champion boxer so he can return home and thrash the nobleman who whipped him in front of the girl he loves. Wallie is in strict training for the role and he thrives on every minute of the workout!

Every morning Wallie runs a mile accompanied by Max Reynolds, reportedly a former trainer and sparring partner of Champion Jack Dempsey. The only problem for fans who'd like Wallie's autograph, is that he trains at 5 A.M. He is on his way back to the studio by the time his fans are getting up. The new picture will be called—what else—*World's Champion.*

"So this is where you live," Polly said as they entered the archway to the white stucco bungalows of the Escondido Court. "Kinda Spanishy, ain't it? Real tile roof. Cute."

In the center of the courtyard a pool of brightly colored Mexican tiles shone in the darkness. Under the surface of the water red and blue lights brightly illuminated some goldfish and a few straggly aquatic plants. Shimmering gleams from the colored lights, reflected by the surface of the water, moved on the undersides of the arches that surrounded the court, giving the impression that everyone lived under water.

Ben led her to the rear of the court and stopped in front of a massive wooden door studded with iron bolts. Above them, birds nesting in the tiled roof rustled, half awakened by their footsteps. Ben opened the door and switched on the lights, and she exclaimed in pleasure.

"Oh, it's really swell!"

"I only just set up housekeeping. You ought to see Bill Taylor's place if you want to see some swell stuff."

She wasn't paying any attention. "These your books? You must read a lot. I love intellectual men." She flashed a smile at him.

"I buy at least one new book a week," he said. "Rain or shine."

"I read a lot, too. On the electric cars riding out to Majestic. *Liberty, Munsey's, Cosmopolitan,* you know, the high-class magazines."

He stood by the kitchen door and watched her wander from object to object like a child.

"There was this teacher I had who loaned books to me, Miss Forbser," she said, fingering a statuette. "You would love her. She's beautiful." She ran her hands over the Spanish Renaissance tufted velvet cushions on the floor. "Ever read *Ramona?*"

"No. Should I?" He was fascinated watching her.

"You'd love it." She looked around the room. "It's early California. Very Spanishy, like your bungalow, Ben. Maybe that's why I love California so much." She roamed about the room, finally running her finger along the surface of a rearing griffon incised into the majolica lamp base.

"I'm going to love being here with you, Ben. I'll pretend I'm Ramona." She looked up at a row of framed photographs hanging on the wall. "Who are these girls? Your girl friends?"

"Oh, models and extra girls, a few actresses. They're rejected publicity photos."

She laughed. "Aren't you the jazz daddy, though?"

"Not really. Tom Bascomb turned them down when he was head of the department. I liked them so I brought them home."

"Why didn't he like them?"

"He thought they were too risqué for hometown newspapers."

"What's 'risqué'?"

338

"It's French for sexy. Not really dirty, just naughty. Bascomb said Ohio and Indiana weren't ready for nipples." He pointed to the ripe brunette in a one-piece bathing suit. "He was always very careful about the kind of pictures we sent into the Bible Belt."

Polly giggled. "I don't know what goes on in Ohio and Indiana, but in Iron City, where I come from, there's plenty going on all the time but everybody pretends it isn't." She laughed. "If you walk past a house on a Sunday afternoon and all the kids are out on the porch looking bored, you can bet the old man has ma down on the bed for a quick one."

"Oh, sure it happens. They just don't want to see it in the evening newspaper or up on their local movie screen." He walked toward the kitchen door and turned. "I'm going to fix myself a drink. I don't have any of that fancy stuff you drink. Just scotch and gin."

"Oh, that's OK, I just want to soak up the atmosphere. Spanish Baronial. That's perfect to describe your place," she called into the kitchen. "I saw it in the *Times*." She took off her wrap, hung it carefully over the back of a chair, and slowly began to unbutton her dress.

He looked out the doorway to see what she was doing. Polly, now in her underwear, had balanced a book on her head, and was walking slowly back and forth swaying gracefully. She saw him and smiled but didn't stop walking.

"It's for my posture. Mr. Taylor says it'll do wonders. It's great coming to a place that has thick books. They work better."

"They're meant to be read, not taken for walks."

She turned haughtily and stalked to the other end of the room.

Back in the kitchen he chipped ice off the block in the ice box. Seeing her in her underwear made his hands tremble. He had thought of little else but touching and getting into that body all evening. He was sure a fifteen-year-old would somehow provide a different experience. Well, soon he'd know.

He took a gulp of his drink and refilled the glass. He must try to remain calm, be nonchalant, and treat Polly like a person. He took a deep breath and walked back into the living room. He stopped in the doorway.

Polly, dressed only in her combination bloomers and camisole, was sitting in his reading chair carefully rolling her silk stockings down her legs. She looked up at him, smiled, and beckoned with one finger.

339

"I need help, sweet poppa. Can't afford to get a run. Come on and give me a hand."

Ben immediately began to swell. In a few seconds he was hard. He drained his glass. Polly kissed his hair as he knelt before her.

"You know," she said dreamily as his hands ran down her legs, "unless you come from a shack, you can't imagine how wonderful all this is." Now she was being Norma Talmadge in *Madame Sans Gêne*.

"The wonderful places are up in the hills. Ever seen Tom Ince's place?" Polly shook her head as he undid her underwear. "Bowling alleys in the basement, an indoor pool for chilly days. The works. Next time I get an invitation, I'll take you along."

"You're always thinking of me, Ben," she sighed archly. "Thank you."

He sat back on his haunches and stared at her small white body with its budding breasts and the dark vee between tender thighs, then up at her lovely face with its great expressive eyes. Polly looked back at him, her eyes growing wider.

"Like it?" she asked.

"Love it," Ben answered huskily. He couldn't believe the innocent look on the face above that nude body.

Gently he touched her between her thighs, then kissed her there.

"Mr. Rubin calls it angel hair. Ain't that crazy?"

"Jesus, Polly, don't tell me what somebody else says about you. Let me have my own ideas." He picked her up and carried her lightly into the bedroom, dropped her gently on the bed. Next to her, on the pillow, sat a long-legged French boudoir doll, dressed in gold lace to resemble Madame Pompadour. Polly squealed in delight.

"Oh, she's beautiful. What's her name?"

"God, I don't know," said Ben, stepping out of his trousers. "Men don't name dolls. Someone gave her to me."

She pressed the doll to her face. "I love her so. We'll have to think up a name."

"Let's do that later." Ben took the doll from her, giving her a little kiss, and sat it on the bureau. Then he snapped off the bed lamp that hung on the headboard. A dim light filtered in from the living room.

She immediately touched his chest and shoulders, running her fingers lightly across them. "You've got nice muscles,

340

Ben. I'm glad you're young. I haven't been with many young men, only older ones. I'm tired of wrinkled, slobby, hairy old men." Her arms reached for him in sudden ardor, her body pressing against his.

"Hey, don't rush it," he cautioned. "We've got all night."

"Oh, sweetheart," she whispered, "I want you to like me, please like me."

"Shh. Be quiet. I do, Polly. I do like you."

She crouched over him, her tongue following the little ridges surrounding his nipples. Then he could feel its stiff wetness darting across the hair of his stomach. He closed his eyes as he felt his penis slide into her mouth. He kept saying over and over to himself, she's so young, so young, so young.

He lay quietly for a long time. She was curled in his arms, her head on his chest. He could feel her short tousled hair lying on his shoulder.

"You don't smoke, do you?"

"Never have. Promised my father I wouldn't until I was twenty-one. Then it didn't seem worthwhile to start. He was dead by then, but I kept my promise."

"Everybody else jumps out of bed to get a cigarette. Except Mr. Droste. He lights up a big cigar. It's awful when he starts kissing me again."

He tried to be patient but couldn't. "Polly," he wailed, "cut it out, for God's sake! It's not nice to talk about other men when you're in bed with me. Are you going to tell Droste and Rubin how I do it, next time you're with them?"

"Maybe," she said, giving it some thought. "Mr. Rubin's pretty good, but Mr. Droste . . ." He rubbed her face in the pillow. They both collapsed laughing.

"Really, Polly, how would you like it if I talked about Mona or Vivian with you?"

She brightened. "Oh, I'd love to hear about them. Do you want to? How do I rate?"

He fell back against the pillow, laughing. "Oh, they'll do in a pinch, but none of them has your experience," he said gravely.

Polly hooted with laughter and picked up a pillow and batted him over the head with it. He pulled her toward him and she fell across his chest, pulled herself up and kissed him, a long throbbing, tonguey kiss.

"Ben, dear, I absolutely love you. Really! Don't laugh."

341

Then she laughed with him. "Really, I do love you. Now," she said, trying to be serious, "I bet you can't do it again."

"You lose."

Later, Polly lay on her stomach, hands propping up her chin, looking at him. "Gosh, you're handsome, Ben. You really ought to be in pictures. I'd sure like to stay here, but Mrs. Bailey'd kill me if I stayed out all night. Do you mind taking me home?"

"Sure," he said, getting up. "Why do you stay there, in a rooming house, for God's sake? That's no place for a budding star. Why don't you move to a court or an apartment?"

"I dunno. I guess I kinda like it there. Mrs. Bailey is like having ma around. It's swell to come home and have a hot dinner ready. I'd never eat, I bet, if I had to work twelve hours then cook, too. Anyway, I'm only fifteen, and I need a home and protection."

Ben roared with laughter. "I've seen you eat, remember? You'd never starve. And just who is it who needs protection? Who the hell told you that?"

"Mr. Rubin," she answered smugly.

"He's a fine one to talk. Who's going to protect you from *him?*" He looked at her. There was a pouty smile on her lips. "You never doubt it, do you?" he said quietly. "Success and fame." He snapped his fingers. "Just like that."

"What do you mean? Look at me. Look where I had to come from and where I am after only a few months."

Ben grinned. "Sure. On your back in my bed."

"Don't be mean." She picked up a corner of the bedspread and wrapped the fringed end around her head and shoulders. "Look—Ramona," she giggled. She fondled him again, laughing.

"You better cut that out. Like they say in the movies, 'Once those passions are unleashed . . .' "

"Unbridled, huh?" she giggled.

" 'They know no bounds.' "

She got up and rummaged through the things on his bureau and started to brush her hair.

"You know, I was perfectly content with older women before tonight."

She caught his eye in the mirror and smiled. "Oh, all anybody seems to want is baby ass. That's what Mr. Rubin calls me," she said absently. "In a couple of years I'll be too old and nobody will want me." She gave him a quick glance to see what effect her remarks were having. He didn't notice.

342

He was watching her buttocks flex as her arm moved up and down.

"Hell, I'll take you. Even if you live to sixteen. When you're tossed aside, too old to be desirable, too worn to be adorable, my bed will still be waiting." She turned from the bureau and made a face at him. He smiled and kissed her breasts. She sat on one of his knees and brushed the hair on his chest.

"You write terrible stuff. Even I can tell that. Does anybody believe all the guff you turn out? Untamed passions and all that?"

"Only about thirty million people a week is all. They run to the nearest movie palace to see the picture." His fingertips ran up her thigh. "You've just experienced some of my untamed passions firsthand." She got up and began to put on her underwear. "I gather the results were satisfactory?"

She looked up. "Oh, sure."

He watched her button her camisole. "My God, you're lovely."

She smiled at him, walked over and buttoned his shirt. "I've already said I love you. You brought me further tonight than anyone else ever has. Nobody ever cared about how *I* felt before." She walked to the bureau and picked up his tieclasp, holding it against her hair as if it were a barrette. Admiring the effect in the mirror, she said, "I guess now that we're more than good friends you'll do extra stories on me and give me special mentions in the press books." She paused. "Right?"

He froze, one trouser leg on. He sat down suddenly on the edge of the bed, looking directly in front of him. He knew that if he turned he would meet her eyes in the mirror. He could tell from the tone of her voice that she was looking at the back of his head, waiting for an answer.

Well, there it was again. And he had been so reluctant to use her, an innocent child. Jesus Christ!

Polly walked over and sat down on his lap and kissed him. "Ben, did you hear me? I asked if you would do special things for me now that we're—you know?"

Ben looked her straight in the eye. "Sure, Polly, you give me special treatment, I'll give it to you."

Just before Christmas, while Will Hays was recuperating from an injury suffered in a train wreck, he was visited by Abe Weiss, Lewis Selznick and Saul Rogers. The three picture executives called at the Wardman Park Hotel in

343

Washington, D.C. hoping that Hays was not too ill to see them. They presented him with a written appeal from the motion picture industry, elaborately hand lettered on a magnificent parchment scroll.

We, the undersigned, are striving to have the Motion Picture Industry accorded the consideration and dignity to which it is justly entitled. This major force in American Life must enjoy proper representation before the people of this country.

We feel that our industry requires further careful up-building and a constructive policy of progress. The forces that would tear it apart must be stopped.

We would ask you to be an industry spokesman, to provide the nation with the true facts of the industry when questioned, to be a bulwark against unfair criticism and attacks.

The compensation we are prepared to pay is the sum of one hundred thousand dollars a year, under a commitment satisfactory to you, for a period of three years.

Along with the scroll was a contract for a hundred thousand dollars a year. The contract could not be canceled except by Hays, who was moved by the responsibility and the honor entrusted to him. He said he would consider the offer when he got back home in Indiana and let the industry representatives know his decision after Christmas.

51

December 1921, The San Fernando Valley

"I had rather be a doorkeeper in the house of my God, than to dwell in the tents of wickedness." The eighty-fourth Psalm gives us the text for today's sermon. "The tents of wickedness"—what are the tents of wickedness here in Dover? Surely, not the tents of the Chautauqua meeting? No, it is a tent on the main street, disguised as a picture house. Wickedness hides itself behind little flickering light bulbs, exotic photos of beautiful women and lustful men. You and your innocent children have been lured into that tent!

> *Sermon delivered by the Reverend Johnson Wilkes*
> *First Community Church, Dover, Ohio.*

Elsie's horse, who had been balky during her ride, was now pawing at the ground.

"I'm convinced he doesn't like me," she said, frowning.

"Oh, shoot!" Kelso said. "You two will make a great pair. He's only mad 'cause you're on top of him, and he can't admire you from where he's standing."

Elsie laughed despite her unsteady seat. "I wish I could stop being nervous. The scenery is so lovely in the winter, that special greenness."

"Let's walk them back to the house, then," he suggested. "We can see better." He dismounted easily, then quieted her horse and helped her down.

"I feel much more secure with two feet on the ground."

"Fraidycat." He held her tightly and kissed her before he let her go.

She took his hand as they walked, leading their mounts.

"One word from you and you could be a partner in all this, you know. As far as you can see from here."

"Oh, Kelso, don't. I'm really not ready to think about it."

345

She walked beside him, happily rubbing her cheek against his sleeve. "I guess I'm not a natural-born rider."

"You're a natural-born woman. That's enough for me, any day."

When they reached the great hacienda, he wrapped the reins around a hitching post. The house sat in the shade of live oaks that cast subtle shadows on the tiled verandah. Square pillars of plastered adobe supported wide arches opening into a broad central courtyard. A fountain spurted its cooling spray into a tiled pool. Elsie sank gratefully into a comfortable chair. Kelso pulled off her boots and she wriggled her toes.

Wong, the Chinese servant, placed a tray of bottles and glasses on the table.

"My goodness, is it that late? I'll have to change to go home."

"Don't you want a drink first, sweetheart?"

"Kelso, I really want to get over that pass before dark."

"A little ride like that don't bother me none. I do it all the time. I wish you'd reconsider and stay."

"Don't, Kelso. You know how I feel. Maybe I'll try a little gin. Not too much." She stretched and put her head back against the chair. "It must cost a lot to live like this. You didn't tell me you were a millionaire."

He laughed and handed her a glass. "Far from it, I'm afraid. I'd sure like to be, but no such luck. This spread takes a lot to keep up." He waved his hand to indicate the white arches and the green lawns surrounding the house. "It takes a lot more than farming will bring." He sipped his drink. "I hope Harding puts his spurs into the economy." He winked at her. "I got to buy you pretty trinkets."

"You do and I'll give them back."

"What else am I going to do with it?"

"Buy contraceptives for my mother to give to the Mexicans."

"Let them buy their own. I got other ideas."

"Braggart. You men are all alike. I hoped you were different."

"I am. I'm keeping myself for you." He was unexpectedly serious. Elsie looked at him steadily. "Life is different out here, not all glittery and foolish like it is in town. I want a wife and a helpmate not a girl friend. I'm holdin' out for the long run."

"I'm beginning to realize something too, Kelso. Maybe it's

346

because of the way you live on a ranch. There is more of a sharing life here for a woman."

He nodded, gazing out to the green fields beyond. "It's still an old-fashioned sort of living, the man and wife are truly partners. He doesn't go away to a job while she's stuck at home with nothing to do except change diapers and wash up. A ranch takes two people to really make it go." He stood up. "When do you want to leave?"

She put her glass down. "As soon as I've changed."

"I'll take you home and stay in town. I'm expecting a shipment of goods I gotta check up on."

Wong interrupted. "Telephone, Miz Ken," he said softly.

"Why don't you change while I take this?"

Before she closed the door of the guest room, she heard his voice rising in impatience, then shouting, then the sound of the receiver being slammed back into place. She quickly closed her door, feeling guilty.

After she'd changed, she found him lounging in a chair by the pool, sipping a drink.

"I'm ready to go, Kelso. Can you still take me?"

"Sure, why not?"

"Well, I thought the call might . . . ."

"It was nothing, sweetheart. Nothing."

The radio crackled and whooped. Taylor tried to stabilize the dial setting at 360 meters. All the twenty or so radio stations in Los Angeles broadcast on the same frequency, sharing time rather than wave lengths. KNX broadcast from seven to eight every evening if the station preceding it did not run over into KNX's time. Finally he was able to sit down, pick up a book and put his earphones on.

Engrossed in his book, listening to the *Mignon Overture*, Bill didn't hear the door open. By the time he became aware of her, Mabel Normand had crossed the room. Ash white, she dropped to her knees and buried her dark head in his lap. Taylor lifted the earphones from his head and gently kissed Mabel's hair, but she refused to be comforted and continued to weep, a crumpled ball of misery. Taylor was not sure what had happened but he suspected she had run out of cocaine.

She had flirted with drugs as long as he'd known her. She blamed her need on a chronic lung condition that had plagued her for years. But he suspected it also stemmed from her tormenting love affair with Mack Sennett, whom on the night before their proposed wedding, she had discovered in bed with Mae Busch, her best and closest friend. Mabel had never forgiven him, although she continued to make films for him.

Taylor tried to raise her face so he could look at her, hoping he might be able to cajole her. But she only pressed her head harder into his lap and began to pound on his leg with her fist. Now it was beginning to develop into a little scene. She might be desperate for coke, but she was still an actress.

At last she looked up at him, her dark eyes troubled, her lovely, expressive face smeared with tears, a perfect mask of wretchedness.

"I'm sorry, Billy. Oh dear," she sniffled. "I have no right to bother you like this. I know how you feel about it." Her eyes searched his face carefully. "But this afternoon I felt so completely hopeless."

"Don't tell me what it was. Let me guess." He furrowed his brow. "Your little dog ran away."

Her eyes flared at him. "I didn't come here to get my leg pulled."

"I'm sure you didn't," he said seriously. "You don't often do this sort of scene. It's not very good casting for you, my dear, although the desire of the clown to play Hamlet is always there, I fear."

"Oh!" She banged her fist down on his leg and stood up. "You're awful! I won't go to bed with you this week. So there! You'll have to find somebody else." She looked at him contemptuously. "As though you'd have any trouble doing that."

Taylor gently placed his hand on her arm. "That was beneath you, Mabel. I thought our relationship was based on a different sort of foundation."

She wandered toward the piano, still clutching a handkerchief. "I'm sorry, Billy." She rested against the instrument, leaning on it with one elbow. "I'm nearly wild." Her eyes pleaded with him for understanding.

"Henry," he called toward the kitchen, "get Miss Normand a whiskey." He sat down and patted the seat beside him on the sofa. "Mabel, I never reproach you about anybody you've been with. It's the last thing I expected from you."

She stood still, her hands on her hips. "That's the most irritating thing about you. Always the complete gentleman." Sighing, she sat next to him and snuggled into his arms. "I just hate you. How can I be bitchy and yell when you're so damned reasonable?"

Henry offered her a cut-glass goblet on a silver tray. There was also an embroidered linen napkin.

Taylor waited until the kitchen door closed.

"Now, suppose you tell me what's wrong?"

"Billy, I've run out of happy dust. It's all I've thought about all day. I wish I'd never said yes to Mack. But he needs help." She kicked her shoes off and tucked her legs up underneath herself. "I was wretched all day, Bill, sitting there with Sennett."

"I'm sorry it's causing you so much anguish, darling. But cocaine is no answer."

She sat up straight and looked at him. "Well, it may not be an answer to you, but it makes the questions a hell of a lot easier to bear. Besides, liking coke is not serious!"

Taylor's face was rigid. "I think it's serious. All dope is serious." He shook his head grimly. "I'd like to get my hands on the bastard who started you on this. I'd kill him."

She shivered with delight. "You *know* him, too," she whispered. "It'd be some match." Smiling, she winked at him.

"Billy, I really tried to go all day without it. I was trying to be good." She puckered up her lips at him and in baby talk said, "Tweetums," then her features hardened. "I went out finally, and missed the son of a bitch. I think the bastard did it deliberately." She jumped up and began to wander about the room. "They all stood and watched me, those Chink bastards. I pleaded with them, but none of them have any hearts. Or maybe he has them scared to death. He's got the Hollywood crowd marked out as his private territory."

"I would have thought that with what you spend," he said carefully, "you'd have a pipeline direct to the source."

"It's as direct as I can find and keep it quiet. I pay for silence as well as dust." She sat down wearily in an armchair and leaned her head back and closed her eyes.

"You mean you pay blackmail, too?"

"Sweetie, I'm famous." She smiled at him, but it was a desperate, lip-biting smile. "How would it look if it got out? They get me coming and going."

"How much?"

"I'd rather not say."

"How much?"

She bowed her head. "Two thousand a week, some weeks." Then, suddenly, she pointed her finger at him and squealed with glee. "Shocked you, didn't I?" She stood up. "Well, I'm going now, Mr. Taylor. I can feel a lecture coming on."

"I can't tell you how appalled I am."

Still laughing, she pulled him to his feet. "You really hate it, don't you? I'm always amazed how Victorian you can be. For a man who's as inventive in bed as you are, you're terribly straightlaced." She backed away, now being serious, even sober. "Thanks for the drink. And the shoulder. I'll call you tomorrow and let you know how the first day's shooting went." She stood on her tiptoes and kissed him. "Maybe, if you're good, I'll spend the night later on in the week and you can be bad." As she moved away she glanced at her framed photo on the piano. "I hate that picture. I can't imagine why I ever gave it to you." She touched the frame with her fingertips. "Pretty frame, though." She was gone in an instant.

Taylor immediately went to the telephone: "Ben? Bill Taylor here. Are you busy tonight? Good. Could you possibly come over to my place? Now? If you haven't eaten, Henry can feed you. I really have to talk to you. It's about that matter. I have some new information." He listened. "Thanks, Ben. It's important. Ta ta."

52

January 1922, Hollywood

Motion Picture Exhibitor, Jan. 14, 1922

**WILL HAYS HIRED AS MORALS CZAR
TO CLEAN UP INDUSTRY
WILL OPEN OFFICE IN NEW YORK**

WASHINGTON. Following an announcement of appreciation from President Harding at the White House, the Motion Picture Producers and Distributors named Will Hays, former Postmaster General, as the new morals czar of the industry. Hays will immediately organize a staff to aggressively clean up Hollywood and the studios. He plans to blanket the 48 states with speakers giving positive views of the industry. Hays will be assisted by Charles Pettijohn, the first man named to the staff.

When asked why he accepted the $100,000-a-year position, Hays said, "I needed the money."

"Mr. Sommers is outside," said Helen. "He says he has to see you."

"Well, send him in," said Rubin. What now, he wondered?

Ben entered and began speaking immediately. Rubin had never seen the cool young Southerner this agitated.

"What I'm going to say, Mr. Rubin, is maybe none of my business," he began, "but it involves a friend. It also involves one of our leading stars and the way people are talking about him, so maybe you should let me know what's happening."

Rubin raised one eyebrow and nodded.

"Something mighty funny is going on with Wallie Reid.

I've been out talking to Dorothy. She's frantic! Wallie doesn't come home anymore, and it isn't a quarrel or anything. He calls her every day but he doesn't tell her anything. *The World's Champion* set is closed. I've been here three years and I've always been able to get onto a set."

Rubin's face remained impassive.

"He rides around in that creepy closed Landau, no one ever sees him walking around, much less playing softball like he used to." Rubin still remained silent, staring at him. "You know, Wallie was a kind of big brother to a lot of people here. Now he's just a spook, straight out of a chapter of *Fantomas.*"

When he finally spoke Rubin's voice had an edge to it. "Ben, you've handled a lot of delicate matters for Majestic. You're very discreet. But you were right the first time. This is none of your business, and you should stop right here. I'm afraid I can't tell you any more."

Ben started to protest, but there was a terrible finality in Rubin's voice that left him at a loss. "The least you could do is to tell the man's wife what you're doing with him."

"Wallace Reid has a problem and we're helping him iron it out." He paused for emphasis. "I want you to leave it alone."

Ben stared at him and then got up and walked out. Helen waited at the door after he had gone.

"Get Dick Brockman for me." She closed the door and the telephone rang.

"Sommers is nosing around. Asking questions," Rubin said in a low, tense voice. "In particular, I don't want him near Reid. Those two were very friendly. Tell that nursemaid, Max, to threaten to cut off Reid's supply if he talks to him."

He hung up abruptly, walked over to the window, and looked out, but his eyes were not focused on anything. He pressed his nose against one of the strips of lead that held the diamonds of glass together. He was risking everything by hiding Reid away. Maybe it couldn't be done anymore in this modern world! He laughed to himself and looked closely at the old glass in the windows, the ancient carved walls of his office, the huge old globe of the world that stood behind his desk, with entire sections of continents empty, unexplored.

When this room was new, when that globe was made a man could be put away into a little dark dungeon, in a castle, the Bastille, a thousand places. *The Count of Monte Cristo. The*

Man in the Iron Mask. They were never heard from again. Or maybe that was only in the movies.

But here in real life? Well, all he could do was to try. God only knew how much it was costing. It was even harder with the most famous face in the country. Those eyebrows. Like a signature. The doctor had recognized him right off. Well, Majestic had the power and the money to pull it off if anyone could. Weiss wouldn't even thank him if he knew.

"Drugs," Bill Taylor said. "You're going to think I'm daft on the subject, but I'll bet a thousand dollars Wallie Reid is on drugs. They're trying to cure him or something."

"It's strange, the way nobody'll talk. Phil Rosen, the director, turned white as a ghost and simply walked away. Practically ran. They must have threatened everybody."

"Blacklisting. One word from Rubin and they never work in Hollywood again. It's that simple. I wonder what the film looks like?"

An idea slowly crept into Ben's mind. "Bill, if I could bribe one of the guys in the vault, maybe somebody they haven't reached yet, to get me the rushes of *Champion,* would you look at them with me?"

"Certainly. Do you think you can?"

Ben grinned. "Sure."

Taylor was already seated in the small screening theater when Ben arrived. He heard laughter from the projection room. Evidently the projectionist was reporting on his experiences of the preceding night. Ben sat down beside Taylor.

"Did he think it was a fair bargain?"

"Said he had to sleep the whole day. They must have been some girls." Ben pressed the buzzer.

Zigzag lines preceded the first pictures. Ben spoke to Taylor in the darkness as they watched the first reels of meaningless shots.

"I asked for the unedited rushes so we could see everything."

Wallace Reid stood on the shore of a small stream unpacking fishing gear. First the master shots, long shots from a distance. Then close-ups.

Ben gasped. "My God. Look at him."

Reid smiled into the sunshine as if looking at the line he had cast out into the water two shots earlier. His cheeks were sunken and there were great hollow circles under his eyes.

Each shot was repeated until the director caught Wallie in a light that made him look as healthy as possible.

"He's trying different angles. Reid looks like a skull. Not much he can do," Taylor muttered. There were as many as twenty shots of each close-up until Wallie looked partly human.

Then came a series of scenes that made Ben sit upright with horror. Wallie, caught poaching on the local duke's estate, was forced to fight him. The nobleman knocked Wallie down again and again.

Although the fight was staged for the cameras, the sight of the hulking duke punching the frail, almost wispy, Wallace Reid was almost too much to endure. Ben felt an impulse to shout out to stop the fight.

"This is awful. They can't possibly release this," Taylor whispered.

Ben pressed the buzzer. "Thanks, Bill. It's just too ghastly to watch. You can count every rib and vertebra."

"Wallie is a very sick man, Ben. But they're being very clever about it."

Ben nodded in agreement. "The official story is booze. But liquor never did that." He sat and silently looked at the empty screen for an instant. "I've got to see him, see him and talk to him."

"You'd better hurry," Taylor said gently, "he may be dead by the time you get there."

53

January 1922, Chinatown, Los Angeles

GOLDWYN PUBLICITY . . .
FOR IMMEDIATE RELEASE

Mabel Wastes Some Time Coming to Gotham

On her recent trip across the country, madcap comedienne Mabel Normand simply threw her diamond wristwatches out of the Pullman window rather than set them forward as she passed from time zone to time zone. Miss Normand went through Western, Mountain, Central, and was wearing her Eastern time zone watch when interviewed by this reporter today.

When asked if she would repeat the stunt going back home to Hollywood, she admitted she would not.

"It's easier to set the time backward than it is to get the darned windows open on the train!"

Anyone who has traveled on a Pullman train knows whereof she speaks.

"Ben, thanks for coming. This is Kum Ying. Her American name is Jean. I asked her to join us, and while we were waiting for you, I told her all about you." The young Chinese girl next to Bill Taylor smiled. Taylor continued.

"Kum was a slave in a brothel in Chinatown in San Francisco. She was freed by an astonishing woman, Donaldina Cameron, a tough-minded old biddy who rescues them regularly. Kum, I mean Jean, has come to Los Angeles to do similar work for the YWCA. I asked her to help us."

"Do what?" Ben was not following Taylor.

"Help us find out who in Chinatown is bringing dope in

and selling it to the picture people. Someone I'm fond of— very fond of—is finally hooked. Mabel Normand."

"God, Bill, I'm sorry. How?"

"I've been snooping around, following little hints and suggestions made by people who wouldn't make them if they knew what I was after. You know, Mabel isn't the only one. There are more than a dozen stars—big names—flirting with the stuff at this moment." Taylor nodded at Kum Ying. "Jean thinks she knows who is the head of vice in China-town."

"Number one man Chung Bow," she said softly, as if afraid she would be overheard. "He have girl and gambling. Girl very high-class slave only for Chinese man, not for American. He have ten or twelve slave work for him all time."

"How do I fit into all this?" asked Ben.

Taylor leaned forward and grasped his arm. "I have an idea. The top man is Chinese, but he must sell to a distributor who sells to the actors and actresses. The man must be Caucasian. I want you to threaten his territory. To go to Chinatown and offer to buy a large amount of drugs and announce that you are going to start selling to movie people. That will drive the dope seller out into the open." He rubbed his hands together in grim satisfaction. "All I need to know is who it is."

"And you want me to make contact?" Ben said.

"The idea is to take Jean along. She can help, maybe translate, ask questions in Chinese."

"But won't it be dangerous for her?"

"It'll be dangerous for you, too."

Ben shook his head. "It wasn't before. . . ." He stopped, feeling stupid. Taylor must suspect he knew more than he was saying about buying dope.

But Taylor pretended not to notice.

Ben turned to Kum Ying. He could feel Taylor watching him, and he had to brazen it out. "Any night OK? I'll have to ask around, make some contacts."

"I always ready." She smiled at him. "We go drink tea."

In New York Abe Weiss could effectively keep three thousand miles between himself and trouble. Saul Rubin was paid to look after the studio. Too bad he didn't do it better. One of the trials of Weiss's periodic trips to California was that everyone at the studio could get at him.

The secretary knocked. "Mr. Weiss, Mrs. Sheldon is here. She's a bit early, do you wish me to ask her to wait?"

"No point to that. Send her in." He stood up and walked around and stood in front of his desk.

Carlotta Sheldon swept in, her hard face framed but not softened by the fur collar of her coat. A heavy woman, she was considerably taller than Weiss.

Taking her hand and smiling, Weiss said, "How nice to see you, dear lady. How well you look." He motioned to a chair. "Let me take your coat, such a coat would be perfect for the East, but January in California is too mild. You'll be too warm." He sat down behind his desk after putting the coat on another chair. She said nothing. Leaning forward on his desk, Weiss smiled. "Now. To what do I owe the distinct pleasure?"

Carlotta set her jaw. She was not going to be sidetracked by pleasantries. "I'm very unhappy with the way my daughter is being handled here at Majestic, Mr. Weiss. She is not getting the attention due a star of her magnitude, the properties being chosen for her are second-rate, and I don't care for her directors." She sat back and waited.

"Is that all? Nothing." Weiss made a small gesture and smiled. "I thought maybe you had serious worries. Dear lady, your Mary is considered the number one feminine star on this lot." He sat back and let that sink in. "Every time a story is considered Mary gets first choice. You won't let us use the director who is best for her, so we *do* use second best. Promotion and publicity is suited perfectly to her talents. The guarantee is unparalleled in the history of this studio or the history of Hollywood."

Mrs. Sheldon's steely eyes never flickered. Weiss had never seen such cold and unfriendly eyes except once—on a snake used as a prop for Bill Hart to shoot. The pale red lipstick only emphasized the grim, hard slash of her mouth, making her look as if she had been eating something bloody.

"She has almost finished the second five pictures on the contract." He glanced at a paper on his desk. "At three hundred thousand each, and the next five will be at three-fifty. That's quite a bit of money for such a little girl, Mrs. Sheldon. Mary is very lucky." He sat back and folded his hands across his stomach. "Only twenty, and look what she earns."

Carlotta Sheldon seemed ready to spring out of her seat. "She's worth every penny of it, you leech. You take my little

357

girl and every time she bats her eye, it's money in your cash register."

His patience was growing short but he was determined to be calm. "It's money in your cash register, too, Mrs. Sheldon. You control Mary's earnings." He nodded in the direction of Los Angeles. "If she didn't make it, you wouldn't be living in that big house or driving in the big motorcar or wearing the coat with the big fur collar." He looked at the coat on the chair and smiled graciously. He leaned forward on the desk. "Now what's really bothering you? All this is so much *shtuss.*"

She regarded him with unconcealed dislike.

"How I wish you Jewish immigrants would learn to talk English," she said. "It would make conversations so much easier."

Weiss stiffened. "I'll try and remember that." He stood up. "Is there anything else? It's almost time for my next meeting."

"Sit down, Mr. Weiss. I haven't finished yet." She clasped her handbag in her lap with both hands. He could see how white her knuckles were. "It's about William Desmond Taylor."

Weiss sat back. So that was it all the time.

She drew her lips back from her teeth. "I believe that he and my Mary are still seeing each other. I can't get Mary to admit it—God knows, I've tried—but I know they've been intimate." Hatred underlined every word. "Mary was a virgin when she came to Majestic, Mr. Weiss. That man took her into his clutches, gained her confidence with his suave Somerset Maugham ways. That accent, those grey eyes." She shook her head as if trying to erase a vision. "No wonder she found herself in his vile bed." She sat up straighter and pounded her fist on the arm of the chair emphasizing each word. "He should be fired! Driven out of Hollywood!" She sat back, her eyes boring into his.

"Is that all, Mrs. Sheldon?" The woman nodded and waited. "If that is all, this may be the end of our conversation." He looked blandly at the grim face opposite him. "There is no way of knowing what happened between Mary and William Taylor." He nodded slowly. "Yes, he has a certain reputation for being attractive to women, especially the stars he directs. But not all of them make fools of themselves over him."

Mrs. Sheldon gasped.

He opened the top drawer of his desk and pulled out a thick contract. "I would like to point out to you that there is a morals clause in this contract between Mary and Majestic. If Mary has not been behaving as you and I would like her to, we can cancel it this minute." He slapped the contract with his hand. "I sincerely hope you are wrong, Mrs. Sheldon. What with Roscoe Arbuckle's troubles in San Francisco, I don't need more scandal here in Hollywood.

"Mr. Taylor directed many of Mary Pickford's best pictures. Miss Pickford didn't succumb. She married Douglas Fairbanks. So he isn't always fatal." He spoke very firmly now. "Taylor is a superior, gifted director. The best pictures that Mary Maxwell has made here at Majestic were directed by William Desmond Taylor. I took him off her pictures because you asked me to do so. No Maxwell picture has been so good since then." A slow smile spread across his face. "I may put him back." He stopped smiling. "Because you do not have the right to name the director of Mary's pictures. If you make any trouble, I can tear up the contract and you can take your little Mary somewhere else. Majestic will announce that she was unable to live up to the morals clause in the contract and we'll see how far you get. You'll never get another deal like this again, I assure you.

"Mrs. Sheldon, the rumors are that you are also in love with Mr. Taylor." He watched red splotches spread across her cheeks. "Don't try and ruin Majestic because Taylor is *shtupping* your daughter instead of you." He gestured in a helpless way. "Oh, I forgot. You want English. The English for *shtup* is *fuck*." He sat back and watched her cover her ears with her hands.

She stood up, her face flushed, eyes flashing.

"I have never been so insulted in my life. Mr. Weiss, if the livelihood of my little girl weren't at stake, I would leave this studio and take Mary with me. . . ."

Weiss interrupted. "It's been very nice seeing you, Mrs. Sheldon. Mary is a lucky little girl to have a mother that looks out for her interests like you do," he said pleasantly, walking toward the door. "I'm glad you have no objections to our putting Mr. Taylor back on Mary's pictures. He understands her in a way that other men evidently do not. Her best performances have been under him."

54

January 1922, The Ambassador Hotel

Section XXXIV

In one typical week of 1921, more than 6,000 American theaters, or approximately one-third of all the motion picture theaters in the United States, showed nothing but Majestic pictures. This number included a substantial percentage of bigger theaters, which means that about sixty-five cents out of every dollar paid as an entrance fee to a motion picture theater was paid to enter those theaters exhibiting Majestic pictures.

> *Federal Trade Commission Hearings on Monopolistic Practices in the Motion Picture Industry. 1922*

The orchestra was playing "Afghanistan," and Elsie was tapping her toes. "Listen," she said, "what a great song!"

Kelso stood up and reached out for her. "Let's dance. We can always eat."

They moved across the dance floor effortlessly, bodies fitted together, swaying lightly. Kelso held her closely, her head leaning against his chest. From time to time he would bend down and kiss her hair. She felt as if she were floating with no will or actions of her own.

When the music finished it was as if she were awakening. They stood in the center of the dance floor for a minute. Still holding hands, they slowly walked back to the table.

The waiter had covered their plates to keep them warm and he whisked the domes off with a flourish.

As they started to eat Kelso asked, "Would you give up your job at Majestic if a better offer came along?"

She stopped eating and looked at him. "It would have to be

a lot better, Kelso. I've worked very hard to get where I am. I'm a department head. That may not mean much to a man, but I had to be twice as good and three times as tough to make it." She shook her head. "I don't think so."

She saw the disappointment in his eyes. He looked down at his plate then up at her as if trying to decide what to say.

"Shoot! You sure spoiled that." He sighed deeply and shook his head slightly as if he didn't want to hear what she said. "OK, you climbed the mountain. You're on top, now." He leaned closer. "But where did it get you, really? You think you're a free woman, but you're pinned down like some pretty butterfly in a collection box. They're still calling the shots." He took her hand and held it gently. "I want to give you a real life. One of your own."

A bellboy laid an envelope by Kelso's plate. Kelso flipped a coin to him and read the message. He looked concerned. "I'm sorry, honey. I can't imagine what this is."

Crumpling the note hurriedly, he stood up. "Please forgive me. But I have to make a call. There's some sort of trouble with a shipment of beef. Gotta find out what's wrong." He patted her hand and stood up, looking around. "I'll only be a minute."

She watched him ask a waiter where the telephones were, then walk briskly to the door of the dining room. He wore his tuxedo as beautifully as he did his Levi's. She sighed.

They drove slowly past the Chinese restaurant. Ben indicated it with a nod of his head as they parked.

"See, I'm not crazy. It doesn't have a name, at least not in English."

Kum Ying translated. "Words there are name. Say Jade Dragon. Beautiful name for bad place." She smiled up at him.

Ben helped Kum Ying out of the motorcar, and said, "Let's go on in and order something to eat. You can read the menu. All I know how to order is chop suey."

She gave him a quick intimate grin. "I order good for you."

The interior was dim. Curtained booths lined the walls on either side of the long room. Torn silk lanterns hung from cords, like rotting melons suspended in mid-air. Potted plants filled the front window, burned yellow on the window side.

The food was delicious. Ben tried chopsticks for the first

time and the two of them laughed. Almost a half hour passed unnoticed. The mission was turning into a date.

In the men's room, as he stood at the tin trough that ran along one wall, a voice startled him.

"Go to your table, please. Man here to see you."

Oh, Jesus, Ben thought. Kum Ying is there alone with him. He looked over his shoulder, but the door had closed.

His contact, a well-dessed Chinese man, was in their booth fingering a bowl of tea. He and Kum Ying were speaking in rapid Chinese. So far, so good. The man smiled at him in a curious way and Ben nodded a greeting.

"You are very lucky to own such a beautiful girl. She serves you well?"

Ben gulped. Kum Ying smiled demurely into her tea cup.

"She serves all my needs very well." Recklessly, he put his hand on her shoulder in a possessive gesture. "She is as talented as she is beautiful."

The man reached across and stroked her bare arm. She didn't move a muscle but Ben could feel her shoulder tense. He sat down.

"She is proud of the high price you pay for her." The man's eyes swept over her in appraisal. "Maybe I arrange to get you new girl. You make big profit." A smile only bared his teeth. "Change is good for a man. Keeps you young." Fingering the rattan handle of the teapot he asked, "Same as always? One ounce?"

"No." Ben leaned back tingling with excitement and danger. "Twenty ounces."

The man raised an eyebrow but it didn't add any expression to his face. "You make many new friends?"

"I have lots of friends in the movie business and make new ones all the time." He sipped his tea deliberately. "I'm thinking of going into business." He stared directly into the blank eyes. "Movie actors got lots of money for cocaine."

"You go into business right away? Twenty ounces is big order."

"You never know. It's as much trouble to order for a few as for many." Ben smiled blandly.

"I better check. Don't like to harm present arrangement."

"I have the cash if you've got twenty ounces."

"I got to call. It will take one hour."

Ben shrugged and nodded at Kum Ying. "We'll finish eating and drink some tea."

"You pay now. I be at your motorcar in one hour."

Ben laid twenty twenty-dollar bills on the table and the man picked them up casually and stuffed them inside his coat pocket.

Ben stared at the curtain through which he had left until it stopped moving. Sitting down, he said, "Let's not waste this good food." He picked up his chopsticks. "You'll have to show me how to hold them again." As she arranged them in his fingers he quietly asked her, "What did he say to you?"

"He think you own me." She giggled and looked at him through lowered eyelashes. "Ask how much you pay. I say three hundred dollar in gold. He surprised. I tell him I proud you like me that much gold." She smiled sweetly. "I say I very happy with you. He not understand why I stay with white man instead of go with rich Chinese. I say you not beat Kum Ying." She popped a piece of water chestnut into her mouth with a delicate gesture. Then she picked up a morsel of fish head from the plate with her chopsticks and put it into his mouth. "That best part." She watched him chew. "Good?"

He chewed thoughtfully. "You're right. It's wonderful. Easily the best part," he said, smiling at her. He looked at the row of platters on the table. "It's all wonderful. I wish I knew how to order all of this."

"I write down. Show paper to waiter next time. You bring girl here. Show off." She giggled.

"Sweetheart, I'm real sorry but I'm gonna have to send you home with my driver. A big load of calves is stranded and they've got to be fed and watered or else they'll die." Kelso kept folding and unfolding the envelope the waiter had given him. "I've got to go way out to the valley and organize a bunch of hands." He took a black leather folder out of his pocket and placed it in her hand. "Kinda spoils my plans. I was going to give you this later." She looked at it, uncertain. "Go ahead. Open it."

Elsie untied the ribbon closure and opened the flaps. A blaze of white fire flashed out of the darkness of the folder. It was a line of diamonds and emeralds. A bracelet. She didn't know what to say and looked up at Kelso's inquiring face with an open mouth.

"If it's not what you want, I can change it for another color. I'm good at buying chaps or a windmill or Spanish bits, but trinkets are a lot harder." He shook his head.

"Oh, Kelso, I can't. I can't take anything this expensive from you."

"Why not?"

"I don't know. I don't have any good reason, really."

"Elsie, you make me very happy. I wanted to say thank you for my happiness, is all. Shoot! I thought girls fell over and did cartwheels when they got diamond bracelets."

"I may do that later, but now—I'm speechless! Oh, Kelso, it's truly beautiful!"

"Then you'll keep it?"

She nodded, looking him full in the eyes.

"Thank the Lord! I got up the nerve to go in and buy the darned thing, I don't think I could muster the nerve to take it back." He looked at his watch. "I'm going to put you in the Marmon and take another car. I'll call you tomorrow and we can have dinner again this week." He kissed her, put her in the car and instructed the driver, then waved her off. She blew him a kiss out the back window.

The street was quiet. A few tourists and a number of Chinese walked slowly past, no one paid any attention to him and Kum Ying as they paused in the doorway of the restaurant they had just left. They walked rapidly to Ben's car to wait for Lum Quong.

It was warm for January and Ben had taken the isinglass curtains down on either side of the front seat, but the rear curtains were still up. He looked for signs of unusual activity on the street. A Chinese in a traditional black costume lounged against a shop window, one heel caught up on the window ledge, gazing at the sidewalk. As Ben watched him another man strolled across the street, his pigtail hanging incongruously from under his western-style slouch hat. Ben put both hands on the steering wheel and waited.

One of the shadows between two buildings materialized into Lum Quong. Slightly behind him walked a portly middle-aged man wearing an embroidered robe. Behind him stood another shadow. The man in the robe came up to the window, studied Ben, then his eyes flickered over Kum Ying. There was no change in his expression.

"The man who sells in Hollywood is on way. We wait for him. Meanwhile, Chung Bow think he know your girl. Interested in buying from you. Give good price. More than you pay. You buy better girl." He held out a red silk square tied around some coins. "Gold," he said standing very close to the side of the Franklin. A faint aroma of incense clung to his clothing. "It is against the law for a white man to own a girl slave. Chinese can claim her as wife. You don't want trouble. Not so?"

A black motorcar approached slowly from the end of the street. When its driver saw the Franklin and the two Chinese standing in conversation, he parked the automobile and opened the door, watching before making any move.

Ben stiffened. The pedestrians were gone. The street was suddenly empty except for the few parked autos. The street-lamps seemed very dim and far apart and the atmosphere was punctuated by shadows, shadows that moved.

"Thank him," Ben said, speaking to Lum Quong, but watching the man getting out of the black car twenty feet down the street. "But I like her fine. She's not for sale at any price."

The two Chinese men spoke for a moment.

"He insists you sell her." Quong's voice took on a polite edge.

Ben wondered how quickly he could start the Franklin. Casually, he advanced the spark lever with one finger while still looking at Chung Bow.

The man emerging from the dark auto was carrying a package in his hand, something white.

Ben laughed. "Why does he want her anyway? They're all alike in the dark."

Lum Quong smiled in appreciation of the joke. "Chung Bow would like to discuss more." He looked across at the man crossing the street. "The man you want is approaching. It would be a meeting very good for business. You become rich and happy."

Neither of the Chinese had more than glanced at Kum Ying, but Ben felt her panic and sensed her hand gripping the seat between them. He pretended to think over the offer. He had to wait long enough to see the approaching drug dealer and get a look at his face. His finger idly fiddled with the gas control on the steering column, never letting his eyes stray to what he was doing.

"Tell Mr. Bow no thanks. I like Kum Ying just fine and don't plan to turn her in on a new model just yet." He tried to sound flippant and unconcerned.

The approaching man stepped into the light and raised the white object to his head. It was a Stetson hat. As the hat went up, Ben realized with a shock that it was Kelso Kennard walking toward them. Kelso! My God! He had a gun on his hip!

Ben froze. He felt Lum Quong grip his arm and heard his polite voice, as if from a long distance.

"Step out, please, Mr. Sommers. Before there is trouble."

At the sound of Ben's name, Kelso stopped in the middle of the street. His body tensed, then sprang to life. Their eyes met and locked, while Kelso's hand flew down from his hat brim to the revolver in his holster.

The Franklin started with a loud roar and backfired from too much gas. Ben aimed it directly at Kelso; the gun hand pulled the Colt out of the holster and snapped it up into position. There was a flash from the gun as the windshield cracked and split apart with a shattering crash.

Kelso, looking amazed, flew into the air as the car struck him; he hit the strut that supported the canvas top, and slid slowly off the hood and dropped behind. The strut sagged and for an instant, while shifting gears, Ben was afraid the canvas top would fall down around his head and blind him. Something hit the canvas top with a ripping sound. Ben drove faster. When he cleared the outer edges of Chinatown, he slowed slightly at cross streets. No one followed.

When they got out in front of the YMCA fragments of glass tinkled on the pavement.

"Like Chinese wind chime," Kum Ying laughed.

Ben looked down at her. "You're very brave," he said softly.

She was pale but she smiled. "Very scared. They want to get me. They call him from San Francisco." She nodded grimly.

Ben walked with her up the steps of the YWCA. A stern-faced matron indicated that the front door was as far as he could come.

Kum Ying took his hand. "I confess to you?" She looked down.

"Sure," Ben said. "We're old friends by now."

"Kum Ying afraid you sell her to Chung Bow." She looked up at him with a radiant smile. "You good man."

"You actually thought that I'd sell you to that highbinder? Jesus Christ! What do you think I am?"

She said softly, "A man."

"Well," Ben said, "as long as we're telling each other everything . . . if you ever decide you want to be owned again, I'd pay lots more than four hundred for you. In gold."

She laughed gaily and waved to him from inside the doors.

The next morning he found the hatchet lying on the backseat where it had fallen through the canvas top of the car. Ben caught his breath, then chuckled. What a swell souvenir.

Later that afternoon he checked in with his buddy at the Los Angeles central police station and explained that he thought he'd accidentally killed a drug dealer. But no one on the Chinatown squad had reported finding a body dressed in a tuxedo and cowboy boots. While the officer was off asking around, Ben slipped an envelope containing 100 dollar bills into the center drawer of the desk. As they shook hands the officer assured him that he would be the first called if anything turned up. But it was more than likely that nothing would, Chinatown being what it was.

55

February 1922, Redondo Beach, California

San Francisco Examiner, Jan. 30, 1922

THIRD TRIAL FOR ARBUCKLE VOWS BRADY

The jury trying the accused comedian for the second time was excused after being deadlocked for forty-five hours. It is reported that ten jurors were for conviction and two were against, but try as hard as they could, the ten could not sway the two hold-outs.

"If it had been the other way around," said District Attorney Brady, "I would let the man go on his way. But as long as ten jurors, good men and true, are so convinced, it is my public duty to try Arbuckle for a third time."

"Hello, Ben. Come on in." Mr. Wright smiled and opened the door wide. Ben hesitated then stepped inside. "You haven't been around much."

"There didn't seem to be much reason for me to come out." He stood there nervously shifting his weight from foot to foot.

"Why don't you sit down for a minute. Elsie and her mother have gone to the store. Be back shortly." He indicated the armchair. "What have you been up to, Ben?"

"Just busy, I guess."

"Oh." Wright sat down, relaxed. "Elsie been leading you on a merry chase?" he asked in a fatherly way. "I mean with this Kennard fellow?"

Ben was startled.

Wright nodded slowly as if his suspicions had been confirmed. "Don't worry, boy. She'll come around." He laughed lightly. "You got her mother on your side, all right. She can't stand that cowboy." He settled back in the chair trying to put Ben at ease. "She wants to keep you around so she can work on you." He laughed at his own joke.

Ben's expression remained grim.

"Something wrong, Ben? You want to tell me?"

Ben nodded. "I have some bad news for Elsie." He started as the back door slammed and the sound of women's voices came from the kitchen. Mr. Wright stared at him and then stood up.

"I'll keep Elsie's mother out in the kitchen," he said quietly. "Or do you two want to go for a walk?"

Ben shook his head. "I don't think she'll walk out with me." He started sharply as he heard the click of the portieres behind him.

"Ben!" Elsie cried. "I saw your machine."

He slowly stood and faced her. "I've got some bad news for you, I'm afraid," he said.

She sat down uncertainly on the arm of a chair, suddenly afraid. She had never seen him look like this.

Mr. Wright stood in the dining room. His wife peered in from the kitchen but he warned her with his hand. "Do you two want me to leave so you can be alone?" Something was terribly wrong.

"Yes, Daddy." She looked at Ben. "No. Maybe you'd better stay. We can always go for a walk on the dunes after, if Ben wants."

"Yes, you'd better stay," Ben said.

Ben took a deep breath. "I think I killed Kelso Kennard night before last. In Chinatown. I drove my motorcar right into him. I'm still not sure what happened." He was clasping his hands tightly in his lap.

Elsie stood up, then sat down again as if unable to manage her legs. Her father got up quickly and sat on the arm of her chair. He took one of her hands in his and held it.

"What happened?" she whispered.

Ben shuddered, then got hold of himself. His voice was now firmer. "Elsie, I found out Kelso was the drug pusher who's been selling to Mabel Normand. And a lot of others. I wasn't sure until he shot at me." His voice was strangely emotionless.

She stared at him. The room was so silent they could hear

the surf a block away on the beach. "How do you know for sure?" she asked slowly. "There's no mistake?"

He shook his head. "No mistake."

"I never did like him," Mrs. Wright said, entering from the kitchen.

"Hush, Mother. Later," Mr. Wright warned. "You better tell us exactly what happened, son."

"I put on a show of trying to muscle in on his drug territory. I bought a big supply of cocaine in Chinatown and announced that I was going to start selling to picture actors. It was Bill Taylor's idea." He looked at Wright. "It worked, too."

"But Kelso was at dinner with me . . ."

"All evening? At about nine-thirty?"

Elsie was silent. She closed her eyes.

"I thought so. He was in Chinatown shooting at me about nine-thirty."

"There was a shipment of calves that would starve. . . ." she said desperately.

"He was lying."

She looked at him as if she wished he would go away. He looked down at the floor.

"I can't help it, Elsie. The Chinese guy I bought cocaine from, Lum Quong, called his dealer and told him someone was cutting into his take. Kelso came running to find out who it was."

She put her hands over her ears to keep his voice out.

"I saw him. I saw him put on his white Stetson," he shouted at her. "He saw me and pulled his gun."

Elsie put her hands down and stared at him in disbelief. "You mean shot, really shot at you? Oh, Ben, Kelso would never do anything like that."

"Oh, for Christ's sake, Elsie!" He wanted to shake her. "He shot the whole goddamned windshield out of the Franklin! Jesus! What do I have to say to convince you?"

"Take it easy, Ben," Mr. Wright said sternly.

Ben looked at him, pleading. "For God's sake. I'm not making this all up. He shot at me and I ran over him with my car." He made his hand into a gun and pointed his finger at Mr. Wright. "Bang! Just like that," he laughed bitterly. "I couldn't believe it. I thought for an instant, My God, he's been over at Universal too long."

No one laughed but Ben.

"Stop it, Ben," Elsie burst out.

"I can't stop it, honey," he said quietly. "I'm still very

jumpy. I wish to Christ I could." He paused and looked at all of them. "But it's done. If I hadn't hit him with the car, he would have killed me."

"Where's your motorcar now?" asked Mr. Wright.

"In a garage. Getting a new windshield and strut. Getting the dents pounded out of it. New paint."

"Destroying evidence?" Mr. Wright asked softly.

"Sure. What else? I'm not certain he's dead. I hit him but there's no dead body. There's been nothing in the papers." He held out his hands, palms up. "Nothing. Like it never happened."

Elsie sat looking at him for a long time. Finally she stood up. "So we still don't know if he's dead, do we?" she asked Ben.

He shook his head.

Her mother put her arm around her. "Put a coat on, dear. You and Ben go out and walk on the beach. It'll do you both good." Elsie nodded dumbly. "You can talk better there."

As they walked away from the house, Ben, almost afraid, said, "I felt the rear wheel hit something with a thump, Elsie."

She stood still and looked up at him. "You like talking about it, don't you?" She shivered. "It's ghoulish."

Ben stopped and watched as she walked away from him toward the beach. They had left the few boarded-up summer cottages behind. He ran after her and caught her arm. She was crying softly.

"That's not true." He whirled her around. "I just wanted you to know." They stared at each other for an instant. "Elsie, what really makes it worse is that I love you so." He let go of her arm and kicked at a clump of sand grass. "Damn it to hell!"

She drew back. "You have a funny way of showing it. Killing my friends." She ran away and stood at the top of a dune, looking down at the surf.

"Oh, Christ! He shot at me first," he shouted into the wind, exasperated. "He was a goddamn drug dealer. He was no friend! We're just lucky he didn't make you into some sort of hophead, too."

She stared back at him. "I don't care," she yelled. "All I know is that a man I liked is dead."

She was brushing the tears off her cheeks. He pulled a handkerchief from his pocket and held it out. She pushed his hand away and turned her back on him.

"I don't understand you at all, Elsie. You broke off with

me because of a little thing like jazzing around with a few girls. Kelso destroyed lives. Honey, he sold drugs. And you still think he was just great." He shook his head.

She sat down in the lea of the dune, hugging her knees. "Oh, Ben, there's a lot more to it than that. For God's sake, I gave you a choice. Choose between me or them. You had to have your little extra girls regularly. So you chose them." She shrugged.

Ben was stunned, realizing the distinction she was making. "You mean I was doing something wrong to you, and Kelso was only doing something wrong to some stranger?"

"You're interpreting it all wrong."

"No, I'm not, Elsie." He sat down beside her and tried to understand her distinction. "He was a criminal. I'm not." He paused. "At least, I wasn't."

"Stop it! Stop it! Stop it!" She pounded on his shoulder with her fists. "I don't know what I mean. I liked two men. One of them has killed the other. How do you expect me to act, for God's sake?" Sobbing, she buried her head in her arms.

The sun went behind a cloud and he could feel how cold the wind was.

"I'll take your hankie now."

He handed it to her and watched her wipe her eyes and then blow her nose. What a pair they must look. He knew his eyes were bloodshot from lack of sleep, now hers were from crying. He smiled at her.

"I'll be all right in a minute," she sniffed.

"I'm so sorry, Elsie. The thing I hate most is making you unhappy."

"I know, Ben," she said sadly. "We do it to each other. We're not good for each other," she added softly.

"I'm still better for you than *he* was," Ben said. She didn't look up, and he thought the sound of the breakers might have drowned out his voice.

"I wouldn't have gone all the way with Kelso," she was almost speaking to herself. She had heard him after all.

"By that time it might have been too late," he muttered grumpily.

Her eyes gleamed. "Oh, Ben, it's hard to explain to a man. He was exciting. An adventure. There was a lot to him." She smiled ruefully. "I asked him, with all he had going for him, why did he pick me out? He could have had the most beautiful girl in California."

"He did," Ben answered simply, reaching out his hand. "He had you."

She shook her head. "Don't, Ben." She stood up and brushed the sand off her skirt. She walked to the top of the dune and stood looking at the sea. "It's all crazy. I don't understand why I feel the way I do." She turned and stretched out her arms to him. "It's not your fault, Ben."

He caught her hand. "Can't we start over again?" he begged.

She looked at him steadily, then shook her head. "Neither of us can change enough."

"You don't know that. We haven't really tried." Somehow it was all slipping away just as he realized how desperately he wanted to hang on. "I'm different. I have changed."

She looked at him fondly. "You haven't really changed. You're just full of remorse. You're still the opportunistic young man who always sways with the wind and grabs with both hands."

He stared at her. Is that what she thought he was?

"You've never killed anybody before, have you?"

He turned to her slowly. "What a lousy thing to say."

"You've done almost everything else for Majestic. It was going to be a killing sooner or later, I figured." She looked at his stricken face for a moment.

He walked down the dune toward the surf, turned suddenly, and shouted at her, "I've got to live with it. You don't, Goddamn it!" He sank to his knees, struck his fists against his thighs, staring at the foaming water as it curled around his legs.

"Get up, Ben. You'll get all wet."

"I don't care!"

"I'll still love you, Ben."

He looked up at her. "Then why are we doing this to each other?"

"Because we're not good for each other. I said it earlier. You just didn't want to hear. Whatever it is I need from a man, I can't get it from you. And I can't give you what you need."

His eyes pleaded with her. "But haven't we drawn closer now than we ever were?"

She shook her head sadly. "We're further away than ever, Ben. You just don't realize it." She shivered. "I'm cold. Let's start back." She walked slowly toward the houses in the distance.

"We love each other! We must be good for each other!" He shouted at her retreating figure.

She turned and waited. "No, I mean it. We're too different. I want to be one thing, you want to be another. You want to be what you want, I want you to be something else. After ten minutes we're at each other's throats."

She walked away more rapidly. He ran after her and caught her hand. "Wait. Please. We complement each other."

She turned away and kept walking. "We're destroying each other."

"You'll think differently in a few days, after the shock is over." She wouldn't wait and listen to him. How could he convince her if she wouldn't wait and listen? Suddenly she stopped and turned.

"No, I won't either." She pulled her hand away as he tried to grasp it.

"Can I call you?" he asked.

"No," she said, and walked on.

"I wish you'd have some ice cream of your own, instead of thieving mine," Bill Taylor said as Mabel Normand took the spoon out of his hand and popped it into her mouth. "Henry could serve you some before he leaves."

"I shouldn't even steal yours. I'll get fat. I ate enough peanuts coming over to feed a zoo. Davis is sweeping out the motorcar now, shells all over the floor in back," she giggled. "Your neighbors will think I arrived on an elephant." She stood up and stretched. "I really must go, Billy. I hope your Ethel M. Dell is soothing. I'm going to read myself to sleep."

Taylor took one of her hands. "Don't worry, dear, and do read *Rosemundy*. It could be a marvelous role for you."

"How will you spend the evening, now that I have declined your bed, Billy?" Mabel ran her finger around the edge of his ear.

"Doing the damned income tax. I'll go through the checks. It's getting outrageous. Four percent! Irresponsible government spending, indeed. I expected better from Harding."

"I know." She shook her head. "My accountant screams about it, too. It seems they only soak the rich."

Holding hands they walked down the path to Mabel's limousine. Davis opened the door and she stepped delicately over the neat pile of peanut shells in the gutter as she got in.

She leaned out of the window and he kissed her on the cheek. "Good-night, sweetheart," he murmured, then watched as the red taillight disappeared down the hill toward Wilshire.

The front door was still standing open. Taylor called out, but Henry Peabody had left for the night. It was now almost dark and he switched on the lamp at the desk and began to go through the pile of canceled checks.

In the bungalow directly across the court, Faith MacLean complained about the cold to her husband, Douglas.

"I'll bring the electric fire down from upstairs and you can put it by your feet," he said, starting up the stairs. Two shattering reports, muffled yet penetrating, sounded from nearby. MacLean ran to the front door and looked out. There was silence.

"Strange," he said, closing the door. "Must have been a backfire. I'll get the heater."

Faith stood up and retrieved the book she had dropped at the sharpness of the sounds. "Didn't sound like any backfire I ever heard." She pulled the lace curtain aside and looked out across the court.

"Douglas, there's somebody standing in Billy Taylor's front door." Her husband didn't answer. "Douglas?" she called out. As she watched, the figure stood in the rectangle of light streaming out of the open door. It turned, leaned into the front room as if saying goodbye, then shut the door. Looking to either side, it hurried into the darkness between the houses. Faith had an impression of a toothy, gleaming smile.

"Douglas," she shouted.

"I'm sure Bill Taylor doesn't appreciate your spying on his women," he said, almost whispering, from the top of the stairs.

"But this one was dressed like a man. I know it was a woman. She had broad hips and was sort of dumpy. You know. Not Billy's type—young and pretty like Mabel or Mary Maxwell."

"Did you recognize her?"

"No. She was wearing a muffler, all bundled up."

"Well," her husband smiled, "we've seen a lot of women go in and out of there. I wouldn't fret about it."

But Faith MacLean couldn't concentrate on her book. The furtive figure still troubled her. Bill Taylor's girls came and went quite openly, traipsing boldly down the walk to waiting motorcars.

Harold Courtnay, Taylor's chauffeur, knocked at the front door just after nine that evening to receive instructions for the following morning. The lights were on in the front window, but no one answered. Courtnay smiled and shrugged. Taylor must be getting some nookie upstairs again. He drove off in Taylor's Marmon.

When the MacLeans went to bed after eleven, the living-room light was still burning across the court.

"One, two. One, two. One, two. Don't overdo, Mr. Reid. One, two." Max counted as Wallie smacked his boxing gloves into the punching bag in the sanitarium gym.

Reid stopped punching. Breathing heavily, he threw two shadow punches at Max. "Few more weeks like this and I'll be able to lick the stuffing out of you, Max."

Max unlaced the gloves. "That's a day I'm looking forward to. I can't imagine anybody I'd rather have knock me down. Better shower. It's almost supper time."

Max followed Wallie into the toilet where he watched him relieve himself, then he stood in the locker room as Wallie disrobed from the sweat suit, followed him to the door of the shower room.

"Ever get tired of watching me, Max?" Wallie asked as he lathered himself. "Wouldn't you rather look at some red-head's cute little ass?"

Max grinned. "You bet. But I'm paid not to take my eyes off you and I don't. I'm betting that you make it and maybe I've helped."

"You have, Max. You're not just my keeper anymore. You've become my friend."

"Do you want a pill?"

Wallie looked up. "No, let me try and get through the night without it. If I can't do it, you can always give me one later." He grinned. "That'll make six days in a row if I can get through tonight." He put his arm around Max's shoulder. "I feel guilty about keeping you awake so much. I'm sure you'd rather sleep than put up with my howling and cold sweats."

"It'll all be worthwhile to see you lick it. I don't begrudge you a single night, Mr. Reid."

"The nights are easier, somehow. I guess it's because I can let go and yell. Daytimes I have to keep hold. I can let it out in the gym, but at the studio, it's terrible."

"I wish they'd let up on you for a few weeks. It's real punishment to make a picture and be going through this too."

"Nothing has ever licked me before. And I'm not going to go down now. My manhood is at stake, Max."

376

"He's going to make it, Dr. Hoffman," Max reported.

Hoffman nodded. "If the strain doesn't kill him. Don't let him exercise too hard."

"Isn't there any way to make the studio let up on his schedule, give him a few weeks' rest?"

"No. That's part of the deal. They will only keep him as long as he works. If they cut him loose, he'd be back on morphine in a few days. Rubin's paying for maintenance. He doesn't know we're trying to cure Reid. That's a bonus."

"Bastards."

"No. Businessmen. But maybe it's all the same."

56

February 1922, South Alvarado Avenue

Motion Picture Daily, Feb. 1, 1922

SHOOTIN' STARS

Item: The rumors, and Hollywood on a clear day has more rumors than most cities ten times its size, continue to circulate that Louis B. Mayer is hobnobbing with Marcus Loew and Joe Godsol, prexy of Goldwyn Pictures. Story goes that Loew needs more product for his picture chain, and Metro isn't up to it. Godsol is in need of cash to finance more Goldwyn pictures, always extravagant but not always profitable. Mayer wants to put it all together with his name on it.

Mayer has inked a good production man in Irving Thalberg. Godsol has the equal in June Mathis. Loew has coin pouring in from his theaters. Putting the entire stable together might take a year or more but would assemble a formidable gang with money, brains and talent.

The voice on the telephone quavered and sounded incoherent.

"Mr. Sommers, this is Henry. Henry Peabody. Mr. Sommers, I think he's dead."

Ben stood up knocking his morning cup of coffee across the desk.

"What the hell do you mean? Who's dead, Henry?"

"Mr. Taylor. He's just lyin' there on the floor as if he just lay down and died. He's lookin' at the ceiling, but he's dead."

"Oh, my God!"

He hurried past his secretary's desk. "Bill Taylor is dead. I'm going right over there. Call Mr. Rubin and see who he wants to notify—a doctor—undertaker—I don't know."

The court on Alvarado Street looked sunny and undisturbed as he walked to the house in the rear corner. Funny, how everything in one life could fall apart and everything else remained unchanged. Henry stood inside the door.

"Miss Purviance, she heard me yell. She came knocking, but she's the only one who knows so far." He pointed into the front room. "Mr. Taylor's in there."

William Desmond Taylor was lying on the floor face up, a chair across his legs. The sightless grey eyes were open and staring, showing no trace of anguish or pain, no grimace of terror. Bill looked calm, gentlemanly, not even startled to be dead. He appeared to be laid out, arms by his sides, fingers almost touching his trousers, clothes arranged without creases, neat and tidy, as if done by an expert.

A sudden peal of the doorbell startled him. "Thank God somebody's here," he called toward the kitchen as he opened the door.

Abe Weiss stood on the steps.

"Who else knows?" he asked, quickly shutting the door. He laid his topcoat on a chair and picked Ben's coat up from the floor and placed it beside his own.

"What are you doing here?" Ben asked.

"I came to see what needs to be done. *Who knows about it?*"

Ben shook his head as if to clear it. "Henry Peabody, the butler. And Edna Purviance, Chaplin's girl friend. She lives next door."

"I know who Edna is." Weiss stepped into the parlor and looked down at the corpse. "That's no stroke. Looks arranged." He glanced around the room. "Something's funny here." Standing in the center, he took command.

"Sooner or later we'll have to call the police, so we only have a short time. You," he pointed at Henry, "empty all of the liquor bottles into the sink, then get rid of them. Even if you have to throw them over the back fence. We don't need revenue agents, too."

Weiss calmly stepped over the body and looked at the papers lying on the desk. "Doing his income tax. Ben, while I look around here, you check upstairs for anything that could look bad for us when the police search. Get going," he waved his hand at them. "Don't miss anything."

Ben couldn't take his eyes off Taylor's face. Could there be

379

some connection between this death and his killing of Kelso? There must be. Damn! He should have called Taylor. A call might have served as a warning. Warning against what? Taylor must have been keeping something back.

"I said snap out of it," Weiss barked. "We've got to comb this house and time's running out." He began to pull open drawers and look through them. Some of them were locked, and Ben watched in horror as Weiss fished a key ring out of the dead man's pocket. "He was shot. There's a bullet hole."

Startled and frightened, Ben raced across the dining room and up the stairs. He had never been upstairs before and was surprised to find the bedroom simple and plain. The double bed had not been slept in. He searched through the drawers absently—nothing but men's furnishings, handkerchiefs, shirts, hosiery, B.V.D.s. Then he examined the closet.

In a box at the rear of the closet Ben found some envelopes of Kodak snaps. Couples having intercourse, lots of nude girls in lewd poses. Ben recognized most of the girls. William Desmond Taylor was the man in most of the pictures.

After listening at the kitchen door, Henry stood at the sink and watched all the beautiful liquor go down the drain. Suddenly he put his hand to his head and ran up the stairs.

"Mr. Sommers? Mr. Sommers, you up here?" he called softly.

"In here, Henry." Ben looked up from the snapshots.

"I just remembered something." He lowered his voice. "A nightgown. I clean forgot. I bought it for Miss Maxwell when Mr. Taylor asked me to. It's got letters across here." Henry ran his fingers across his chest. "She embroidered them herself, sitting right on that sofa." He pointed at the floor indicating the living room below.

"Where did he keep it?"

"In the chifforobe. Third drawer, in a green paper box."

"Well, it's not there now. I'd better tell Mr. Weiss."

The corpse had been covered with the Spanish shawl from the piano and the bright colors made it look more grotesque than before. Weiss sat behind the desk reading from a pile of letters. Ben explained about the nightgown.

"*Meshuggeneh!* Of all the stupid things." He shook his head. "First lesson to a star should be never put your name on your underwear. The whole damn house is probably filled with little souvenirs."

"I found these." Ben held out the pictures. Weiss glanced at them and put them on the little pile of papers he was accumulating. Then he picked up the top photo and looked at it closely.

"I could never understand why some men want to see themselves while they're *shtupping* some *tsataske*." He examined some of the pictures. "No one looks good, ever."

"What did you find?" asked Ben indicating the letters.

"Oh, these are just from Mabel Normand. Harmless. Besides, she's not a Majestic star."

"What do you mean?" Ben asked, puzzled.

"What do I care if Normand is incriminated or whatever? These are not so dirty. Hearst will print them gladly. I don't think they were really in love. Not enough passion in them."

"You mean you'd leave them for the police to find?"

"Of course. We're only interested in those things that might embarrass Majestic."

"Mabel is a really nice woman." He felt nervous and apologetic. "Those letters might ruin her career. Could taking them really do us any harm?"

"So let her career get ruined." Weiss slowly replaced the letters in the drawer. "Little fool! That'll teach her to write letters. Let Goldwyn take care of his own. Normand is not mine. She's his, Goldwyn's. I only protect Majestic, not all of Hollywood." He tossed the keys to Ben. "Lock the drawers and come upstairs." Weiss moved rapidly across the room, stepping over the body on his way.

Ben, feeling spasms in his stomach, sat down. Slowly he opened the drawer and looked at Mabel's letters It was almost as if she were in the drawer reaching out to him. Without hesitation, he took them up, selected a few papers from the pile on the desk, and put them in the empty drawer. He knew Bill Taylor would have approved. He locked all the desk drawers, laid the keys on the top of the desk, and arranged a few canceled checks on them to make it look casual.

The bundle of letters was too bulky to fit into his jacket, so he stuffed it into the pocket of his topcoat lying on the chair. Then he edged around the body and went upstairs.

"I thought you went through these drawers," Weiss snapped.

"Henry interrupted me. What else did you find?"

"Enough *Merry Widows* to supply the U.S. Navy. He must have got them wholesale. Here." Weiss tossed the packages of condoms at him. "Put them to good use." Nodding at the floor below, he said, "He won't need them anymore."

They found some women's undergarments and a few more photographs. Weiss was disgusted and handled the panties with his fingertips.

They collected all the things they were taking away and put on their topcoats. Ben could feel the bundle of letters in his pocket. He stuffed the photos and condoms into his other pocket and hoped he looked balanced.

"Give us a few minutes, Henry," he said, "then yell." The Spanish shawl was still covering the body. He forced himself to pull it off and throw it back over the piano. He could swear that Taylor was watching him.

"I'm Edna Purviance. Get Miss Normand up."

When the maid looked blank, Edna shouted, "Now!"

The maid was acting stubborn. "You can't just come barging in here like this. Miss Normand is still asleep."

Edna pushed her hard. "Out of my way, sister. It's a matter of life and death." The maid didn't budge. "Look, if you don't wake her up and get her out here, I'm going to start smashing things." She picked up a delicate china figurine and waved it in the air.

The maid ran down the hall and in a few minutes Mabel stood in the doorway looking sleepy and frightened.

"Oh, Edna, it's you," she said, relieved. "What the hell are you doing up at this hour?"

Edna put her arm around Mabel. "Honey, you better sit down."

Within a half hour of Henry Peabody's running up and down the walk, screaming, the bungalow court was filled with a crowd of spectators and police. Ben and Weiss sat in Ben's automobile up the block and looked down the hill at the crowd as it gathered and spilled over the sidewalk and out into the street. Then they walked up to the police line and Weiss presented his card to the officer standing there.

"I'm Abe Weiss of Majestic Pictures, Officer. I understand there's been an accident? Who's in charge?"

The burly man turned around and smiled. "Morning, Mr. Weiss. You probably don't remember me. I'm Chief of Detectives Riccardi." The smile broadened. "We sat at the same table once at a Widows' and Orphans' Benefit dinner."

Weiss's eyes widened as if in recognition. "Yes. Yes, I remember now. How have you been?"

"Fine." He jerked his head toward the back of the court. "Until this. Mr. Weiss, this ain't no accident. It's murder. Taylor's been shot. Twice, with a thirty-eight. The D.A.'s inside. I suppose you want to look? You know Woolwine, don't you?"

The thinnest line of a smile forced its way across the studied look of concerned horror on Weiss's face. "I ought to. I contributed enough to help get him elected." He stopped, as if just struck by a realization. "Did you say murder?"

Riccardi grinned. "Yeh, it's murder all right. Clean, though. Place looks real neat." He drew closer, confidential. "You wouldn't believe how messy some murders are."

"I'll take your word for it."

They followed the detective into the front room, now filled with policemen. Taylor's body had been turned over, and the coroner was examining two bullet holes in the back of the suit coat. He was probing into one of them with a yellow pencil. A flattened handkerchief lay on the Turkish carpet as if it had lain under the corpse. A policeman idly picked it up and placed it on a table.

Riccardi cleared his throat and everyone turned expectantly.

"Mr. Weiss is here, Mr. Woolwine."

Woolwine nodded a greeting. "How've you been, Mr. Weiss?" He stood up and they shook hands. "Looks like you lost one of your boys." He stepped aside thoughtfully so as not to block their view of the corpse. "I'm sorry."

Weiss looked appropriately grief stricken. "I am, too. He was a great director."

Ben thought that if Weiss had been wearing a hat he'd have taken it off and held it over his heart.

Weiss nodded at Ben. "This is my press chief, Ben Sommers. He'll need information for the reporters."

Woolwine looked Ben up and down. "He'll get it as soon as we have any to give him." He paused dramatically. "Lots of mysterious things went on here." He looked around the room. "Somebody really cleaned this place out." He stared at both of them. Weiss met the look without blinking. Ben had to sit down. "I'd sure like to know what went on around here. Nothing matches up."

The coroner looked up. "Not even the bullet holes. The ones in his suit coat don't match the ones in his vest." He sounded cross. "He either had his hands up or was leaning over."

"Maybe embracing some broad," Riccardi smirked. Weiss

383

looked at him disapprovingly. They bent over the body to see what the coroner was pointing at with his pencil. Ben watched with fascinated horror as Abe Weiss stood beside the little table and deftly picked up the handkerchief.

One of the policemen, diligently leafing through all of the books in the bookcases, was rewarded with a flutter of notepaper falling to the floor. The stationery was engraved with a butterfly and the three initials, MMM. The policeman picked up one of the notes, then blushed as he read it. Ben watched Weiss turn white with fury.

Mabel Normand stood on the porch, her face puffy with weeping, her hair disheveled.

"Mr. Policeman, I must have my letters!" She shouted through the open doorway. "You must let me have them. They're private. No one has a right to read them. Please." She began sobbing and sank down on the stoop, beyond caring about the spectacle she was creating for the crowd.

Reporters surged about her, breaking through the line of police guards. Woolwine helped her to her feet and through the doorway, pulling her into the parlor. She drew back as the stretcher, covered with a white sheet, was carried past. Without warning, Woolwine jerked back the sheet and the cool grey eyes of William Desmond Taylor stared up at the hysterical Mabel Normand, who screamed once, then slumped to the floor. Woolwine calmly replaced the sheet. Ben sat down unsteadily.

Recovered, a distraught Mabel reclined on the sofa as the chief of detectives tried to explain that they'd found no letters.

"But I saw them in that desk just last week. We laughed over how the pile was growing. I know they were in that drawer."

"They're not there now," said Woolwine.

Ben, not daring to move, felt the hairs on his neck start to prickle as he realized that Abe Weiss was staring at him intently.

There was a terrible scream from outside. Everyone in the room froze. Mary May Maxwell was fighting with an officer who was keeping her away from the front door. Ben beckoned to Weiss and they watched as she tore at her long blonde curls and pounded her fists on the policeman's chest.

"I loved him. Don't you understand? I loved him."

Ben started for the front door. "She needs help. That's my job," he protested to the district attorney who had stepped in front of him and put his hand on his chest to bar his way.

Mary looked to the skies. "Oh, God, why didn't you take me instead? Take me now! I don't want to live. I don't want to live." Falling to her knees, she continued to scream until she collapsed in a heap. Ben fumed helplessly as Woolwine called for an ambulance to take her away.

The district attorney nodded to Weiss. "If we stay long enough, every star in Hollywood will turn up to have hysterics."

Weiss didn't reply.

Ben was numb with desolation driving back to Majestic. He felt edgy and kept glancing at his passenger who stared straight ahead with an emotionless face.

Ben cleared his throat. "Who do you suppose did it?" His voice sounded like a croak.

"One of his women, most likely. Any man with messy sex habits like that, sooner or later, it catches up."

"But murder?"

"Who knows?" Weiss drummed his fingers on the dashboard. *"The Top of New York* is finished shooting. So that will go on the schedule all right. If Rubin can arrange it, Mickey Neilan maybe can take over on Taylor's next picture. Good women's directors are hard to find. I hope Rubin has some ideas." He turned slightly and looked at Ben. "Why did you take the letters?"

Oh, Christ, here it was. He looked over at Weiss who was staring straight ahead, emotionless.

"I felt sorry for her. She's had a sad life. The Sennett love affair, her drug addiction. I just figured she'd had enough trouble. How was I to know she'd come around demanding the goddamn letters back?"

Weiss nodded. "You'll have to put them back. Now there'll be more damage if they can't be read. They're dynamite. People will imagine all sorts of dirty things. Her career is finished anyway. No matter how innocent the letters turn out to be."

"I'm sorry, Mr. Weiss." Ben was at a loss to explain his rash act. "I just took them on the spur of the moment."

Weiss cleared his throat. It was almost a signal to change the mood of their conversation. "When you return the letters to Taylor's bungalow tonight, you can also hang a nightgown in the closet, just like the one the butler described. Go buy one—lacy, transparent, disreputable. Get Grace to initial it with three Ms. On the bosom."

Ben let the wheels swerve as he stared at Weiss. An

oncoming car honked at him and he straightened out. "Why, in God's name," he said, outraged. "We just broke all sorts of laws stealing any evidence that might tie Mary to the killing."

"Wasted effort now. Little Mary tied herself to it." He let go of the windshield strut. "With those letters and all that play-acting." He shook his head as if unable to believe what had taken place. "Why do actresses always have to play big scenes?" he asked quietly, as if to himself. His voice was so soft Ben glanced at him.

"You just watch how I handle this, Ben, boy. Mary's contract is for millions of dollars and has two years to run at increasing figures." He smiled grimly. "Carlotta Sheldon is a shark and will hold me to every cent of it. If I can tie little Mary to the murder, the contract has a morals clause in it. Escape clauses." The smile broadened. "And Majestic is rid of a failing, expensive star who couldn't stay out of a middle-aged director's bed." He laughed out loud. "And a mother who is an insult and a pain in the ass."

Ben was stunned. "But Mary is one of our greatest assets!"

Weiss put his hand on Ben's arm. "Don't believe everything you write, boy. She's been a flop ever since her mother forced me to take William Taylor off of her pictures." He was silent for a moment. "That was a stupid move on my part. I never should have given in." He shook a finger at Ben. "Not one hit since then. Taylor directed with his *putz*. That's why he was so great with women." He shrugged. "But it led to trouble, too. As we just saw."

Ben stamped on the brake in front of the executive bungalow. "Mr. Weiss," he said evenly, "I wish you wouldn't talk like that. The man is dead."

"You're right," he nodded piously. "Terrible thing." As he opened the door of the motorcar he fished in his pocket and held up the handkerchief Ben had seen him pick up. Opening it, he showed the embroidered initials in the corner, *C.S.* "It runs in the family. The daughter initials her love letters and her nightgown." He clucked his tongue in disapproval. "Now who do we know who has the initials, *C.S.?*" He held up his hand as Ben was about to speak. "No, don't answer that question." He grinned. "When you return the letters, hang the nightgown in the closet. Hide it a little so the police will think they just overlooked it. The newspapers will have a field day." He carefully folded the handkerchief and put it back in his

386

inside pocket. "Poor Mrs. Sheldon." He laughed. "She's in my pocket for good." He was suddenly serious. "You see, Ben, there is a sort of justice, after all. Crime definitely does not pay."

57

March 1922, Hollywood

The Los Angeles Examiner, March 4, 1922

SLAIN MAN HID PAST
AMAZING DUAL LIFE OF TAYLOR
BARED IN NEW YORK

SPECIAL TO THE EXAMINER. Amazing details were revealed tonight about the mysterious life led by slain motion picture director William D. Taylor. Although he had become famous as a film director and was popular with his associates among the film folk, it was remarked that he had few intimates, and a shadow lay over his past that he never discussed.

It has been disclosed that Taylor was known in New York prior to 1908 as William Deane Tanner, that he was married to Ethel Mae Harrison, a member of the famous Floradora dancers, and was the proprietor of a well-known and very successful Fifth Ave. Art and Antique Studio.

Taylor simply disappeared one day and never returned. Reports that he was shanghaied to the Yukon have not been verified as yet.

Tanner's (Taylor's) wife was granted a divorce in 1912 and remarried to a wealthy New York merchant, owner of Delmonico's Restaurant, on Fifth Avenue. Taylor was the father of one daughter.

"But *Thirty Days* is going to be a very good picture. You just wait and see," Ben said confidently as he poured gin from his flask into their coffee cups. He drank it straight. Polly filled hers up with the lemon rickey from the coffee pot.

"I know. It's a real cute story and Wallie Reid is a wonderful leading man. I just worry, is all." She cupped her chin in her hand. "I can hardly wait to finally meet him." She smiled dreamily as if remembering rapturous evenings. "I've loved him for just ages."

"You've got a swell supporting cast and, God knows, Jimmie Cruze has done a whole string of good pictures with Reid." He touched her hand reassuringly, and she let it nestle within his. "Don't you worry, now, everything'll be all right." He realized that she was distracted and he followed her eyes darting from place to place in the room. Neither of them spoke for a while, Polly fidgeting, Ben watching. "What's really bothering you?" he finally asked. "Tell ole brother Ben."

Her eyes appealed to him for help. "I'm scared. I feel kind of alone again."

A little wary, he said, "Whatever for? You're the one person in this world that I think of as being able to take care of herself."

She pouted. "Look, I'm an actress. I just act self-assured." She looked at him with her enormous expressive eyes. "Inside, I'm just a frightened kid."

"Aw, come on, Polly. This is Ben you're talking to. We know each other better than that. No soft soap. OK?"

"OK."

He made a guess. "Is it because of Bill Taylor? He wasn't even assigned to your picture."

"Maybe." She was suddenly very busy stirring her food around on her plate. "I just feel all alone at the studio, is all." She leaned closer. "Nobody calls me. Mr. Rubin doesn't take me out anymore. Nobody cares."

He sat back trying to look cheerful. "Don't worry. Your career is just at an in-between stage Look, you've achieved featured player status in your third picture. You're beginning to get mail and requests from fans for pictures. After *Thirty Days* with Wallie you'll be co-starred with Richard Barthelmess in *The Old Farm*. Not bad, I'd say." He stopped patting her hand sympathetically and held it firmly, reassuringly. "You're no longer a new discovery and not quite a star yet. Just be a little patient. It'll come."

She looked at him as if she was uncertain whether or not to believe him. "You're not just trying to make me feel better?"

"You know me better than that."

"I do?"

"A few more pictures and things will change. These next few pictures are terribly important. You'll see." He smiled with confidence.

"Do you really think so?"

"Absolutely."

She breathed deeply as a sense of confidence swept over her. "God, I'm glad you're around to buck me up when I need it." She jumped up. "Let's dance. I got new steps to show you."

"Wallie, this is your new co-star, Polly McCormack. Polly, meet Wallace Reid." James Cruze stepped back smiling with pleasure. He'd lay even money that they'd make a swell team. The girl had lots of spark and would give that dash of spirit to *Thirty Days* that was so hard for Wallie to get up these days. Pep. The Pep King. Only he didn't have much anymore.

"I'm delighted, Polly," Reid said graciously. "I'm looking forward to working with you." He was a little disconcerted by the way she stared at him. He was used to being stared at but not by another professional.

She was unable to believe that the sick-looking man shaking her hand, smiling at her, was really Wallace Reid. Sure, actors looked different without their makeup. Everybody did. But this must be some trick. No makeup man could create Wallace Reid out of this ghost.

"I'm pleased to meet you, Mr. Reid. I've always wanted to work with you." She managed a smile. He smiled back at her. Well, maybe it could be Wallace Reid after all. That was the trouble with the studio. Nothing was what you thought it was. Nobody you saw on the screen was real.

"Why, thank you, Polly." He gave her an appreciative glance. "You're every bit as pretty as they said you'd be." He chuckled. "I understand you've taken aim right at the top." He winked at her cheerfully. The hollow bravado in his attitude made her embarrassed for him.

"Well, working with you will be a swell boost for my career. Improve my rep." It was the best she could do. She laughed prettily and he felt flattered.

He needed any encouragement he could get. It was sweet of her to want to play opposite him. He only hoped he could get through the picture. He was constantly tired—exhausted, really—and the long grinding days of making another picture seemed almost too much to bear. He felt worn down no matter how early he got to bed, how cautiously he ate, how careful he was. What he wouldn't give for a month off!

As they stood waiting for the photographer, talking and laughing politely, Polly was seized by a terrible sadness. She wanted to tell this pathetic old man that he had been the first, the first movie star she had ever seen. That beautiful young man who had stood at the top of the pyramid in silver armor and raised the hilt of his sword to the sun—some fleeting trace of him still lurked in those hollow eyes, but that was all.

They stood together, arms around each other, and a photograph was taken for *Photoplay*. A fragment of a memory—Mavis's *Photoplay*—flashed through her mind. She wanted him to know that she had once loved him, that he was the real reason she was here now, talking to him on a Hollywood set. But the words wouldn't come.

Not since they had lost Mary Pickford had Rubin known Weiss to be so furious. He looked away rather than endure the expression on his face.

Weiss's voice had a sharp edge to it. "I never heard such a piece of *mishegoss*. Oh, you got away with it. So far. But what a gamble."

"I gamble every morning when I get out of bed. Some days the odds are worse than others."

"If anybody had talked, we wouldn't have been able to whitewash it."

"That was part of the gamble. I figured that Wallie and his family wanted to keep his addiction quiet, too. And everybody did—no one wanted it to get out." He sat back with the smug self-satisfaction of a man who has won.

Weiss leaned forward, a stern warning in every word. "You had no right to gamble with my company."

Rubin laughed bitterly. "While I was trying to decide what to do, I said to myself that even if you knew about it, you wouldn't say thanks." He stood up and looked out over the back lot through the window. "And I was right," he said to the leaded panes of glass.

"I like to look at the man I'm talking to," Weiss said.

Rubin turned and sat down sulkily. "Did you use Ben to handle the details?" Weiss demanded.

"Why should I need help with details? No one knew except Brockman and Stein." His patience was wearing thin.

"And the male nurse and the people at the sanitarium and

the chauffeur and everybody on the sets of the pictures." Weiss sat back and smiled genially. "Oh, such a secret." Then he snapped. "Get Sommers in here."

"What can he do now?"

"He kept you from having to get a divorce, didn't he?"

Rubin stared at Weiss, uncertain whether to tell him about Ben's involvement in the Taylor-Maxwell affair. He decided not to. That was water under the bridge. "Get Ben Sommers in here," he barked into the speaker. He leaned back, his fingertips touching as if in prayer. "Dr. Hoffman thinks Wallie is cured of his habit. So now we have our number one box-office star back in action again." His tone implied that he'd gained the edge in this battle.

Weiss sighed. "I don't understand why nobody noticed. He looks terrible. Like a skeleton." He laughed humorlessly. "The funny thing is that for one year he has looked terrible and not one patron ever complained to a theater manager or wrote a letter to the studio."

Ben stood in the doorway. Weiss looked over his shoulder and beckoned him to sit down beside him. "We're talking about Wallie Reid."

"It's about time somebody did," Ben said sharply as he sat down.

Weiss looked at Rubin. "So nobody knew?"

"Everybody knew something," Ben continued. "I found out in January. Everybody likes Wallie enough so nobody wanted to blow the whistle. I think it was despicable."

Weiss smiled at Rubin.

"You don't know the facts," Rubin protested. "He's cured, back to normal."

"You call that normal?" Ben glared at Rubin.

Weiss grabbed Ben around the shoulder. "Come on. I want to find Wallie Reid. Tell him he should eat a little, get some meat back on his bones."

Ben wanted to shake off that hand but couldn't quite bring himself to do it. But he did manage to ask, "Doesn't it bother you a little that Majestic made him an addict?"

Weiss shrugged. "Majectic made him a star," he said as he walked toward the doorway.

58

April 1922, Hollywood

San Francisco Chronicle, April 17, 1922

WILL HAYS BARS ARBUCKLE PICTURES
FOREVER FROM SCREENS OF THE NATION

NEW YORK, Apr. 16. Any hope that Majestic Pictures would be free to release the three Arbuckle comedies in their vault was dashed yesterday when Will Hays, morals "Czar" of the industry, said that the pictures must never be shown "to protect the youth of our nation."

Hollywood seemed stunned by the order, which came as a complete surprise. No spokesman for Majestic Pictures was available but many of the rotund comedian's friends were outraged and voiced protests. Last week, when Arbuckle was declared innocent by the third jury to hear the evidence, a statement read by the foreman said, in part, "We hope that the American people will take the judgement of fourteen men and women who have sat listening for thirty-one days to the evidence, that Roscoe Arbuckle is entirely innocent and free from all blame."

Tables and chairs had been packed closely together under the glass ceiling of the largest stage. There was barely enough room for the waitresses to pass out glasses of iced lemonade and collect the ruins of the box lunches. Saul Rubin, seated on the dais to the left of Hays, looked at the confusion with dismay. He had been against this crazy lunch from the start. The idea! Shutting down the entire studio for two hours to listen to that pile of crap Hays had written.

"We didn't hire him to talk to *us*, for God's sake!" he muttered out of the side of his mouth to Weiss not really trying to keep Hays from overhearing. "Why the hell isn't he out on the road talking to the troublemakers who are shutting up the picture houses, raising hell with our exhibitors. I know what happens up there on the screen. We never made a dirty picture. I don't need to be told how to make a clean one."

Weiss sat patiently, looking straight ahead, smiling. "It's important for the man to feel welcome. To make him feel that he's part of the Majestic family." Weiss continued to smile straight ahead. Rubin scowled. Weiss nudged him with his elbow. "Now."

Rubin stood up and smiled at his employees. "Thank you for making time in your busy schedules to hear this important talk from an important man. Important to all of us and to this great industry of ours. Here to introduce him is our chairman of the board of Majestic Pictures, Abraham Weiss." He led the sparse applause.

Although the ceiling curtains had been drawn against the sun, the stage was unbearably hot. Someone opened the scenery doors at either end hoping a breeze would move through. Flies buzzed against the glass walls and people nodded.

Weiss glanced around the crowd. "As you probably know, a few producers who are as poor in imagination as they are in their pocketbooks have been releasing dirty pictures that have drawn the wrath, and rightfully so, of all good-minded parents, teachers, and clergymen in this great nation of ours. Our industry, ever vigilant, seeking ways to better our product, has hired a man to be the head of a new organization, an organization that will police those producers who habitually offend against morality and assure the patrons of our theaters that we are out to provide only the best in family entertainment that money can produce." He paused and looked proud. "And genius." Indicating Hays, seated beside the lectern, he concluded, "Ladies and gentlemen, I take great pride in introducing Will Hays."

The short scrawny man with big ears stood up and smiled at the light wave of applause that greeted him. His teeth were grotesquely crooked and his smile had a distinctly chilling effect. He nodded at Weiss.

"Thank you, Mr. Weiss, for this fine meeting and gracious reception. Fellow members of the moving picture industry, I'd like to begin reading the new production code to you without delay, so as not to take you away from your important work any longer than is necessary. You can, however, when you return to shooting pictures today, begin immediately to put these revolutionary concepts to work for Majestic and the people of the United States." He smiled, paused, hoped for applause. None came. He cleared his throat. "You will, of course, each get a copy of the code for reference.

"*VULGARITY*. The treatment of low, disgusting, unpleasant, though not necessarily evil subjects, should be subject always to the dictates of good taste and regard for the sensibilities of the audience." There was a titter and Hays looked up.

"Any questions?" he asked quickly, then waited, smiling his ghastly smile. No one moved. No one even looked at each other, much less at Hays. Rubin shot an accusing glance at Weiss who calmly gazed straight ahead.

"*OBSCENITY*." Hays plunged ahead fearlessly.

Weiss felt a tap on his shoulder and his secretary put a note into his hand. He looked up at her in surprise. She shook her head slowly and closed her eyes. It was serious whatever it was. He opened the note and read it.

"Klein has called from Washington three times during the hour," he muttered to Rubin. "Something's happened."

"*PROFANITY*," Hays croaked.

Someone at a table up near the front softly said, "Shee-it."

Hays pretended not to hear.

"Cut! That was very good, Wallie. Why don't you sit down for a few minutes and I'll get a couple of close-ups of Polly."

James Cruze knelt down by her. "I need more concern from you, sweetheart. Your boy friend is in jail. You don't know that he had himself put there. You think he has become a criminal. It's a comedy sure, but you're in love with him and worried sick. You don't know what to expect, and furthermore, you don't know how he will have changed. Now I want to get some close-ups over Wallie's shoulder. Look into his eyes, search there to see if it's the same John Floyd who left you a day ago." Cruze turned and called out, "Ready, Wallie? We'll do those reverses now and then break for the next shots."

Reid pushed himself up out of the canvas chair and walked toward the set of the prison visitors' room. In the center of the studio he faltered. Then, as if someone had tied a rope to one leg and tugged sharply, he staggered and fell in a heap.

Polly's hand went to her mouth. Wallie's fall was not just a clumsy stumble; it had a look of finality about it. For an instant, James Cruze thought someone had shot him.

Crew members crowded around him. Someone brought a paper cup of water and another brandished a hip flask.

"Get back! He needs air. Call Doc Stein. Get him up on that table. Air. Stop crowding, for God's sake!"

Two grips carried the stretcher through the streets of the lot to the Hospital Bungalow, where they laid Reid on the cot. Dr. Stein closed the door, then raised one eyelid and peered in. He waved a bottle of ammonia salts under Reid's nose and his eyelids fluttered.

Dr. Stein looked around to make sure they were alone and whispered, "I want the truth. Are you on morphine again?"

Reid looked up at him sadly. "Honest to God, no," he whispered. "Please believe me. I think it may be some kind of flu. I felt rotten this morning and Dottie wanted me to stay home." He coughed. "Call her, will you? She'll come and get me."

Dr. Stein examined Wallie without saying a word. "You look tired. Back to the old merry-go-round?"

"Christ no," he said wearily. "I'm in bed by nine o'clock."

The doctor listened with his stethoscope again. "Well, I don't like what I hear in there." He tapped Wallie's chest. "I wouldn't want it to turn into pneumonia. Better safe than sorry," he added cheerfully. "I'll call an ambulance."

"Hospital?"

Dr. Stein nodded and smiled reassuringly.

Reid closed his eyes. Was this how it would always be? Every time he tumbled they thought he was back on dope again. Thank God only a few people knew. He couldn't face it if the whole world knew. Nobody would give him credit for what he'd done. How many men had gone the cure? Well, he'd proved himself. If it was weakness that made him tumble to begin with, it was strength that brought him back. He had more than a pretty face and an even smile. What counted was underneath, and he had it there.

59

April 1922, Hollywood

Moving Picture Daily, April 18, 1922

SHOOTIN' STARS

Item: Kathleen O'Brian, pretty daughter of theater magnate Charles (Cholly) O'Brian, biggest independent exhibitor in St. Louis, is in town. Papa pulled strings, and Kathleen, accompanied by her mother, is making the rounds, getting screen tests at all the studios. Why the interest? Read on.

BIGGER ITEM: Momma O'Brian's big brother is Cardinal Moynihan of the St. Louis archdiocese and a loud supporter of movie censorship. Could it be that the studio that lands little Kathleen might gain a friend behind the pulpit? Who cares if the kid can act.

Polly waited in the outer office. From time to time Helen looked over at her and smiled, then returned to her work. Polly, bored, riffled through the trade papers and magazines on the table for the third time.

At the sound of the buzzer Helen looked at her and smiled again. "He's off the phone, honey, go on in." She pressed a button and the door clicked.

Saul Rubin stood behind his desk, a welcoming grin on his face. "Come on in, Polly, sweetheart, come in."

She plopped herself into the deep chair opposite the desk and stretched like a cat.

"I thought it was about time for us to have a little talk, dear," he said softly as he sat down behind his desk.

Her eyes involuntarily flicked toward the door to the bedroom. It was closed. He caught the glance and laughed.

"Not that kind of talk, I'm afraid, my dear. I'm much too busy right now for your kind of fun." His voice turned serious. "No, it's about your career. It's time we talked about Polly McCormack and where she is going."

She felt slightly apprehensive.

"Were you on the set of *Thirty Days* yesterday when Wallie collapsed?" he asked.

She nodded, eyes wide.

Rubin looked grave. "Well, we're going to finish the picture with a stand-in." He sat back gloating. "Jimmie Cruze tells me that we can do it. There's only a week's shooting left. All the major scenes are finished, and Jimmie can rearrange all of the rest so that a stand-in, wearing Wallie's costumes, can stand with his back and shoulders to the camera." He leaned forward earnestly. "It'll mean that the rest of the cast will have to work harder to be convincing."

"Oh, sure. That's OK. I was afraid it'd be canceled."

"We don't cancel when we've got this many thousand dollars already invested." He nodded reassuringly. "It may take a few days longer in the event the scenario has to be slightly rewritten."

"Does that mean that *The Old Farm* will be delayed?"

"That's the other thing I wanted to talk to you about, dear." His smile faded. "We'll have to recast that part so we don't delay production."

She stared at him as if splashed by cold water. "But that part was written for me!"

"Well, not really. Oh, I guess the scenarist maybe had you in mind." He was all business now, no smiles, no reassurance. "But it can certainly be handled by another actress." He fiddled with the ivory letter opener. "Besides, it's just not right for your career, sweetheart. Too big a jump, Polly. We don't want you to undertake anything that might be beyond your talents at this moment." He smiled now. "The studio must protect its stars, not let them run before they can walk."

His smile looked frozen. So much for all her favors. He knew who she was, and it didn't make any difference.

"Your fan mail just doesn't merit a starring role at this time," he said. "That's a good girl. I knew you'd understand and realize that we have your best interests at heart."

"Who are you going to give my part to?"

There was an edge of irritation. "It's not really your part, sweetheart. You've got to stop thinking of it like that. Besides, we don't know yet."

"What are you going to do with me?"

He shook his head. "I wish you wouldn't say it just like that. You're part of the Majestic family, Polly. What is in the best interests of the studio is best for all of us." He beamed at her. "There's a grand part in *The Bachelor Daddy*. It would be ever so much better suited to you at this point in your development."

"What's the part?" she asked warily.

"The story is wonderful. Heartwarming. Tommy Meighan plays the owner of a coal mine. He adopts an orphan family of five children. Can you picture that? Five wonderful kids, bravely on their own after their miner father is killed. Well, Tommy's girl friend won't have anything to do with these grubby kids. She's society. So in the end Tommy marries his secretary who loves the children and nurses them through an epidemic." His face glowed with warm sentimentality.

Polly bubbled with enthusiasm. "What's my part? The girl friend or the secretary."

He hesitated. "Neither one. I think you'd add real lustre and depth to the role of Nita, the oldest of the children." He tried to look encouraging and winked cheerily at her.

"Who's playing the other two?"

"Well, Leatrice Joy has been cast as Sally, the secretary, and Maude Wayne is Ethel, the girl friend." He paused. "The only part left with any character and some good scenes is that of Nita." Their eyes met. "There are a number of other young actresses who'll jump at it if you are foolish enough to turn it down." His voice had turned icy.

"Of course I won't turn it down." She spoke very slowly so her voice wouldn't break. "But I'm disappointed." She stood up and shook her dress straight. "I was promised a starring role and I get a minor feature bit." She put her hand on the desk to steady herself. "Who's directing?"

"Al Green. He's brand new, but we think he's going to be tops."

"Thanks, Mr. Rubin." She walked slowly to the door, turned and flashed a brave smile. "See ya around."

"Polly," he called out, "remember you got a friend in this office. The door is always open. If any little thing troubles you, just come and tell Uncle Saul." He grinned at her and wriggled his fingers in a little wave.

She looked at him for an instant, then let the door close and it clicked behind her.

Once outside, she walked to a bench and sat down. She

didn't know whether she wanted to weep or spit in Rubin's face.

Why did Mr. Taylor have to up and get himself killed, just when everything was going so well? There was still Ben but he hadn't been in the mood for much talking or anything else since they'd put Wallace Reid in the hospital. She suddenly felt like an orphan. An orphan child in a dirty dress living in some shack on the edge of a coal mine. So that's what they thought was good casting, did they? It was dirt they wanted. Well, she could run grubby rings around anyone else. She'd show them. They'd see. She wiped her eyes and blew her nose. Right now she'd better pick up her costume from Grace.

Abe Weiss, halfway across Nebraska, drummed his fingers on the arm of the chair in the lounge. He was too nervous to sit in his parlor car. He needed the hum of conversation and the activity of people to keep him from brooding and to steady his nerves. He wished he was in New York, walking the dark streets at four in the morning.

Who could guess that the Federal Trade Commission would smite him down. Smite. That's what a stern Jehovah did to transgressors. He laid his head back against the chair and closed his eyes. Had he been too ambitious? Had he broken laws? Must he now be punished?

Those bastards, Selznick and Goldwyn. They must be behind this. It couldn't be anyone from First National. They had their own theaters. It had to be some jealous *schmuck* who didn't have a theater to his name and no place to show his pictures. Restraint of trade! The very idea! That was the big thing! Keep your competitor from competing. If everybody was on an even footing, then nobody had an edge and got to the top. That was hardly the American way. It *wasn't* American. Bolsheviks!

Well, they'd tried to stop him before and they hadn't been able to. He was on top now and he'd hang on. There must be a way. A stray thought chilled him. Walter Falcon and that whole greedy bunch of bankers had to be kept at bay. They were almost in control as it was. If they saw an opportunity, a minute of weakness . . . *Gevalt!* They would leap at his throat. He decided to walk back to his suite. A plan had to be made and ready by the time the train reached New York. Three days. He had three days to think. A smile broke over his face. He'd solved worse problems in three hours! He could do this one, easy.

A hardwood dance floor had been constructed on the croquet lawn. Great buffet tables stretched the length of the stone terrace behind the English cottage, which had fifty rooms. On the surface of the oval swimming pool floated hundreds of large blown glass bubbles reflecting the colored lanterns clustered in the branches of each huge oak tree. But Polly loved the gardenias best. They floated by the thousand on the waters of the Canoe Run that meandered along the edge of the lawns, filling the night air with their fragrance.

Nursery rhymes were the theme of the party and she had borrowed a Bo Peep costume from Grace. Puffed paniers lay above a checked and beaded skirt that came to her knees. She wore blue and white striped stockings and her dark bangs peeped out from under a white mobcap. She carried the gold mesh evening bag with the sapphire clasp that she had earned from Saul Rubin.

Wandering through the crowds of people, all in fanciful costumes, she walked up to groups and listened or joined the conversations. Several men had tried to become familiar but as she didn't know who they were or if they were important, she had fended them off. Anyway, she didn't feel like talking.

The food was marvelous and Polly returned repeatedly to the buffet tables. As she walked through the gardens she recognized all of the faces she had seen on the screen of the Million Dollar. Others that she had never seen in a movie came alive from photos in *Photoplay*.

A voice from behind startled her as she finished a bit of chicken salad served in half a cantaloupe.

"I haven't seen you around before, you beautiful child. Who are you?" It was Jack-Be-Nimble-Jack-Be-Quick carrying his candlestick. It was also Charlie Chaplin without his moustache and looking very handsome.

She nearly choked on the piece of chicken in her mouth. The most famous man in the world. Speaking to her.

"Cat got your tongue?"

"My name is Polly. Polly McCormack. I know who you are. You're the little tramp."

He smiled, the lines around his eyes crinkling. "Everyone does." He stepped closer to her. "How old are you?" He was only an inch taller than she.

"I was fifteen last week." She didn't know what to do with the plate and the empty melon shell. He took them from her hand and tossed them behind the tree with an airy gesture.

"Congratulations, dear. So lovely. So young." His hand touched her face and lingered on her throat.

401

"Has anyone taught you to act yet, lovely child?"

She looked at him steadily. "Yes. But only if it's worth my while."

He laughed and took her by the arm. "That's appealing, dear. We'll see what we can do to make acting worth your while. Lots of girls like to act with me because of what they've heard about me. I assume you want a part?"

It was a miracle. Only this afternoon she'd been sure that she was all washed up at Majestic. Now the Little Tramp himself was interested in her. She smiled prettily.

"Well, I do have a contract with Majestic, but they might lend me out, if you asked for me."

He smiled encouragingly. "You sweet little thing, you just walk along with me and we'll see if you can do better than Majestic. It's a bloody awful place, I hear. I could never tolerate that man Rubin."

Polly giggled. "I can't tolerate that bloody man myself!"

He looked at her delightedly. "Wonderful! You're a mimic!" He stopped suddenly and turned to her taking both of her hands in his. "Would you like to come home with me?"

Polly turned her head and looked at the still figure beside her. His eyes were closed and he was breathing regularly, but she didn't think he was asleep. Just resting up. She put her hand on his leg and felt the muscles tighten. Yep, he was awake.

She looked around the dimly lit room. What a crazy room. Didn't look like a man's bedroom, all apricot silk and swoops of chiffon and organdy ruffles. Lamps that looked like rose trees threw off a feeble pink glow from a tiny light concealed in each silk flower. Maybe he thought it was sexy. No. She had it. The ex-wife had done the room. The one that was in all the papers. Well, here today, et cetera. She was gone and little Polly McCormack was in the bed now.

She ran her hand over the satin sheet. First time on satin. She'd had it in the back seat of limousines, on dusty draperies, on the floor, but on satin sheets was really something. If you had to do it to get ahead, on satin sheets was positively the best way.

She wondered what his next picture would be about. What kind of part would he give her? She looked at her reflection in the mirror on the ceiling. That had been a surprise. She had tried to remember to watch, but she'd closed her eyes and had been too busy and forgot. Besides, he liked such crazy things she had to keep her mind on it. Well, next time around. She sighed.

So this is what it was like with the most famous man in the world. Most famous? But what about Doug Fairbanks? Or President Harding? Or even General Pershing? Or what about some foreigner like King George or Clemenceau? No, Charlie was definitely the most famous man in the world. And here was little Polly, full of his come, lying on his satin sheets, waiting for him to rest up for another one.

She wished she had some gum. Juicy Fruit would be swell right now, but there didn't seem to be any lying around. If she had all his money she would have lots of everything just lying around just in case a person wanted some. Well, she was on her way. One of these days she'd only go to bed with guys she liked. In the meantime—something good better come of this.

Maybe it wouldn't. Everybody in Hollywood knew he liked a different girl every night. And he was only making a couple of pictures a year. That meant, she stopped and figured silently, three hundred and fifty girls had to put up with his weird ideas and go away empty-handed. Maybe he gave them jewelry or something instead. She wondered what Edna had to do to him to get all those parts. She must have been something in bed. If I ever meet her I'll ask her. She giggled softly. No, she wouldn't either.

She looked over at him. God, he had pretty curls. Lots of girls would give their eyeteeth for curls like that. He was little, though. The white hairless body was strong but thin and stringy. Not much of a physique, but muscles like wires.

She thought of the men in the *Photoplay* ads for muscle building, men like Strongfort and them. That's what she liked men to look like. But she never seemed to get one. Men who looked great naked didn't give jobs to girls, they needed jobs themselves.

The still figure beside her began to stir. His hand moved over slowly and then lay casually on her crotch. She turned on her side, facing him and leaned back on one elbow. With her other hand she started to draw little circles on his chest. His eyes didn't open. His hand lay on the sheet, relaxed, where it had fallen when she turned over.

"That was such a good joke tonight," she whispered. "It was really funny when Peggy Hopkins Joyce walked up to you and said, 'I understand you're hung like a horse,' and you just stood there and neighed at her." Polly giggled.

He didn't move or give any indication that he heard. She reached down. Her hand sought him out.

"You're not really like a horse. More like a pony." She laughed lightly.

She felt his body stiffen. His eyes snapped open. With a sudden convulsive movement and a strange sound that was half cough, half snarl, he suddenly drew himself up. Crouching on the ruffled pillows, he sat on his haunches, looking at her intently, black eyes all pupil. He began to exhale in a slow hiss. Startled and confused by his terribly quick movements, she sat up. He exploded arms and legs flung wide. His legs, like uncoiling springs, kicked into her and she was flung off the bed. Clutching at the bedclothes, she slid on the satin sheets and landed with a bump on the floor.

"Hey! You kicked me! What's the big idea?"

"Exactly, my dear."

"That isn't very nice after what I let you do to me tonight."

Crouching on the bed above her, shaking with rage, he began to tug on the sheets, pulling them back onto the bed, dumping her onto the carpet.

"Hey, what do you think you're doing?"

"I'm kicking you out. That's what I'm doing. No bloody little twat talks to me like that."

"But, Charlie, I was just making a joke, just trying to be funny."

He narrowed his eyes wickedly.

"I'm the bloody comedian in this bed. No one else makes jokes around here. They pay me to make jokes. What do they pay you for? You don't even get paid to fuck." He sat up straight with a fixed stare.

"I'm the King of Comedy. I'm the King of Hollywood. I'm the King of the World." He leaned over her and screamed, "And I'm the King of Fucking. A pony! A bloody pony! Get out!"

She sat on the floor puzzled. Boy, had she said the wrong thing. What a little thing to set him off like this. Little thing, that was it. She said he had a little thing. Well, he did. He was little all over. Lots of men were little. No reason to go crazy.

"Aw, honey, don't be mean to little me. I didn't mean nothin' by it. Listen, I did everything you wanted, didn't I?"

"One gash is just like another. You're all just meat."

"You're just mad," she pouted. "Trying to hurt my feelings." He had, and now she just wondered how to get her clothes and get out.

He leaned over her. Really frightened, she pulled back, then thought better of it and, trying to smile, forced herself to lean back toward him, to seem intimate. There was a terrible look in those eyes.

She had seen his eyes a hundred times. Up on the screen, merry, twinkling, devilish, sad, famous eyes. Eyes that millions thought were just wonderful. Well, they weren't. They were awful. She had to look away. No audience had ever seen them look like that. All she saw there was absolute contempt. He wasn't just acting, this was real. He wasn't the tragic lonely Little Tramp who lost the girl to someone else. He was a monster who hated women. Most of all, he hated her.

"Get out!" he screamed. "Get out! Get out!"

She put her hand on the edge of the bed to help herself up. A nimble foot shot out and pushed it off. He stood on the bed, ready to stamp on her fingers in case she touched it again. His erection was coming back. This was what he really liked.

She stood up and backed away. Her costume was across the room on the chaise where he had put it. He saw her looking at the chaise and suddenly, with a single leap, he bounded out into the middle of the floor. Pirouetting like a ballet dancer, he whirled on his toes toward the chaise. It was grotesque. He was leaping and dancing as if this were a charming scene from one of his pictures. He paused, bowing low to the clothes. With a delicate gesture, he picked up her things, shaking each garment out carefully. Beautiful movement, so quick she couldn't follow them. It was really all a game and it might end at any moment, and everything would be all right. Despite her fear she smiled at him.

He flung the costume at her. Standing on tiptoe like some fragile faun, he sneered at her, his face contorted into an ugly mask. The Bo Peep costume floated through the air toward her. Beaded fringe glittered in the pale light. Everything suddenly looked as though it were in slow motion. The gown fell at her feet. She caught her step-ins and struggled with the costume. She heard it rip.

"Oh, God. It's torn," she whispered to him. "Grace will be furious."

He began to laugh. Now she was really frightened. He looked insane and danced around the room chanting.

405

"Get out get out get out get out get out."

Suddenly, on the other side of the bed, he stopped and picked up something from the floor. He threw it at her.

The object hit her on the shoulder and fell to the floor. In the dark she couldn't see what it was. She bent over and felt on the carpet. It was a diaphragm. It couldn't be hers. How could it be? Involuntarily she put her hand between her legs. It just couldn't be. Polly looked at his face and knew it was hers.

"How? When? How could it? How could you? Why?" She stopped stammering and her face felt hot and she began to cry softly. In her mind she could see Mavis' big belly, see her ungainly walk, hear her complain about her aching back. "Oh, my God. What did you do?"

He stood laughing. "I pulled it out. That's what I did. When you weren't looking. It's my best trick, I only do it to girls I really want to get a thrill from." He looked like a naughty boy.

"Great passions, like great comedy, must always have an edge of danger, an underlying sense of tragedy. I get a bigger kick out of it when someone takes a risk. Oh, nothing may happen." His voice grew consoling, soothing. "Probably nothing will happen. No one's come back yet and laid a bloody brat on the doorstep."

"But I'm taking the risk. You had no right!"

"Of course, yes, you take the risk. You don't expect me to take a risk do you?" He twirled around. "And you are wrong. I do have the right." He was speaking slowly, separating each word. "I have all the bloody rights here." He picked up one of her shoes and threw it at her, giving a small graceful leap as he did so.

"I want my handbag," she said, sniffling. "Mr. Rubin gave it to me and I want it." A cold chill grabbed at her. What if he told Mr. Rubin about tonight? That would really kill off her chances. Why had she been so stupid?

"Take it." He picked it up and threw it at her. "Doesn't suit me anyway. Probably fake."

"What about the part you promised me?" Her voice broke as she spoke. "You made a promise to me." Tears were making ugly black smudges on her cheeks as her mascara ran.

He laughed, a cascade of musical notes. "A lot of people will promise you. Promises are only made to be broken. You'd better get used to it."

The door opened behind her, and the Japanese houseman gestured to her to follow him out.

"But I only have one shoe," she tried to explain to him, tugging on his clothes, trying to get him to wait. She turned to the Little Tramp. "You have my other shoe. I only have one shoe."

"Get out!"

60

June 1922, Hollywood

The New York Times, June 14, 1922

WALLIE REID HOSPITALIZED
STAR SECRET DRUG FIEND
WIFE TELLS OF CASE
SAYS HE USED DRUGS BUT BELONGED
TO NO RING AND WENT TO NO DOPE
PARTIES.

LOS ANGELES. Wallace Reid, well-loved motion picture actor, was hospitalized this morning when he collapsed on the set of his latest moving picture. Reid has been in a sanitarium for several months with what was thought to be a nervous breakdown. In the early afternoon his wife, Dorothy, stunned reporters at the hospital by disclosing that Reid had been a morphine addict but had cured himself.

Majestic Pictures will not confirm or deny the statement by Mrs. Reid. The handsome star does not know that his wife has revealed his secret to his faithful fans. "He would die if he knew that the world had been told of his shame. I did it to try and stop this scarlet traffic in souls," the tiny brave woman said, brushing back a tear.

Hourly bulletins are issued by the hospital staff.

Hearst's *Los Angeles Examiner* handled the story on Wallace Reid's death austerely and ran a sympathetic editorial. "He Held On Gamely," the headlines read. While Wallie was still alive a special edition of *The Los Angeles Examiner* was printed each morning on Hearst's personal order. Every mention of Reid's addiction and illness was replaced by special news inserts. The single copy was delivered to Wallie's hospital room for him to read with his breakfast. When he died he never knew that his terrible and shameful secret had been revealed.

At the premiere of *Thirty Days*, Reid's final film, the audience stood for a minute of silent prayer. In theaters all over the United States, audiences stood and applauded when his name flashed on the screen, then wept openly as he made his last appearance.

Majestic gave Reid a splendid funeral. Twenty-five thousand fans filed past the casket in two days. The crowds were kept orderly by a line of mounted policemen—every single mounted man in southern California had been called in. A number of grief-stricken actors and actresses spoke of Wallie's goodness and the joy of working with him. Abe Weiss delivered a moving eulogy and Wallie's favorite songs, "Keep the Home Fires Burning" and "At the End of a Perfect Day," were performed on Wallie's own violin by Fritz Kreisler.

Wallie was laid out by Majestic makeup artist, Herbert Weinstock, who did a superb and affectionate job. It was hard to tell that Reid had been ravaged by his illness. Lying in a pewter casket, covered by a blanket of yellow roses, he looked young, handsome, strong, and healthy. Ready to jump behind the wheel of a fast-moving car, flash a smile at a pretty girl waving to him from the stands, and race off to love, fame and fortune—burning up the road, white teeth gleaming, eyes sparkling with fun and adventure—a true American hero.

The silver Lagonda dropped down to seventy as Ben drove through Redondo Beach, and then took the first curve on the coast highway leading up to the Palisades overlooking the Pacific Ocean. He was feeling the narcotic effect of speeding through the night, and more relaxed than he'd been in weeks. Wallace Reid had once told him that driving at night—the escape from reality represented by the flash of the headlamps on ordinary objects, dark cottages, fences, beach grass—was great for thinking out problems. Perhaps that was why Wallie had gone to dope. Now he was dead.

Ben parked at the deserted turnoff, stepped out of the racer and sat on a whitewashed rock at the edge of the cliff. Below him the lines of waves broke in a soothing rhythm, long luminous lines in the early light. Dawn glinted on fragments of broken gin bottles that looked as if someone had snapped a diamond necklace in the dirt. Just like this town, he thought, and just as real.

Ben had been drinking and grieving for two days now. Neither seemed to do much good; if anything he felt more disturbed by his thoughts than he had been by Wallie's death and funeral. These thoughts had come slowly but persuasively to make him feel accountable for his friend's death. He figured he was about as guilty as Weiss was. True, it was Rubin who had kept Wallie on that deadly schedule of overwork and drugs, but he, like Weiss, had known about it in time to make Rubin stop, while there was still some life left in Wallie to save. And he hadn't—for the same reason Weiss hadn't. He worked for Majestic, too. He took its blood-stained money just as eagerly as everyone else did. He bought sleek motorcars, he'd fucked more girls in three months than most men had in a lifetime, lived in a fancy bungalow filled with Spanish antiques. No telling how many men had died or been crippled so Rubin and Weiss could make the big profits that paid Ben Sommers as much every week as would keep most families for months.

The whole goddamned business was nothing but greed. People killed themselves to get to Hollywood. Suffered all kinds of cruelty, endured any punishment to get inside those gates. They pounded on the doors, climbed the lousy walls, groveled, prostituted themselves, lied, cheated, and betrayed to stay once they were inside. Everyone who worked in the movies was willing to submit to degradation as the price of success.

Of course there was power. It radiated down from Weiss. It was corrosive, that taste of power. Power over life and death, shocking, absolute. Men who had never commanded as much as a pet dog took human lives in their hands. Sick men, freaks, who twisted other lives to fit their own warped desires. As his anger flowed, his guilt ebbed. Finally, he began to grow calm. He'd reached a decision almost without having tried. He would get out while there was still something of himself worth saving.

For the next hour he prepared himself for the confrontation to come. As the dazzling California sun rose, gleaming off the tooled steel dial face on the dashboard, he drove back to his bungalow and to the rest he had been searching for.

Ben waited patiently outside the closed door of Weiss's office. At the funeral Weiss had put his arm around him and told him to call at his office. Well, here he was. The secretary smiled and beckoned. It was time.

"Ben, boy. I'm glad to see you. The campaign for *World's Champion* was very good. I'm proud of you. Wallie looked terrible but audiences still ate him up. Now we've got to figure out how to make something good out of his tragic and so unfortunate death." He waved him into a chair.

Ben sat down. Then he stood up again. "Mr. Weiss, I decided this morning to quit. Now I'm even more sure that it's a good idea." He paced back and forth in front of the desk almost ill with agitation.

Weiss very slowly let his reclining chair go upright. He realized that Ben was deadly serious. "What's the matter?" he asked, mystified.

Ben walked away a few feet, then whirled. "You think ten thousand a week is enough to pay a man for ruining his life?"

Weiss frowned. "You don't know what you're talking about."

Ben spoke slowly making each syllable distinct. "I'm talking about a lot of things. I'm talking about dumping Roscoe Arbuckle straight down a chute to hell. I'm also talking about a girl whose life and career have been destroyed by a nightgown I planted." He paused and his voice broke. "I think Mrs. Sheldon killed William Desmond Taylor, and that's why you were so anxious to clean up that place. Then you suddenly realized that you could take advantage of it to break Mary's contract. But now that we've destroyed all of the evidence, nobody'll ever know. Right?"

He leaned across the desk but Weiss didn't retreat. "But what I'm really talking about is a man who was slowly killed to meet commitments to a bunch of exhibitors. Wallie Reid is dead because of you." He pushed against a chair, it teetered but did not fall over.

Ben slowly shook his head. "I really admired you, thought you were a great man, a genius in this business. All that crap. Now I only hate you. What I really hate about you is how I went along with you. Jesus Christ! I knew better! But I went along anyway. You're not only foul yourself, but everybody in your path gets contaminated, like a fucking Typhoid Mary."

Weiss spoke softly. "I can see you're not yourself, and I

can understand why." He sat straighter in his chair. "I don't have to justify myself to anyone, Ben. Much less you. And I don't have to listen to any more of this crap. If you were anyone else, you'd have been thrown out the front gate by now."

"Don't you try. I know what I know." Ben bristled. "Don't forget I used to work for a newspaper."

Weiss sighed. He had really liked this raw but resourceful young man. He regretted what was happening.

"Listen." He would make one last try.

"Ben, grow up. I got no sympathy for a man whose dream comes true, who gets paid ten thousand dollars a week, and who only dreams to take drugs or drink himself insensible every night. You know who I feel sorry for? Well, I'll tell you. I think about shopgirls, working men and their worn out wives trying to bring up decent kids, those millions who still live in the stinking ghettoes I came out of or on lonely farms."

He leaned forward, intense, his eyes remembering. "Ben, you never once asked me if I had a dream, of if I did, what it was. Did it ever occur to you that men like myself have dreams?"

Ben looked at him, puzzled.

"I thought so," Weiss said. "My dream is a dream of America, Ben. When I first got here, I was filled with expectations, with an idea in my head about what it was going to be like, this America." He shrugged. "Well, it was and then again it wasn't."

"You've done all right for yourself. Several times over."

"But I have special abilities. Special dreams. Ambitions. Ben, for every opportunity I saw and took advantage of, millions didn't get a chance. Millions are still living in rags. I want to show them what I think America can be like if only they'll try and make it that way. My dream was to give dreams to twenty million Americans each week. Let them see grit and determination. Mary Pickford. Let them sense adventure. Wallie Reid and Doug Fairbanks. Let them feel luxury and success. Gloria Swanson. Inspire them. Little people who live grinding lives, who got no chance to find a dream. I give them dreams every week and they take care of me. Sure, I feel bad about Roscoe. But he created that scandal. I didn't make him go to San Francisco. I dream about a better America. All Roscoe dreamed about was his gut and his *putz*."

Ben knew he was being manipulated but there was a grain of truth to what Weiss was saying.

"Ben, boy, they all lose control of themselves. All I can do is to find stars and then pay them enough so they won't walk next door and work there for more money. I can't tell them when to stop drinking, or not to sniff cocaine, don't take pills, or stop smoking opium, or that one girl a night is enough for any man." He sighed deeply. "Appetites," he said softly.

Ben stirred uneasily, thinking of his own.

"Appetites. That's all they're interested in. Satisfying every desire they've ever had and new ones they learn about along the way." He gazed sadly into the distance. "When they finish here for the day, all I can hope is that they will stay alive and out of jail until the next morning. If they can manage that, they'll be rich and famous. If they don't, they end up broke or dead, sometimes both. I'm not God. I'm only Abe Weiss. I can only create people on a silver screen. Off of it, they're on their own. It's enough already that I should keep Majestic on top. I can't do more."

"I can fix that," Ben said quietly. Weiss looked up sharply. "I know enough to sink this ship."

Weiss coldly measured him. "That's very foolish of you, Ben. You know that I'm not going to sit by and let you wreck the work of a lifetime. I'm very disappointed that you fail to understand the need of whitewashing a murder or even capitalizing on it when the unfortunate event occurs." He shook his head. "Ben, it just fell into our laps and it saved millions." He sat back, face grave. "I was truly sorry to lose Bill Taylor. He was a gifted director." He shrugged. "But others will come along and I had to get rid of that millstone, Maxwell."

He looked away for a long moment. "The only move that might have been personally motivated," he said softly, "and here I'm being very frank with you, was Roscoe. I never really forgave him for that Woburn mess, getting me into a whorehouse. But the rest weren't petty or mean. I'm not a mean man."

He again looked Ben squarely in the eyes. "But I'll tell you one thing, Ben, if you don't leave Majestic quietly and keep your mouth shut, I'll have to make another decision, one I don't relish."

Ben stood up. "I'll just have to take that into consideration, I guess." The two men stared at each other, testing wills.

"I'm sorry to hear that," Weiss said ominously. "Think it

413

over. In the event you do change your mind and leave town quietly, there'll be a check for twenty-five thousand dollars waiting for you to help you start over somewhere else."

Ben put both hands on the front edge of the desk and leaned forward. "You rotten bastard! You think you can buy anything."

Weiss put the tips of his fingers together and leaned back in the chair. "Ben, I learned over the years that anything, anyone can be bought. I even bought you for a while, didn't I?" His smile faded. "After today you're barred from the lot. You have an hour to get off, then the studio security guards will start looking for you." He stood up. "Too bad. I thought you had real promise." There was genuine regret in his voice.

Quite calmly Ben picked up the chair he'd been sitting in and threw it into the oil portrait of Weiss that hung on the wall. The chair leg ripped through the face on the painting. Falling, it knocked over a lamp and the table it stood on. The lamp bulb broke in a shower of sparks. Weiss stepped back, placing his chair between Ben and himself. For the first time Ben saw a look of fright on his face. He pressed the button on his desk.

Ben gave the brocade covering on the long awards table a powerful jerk and all of the framed photographs, the testimonials, the plaques indicating recognition from the industry as a pioneer and leader, the statuettes for humanitarian achievement, cascaded to the floor in a shower of shattering glass and crashing metal. The secretary opened the door, looked in, then quickly shut it.

"I feel better," he said, breathing heavily.

"Get out of town, Ben," Weiss said evenly. "A word to the wise is already plenty."

The long line in front of the Million Dollar Theatre moved slowly inside for the next showing of *The Old Farm*. Polly walked up the familiar Grand Staircase, down the Long Gallery, and up to the fifth balcony. She could have done it with her eyes closed. The theater seemed more beautiful than ever. The usherette handed her the flashlight clumsily, though. Must've just started working here.

After a few minutes, the blue sky overhead deepened, sunset occurred over the proscenium arch, and tiny light-bulb stars could be seen twinkling on the ceiling. No matter how many times she'd seen it happen, it still was thrilling. With a rolling chord that might have announced Doomsday, the mighty Wurlitzer organ rose on its pedestal, bathed in a rosy glow, and the overture commenced, a clever potpourri of farm songs.

The spotlights on the organ dimmed, the audience settled down, and the tasseled curtains parted. The black screen gradually filled with glittering silver stars, the Constellation of the Big Dipper shining brightest among them. Shimmering silver letters rushed forward.

A MAJESTIC PICTURE

presented by

ABE WEISS

The signature dissolved into a lovely rural landscape. The camera, in a long tracking shot, moved past mounded haystacks, gnarled fruit trees, gliding always toward a picturesque tumble-down barn. Over the barn appeared:

THE OLD FARM
Starring
RICHARD BARTHELMESS

And Introducing
KATHLEEN O'BRIAN
as
Little Kitty Kelly

A circular insert of the face of a pretty dark-haired girl dissolved into the center of the screen. Kathleen's face, thirty feet high and looking absolutely enchanting, lowered its eyelashes and smiled at the audience. There was some applause from here and there in the theater.

Polly felt an aching stab. It should be me up there! It was my part! She stood up, climbed to the top of the balcony, wandered aimlessly down the long baroque corridors, running her hands slowly over the velvet-covered handrails on the stairways, saying good-bye.

61

September 1922, Hollywood

The Blue Cafe was as crowded as usual for the Sunday afternoon *Thé Dansant,* the orchestra blaring out a hot version of "Swanee."

"It was swell of you to come out on such short notice, Bunny," Ben said, grasping her by the elbow to guide her down the steps into the cafe lounge.

"A girl's got to eat." Her beaded dress made a metallic swish as she moved. "And the chow here's better than the

416

eggs I'd scramble for myself at home." She smiled up at him. "Besides, I like you." She winked and he wondered how she got that little black bead on the end of each eyelash.

"It pays to stay in good," he said in mock seriousness. "I won't always be down and out." He gave her arm a playful squeeze and she retaliated with a hard poke in the ribs.

"I don't care how down and out you are as long as you can pay for lunch."

Chester, the maitre d', broke into a beaming smile as he saw him. "Welcome, Mr. Sommers. Long time you not been here." His voice became confidential. "We all thought you deserted us."

"Not at all, Chester. I been home in New Orleans for a few months but I couldn't stay away. Once you've been here, there's no other place to be. Besides, where else can you get your eardrums cracked and gag on a lot of smoke on a Sunday afternoon?"

Chester leaned closer. "Lots of places. But if you want to do it expensive, you got to come here." He cackled at his joke, leading them around the edge of the packed dance floor to a table. He pulled Bunny's chair out for her and flourished the menus. "You want ice in your teacups?"

"Sure, thanks." Ben took out his silver flask and poured gin into her cup after the waiter spooned chipped ice into it.

She smacked her lips. "Mmmm. Good stuff. I bet that dissolved the ring out of the bathtub."

He laughed. "Actually, it ate the bottom out of the boat."

Bunny looked around. "I wondered why we were coming here. Now I can see why. Everybody who's anybody's here. The joint is absolutely infested." She blew a kiss to a couple she seemed to know, then spotted more friends and waved to them.

"I figured it was time to let everybody see that I'm back in town," he said. "And this is the best place to let them all see me at once."

Bunny emptied her teacup. "Hey, I'd like to dance—how about it?"

They danced close together, partly because the dance floor was filled with couples, partly because Ben was hungry for the feel of a woman's body against his.

"You cur," she murmured into his chest, "you never told me you were such a good dancer." She pinched him lightly. "You could have taken me out once in a while. All you ever wanted to do was canoe."

417

"And what's wrong with that? Perfectly healthy and normal, I'd say."

"I'd rather dance, that's what," she giggled.

Ben ordered *huevos rancheros* and Bunny ordered a big steak.

He sat back in mock amazement. "Why is it that the littlest ones eat the most?" he asked her. "I ought to remember and only take out girls who are on diets."

"Don't get up, Ben. I just wanted to say hello." A solid, athletic looking man with a square jaw smiled and held out his hand. Ben stood up and they shook hands.

"Hiya, Tom. Nice to see you. Meet Bunny Roberts. Bunny, Tom Ince."

Bunny smiled an absolutely radiant smile. "Hello, Big Boy."

Ince nodded, impervious to her message.

"I just wanted to say that I'm glad to see you out and around." He leaned closer as if speaking in confidence. Actually, he was shouting over the din of the band. "Everyone knows what happened. We independents salute you. The industry needs more guys with guts." He stepped back and grinned at Ben. "Weiss is going to get his. I hope the FTC grinds his balls."

"It'll be interesting to see how he fights back," Ben said. "I know him well enough not to count him out."

Ince laughed. "I know damn well what you mean. Uncle Sam is more abrasive, though. He has ways of wearing you down. Not even Abe has that hard a shell." He started to walk away then turned back as if in afterthought. "If you're looking, you might give Louis B. Mayer a call. I hear that he and Loew are talking merger of Mayer's studio and Metro. The Goldwyn studio is involved too, somehow. You put Mayer, Metro, and Goldwyn together and while it'd be like working for a volcano, *you* might just consider it a vacation." He clapped Ben on the shoulder. "Good luck. If I can be of any help, give me a call." With a cheery wave he disappeared into the crowd of dancers.

Bunny looked at Ben with shrewd appraisal. "Down and out, my ass. So that's why you're here." She wiggled gleefully. "I wish I'd ordered two steaks," she added, smacking her lips and cutting into the meat with relish.

"A friend of mine once told me that getting fired by Abe Weiss was a good enough reason to get hired by somebody else."

The band stopped for a break and a pianist took over. As the dance floor cleared, Ben's fork wavered, then he laid it down on his plate. Polly was sitting across the room at a crowded table. His first impulse was to get up and walk out. That's stupid, he thought. I've made up my mind to come back and work in this town, and I'm going to run into everybody I ever knew, sooner or later. At least those who are still alive. He glanced back at Polly.

Bunny followed his glance. "You two see a lot of each other?" she asked speculatively.

"Yeh. A lot. Everything," he breathed.

"I get it." She searched in her bag and brought out a compact. Then she took the cap off her lipstick and held it to her carefully drawn Cupid's bow mouth. "She's cute." He realized that Bunny was studying Polly in her compact mirror. "You want to go?"

"Yes," he murmured. "But I'm not going to." He drew in a deep breath and leaned across the table. "Bunny, I got involved with a bunch of people at Majestic and it all fell apart. Too involved. I'll never do that again."

She looked at him over the edge of her powder puff. "You gotta be involved, sugar." She snapped the lid of her compact closed. "Either you're with people, or you're against 'em. You can't avoid 'em. The world's too full of them." She smiled. "You've got a rep around town of being a nice decent guy who doesn't use or abuse people. Keep it that way." She turned her chair a bit so she could look across the empty dance floor. "That's my deep thought for the day," she whispered huskily and turned to watch Polly.

"I'd say she isn't having a very good time," she said after a moment. "She's laughing too hard."

Ben nodded in agreement. *The Old Farm* was supposed to be her part. Maude wrote it for her. I bet those rave reviews for that O'Brian girl almost killed her."

"Poor kid," Bunny added, leaning back in her chair and clucking her tongue sympathetically. Ben could see the curve of her breast through the armhole of her sleeveless dress. She went on. "I bet she laid out plenty to make it to where she is. Too bad it isn't working out."

As the musicians ambled back to their places a dark wiry man stepped up to their table and cleared his throat. "You were just pointed out to me, Mr. Sommers. It is Mr. Sommers, isn't it?" He held out a card with clawlike fingers.

"Yes, I am." Ben took the card and looked at it.

"I'm Edwin LeGrand, the probate attorney for William Desmond Taylor's estate. I handled all of Bill's affairs while he was alive, and the courts appointed me when he died."

419

"Pleased to meet you," Ben said uncertainly.

"I'll only take a moment of your time," said LeGrand with a nod at Bunny. "Bill's daughter has authorized me to sell any of his personal posessions that I can. I know you were friends and thought you might want a memento. You can call me at that number." He nodded at the card. Bowing to Bunny, he said, "Sorry to have interrupted your tea dancing, Miss." He looked at her appreciatively, turned and walked back through the dancers.

Ben sat back and breathed more easily.

"Lemme see that," Bunny said, snatching the card away from him. She shrugged. "Looks legit." Filled with curiosity she said, "I bet he had swell stuff. Maybe he'd let us go and look at the place." She paused then slowly said, "I never been to a place where there's been a murder."

Ben grinned. "You little ghoul. I promise, Bunny," he raised his right hand, "if I go and look at the stuff, I'll take you along."

She wiggled gratefully. "You're a real pal, Ben."

He leaned forward, and in a conspiratorial voice said, "I got the best things already. I swiped 'em that morning when the police weren't looking."

"What?" she asked breathlessly.

"Condoms. He bought them by the gross." He leaned back laughing.

Bunny started to smile, then, straight-faced, said. "You can wear them in memory." Then she broke up and giggled.

"No, seriously, what I'd really like is his big Marmon limousine."

"Nifty, huh?"

"Classiest motorcar in all Hollywood, besides my Lagonda. It's got wickerwork sides, like those basket chairs they push you in on the broadwalk at Atlantic City." He sighed. "It's the cat's pajamas."

As they moved around the floor Ben felt Bunny tugging at his jacket. "Wouldja look at your little friend, now." She jerked her head across the crowd at Polly and her dance partner. "That guy knows all the places to grab. Jeez look at him. In public, yet."

He watched Polly and her partner dance. "If he's from Majestic, he's new. I never saw him before," he said softly.

"Probably your replacement, in more ways than one." She was sorry as soon as she said it. "Forget I said that."

He shrugged. "Probably true."

She stopped near their table. "I'm ready to go whenever

you are," she said. "Let's go to your place, sweetie. I could use a laugh." She looked up at him. "And you could try out a little memorial to Billy Taylor." She picked up her handbag from the table and looked at him appealingly.

He took her hand. "Bunny, you're a good kid. You don't have to." Then, with sudden realization he added, "Hell, I don't have to either. I'm free! I got no more jobs to give out anymore." He laughed. "It's a whole new ball game."

She gently laid her hand on his. "I know I don't hafta." She looked up at him, her eyes filled with tenderness. "What if I said I wanted to?"

Ben smiled at her. "If that's so, then so do I."

Several of the patrons stood up and greeted him as they wound their way through tables on their way out.

"Glad to see you back, Ben."

"Whatcha doin', Benny Boy?"

"Trying to stay out of trouble."

Laughter.

"I know whatcha mean."

"Give me a call, Ben."

"I will. Next week, Al."

Standing close as the hatcheck girl retrieved her coat, Bunny asked, "Where were they when we came in?"

Ben grinned. "Waiting for someone else to make the first move. Tom Ince did it. He came over and said hello. Made all the difference." He held her coat for her. "I came here to be seen. They saw me."

Bunny smiled, her eyes bright. "I wish somebody knew I was available." Ben started to speak. "Besides you."

"Stick with me and I'll have your name up in lights."

"Yeh? I heard that before. Wait a jiff. I want to go to the Ladies. Give me something for the maid." She held out her hand and Ben put a five-dollar bill in it. As she disappeared down the corridor Chester suddenly appeared and placed a folded paper in Ben's hand.

"A lady asked me to give this to you as you were leaving, Mr. Sommers. She said there wouldn't be an answer." He walked away.

Ben opened the folded note. Written in careful schoolgirl penmanship were the words, "I would rather be dancing with you."

Ben stepped back to the top of the stairs and looked across the smoky cafe. Polly was talking to the man next to her. Deliberately he inhaled deeply on his cigarette and exhaled a cloud of smoke into her face. She inhaled as much as she

421

could and blew a little back at him. If ever she had been a little girl, she wasn't one any longer. The man held out the cigarette inviting her to take a puff. Laughing flirtatiously, she pushed his hand away, shaking her head. Too young. He saw her lips form the words. Too young to smoke.

Ben leaned against the pillar and watched. That was the difference between Polly and other girls. She was willing to walk on the edge. And that's what was needed. She was dangerous, willing to take risks, constantly flirting with the outrageous, giving more than anyone asked or expected. Most girls had fears, inhibitions, built-in danger signals beyond which they wouldn't budge. Polly didn't. She walked right up to the edge and looked over. That's what set her apart, made her star material. Somebody'd spot it. Sooner or later she'd get a part that would let her show what she could do. Then, watch out! Nothing could keep her back.

He turned and saw Bunny looking at him. He smiled apologetically. "I'm sorry, Bunny. I didn't hear you come up behind me."

In the automobile, as Ben drove back down Hollywood Boulevard, she said, "That Polly really got under your skin, didn't she?"

He nodded, then said, "In a way. She has this uncanny knack of making a guy feel absolutely marvelous about himself. You know it isn't true while she's doing it, but it feels so good, and she does it so well. You've got to be a little in love with someone who can do that for you." He laughed. "Then, she always turns the tables just a little bit. Throws a guy off balance." He sighed. "She was exciting."

Bunny looked straight ahead and smiled. "Aren't we all," she said, almost to herself.

"How did you find me, sir?" the chauffeur asked.

"There aren't too many Courtnays in the phone book spelled your way." Ben smiled. "I'd like you to start at the end of the week if you can."

Courtnay nodded. "What kind of machine will I be driving, sir?"

"Mr. Taylor's Marmon. The one with the basketwork sides."

The chauffeur beamed. "Splendid, sir. She's a grand girl. I've missed her."

"The attorney will deliver her Thursday. I'll want to drive out on Friday morning."

He saluted. "Thank you, sir. It'll be a pleasure to be driving again."

On Friday morning Ben, dressed in a conservative pin-striped suit, sat in the backseat of the Marmon limousine as it turned into the gate of the Mayer Studios of Mission Avenue. Louis B. Mayer stood in the window of his second-floor office and watched as Courtnay opened the automobile door.

Mayer turned to Irving Thalberg, his production supervisor, who was seated in a chair in front of the desk. "You're right. He's got class." He rubbed his hands together. "If this damned thing comes together, he'll be just what we need." He laughed gleefully. "Weiss will shit!" He turned toward the door as he heard his secretary buzz a warning.

"Come in, Mr. Sommers." He walked forward to shake hands. "Can I call you Ben?"

Ben smiled. "Please do."

"You know Irving?" He nodded at Thalberg. The slight, dark man stood up.

"Only by reputation." Ben walked over to him and they shook hands. "No one from this side of the hills gets over to Universal very often."

Thalberg laughed. "You got over once too often, as far as I was concerned. You stole my best publicity man right out from under my nose one afternoon."

Ben forced himself to keep smiling. "Yes, I did. And I was lucky to get him," he said evenly, still smiling.

"You've got good taste," Thalberg answered. "You handled that very smoothly. We'll have to do a lot of stealing to build a good staff. I'm glad you're experienced." He sat down and crossed his legs casually. Ben breathed easier.

Mayer motioned him into a chair. "So. You looking? You and Abe have a falling out?"

Ben smiled politely. "You might call it that." No one spoke.

Mayer waited, then looked at him intently. The subject was closed. He liked a man who could keep his mouth shut.

He sat down behind his desk, leaned back in the swivel chair, and folded his hands across his portly stomach.

"I'm trying to put together what may turn out to be the greatest studio in the industry. We'll turn out class A, big budget pictures with outstanding casts, wonderful stories, and great production values." He sat back to see how the news would affect Ben.

Ben smiled and cocked his head alertly showing great enthusiasm. "It sounds exactly like what I'm looking for. I'm very good at publicizing product. I'm sure you know my work at Majestic for the past three years. You give me the goods, and I can move them."

Mayer leaned forward, his face wreathed with concern. "Product? Goods? Ben, we—Irving, here, is going to turn out works of art. My company will never make mere products." He looked as if he had been wounded.

Ben did not blink. "Whatever you call it, Mr. Mayer, you make it, and I'll get the public to come and see it. They don't care if it's art or product. They only want it great."

Thalberg tapped the fingers of one hand on the palm of the other in silent applause.

ABOUT THE AUTHOR

RAY HUBBARD was born in Los Angeles and has a Master's degree from Stanford University. After spending a few years teaching art at a high school in California, Mr. Hubbard joined the staff of KPIX, one of the pioneer television stations in San Francisco in 1951. Among other positions he has held in the field of broadcasting, he has been national program director for the Westinghouse Broadcasting Company and vice president of programming and production for Post Newsweek Stations. He has been the recipient of many television production and writing awards, including the Emmy and the Dupont Award. He is also known for having hired the first female news anchorperson in television. In 1976, Mr. Hubbard retired to concentrate on his writing and began his own television production company. He is an avid collector of Tiffany lamps, glass and bronze candleholders and African sculpture. He enjoys pottery and handweaving, binds books and makes jewelry. In addition, he owns a collection of over a thousand books on the history of the movies. Mr. Hubbard lives with his wife in a home he designed in Potomac, Maryland.

THE LATEST BOOKS
IN THE BANTAM
BESTSELLING TRADITION